NEBULA AWARDS
SHOWCASE
2012

NEBULA AWARDS
SHOWCASE
2012

Edited by
JAMES PATRICK KELLY
& JOHN KESSEL

an imprint of **Prometheus Books**
Amherst, NY

Published 2012 by Pyr®, an imprint of Prometheus Books

Cover illustration © Michael Whelan
Cover design by Grace M. Conti-Zilsberger

Inquiries should be addressed to
Pyr
59 John Glenn Drive
Amherst, New York 14228–2119
VOICE: 716–691–0133
FAX: 716–691–0137
WWW.PYRSF.COM

16 15 14 13 12   5 4 3 2 1

Library of Congress Cataloging-in-Publication Data

Nebula Awards showcase 2012 / edited by James Patrick Kelly and John Kessel.
    p. cm.
  ISBN 978–1–61614–619–1 (pbk. : alk. paper)
  ISBN 978–1–61614–620–7 (ebook)
  1. Science fiction, American. I. Kelly, James P. (James Patrick) II. Kessel, John.

PS648.S3A16 2012
813'.0876208—dc23

2012000382

Printed in the United States of America on acid-free paper

PERMISSIONS

IN MEMORIAM

Christopher Anvil
Kage Baker
Everett F. Bleiler
Martin Gardner
James P Hogan
F. Gwynplaine MacIntyre
Jeanne Robinson
George Scithers
William Tenn, pen name of Phillip Klass
EC Tubb
Sharon Webb

and our agent
Ralph Vicinanza

CONTENTS

Introduction: In Which Your Editors Consider the Nebula Awards
of Yesterday, Today, and Tomorrow
    James Patrick Kelly and John Kessel   *11*

Ponies
    Kij Johnson   *19*

The Sultan of the Clouds
    Geoff Landis   *25*

Map of Seventeen
    Chris Barzak   *75*

And I Awoke and Found Me Here on the Cold Hill's Side
    James Tiptree, Jr.   *99*

In the Astronaut Asylum
    Kendall Evans and Samantha Henderson   *109*

Pishaach
    Shweta Narayan   *117*

excerpt from *Blackout/All Clear*
    Connie Willis   *139*

Bumbershoot
    Howard Hendrix   *159*

Arvies
    Adam Troy-Castro   *161*

CONTENTS

How Interesting: A Tiny Man
    Harlan Ellison   177

The Jaguar House, in Shadow
    Aliette de Bodard   185

The Green Book
    Amal El-Mohtar   209

That Leviathan, Whom Thou Hast Made
    Eric James Stone   223

excerpt from *I Shall Wear Midnight*
    Terry Pratchett   247

To Theia
    Ann K. Schwader   263

The Lady Who Plucked Red Flowers beneath the Queen's Window
    Rachel Swirsky   265

2011 Nebula Awards Nominees and Honorees   315

Past Nebula Winners   319

About the Cover   333

About the Editors   335

IN WHICH YOUR EDITORS CONSIDER THE NEBULA AWARDS OF YESTERDAY, TODAY, AND TOMORROW

James Patrick Kelly and John Kessel

Jim: When you compare the very first Nebula ballot to our 2011 ballot, you see a lot of differences. One is that the 1966 ballot was much, much longer—there was no preliminary winnowing back then. For example, Nebula voters had to choose a winner from thirty-one nominees in the short story category alone! This year there are just twenty-six nominees in the four fiction categories combined. Another difference was that there were just four awards given, Novel, Novella, Novelette, and Short Story. No Ray Bradbury Award for Outstanding Dramatic Presentation or Andre Norton Award for Young Adult Science Fiction and Fantasy. The Bradbury was started in 1992, but then went dormant until it was rebooted in 1999. The Norton was first given in 2006. Another difference was that there was just one woman nominated in any category: Jane Beauclerk, a pseudonym for M. J. Engh. Yikes! Note that the 2011 ballot has more women than men. And all five winners in 1966 were science fiction stories, as were the vast majority of the nominees. For the record, the winner for best novel was Frank Herbert's *Dune*, the tied winners for novella were "The Saliva Tree" by Brian W. Aldiss and "He Who Shapes" by Roger Zelazny, the novelette category was won by Zelazny's "The Doors of His Face, the Lamps of His Mouth," and the short story award went to Harlan Ellison's "'Repent, Harlequin!' Said the Ticktockman." In the four plus decades since, we have seen a proliferation of subgenres in our little corner of literature, but clearly we have nominated more fantasy than science fiction this year.

Of course, in 1966 there wasn't nearly as much fantasy as science fiction being published. So you would expect the Nebulas to track a publishing trend that reflects changes in popular tastes. And the two of us have certainly written plenty of fantasy, even though we're primarily known as science fiction writers. So has the rise of fantasy been at the expense of science fiction?

John: "At the expense of . . ." is a loaded phrase; after all, this is now the Science Fiction *and Fantasy* Writers of America. But even then I think the answer is not simple. The geography of our genre(s) has changed drastically over the last forty-five years, and the consequences are evident everywhere. Consider, as a minor example but a reflection of the larger movement, the term "speculative fiction." In both 1966 and 2011 the term was in widespread use, but its meaning has changed drastically. In 1966 it was already in its second incarnation. Originally the term was coined by Robert Heinlein (in 1947) to describe a subset of science fiction extrapolating from known science and technology; what he meant by it is what we today essentially mean by science fiction. By 1966 the term was being hijacked by New Wave writers and editors—notably by Judith Merril—to indicate SF that de-emphasized the science and focused on sociological extrapolation and stylistic experimentation. Today "spec fic" has lost almost all rigor and is used as an umbrella term to describe any fiction, SF or fantasy or horror or slipstream, that is not mimetic fiction. So Vernor Vinge and N. K. Jemisin and Kelly Link and Paolo Bacagalupi and Holly Black and China Miéville are all "speculative fiction" writers in one big happy family.

Or is the family such a happy one? As many commentators have noted, there is no longer an easily identifiable center that can be used to, say, identify all the stories nominated for the Nebula Award in any year. Hard science stories compete with liminal fantasies, which compete with horror fictions, which compete with sociological extrapolations, which compete with nostalgic exercises in pulp adventure. Many SF writers bemoan the very fact you note, that fantasy is overwhelming science fiction in sales and popularity, and that the things that are called science fiction today would not have passed muster as SF in John W. Campbell's *Astounding*. But perhaps it's only the dinosaurs who have even heard of John W. Campbell. Is the field losing all coherence, or are these changes just the natural effects of time passing and the world changing? Is any of this something that Nebula voters and readers should worry about? Does the reader who picks up this volume have any reason to know what she is going to get when she reads its contents?

Jim: It's a good question. The boundaries of "speculative fiction"—or as the critic John Clute calls it, *fantastika*—have expanded to include a lot of literary territory. But to mix metaphors, I actually like the "Big Tent" we've set up for our readers here. It fits with my own writerly sensibilities, and yours as well, I'll bet. Sure, fantasy and its many subgenres have captured some readers who might once have been exclusively science fiction fans, but I like to think that many fantasy readers retain a lively interest in what's happening in SF—and vice versa. Certainly there are editors who publish short fiction in print and online who still welcome a variety of genres to their table of contents. Many of the short fiction nominees first appeared in magazines featuring stories that are as likely to explore Venus as they are to visit Faerie. I wonder if speculative fiction's many awards, but the Hugo and Nebula especially, are not the center of our sprawling genre, at least at this point in history. Were the science fiction novels of Connie Willis and Paolo Bacigalupi awarded Nebulas in 2010 and 2009 respectively? Well, Ursula Le Guin's fantasy and Michael Chabon's alternate history took the novel Nebs in 2008 and 2007. So if we're keeping score, which genre is ahead? Fantasy or science fiction?

My answer is *yes*.

John: When the Nebulas were founded there were two reasons for their founding, and I think the difference between those reasons is illuminating and still relevant. Science Fiction Writers of America was a fledgling organization, dedicated to improving the situation of SF writers, but it had no money. Lloyd Biggle, the SFWA secretary-treasurer, suggested that SFWA sell an annual anthology to publishers with the proceeds going to support the organization. This rapidly became a plan to create a new SF award, voted on by writers, and thus the Nebulas were born. But the other reason, according to Damon Knight, was to improve the breed, to "show the quality of modern science fiction, its range, and . . . its growing depth and maturity." Knight was a critic and teacher as well as an editor and writer, and I believe he saw the Nebulas not simply as a way to honor the best work in the field, but to encourage writers to set their sights higher.

In the event, the trophies cost more than the amount raised by the anthology. But what of Knight's other purpose? Have the awards spurred us on to write better SF and fantasy? Have they been good for the reputation of the genre?

I think it's demonstrable that some of the best work written in the last forty years has been recognized by the Nebulas. And the awards have gone to grizzled old pros and to newcomers, to Ursula Le Guin's *Powers*, published in the forty-eighth year of her career, and to Ted Chiang's "Tower of Babylon," the first story he ever published. To classics like *Dune*, *The Left Hand of Darkness*, *Neuromancer*, "Aye, and Gomorrah," "When it Changed," "Houston, Houston, Do You Read?" "Beggars in Spain," "Bears Discover Fire," "Fire Watch," "Behold the Man," "R&R," and "Magic for Beginners." To names who could not be more famous (Isaac Asimov) and to those who could (Jack Cady). I find it reassuring that the race does not always go to the best-known competitor; that every year there are new names on the final ballot.

I don't suppose there's anyone who would maintain that the winners have been without question the best stories of the year. Just as the Oscars go to films chosen for reasons that, in retrospect, seem inexplicable, sometimes factors other than literary merit influence the outcome of the voting. Or people's judgment just changes over time. Or there just isn't room to give awards to all the worthy stories. At the 2011 Academy Awards Stephen Spielberg acknowledged these realities when he presented the best picture award, saying, "In a moment one of these ten movies will join a list that includes *On the Waterfront*, *Midnight Cowboy*, *The Godfather*, and *The Deer Hunter*. The other nine will join a list that includes *The Grapes of Wrath*, *Citizen Kane*, *The Graduate*, and *Raging Bull*."

Past Nebula nominee Andy Duncan recently made a provocative point about awards:

Over the years, I have decided the primary purpose of an award is not to celebrate individuals, but to celebrate the field those individuals work in. We squirm when this is made overt, as in the sanctimonious aren't-we-great speeches about the universal appeal of motion pictures at the Oscars every year, or that endless Grammys tribute this year to the music charities supported by the recording industry. Yet it's true anyway; it's less important who wins, say, the Hugos in any given year than the fact that, once again, the Hugos are given out, generating another opportunity to see one another, and applaud one another, and talk to one another about our field and how it's doing—and, yes, to kvetch about who got robbed and who's overrated and who the real winner is.

Jim: We don't have to go to the history books for reassurance that the race does not always go to the best-known competitor: it seems to me that the takeaway from this year's list of nominees is that fresh voices will be heard. With wins in novella and novelette, new writers Rachel Swirsky and Eric James Stone have posted their names on the marquee just a few years into their careers. Reminds me of 1982 when a couple of tyros named Connie Willis and John Kessel swooped out of nowhere and won all three short fiction Nebulas. And first time nominees like Vylar Kaftan, Amal El-Mohtar, Felicity Shoulders, Aliette de Bodard, Shweta Narayan, Christopher Kastensmidt, Caroline M. Yoachim, J. Kathleen Cheney, M. K. Hobson, N. K. Jemisin, Mary Robinette Kowal, and Nnedi Okorafor represent almost half of the ballot. It's the largest such group in the history of the award.

Speaking from personal experience, the impact of a nomination on a new writer can be profound. It's hard for any writer to know exactly how she is doing, once she starts selling regularly. Income doesn't necessarily tell the story. Reviews are a crapshoot—are bad reviews worse than no reviews? Readers may or may not check in. And there are no promotions. Nobody gets to be Vice President of Slipstream or Project Manager for Space Opera or Director of the Zombie Division. Yes, we have to believe in ourselves and know in our hearts that what we have to say is worth saying, but it helps when our colleagues offer some validation. Best-of-the-year editors certainly have this power, but they are individuals whose sensibilities are theirs alone. But when an organization of your colleagues proclaims to the world that you have written an elite story, you have to believe them. I think that helps the next time your curl your fingers over a keyboard.

And that's precisely why there is so much kvetching about the Nebulas. *They matter.* If we get it wrong, if the process of nominating stories and anointing one of the nominees does not spur the collective effort to write better SF and fantasy, then we've lost our way. My mentor Damon Knight would not be pleased.

I don't think this is the case, obviously. But the problem is that there is no consensus about how to write better SF and fantasy. Do we honor stories that are in dialogue with stories from our past, as has been our tradition, or is all that stuff old-fashioned now? Should we seek to break down the walls between the genres, or between genre and the literary mainstream, or is that turning our backs on our mission? And just what is our mission? Do we even have one? The discussions and, yes, *controversies* that sometimes swirl around the Nebulas are as important a part of our continuing self-evaluation as the awards themselves.

John: If the impact of a nomination on a young writer can be profound, I can say from similar personal experience that winning a Nebula can be a test of character. When I wrote "Another Orphan," which won me a Nebula on my first nomination, I paid less attention to marketability, and more to my own obsessive interests than I had for any story I had written up to that point. After I won, I spent a year spinning my wheels trying to figure out what winning meant I should write next. What did people expect to see from me? What was I *supposed* to write? It took me some time to find myself again after that experience.

The attention of your peers is powerful, for good or ill. As E. B. White reminds us when Wilbur the pig wins an award at the country fair in *Charlotte's Web*, "It is deeply satisfying to win a prize in front of a lot of people." The stress of winning causes poor Wilbur to faint dead away, for "he is modest and can't stand praise." Fortunately, winning a prize does not mean that Wilbur must be slaughtered and eaten; instead, he goes back to his barn at the end and lives pretty much as he did before. Let us choose Wilbur as our role model.

Jim: There are many paths to greatness. (Uh-oh, I'm starting to sound like a fortune cookie!) And we would be foolish to say that being nominated for a Nebula or even winning one was the only honor that counted in this or any other year. It is instructive to note that two of the awards given at the Nebula ceremony, the Bradbury and the Norton, are named for great writers who, while celebrated as SFWA Grandmasters, have never made the short list for the award, let alone won. That's right: Ray Bradbury and Andre Norton have never appeared on the final ballot. Ever. And in their distinguished company are some of the most talented writers ever to grace our genre. For example: Iain Banks, Elizabeth Bear, Jonathan Carroll, Greg Egan, M. John Harrison, Alexander Jablokov, Jay Lake, Kit Reed, Rudy Rucker, and Sherri Tepper— to name but ten.

What does this tell us? Only that proximity to the stories of any given year distorts our vision. In our opinion, these are *some* of the very best stories of 2011, but it is up to future generations of readers to decide—fifty or a hundred years from now—which ones speak to the ages.

Until then, we are very proud to present this year's *Nebula Awards Showcase*.

AUTHOR'S INTRODUCTION

Children are not all monsters, but many little girls are. In my small town elementary school, I was informally seeded 22nd in my class of 24. I played with numbers 23 and 24 because they were the ones willing to play with me, and I like to think that I would not have thrown them under the bus if that had been the price for improving my position—but it never came up, and I'm grateful, now.

"Ponies" is about that, and the maiming so many little girls subject themselves to, just to survive childhood. My first published short stories were horror, the literature of effect. Later I moved into fantasy and other things, but last year I returned to horror with the science fiction story "Spar," and found that I had more to learn about how fiction gets under the skin. "Ponies" is another exploration of that.

NEBULA AWARD, SHORT STORY (TIE)

PONIES

Kij Johnson

The invitation card has a Western theme. Along its margins, cartoon girls in cowboy hats chase a herd of wild Ponies. The Ponies are no taller than the girls, bright as butterflies, fat, with short round-tipped unicorn horns and small fluffy wings. At the bottom of the card, newly caught Ponies mill about in a corral. The girls have lassoed a pink-and-white Pony. Its eyes and mouth are surprised round Os. There is an exclamation mark over its head.

The little girls are cutting off its horn with curved knives. Its wings are already removed, part of a pile beside the corral.

> You and your Pony ____[and Sunny's name is handwritten here, in puffy let-
> ters]____ are invited to a cutting-out party with TheOtherGirls! If we like
> you, and if your Pony does okay, we'll let you hang out with us.

Sunny says, "I can't wait to have friends!" She reads over Barbara's shoulder,
rose-scented breath woofling through Barbara's hair. They are in the backyard
next to Sunny's pink stable.

Barbara says, "Do you know what you want to keep?"

Sunny's tiny wings are a blur as she hops into the air, loops and then
hovers, legs curled under her. "Oh, being able to talk, absolutely! Flying is
great, but talking is way better!" She drops to the grass. "I don't know why
any Pony would keep her horn! It's not like it does anything!"

This is the way it's always been, as long as there have been Ponies. All
ponies have wings. All Ponies have horns. All Ponies can talk. Then all Ponies
go to a cutting-out party, and they give up two of the three, because that's what
has to happen if a girl is going to fit in with TheOtherGirls. Barbara's never
seen a Pony that still had her horn or wings after her cutting-out party.

Barbara sees TheOtherGirls' Ponies peeking in the classroom windows
just before recess or clustered at the bus stop after school. They're baby pink
and lavender and daffodil-yellow, with flossy manes in ringlets, and tails that
curl to the ground. When not at school and cello lessons and ballet class and
soccer practice and play group and the orthodontist's, TheOtherGirls spend
their days with their Ponies.

*   *   *

The party is at TopGirl's house, which has a mother who's a pediatrician and
a father who's a cardiologist and a small barn and giant trees shading the grass
where the Ponies are playing games. Sunny walks out to them nervously.
They silently touch her horn and wings with their velvet noses, and then the
Ponies all trot out to the lilac barn at the bottom of the pasture, where a bale
of hay has been broken open.

TopGirl meets Barbara at the fence. "That's your Pony?" she says without
greeting. "She's not as pretty as Starblossom."

Barbara is defensive. "She's beautiful!" This is a misstep so she adds,
"Yours is so pretty!" And TopGirl's Pony *is* pretty: her tail is every shade of

purple and glitters with stars. But Sunny's tail is creamy white and shines with honey-colored light, and Barbara knows that Sunny's the most beautiful Pony ever.

TopGirl walks away, saying over her shoulder, "There's RockBand in the family room and a bunch of TheOtherGirls are hanging out on the deck and Mom bought some cookies and there's CokeZero and DietRedBull and diet lemonade."

"Where are you?" Barbara asks.

"*I'm* outside," TopGirl says, so Barbara gets a CrystalLight and three frosted raisin-oatmeal cookies and follows her. TheOtherGirls outside are listening to an iPod plugged into speakers and playing Wii tennis and watching the Ponies play HideAndSeek and Who'sPrettiest and ThisIsTheBestGame. They are all there, SecondGirl and SuckUpGirl and EveryoneLikesHerGirl and the rest. Barbara only speaks when she thinks she'll get it right.

And then it's time. TheOtherGirls and their silent Ponies collect in a ring around Barbara and Sunny. Barbara feels sick.

TopGirl says to Barbara, "What did she pick?"

Sunny looks scared but answers her directly. "I would rather talk than fly or stab things with my horn."

TopGirl says to Barbara, "That's what Ponies always say." She gives Barbara a curved knife with a blade as long as a woman's hand.

"*Me?*" Barbara says. "I thought someone else did it. A grownup."

TopGirl says, "Everyone does it for their own Pony. I did it for Starblossom."

In silence Sunny stretches out a wing.

It's not the way it would be, cutting a real pony. The wing comes off easily, smooth as plastic, and the blood smells like cotton candy at the fair. There's a shiny trembling oval where the wing was, as if Barbara is cutting rose-flavored Turkish Delight in half and sees the pink under the powdered sugar. She thinks, *It's sort of pretty*, and throws up.

Sunny shivers, her eyes shut tight. Barbara cuts off the second wing and lays it beside the first.

The horn is harder, like paring a real pony's hooves. Barbara's hand slips and she cuts Sunny, and there's more cotton-candy blood. And then the horn lies in the grass beside the wings.

Sunny drops to her knees. Barbara throws the knife down and falls beside her, sobbing and hiccuping. She scrubs her face with the back of her hand and looks up at the circle.

Starblossom touches the knife with her nose, pushes it toward Barbara with one lilac hoof. TopGirl says, "Now the voice. You have to take away her voice."

"But I already cut off her wings and her horn!" Barbara throws her arms around Sunny's neck, protecting it. "Two of the three, you said!"

"That's the cutting-out, yeah," TopGirl says. "That's what *you* do to be OneOfUs. But the Ponies pick their *own* friends. And that costs, too." Starblossom tosses her violet mane. For the first time, Barbara sees that there is a scar shaped like a smile on her throat. All the Ponies have one.

"I won't!" Barbara tells them all, but even as she cries until her face is caked with snot and tears, she knows she will, and when she's done crying, she picks up the knife and pulls herself upright.

Sunny stands up beside her on trembling legs. She looks very small without her horn, her wings. Barbara's hands are slippery but she tightens her grip.

"No," Sunny says suddenly. "Not even for this."

Sunny spins and runs, runs for the fence in a gallop as fast and beautiful as a real pony's; but there are more of the others, and they are bigger, and Sunny doesn't have her wings to fly or her horn to fight. They pull her down before she can jump the fence into the woods beyond. Sunny cries out and then there is nothing, only the sound of pounding hooves from the tight circle of Ponies.

TheOtherGirls stand, frozen. Their blind faces are turned toward the Ponies.

The Ponies break their circle, trot away. There is no sign of Sunny, beyond a spray of cotton-candy blood and a coil of her glowing mane torn free and fading as it falls to the grass.

Into the silence TopGirl says, "Cookies?" She sounds fragile and false. TheOtherGirls crowd into the house, chattering in equally artificial voices. They start up a game, drink more DietCoke.

Barbara stumbles after them into the family room. "What are you playing?" she says, uncertainly.

"Why are *you* here?" FirstGirl says, as if noticing her for the first time. "You're not OneOfUs."

TheOtherGirls nod. "You don't have a pony."

ABOUT THE AUTHOR

Kij Johnson is a novelist and short-story writer who has also won the World Fantasy and Theodore Sturgeon Awards. Currently she lives in Raleigh, North Carolina, and is at work on a novel and a collection of short stories.

AUTHOR'S INTRODUCTION

Although I'm a science fiction writer in my spare time, in my "day job" I work on real science and spaceflight, including both working on existing missions (such as the Mars Rovers—still roving after all these years!) and developing concepts and technologies for future missions. Although much of my work is on Mars, I've long been interested in the planet Venus, very much the neglected planet in both science and science fiction. I've been struck by the fact that, although the surface of Venus is a good analogue of hell, when you get about 50 kilometers up on the atmosphere, the environment is in many ways the most Earthlike place in the solar system (other than Earth, of course), with temperature and pressure at values close to what humans like to live at. And in the carbon dioxide atmosphere of Venus, breathable air is a lifting gas. So I've been fascinated with the possibility of habitats that float in the atmosphere of Venus. Another fascination I've had is with terraforming, an idea that the late astronomer Carl Sagan proposed for Venus and Mars. It turns out that terraforming Venus would be incredibly difficult; a lot more difficult than Sagan thought it would be, back in 1962. In an earlier story ("Ecopoiesis"), my characters Leah Hamakawa and David Tinkerman looked at the (not very successful) attempt at partial terraforming of Mars. In "The Sultan of the Clouds," I brought them to Venus.

THE SULTAN OF THE CLOUDS

Geoff Landis

When Leah Hamakawa and I arrived at Riemann orbital, there was a surprise waiting for Leah: a message. Not an electronic message on a link-pad, but an actual physical envelope, with *Doctor Leah Hamakawa* lettered on the outside in flowing handwriting.

Leah slid the note from the envelope. The message was etched on a stiff sheet of some hard crystal that gleamed a brilliant translucent crimson. She looked at it, flexed it, ran a fingernail over it, and then held it to the light, turning it slightly. The edges caught the light and scattered it across the room in droplets of fire. "Diamond," she said. "Chromium impurities give it the red color; probably nitrogen for the blue. Charming." She handed it to me. "Careful of the edges, Tinkerman; I don't doubt it might cut."

I ran a finger carefully over one edge, but found that Leah's warning was unnecessary; some sort of passivation treatment had been done to blunt the edge to keep it from cutting. The letters were limned in blue, so sharply chiseled on the sheet that they seemed to rise from the card. The title read, "Invitation from Carlos Fernando Delacroix Ortega de la Jolla y Nordwald-Gruenbaum." In smaller letters, it continued, "We find your researches on the ecology of Mars to be of some interest. We would like to invite you to visit our residences at Hypatia at your convenience and talk."

I didn't know the name Carlos Fernando, but the family Nordwald-Gruenbaum needed no introduction. The invitation had come from someone within the intimate family of the Satrap of Venus.

Transportation, the letter continued, would be provided.

The Satrap of Venus. One of the twenty old men, the lords and owners of the solar system. A man so rich that human standards of wealth no longer had any meaning. What could he want with Leah?

I tried to remember what I knew about the sultan of the clouds, satrap of the fabled floating cities. It seemed very far away from everything I knew. The society, I thought I remembered, was said to be decadent and perverse, but I knew little more. The inhabitants of Venus kept to themselves.

Riemann station was ugly and functional, the interior made of a dark anodized aluminum with a pebbled surface finish. There was a viewport in the lounge, and Leah had walked over to look out. She stood with her back to me, framed in darkness. Even in her rumpled ship's suit, she was beautiful, and I wondered if I would ever find the clue to understanding her.

As the orbital station rotated, the blue bubble of Earth slowly rose in front of her, a fragile and intricate sculpture of snow and cobalt, outlining her in a sapphire light. "There's nothing for me down there," she said.

I stood in silence, not sure if she even remembered I was there.

In a voice barely louder than the silence, she said, "I have no past."

The silence was uncomfortable. I knew I should say something, but I was not sure what. "I've never been to Venus," I said at last.

"I don't know anybody who has." Leah turned. "I suppose the letter doesn't specifically say that I should come alone." Her tone was matter of fact, neither discouraging nor inviting.

It was hardly enthusiastic, but it was better than no. I wondered if she actually liked me, or just tolerated my presence. I decided it might be best not to ask. No use pressing on my luck.

The transportation provided turned out to be the Sulieman, a fusion yacht.

Sulieman was more than merely first-class, it was excessively extravagant. It was larger than many ore transports, huge enough that any ordinary yacht could have easily fit within the most capacious of its recreation spheres. Each of its private cabins—and it had seven—was larger than an ordinary habitat module. Big ships commonly were slow ships, but Sulieman was an exception, equipped with an impressive amount of delta-V, and the transfer orbit to Venus was scheduled for a transit time well under that of any commercial transport ship.

We were the only passengers.

Despite its size, the ship had a crew of just three: captain, and first and second pilot. The captain, with the shaven head and saffron robe of a Buddhist novice, greeted us on entry, and politely but firmly informed us that the crew were not answerable to orders of the passengers. We were to keep to the passenger section, and we would be delivered to Venus. Crew accommodations were separate from the passenger accommodations, and we should expect not to see or hear from the crew during the voyage.

"Fine," was the only comment Leah had.

When the ship had received us and boosted into a fast Venus transfer orbit, Leah found the smallest of the private cabins and locked herself in it.

Leah Hamakawa had been with the Pleiades Institute for twenty years. She had joined young, when she was still a teenager—long before I'd ever met her—and I knew little of her life before then, other than that she had been an orphan. The institute was the only family that she had.

It seems to me sometimes that there are two Leahs. One Leah is shy and childlike, begging to be loved. The other Leah is cool and professional, who can hardly bear being touched, who hates—or perhaps disdains—people.

Sometimes I wonder if she had been terribly hurt as a child. She never talks about growing up, never mentions her parents. I had asked her, once, and the only thing she said was that that is all behind her, long ago and far away.

I never knew my position with her. Sometimes I almost think that she must love me, but cannot bring herself to say anything. Other times she is so casually thoughtless that I believe she never thinks of me as more than a technical assistant, indistinguishable from any other tech. Sometimes I wonder why she even bothers to allow me to hang around.

I damn myself silently for being too cowardly to ask.

While Leah had locked herself away, I explored the ship. Each cabin was spherical, with a single double-glassed octagonal viewport on the outer cabin wall. The cabins had every luxury imaginable, even hygiene facilities set in smaller adjoining spheres, with booths that sprayed actual water through nozzles onto the occupant's body.

Ten hours after boost, Leah had still not come out. I found another cabin and went to sleep.

In two days I was bored. I had taken apart everything that could be taken apart, examined how it worked, and put it back together. Everything was in perfect condition; there was nothing for me to fix.

But, although I had not brought much with me, I'd brought a portable office. I called up a librarian agent, and asked for history.

In the beginning of the human expansion outward, transport into space had been ruinously expensive, and only governments and obscenely rich corporations could afford to do business in space. When the governments dropped out, a handful of rich men bought their assets. Most of them sold out again, or went bankrupt. A few of them didn't. Some stayed on due to sheer stubbornness, some with the fervor of an ideological belief in human expansion, and some out of a cold-hearted calculation that there would be uncountable wealth in space, if only it could be tapped. When the technology was finally ready, the twenty families owned it all.

Slowly, the frontier opened, and then the exodus began. First by the thousands: Baha'i, fleeing religious persecution; deposed dictators and their sycophants, looking to escape with looted treasuries; drug lords and their retinues, looking to take their profits beyond the reach of governments or rivals. Then, the exodus began by the millions, all colors of humanity scattering from the Earth to start a new life in space. Splinter groups from the Church of John the Avenger left the unforgiving mother church seeking their prophesied destiny; dissidents from the People's Republic of Malawi, seeking freedom; vegetarian communes from Alaska, seeking a new frontier; Mayans, seeking to reestablish a Maya homeland; libertarians, seeking their free-market paradise; communists, seeking a place outside of history to mold the new communist man. Some of them died quickly, some slowly, but always there were more, a never-ending flood of dissidents, malcontents and rebels, people willing to sign away anything for the promise of a new start. A few of them survived. A few of them thrived. A few of them grew.

And every one of them had mortgaged their very balls to the twenty families for passage.

Not one habitat in a hundred managed to buy its way out of debt—but the heirs of the twenty became richer than nations, richer than empires.

The legendary war between the Nordwald industrial empire and the Gruenbaum family over solar-system resources had ended when Patricia Gruenbaum sold out her controlling interest in the family business. Udo Nordwald, tyrant and patriarch of the Nordwald industrial empire—now Nordwald-Gruenbaum—had no such plans to discard or even dilute his hard-battled wealth. He continued his consolidation of power with a merger-by-marriage of his only son, a boy not even out of his teens, with the shrewd and calculating heiress of la Jolla. His closest competitors gone, Udo retreated from the outer solar system, leaving the long expansion outward to others. He established corporate headquarters, a living quarters for workers, and his own personal dwelling in a place which was both central to the inner system, and also a spot that nobody had ever before thought possible to colonize. He made his reputation by colonizing the planet casually called the solar system's Hell planet.

Venus.

The planet below grew from a point of light into a gibbous white pearl, too bright to look at. The arriving interplanetary yacht shed its hyperbolic excess in a low pass through Venus' atmosphere, rebounded leisurely into high elliptical orbit, and then circularized into a two-hour parking orbit.

Sulieman had an extravagant viewport, a single transparent pane four meters in diameter, and I floated in front of it, watching the transport barque glide up to meet us. I had thought Sulieman a large ship; the barque made it look like a miniature. A flattened cone with a rounded nose and absurdly tiny rocket engines at the base, it was shaped in the form of a typical planetary-descent lifting body, but one that must have been over a kilometer long, and at least as wide. It glided up to the Sulieman and docked with her like a pumpkin mating with a pea.

The size, I knew, was deceiving. The barque was no more than a thin skin over a hollow shell made of vacuum-foamed titanium surrounding a vast empty chamber. It was designed not to land, but to float in the atmosphere, and to float it required a huge volume and almost no weight. No ships ever landed on the surface of Venus; the epithet "hell" was well chosen. The transfer barque, then, was more like a space-going dirigible than a spaceship, a vehicle as much at home floating in the clouds as floating in orbit.

Even knowing that the vast bulk of the barque was little more substantial than vacuum, though, I found the effect intimidating.

It didn't seem to make any impression on Leah. She had come out from her silent solitude when we approached Venus, but she barely glanced out the viewport in passing. It was often hard for me to guess what would attract her attention. Sometimes I had seen her spend an hour staring at a rock, apparently fascinated by a chunk of ordinary asteroidal chondrite, turning it over and examining it carefully from every possible angle. Other things, like a spaceship nearly as big as a city, she ignored as if they had no more importance than dirt.

Bulky cargos were carried in compartments in the hollow interior of the barque, but since there were just two of us descending to Venus, we were invited to sit up in the pilot's compartment, a transparent blister almost invisible at the front.

The pilot was another yellow-robed Buddhist. Was this a common sect for Venus pilots, I wondered? But this pilot was as talkative as Sulieman's pilot had been reclusive. As the barque undocked, a tether line stretched out between it and the station. The station lowered the barque toward the planet.

While we were being lowered down the tether, the pilot pointed out every possible sight—tiny communications satellites crawling across the sky like turbocharged ants; the pinkish flashes of lightning on the night hemisphere of the planet far below; the golden spider's web of a microwave power relay. At thirty kilometers, still talking, the pilot severed the tether, allowing the barque to drop free. The Earth and Moon, twin stars of blue and white, rose over the pearl of the horizon. Factory complexes were distantly visible in orbit, easy to spot by their flashing navigation beacons and the transport barques docked to them, so far away that even the immense barques were shrunken to insignificance.

We were starting to brush atmosphere now, and a feeling of weight returned, and increased. Suddenly we were pulling half a gravity of overgee. Without ever stopping talking, the pilot-monk deftly rolled the barque inverted, and Venus was now over our heads, a featureless white ceiling to the universe. "Nice view there, is it not?" the pilot said. "You get a great feel for the planet in this attitude. Not doing it for the view, though, nice as it is; I'm just getting that old hypersonic lift working for us, holding us down. These barques are rather a bit fragile; can't take them in too fast, have to play the atmosphere like a big bass fiddle. Wouldn't want us to bounce off the atmosphere, now, would you?" He didn't pause for answers to his questions, and I wondered if he would have continued his travelogue even if we had not been there.

The gee level increased to about a standard, then steadied.

The huge beast swept inverted through the atmosphere, trailing an ionized cloud behind it. The pilot slowed toward subsonic, and then rolled the barque over again, skipping upward slightly into the exosphere to cool the glowing skin, then letting it dip back downward. The air thickened around us as we descended into the thin, featureless haze. And then we broke through the bottom of the haze into the clear air below it, and abruptly we were soaring above the endless sea of clouds.

Clouds.

A hundred and fifty million square kilometers of clouds, a billion cubic kilometers of clouds. In the ocean of clouds the floating cities of Venus are not limited, like terrestrial cities, to two dimensions only, but can float up and down at the whim of the city masters, higher into the bright cold sunlight, downward to the edges of the hot murky depths.

Clouds. The barque sailed over cloud-cathedrals and over cloud-mountains, edges recomplicated with cauliflower fractals. We sailed past lairs filled with cloud-monsters a kilometer tall, with arched necks of cloud stretching forward, threatening and blustering with cloud-teeth, cloud-muscled bodies with clawed feet of flickering lightning.

The barque was floating now, drifting downward at subsonic speed, trailing its own cloud-contrail, which twisted behind us like a scrawl of illegible handwriting. Even the pilot, if not actually fallen silent, had at least slowed down his chatter, letting us soak in the glory of it. "Quite something, isn't it?" he said. "The kingdom of the clouds. Drives some people batty with the immensity of it, or so they say—cloud-happy, they call it here. Never get tired of it, myself. No view like the view from a barque to see the clouds." And to prove it, he banked the barque over into a slow turn, circling a cloud pillar that rose from deep down in the haze to tower thousands of meters above our heads. "Quite a sight."

"Quite a sight," I repeated.

The pilot-monk rolled the barque back, and then pointed, forward and slightly to the right. "There. See it?"

I didn't know what to see. "What?"

"There."

I saw it now, a tiny point glistening in the distance. "What is it?"

"Hypatia. The jewel of the clouds."

As we coasted closer, the city grew. It was an odd sight. The city was a dome, or rather, a dozen glistening domes melted haphazardly together, each one faceted with a million panels of glass. The domes were huge; the smallest nearly a kilometer across, and as the barque glided across the sky the facets caught the sunlight and sparkled with reflected light. Below the domes, a slender pencil of rough black stretched down toward the cloudbase like taffy, delicate as spun glass, terminating in an absurdly tiny bulb of rock that seemed far too small to counterbalance the domes.

"Beautiful, you think, yes? Like the wonderful jellyfishes of your blue planet's oceans. Can you believe that half a million people live there?"

The pilot brought us around the city in a grand sweep, showing off, not even bothering to talk. Inside the transparent domes, chains of lakes glittered in green ribbons between boulevards and delicate pavilions. At last he slowed to a stop, and then slowly leaked atmosphere into the vacuum vessel that provided the buoyancy. The barque settled down gradually, wallowing from side to side now that the stability given by its forward momentum was gone. Now it floated slightly lower than the counterweight. The counterweight no longer looked small, but loomed above us, a rock the size of Gibraltar. Tiny fliers affixed tow-ropes to hardpoints on the surface of the barque, and slowly we were winched into a hard-dock.

"Welcome to Venus," said the monk.

The surface of Venus is a place of crushing pressure and hellish temperature. Rise above it, though, and the pressure eases, the temperature cools. Fifty kilometers above the surface, at the base of the clouds, the temperature is tropical, and the pressure the same as Earth normal. Twenty kilometers above that, the air is thin and polar cold.

Drifting between these two levels are the ten thousand floating cities of Venus.

A balloon filled with oxygen and nitrogen will float in the heavy air of Venus, and balloons were exactly what the fabled domed cities were. Geodetic structures with struts of sintered graphite and skin of transparent polycarbonate synthesized from the atmosphere of Venus itself, each kilometer-diameter dome easily lifted a hundred thousand tons of city.

Even the clouds cooperated. The thin haze of the upper cloud deck served to filter the sunlight so that the intensity of the sun here was little more than the Earth's solar constant.

Hypatia was not the largest of the floating cities, but it was certainly the richest, a city of helical buildings and golden domes, with huge open areas and elaborate gardens. Inside the dome of Hypatia, the architects played every possible trick to make us forget that we were inside an enclosed volume.

But we didn't see this part, the gardens and waterfalls, not at first. Leaving the barque, we entered a disembarking lounge below the city. For all that it featured plush chaise lounges, floors covered with genetically engineered pink grass, and priceless sculptures of iron and of jade, it was functional: a place to wait.

It was large enough to hold a thousand people, but there was only one person in the lounge, a boy who was barely old enough to have entered his teens, wearing a bathrobe and elaborately pleated yellow silk pants. He was slightly pudgy, with an agreeable, but undistinguished, round face.

After the expense of our transport, I was surprised at finding only one person sent to await our arrival.

The kid looked at Leah. "Doctor Hamakawa. I'm pleased to meet you." Then he turned to me. "Who the hell are you?" he said.

"Who are you?" I said. "Where's our reception?"

The boy was chewing on something. He seemed about to spit it out, and then thought better of it. He looked over at Leah. "This guy is with you, Dr. Hamakawa? What's he do?"

"This is David Tinkerman," Leah said. "Technician. And, when need be, pilot. Yes, he's with me."

"Tell him he might wish to learn some manners," the boy said.

"And who are you?" I shot back. "I don't think you answered the question."

The not-quite-teenager looked at me with disdain, as if he wasn't sure if he would even bother to talk to me. Then he said, in a slow voice as if talking to an idiot, "I am Carlos Fernando Delacroix Ortega de la Jolla y Nordwald-Gruenbaum. I own this station and everything on it."

He had an annoying high voice, on the edge of changing, but not yet there.

Leah, however, didn't seem to notice his voice. "Ah," she said. "You are the scion of Nordwald-Gruenbaum. The ruler of Hypatia."

The kid shook his head and frowned. "No," he said. "Not the scion, not exactly. I am Nordwald-Gruenbaum." The smile made him look like a child again; it make him look likable. When he bowed, he was utterly charming. "I," he said, "am the sultan of the clouds."

Carlos Fernando, as it turned out, had numerous servants indeed. Once we had been greeted, he made a gesture and an honor guard of twenty women in silken doublets came forward to escort us up.

Before we entered the elevator, the guards circled around. At a word from Carlos Fernando, a package was brought forward. Carlos took it, and, as the guards watched, handed it to Leah. "A gift," he said, "to welcome you to my city."

The box was simple and unadorned. Leah opened it. Inside the package was a large folio. She took it out. The book was bound in cracked, dark red leather, with no lettering. She flipped to the front. "Giordano Bruno," she read. "On the Infinite Universe and Worlds." She smiled, and riffled through the pages. "A facsimile of the first English edition?"

"I thought perhaps you might enjoy it."

"Charming." She placed it back in the box, and tucked it under her arm. "Thank you," she said.

The elevator rose so smoothly it was difficult to believe it traversed two kilometers in a little under three minutes. The doors opened to brilliant noon sunlight. We were in the bubble city.

The city was a fantasy of foam and air. Although it was enclosed in a dome, the bubble was so large that the walls nearly vanished into the air, and it seemed unencumbered. With the guards beside us, we walked through the city. Everywhere there were parks, some just a tiny patch of green surrounding a tree, some forests perched on the wide tops of elongated stalks, with elegantly sculpted waterfalls cascading down to be caught in wide fountain basins. White pathways led upward through the air, suspended by cables from impossibly narrow beams, and all around us were sounds of rustling water and birdsong.

At the end of the welcoming tour, I realized I had been imperceptibly but effectively separated from Leah. "Hey," I said. "What happened to Dr. Hamakawa?"

The honor guard of women still surrounded me, but Leah, and the kid who was the heir of Nordwald-Gruenbaum, had vanished.

"We're sorry," one of the woman answered, one slightly taller, perhaps, than the others. "I believe that she has been taken to her suite to rest for a bit, since in a few hours she is to be greeted at the level of society."

"I should be with her."

The woman looked at me calmly. "We had no instructions to bring you. I don't believe you were invited."

"Excuse me," I said. "I'd better find them."

The woman stood back, and gestured to the city. Walkways meandered in all directions, a three-dimensional maze. "By all means, if you like. We were instructed that you were to have free run of the city."

I nodded. Clearly, plans had been made with no room for me. "How will I get in touch?" I asked. "What if I want to talk to Leah—to Doctor Hamakawa?"

"They'll be able to find you. Don't worry." After a pause, she said, "Shall we show you to your place to domicile?"

The building to which I was shown was one of a cluster that seemed suspended in the air by crisscrossed cables. It was larger than many houses. I was used to living in the cubbyholes of habitat modules, and the spaciousness of the accommodations startled me.

"Good evening, Mr. Tinkerman." The person greeting me was a tall Chinese man perhaps fifty years of age. The woman next to him, I surmised, was his wife. She was quite a bit younger, in her early twenties. She was slightly overweight by the standards I was used to, but I had noticed that was common here. Behind her hid two children, their faces peeking out from behind her and then darting back again to safety. The man introduced himself as Truman Singh, and his wife as Epiphany. "The rest of the family will be about to meet you in a few hours, Mr. Tinkerman," he said, smiling. "They are mostly working."

"We both work for His Excellency," Epiphany added. "Carlos Fernando has asked our braid to house you. Don't hesitate to ask for anything you need. The cost will go against the Nordwald-Gruenbaum credit, which is," she smiled, "quite unlimited here. As you might imagine."

"Do you do this often?" I asked. "House guests?"

Epiphany looked up at her husband. "Not too often," she said, "not for His Excellency, anyway. It's not uncommon in the cities, though; there's a lot of visiting back and forth as one city or another drifts nearby, and everyone will put up visitors from time to time."

"You don't have hotels?"

She shook her head. "We don't get many visitors from outplanet."

"You said 'His Excellency,'" I said. "That's Carlos Fernando? Tell me about him."

"Of course. What would you like to know?"

"Does he really—" I gestured at the city— "own all of this? The whole planet?"

"Yes, certainly, the city, yes. And also, no."

"How is that?"

"He will own the city, yes—this one, and five thousand others—but the planet? Maybe, maybe not. The Nordwald-Gruenbaum family does claim to own the planet, but in truth that claim means little. The claim may apply to the surface of the planet, but nobody owns the sky. The cities, though, yes. But, of course, he doesn't actually control them all personally."

"Well, of course not. I mean, hey, he's just a kid—he must have trustees, or proxies or something, right?"

"Indeed. Until he reaches his majority."

"And then?"

Truman Singh shrugged. "It is the Nordwald-Gruenbaum tradition—written into the first Nordwald's will. When he reaches his majority, it is personal property."

There were, as I discovered, eleven thousand, seven hundred and eight cities floating in the atmosphere of Venus. "Probably a few more," Truman Singh told me. "Nobody keeps track, exactly. There are myths of cities that float low down, never rising above the lower cloud decks, forever hidden. You can't live that deep—it's too hot—but the stories say that the renegade cities have a technology that allows them to reject heat." He shrugged. "Who knows?" In any case, of the known cities, the estate to which Carlos Fernando was heir owned or held shares or partial ownership of more than half.

"The Nordwald-Gruenbaum entity has been a good owner," Truman said. "I should say, they know that their employees could leave, to another city, if they had to, but they don't."

"And there's no friction?"

"Oh, the independent cities, they all think that the Nordwald-Gruenbaums have too much power!" He laughed. "But there's not much they can do about it, eh?"

"They could fight."

Truman Singh reached out and tapped me lightly on the center of my forehead with his middle finger. "That would not be wise." He paused, and then said more slowly, "We are an interconnected ecology here, the independents and the sultanate. We rely on each other. The independents could declare war, yes, but in the end nobody would win."

"Yes," I said. "Yes, I see that. Of course, the floating cities are so fragile—a single break in the gas envelope—"

"We are perhaps not as fragile as you think," Truman Singh replied. "I should say, you are used to the built worlds, but they are vacuum habitats, where a single blow-out would be catastrophic. Here, you know, there is no pressure difference between the atmosphere outside and the lifesphere inside; if there is a break, the gas equilibrates through the gap only very slowly. Even if we had a thousand broken panels, it would take weeks for the city to sink to the irrecoverable depths. And, of course, we do have safeguards, many safeguards." He paused, and then said, "but if there were a war . . . we are safe against ordinary hazards, you can have no fear of that . . . but against metastable bombs . . . well, that would not be good. No, I should say that would not be good at all."

The next day I set out to find where Leah had been taken, but although everyone I met was unfailingly polite, I had little success in reaching her. At least I was beginning to learn my way around.

The first thing I noticed about the city was the light. I was used to living in orbital habitats, where soft, indirect light was provided by panels of white-light diodes. In Hypatia City, brilliant Venus sunlight suffused throughout the interior. The next thing I noticed were the birds.

Hypatia was filled with birds. Birds were common in orbital habitats, since parrots and cockatiels adapt well to the freefall environment of space, but the volume of Hypatia was crowded with bright tropical birds, parrots and cockatoos and lorikeets, cardinals and chickadees and quetzals, more birds than I had names for, more birds than I had ever seen, a raucous orchestra of color and sound.

The floating city had twelve main chambers, separated from one another by thin, transparent membranes with a multiplicity of passages, each chamber well-lit and cheerful, each with a slightly different style.

The quarters I had been assigned were in sector Carbon, where individual living habitats were strung on cables like strings of iridescent pearls above a broad fenway of forest and grass. Within sector Carbon, cable-cars swung like pendulums on long strands, taking a traveler from platform to platform across the sector in giddy arcs. Carlos Fernando's chambers were in the highest, centermost bubble—upcity, as it was called—a bubble dappled with colored light and shadow, where the architecture was fluted minarets and oriental domes. But I wasn't, as it seemed, allowed into this elite sphere. I didn't even learn where Leah had been given quarters.

I found a balcony on a tower that looked out through the transparent canopy over the clouds. The cloudscape was just as magnificent as it had been the previous day; towering and slowly changing. The light was a rich golden color, and the sun, masked by a skein of feathery clouds like a tracery of lace, was surrounded by a bronze halo. From the angle of the sun it was early afternoon, but there would be no sunset that day; the great winds circling the planet would not blow the city into the night side of Venus for another day.

Of the eleven thousand other cities, I could detect no trace—looking outward, there was no indication that we were not alone in the vast cloudscape that stretched to infinity. But then, I thought, if the cities were scattered randomly, there would be little chance one would be nearby at any given time. Venus was a small planet, as planets go, but large enough to swallow ten thousand cities—or even a hundred times that—without any visible crowding of the skies.

I wished I knew what Leah thought of it.

I missed Leah. For all that she sometimes didn't seem to even notice I was there . . . our sojourn on Mars, brief as it had been . . . we had shared the same cubby. Perhaps that meant nothing to her. But it had been the very center of my life.

I thought of her body, lithe and golden-skinned. Where was she? What was she doing?

The park was a platform overgrown with cymbidian orchids, braced in the air by the great cables that transected the dome from the stanchion trusswork. This seemed a common architecture here, where even the ground beneath was suspended from the buoyancy of the air dome. I bounced my weight back and forth, testing the resonant frequency, and felt the platform move infinitesimally under me. Children here must be taught from an early age not to do that; a deliberate effort could build up destructive oscillation. I stopped bouncing, and let the motion damp.

When I returned near the middle of the day, neither Truman nor Epiphany were there, and Truman's other wife, a woman named Triolet, met me. She was a woman perhaps in her sixties, with dark skin and deep grey eyes. She had been introduced to me the previous day, but in the confusion of meeting numerous people in what seemed to be a large extended family, I had not had a chance to really meet her yet. There were always a number of people around the Singh household, and I was confused as to how, or even if, they were related to my hosts. Now, talking to her, I realized that she, in fact, was the one who had control of the Singh household finances.

The Singh family were farmers, I discovered. Or farm managers. The flora in Hypatia was decorative, or served to keep the air in the dome refreshed, but the real agriculture was in separate domes, floating at an altitude that was optimized for plant growth, and had no inhabitants. Automated equipment did the work of sowing and irrigation and harvest. Truman and Epiphany Singh were operational engineers, making those decisions that required a human input, watching that the robots kept on track and were doing the right things at the right times.

And, there was a message waiting for me, inviting me in the evening to attend a dinner with His Excellency, Carlos Fernando Delacroix Ortega de la Jolla y Nordwald-Gruenbaum.

Triolet helped me with my wardrobe, along with Epiphany, who had returned by the time I was ready to prepare. They both told me emphatically that my serviceable but well-worn jumpsuit was not appropriate attire. The gown Triolet selected was far gaudier than anything I would have chosen for myself, an electric shade of indigo accented with a wide midnight-black sash. "Trust us, it will be suitable," Epiphany told me. Despite its bulk, it was light as a breath of air.

"All clothes here are light," Epiphany told me. "Spider's silk."

"Ah, I see" I said. "Synthetic spider silk. Strong and light; very practical."

"Synthetic?" Epiphany asked, and giggled. "No, not synthetic. It's real."

"The silk is actually woven by spiders?"

"No, the whole garment is." At my puzzled look, she said, "Teams of spiders. They work together."

"Spiders."

"Well, they're natural weavers, you know. And easy to transport."

I arrived at the banquet hall at the appointed time and found that the plasma-arc blue gown that Epiphany had selected for me was the most conservative dress there. There were perhaps thirty people present, but Leah was clearly the center. She seemed happy with the attention, more animated than I'd recalled seeing her before.

"They're treating you well?" I asked, when I'd finally made it through the crowd to her.

"Oh, indeed."

I discovered I had nothing to say. I waited for her to ask about me, but she didn't. "Where have they given you to stay?"

"A habitat next section over," she said. "Sector Carbon. It's amazing— I've never seen so many birds."

"That's the sector I'm in," I said, "but they didn't tell me where you were."

"Really? That's odd." She tapped up a map of the residential sector on a screen built into the diamond tabletop, and a three-dimensional image appeared to float inside the table. She rotated it and highlighted her habitat, and I realized that she was indeed adjacent, in a large habitat that was almost directly next to the complex I was staying in. "It's a pretty amazing place. But mostly I've been here in the upcity. Have you talked to Carli much yet? He's a very clever kid. Interested in everything—botany, physics, even engineering."

"Really?" I said. "I don't think they'll let me into the upcity."

"You're kidding; I'm sure they'll let you in. Hey—" she called over one of the guards. "Say, is there any reason Tinkerman can't come up to the centrum?"

"No, madam, if you want it, of course not."

"Great. See, no problem."

And then the waiters directed me to my place at the far end of the table.

The table was a thick slab of diamond, the faceted edges collecting and refracting rainbows of color. The top was as smooth and slippery as a sheet of ice. Concealed inside were small computer screens so that any of the diners who wished could call up graphics or data as needed during a conversation. The table was both art and engineering, practical and beautiful at the same time.

Carlos Fernando sat at the end of the table. He seemed awkward and out of place in a chair slightly too large for him. Leah sat at his right, and an older woman—perhaps his mother?—on his left. He was bouncing around in his chair, alternating between playing with the computer system in his table and sneaking glances over at Leah when he thought she wasn't paying attention to him. If she looked in his direction, he would go still for a moment, and then his eyes would quickly dart away and he went back to staring at the graphics screen in front of him and fidgeting.

The server brought a silver tray to Carlos Fernando. On it was something the size of a fist, hidden under a canopy of red silk. Carlos Fernando looked up, accepted it with a nod, and removed the cloth. There was a moment of silence as people looked over, curious. I strained to see it.

It was a sparkling egg.

The egg was cunningly wrought of diamond fibers of many colors, braided into intricate lacework resembling entwined Celtic knots. The twelve-year-old Satrap of Venus picked it up and ran one finger over it, delicately, barely brushing the surface, feeling the corrugations and relief of the surface.

He held it for a moment, as if not quite sure what he should do with it, and then his hand darted over and put the egg on the plate in front of Leah. She looked up, puzzled.

"This is for you," he said.

The faintest hint of surprise passed through the other diners, almost sub-vocal, too soft to be heard.

A moment later the servers set an egg in front of each of us. Our eggs, although decorated with an intricate filligree of finely painted lines of gold and pale verdigris, were ordinary eggs—goose eggs, perhaps.

Carlos Fernando was fidgeting in his chair, half grinning, half biting his lip, looking down, looking around, looking everywhere except at the egg or at Leah.

"What am I to do with this?" Leah asked.

"Why," he said, "perhaps you should open it up and eat it."

Leah picked up the diamond-laced egg and examined it, turned it over and rubbed one finger across the surface. Then, having found what she was looking for, she held it in two fingers and twisted. The diamond eggshell opened, and inside it was a second egg, an ordinary one.

The kid smiled again and looked down at the egg in front of him. He picked up his spoon and cracked the shell, then spooned out the interior.

At this signal, the others cracked their own eggs and began to eat. After a moment, Leah laid the decorative shell to one side and did the same. I watched her for a moment, and then cracked my own egg.

It was, of course, excellent.

Later, when I was back with the Singh family, I was still puzzled. There had been some secret significance there that everybody else had seen, but I had missed. Mr. Singh was sitting with his older wife, Triolet, talking about accounts.

"I must ask a question," I said.

Truman Singh turned to me. "Ask," he said, "and I shall answer."

"Is there any particular significance," I said, "to an egg?"

"An egg?" Singh seemed puzzled. "Much significance, I would say. In the old days, the days of the asteroid miners, an egg was a symbol of luxury. Ducks were brought into the bigger habitats, and their eggs were, for some miners, the only food they would ever eat that was not a form of algae or soybean."

"A symbol of luxury," I said, musing. "I see. But I still don't understand it." I thought for a moment, and then asked, "is there any significance to a gift of an egg?"

"Well, no," he said, slowly, "not exactly. An egg? Nothing, in and of itself."

His wife Triolet, asked, "You are sure it's just an egg? Nothing else?"

"A very elaborate egg."

"Hmmm," she said, with a speculative look in her eye. "Not, maybe, an egg, a book, and a rock?"

That startled me a little. "A book and a rock?" The Bruno book—the very first thing Carlos Fernando had done on meeting Leah was to give her a book. But a rock? I hadn't see anything like that. "Why that?"

"Ah," she said. "I suppose you wouldn't know. I don't believe that our customs here in the sky cities are well known out there in the outer reaches."

Her mention of the outer reaches—Saturn and the Beyond—confused me for a moment, until I realized that, viewed from Venus, perhaps even Earth and the built worlds of the orbital clouds would be considered "outer."

"Here," she continued, "as in most of the ten thousand cities, an egg, a book, and a rock is a special gift. The egg is symbolic of life, you see; a book symbolic of knowledge; and a rock is the basis of all wealth, the minerals from the asteroid belt that built our society and bought our freedom."

"Yes? And all three together?"

"They are the traditional gesture of the beginning of courtship," she said.

"I still don't understand."

"If a young man gives a woman an egg, a book, and a rock," Truman said, "I should say this is his official sign that he is interested in courting her. If she accepts them, then she accepts his courtship."

"What? That's it, just like that, they're married?"

"No, no, no," he said. "It only means that she accepts the courtship— that she takes him seriously and, when it comes, she will listen to his pro-posal. Often a woman may have rocks and eggs from many young men. She doesn't have to accept, only take him seriously."

"Oh," I said.

But it still made no sense. How old was Carlos Fernando, twenty Venus years? What was that, twelve Earth years or so? He was far too young to be proposing.

"No one can terraform Venus," Carlos Fernando said.

Carlos Fernando had been uninterested in having me join in Leah's dis-cussion, but Leah, oblivious to her host's displeasure (or perhaps simply not caring), had insisted that if he wanted to talk about terraforming, I should be there.

It was one room of Carlos Fernando's extensive palaces, a rounded room, an enormous cavernous space that had numerous alcoves. I'd found them sit-ting in one of the alcoves, an indentation that was cozy but still open. The ubiquitous female guards were still there, but they were at the distant ends of the room, within command if Carlos Fernando chose to shout, but far enough to give them the illusion of privacy.

The furniture they were sitting on was odd. The chairs seemed sculpted of sapphire smoke, yet were solid to the touch. I picked one up and discov-ered that it weighed almost nothing at all. "Diamond aerogel," Carlos Fer-nando said. "Do you like it?"

"It's amazing," I said. I had never before seen so much made out of diamond. And yet it made sense here, I thought; with carbon dioxide an inexhaustible resource surrounding the floating cities, it was logical that the floating cities would make as much as they could out of carbon. But still, I didn't know you could make an aerogel of diamond. "How do you make it?"

"A new process we've developed," Carlos Fernando said. "You don't mind if I don't go into the details. It's actually an adaptation of an old idea, something that was invented back on Earth decades ago, called a molecular still."

When Carlos Fernando mentioned the molecular still, I thought I saw a sharp flicker of attention from Leah. This was a subject she knew something about, I thought. But instead of following up, she went back to his earlier comment on terraforming.

"You keep asking questions about the ecology of Mars," she said. "Why so many detailed questions about Martian ecopoiesis? You say you're not interested in terraforming, but are you really? You aren't thinking of the old idea of using photosynthetic algae in the atmosphere to reduce the carbon dioxide, are you? Surely you know that that can't work."

"Of course." Carlos Fernando waved the question away. "Theoretical," he said. "Nobody could terraform Venus, I know, I know."

His pronouncement would have been more dignified if his voice had finished changing, but as it was, it wavered between squeaking an octave up and then going back down again, ruining the effect. "We simply have too much atmosphere," he said. "Down at the surface, the pressure is over ninety bars—even if the carbon dioxide of the atmosphere could be converted to oxygen, the surface atmosphere would still be seventy times higher than the Earth's atmospheric pressure."

"I realize that," Leah said. "We're not actually ignorant, you know. So high a pressure of oxygen would be deadly—you'd burst into flames."

"And the leftover carbon," he said, smiling. "Hundreds of tons per square meter."

"So what are you thinking?" she asked.

But in response, he only smiled. "Okay, I can't terraform Venus," he said. "So tell me more about Mars."

I could see that there was something that he was keeping back. Carlos Fernando had some idea that he wasn't telling.

But Leah did not press him, and instead took the invitation to tell him about her studies of the ecology on Mars, as it had been transformed long ago by the vanished engineers of the long-gone Freehold Toynbee colony. The Toynbee's engineers had designed life to thicken the atmosphere of Mars, to increase the greenhouse effect, to melt the frozen oceans of Mars.

"But it's not working," Leah concluded. "The anaerobic life is being out-competed by the photosynthetic oxygen-producers. It's pulling too much carbon dioxide out of the atmosphere."

"But what about the Gaia effect? Doesn't it compensate?"

"No," Leah said. "I found no trace of a Lovelock self-aware planet. Either that's a myth, or else the ecology on Mars is just too young to stabilize."

"Of course on Venus, we would have no problem with photosynthesis removing carbon dioxide."

"I thought you weren't interested in terraforming Venus," I said.

Carlos Fernando waved my objection away. "A hypothetical case, of course," he said. "A thought exercise." He turned to Leah. "Tomorrow," he said, "would you like to go kayaking?"

"Sure," she said.

Kayaking, on Venus, did not involve water.

Carlos Fernando instructed Leah, and Epiphany helped me.

The "kayak" was a ten-meter long gas envelope, a transparent cylinder of plastic curved into an ogive at both ends, with a tiny bubble at the bottom where the kayaker sat. One end of the kayak held a huge, gossamer-bladed propeller that turned lazily as the kayaker pedaled, while the kayaker rowed with flimsy wings, transparent and iridescent like the wings of a dragonfly.

The wings, I discovered, had complicated linkages; each one could be pulled, twisted, and lifted, allowing each wing to separately beat, rotate, and camber.

"Keep up a steady motion with the propeller," Epiphany told me. "You'll lose all your maneuverability if you let yourself float to a stop. You can scull with the wings to put on a burst of speed if you need to. Once you're comfortable, use the wings to rise up or swoop down, and to maneuver. You'll have fun."

We were in a launching bay, a balcony protruding from the side of the city. Four of the human-powered dirigibles that they called kayaks were docked against the blister, the bulge of the cockpits neatly inserted into docking rings so that the pilots could enter the dirigible without exposure to the outside atmosphere. Looking out across the cloudscape, I could see dozens of kayaks dancing around the city like transparent squid with stubby wings, playing tag with each other and racing across the sky. So small and transparent compared to the magnificent clouds, they had been invisible until I'd known how to look.

"What about altitude?" I asked.

"You're about neutrally buoyant," she said. "As long as you have airspeed, you can use the wings to make fine adjustments up or down."

"What happens if I get too low?"

"You can't get too low. The envelope has a reservoir of methanol; as you get lower, the temperature rises and your reservoir releases vapor, so the envelope inflates. If you gain too much altitude, vapor condenses out. So you'll find you're regulated to stay pretty close to the altitude you're set for, which right now is," she checked a meter, "fifty-two kilometers above local ground level. We're blowing west at a hundred meters per second, so local ground level will change as the terrain below varies; check your meters for altimetry."

Looking downward, nothing was visible at all, only clouds, and below the clouds, an infinity of haze. It felt odd to think of the surface, over fifty kilometers straight down, and even odder to think that the city we were inside was speeding across that invisible landscape at hundreds of kilometers an hour. There was only the laziest feeling of motion, as the city drifted slowly through the ever-changing canyons of clouds

"Watch out for wind shear," she said. "It can take you out of sight of the city pretty quickly, if you let it. Ride the conveyor back if you get tired."

"The conveyor?"

"Horizontal-axis vortices. They roll from west to east, and east to west. Choose the right altitude, and they'll take you wherever you want to go."

Now that she'd told me, I could see the kayakers surfing the wind-shear, rising upward and skimming across the sky on invisible wheels of air.

"Have fun," she said. She helped me into the gondola, tightened my straps, looked at the gas pressure meter, checked the purge valve on the emergency oxygen supply, and verified that the radio, backup radio, and emergency locator beacons worked.

Across the kayak launch bay, Leah and Carlos Fernando had already pushed off. Carlos was sculling his wings alternatingly with a practiced swishing motion, building up a pendulum-like oscillation from side to side. Even as I watched, his little craft rolled over until for a moment it hesitated, inverted, and then rolled completely around.

"Showing off," Epiphany said, disdainfully. "You're not supposed to do that. Not that anybody would dare correct him."

She turned back to me. "Ready?" she asked.

"Ready as I'm going to be," I said. I'd been given a complete safety briefing that explained the backup systems and the backups to the backups, but still, floating in the sky above a fifty-two kilometer drop into the landscape of hell seemed an odd diversion.

"Go!" she said. She checked the seal on the cockpit, and then with one hand she released the docking clamp.

Freed from its mooring, the kayak sprang upward into the sky. As I'd been instructed, I banked the kayak away from the city. The roll made me feel suddenly giddy. The kayak skittered, sliding around until it was moving sideways to the air, the nose dipping down so that I was hanging against my straps. Coordinate the turn, I thought, but every slight motion I made with the wings seemed amplified drunkenly, and the kayak wove around erratically.

The radio blinked at me, and Epiphany's voice said, "You're doing great. Give it some airspeed."

I wasn't doing great; I was staring straight down at lemon-tinted haze and spinning slowly around like a falling leaf. Airspeed? I realize that I had entirely forgotten to pedal. I pedaled now, and the nose lifted. The sideways spin damped out, and as I straightened out, the wings bit into the air. "Great," Epiphany's voice told me. "Keep it steady."

The gas envelope seemed too fragile to hold me, but I was flying now, suspended below a golden sky. It was far too complicated, but I realized that as long as I kept the nose level, I could keep it under control. I was still oscillating slightly—it was difficult to avoid overcontrolling—but on the average, I was keeping the nose pointed where I aimed it.

Where were Leah and Carlos Fernando?

I looked around. Each of the kayaks had different markings—mine was marked with gray stripes like a tabby cat—and I tried to spot theirs.

A gaggle of kayaks was flying together, rounding the pylon of the city. As they moved around the pylon they all turned at once, flashing in the sunlight like a school of fish suddenly startled.

Suddenly I spotted them, not far above me, close to the looming wall of the city; the royal purple envelope of Carlos Fernando's kayak and the blue and yellow stripes of Leah's. Leah was circling in a steady climb, and Carlos Fernando was darting around her, now coming in fast and bumping envelopes, now darting away and pulling up, hovering for a moment with his nose pointed at the sky, then skewing around and sliding back downward.

Their motions looked like the courtship dance of birds.

The purple kayak banked around and swooped out and away from the city; and an instant later, Leah's blue and yellow kayak banked and followed. They both soared upward, catching a current of air invisible to me. I could see a few of the other fliers surfing on the same updraft. I yawed my nose around to follow them, but made no progress; I was too inexperienced with the kayak to be able to guess the air currents, and the wind differential was blowing me around the city in exactly the opposite of the direction I wanted to go. I pulled out and away from the city, seeking a different wind, and for an instant I caught a glimpse of something in the clouds below me, dark and fast moving.

Then I caught the updraft. I could feel it, the wings caught the air and it felt like an invisible giant's hand picking me up and carrying me—

Then there was a sudden noise, a stuttering and ripping, followed by a sound like a snare drum. My left wing and propeller ripped away, the fragments spraying into the sky. My little craft banked hard to the left. My radio came to life, but I couldn't hear anything as the cabin disintegrated around me. I was falling.

Falling.

For a moment I felt like I was back in zero-gee. I clutched uselessly to the remains of the control surfaces, connected by loose cords to fluttering pieces of debris. Pieces of my canopy floated away and were caught by the wind and spun upward and out of sight. The atmosphere rushed in, and my eyes started to burn. I made the mistake of taking a breath, and the effect was like getting kicked in the head. Flickering purple dots, the colors of a bruise, closed in from all directions. My vision narrowed to a single bright tunnel.

The air was liquid fire in my lungs. I reached around, desperately, trying to remember the emergency instructions before I blacked out, and my hands found the emergency air-mask between my legs. I was still strapped into my seat, although the seat was no longer attached to a vehicle, and I slapped the breathing mask against my face and sucked hard to start the airflow from the emergency oxygen. I was lucky; the oxygen cylinder was still attached to the bottom of the seat, as the seat, with me in it, tumbled through the sky. Through blurred eyes, I could see the city spinning above me. I tried to think of what the emergency procedure could be and what I should do next, but I could only think of what had gone wrong. What had I done? For the life of me I couldn't think of anything that I could have done that would have ripped the craft apart.

The city dwindled to the size of an acorn, and then I fell into the cloud layer and everything disappeared into a pearly white haze. My skin began to itch all over. I squeezed my eyes shut against the acid fog. The temperature was rising. How long would it take to fall fifty kilometers to the surface?

Something enormous and metallic swooped down from above me, and I blacked out.

Minutes or hours or days later I awoke in a dimly lit cubicle. I was lying on the ground, and two men wearing masks were spraying me with jets of a foaming white liquid that looked like milk but tasted bitter. My flight suit was in shreds around me.

I sat up, and began to cough uncontrollably. My arms and my face itched like blazes, but when I started to scratch, one of the men reached out and slapped my hands away.

"Don't scratch."

I turned to look at him, and the one behind me grabbed me by the hair and smeared a handful of goo into my face, rubbing it hard into my eyes.

Then he picked up a patch of cloth and tossed it to me. "Rub this where it itches. It should help."

I was still blinking, my face dripping, my vision fuzzy. The patch of cloth was wet with some gelatinous slime. I grabbed it from him, and dabbed it on my arms and then rubbed it in. It did help, some.

"Thanks," I said. "What the hell—"

The two men in face masks looked at each other. "Acid burn," the taller man said. "You're not too bad. A minute or two of exposure won't leave scars."

"What?"

"Acid. You were exposed to the clouds."

"Right."

Now that I wasn't quite so distracted, I looked around. I was in the cargo hold of some sort of aircraft. There were two small round portholes on either side. Although nothing was visible through them but a blank white, I could feel that the vehicle was in motion. I looked at the two men. They were both rough characters. Unlike the brightly colored spider-silk gowns of the citizens of Hypatia, they were dressed in clothes that were functional but not fancy, jumpsuits of a dark gray color with no visible insignia. Both of them were fit and well-muscled. I couldn't see their faces, since they were wearing breathing masks and lightweight helmets, but under their masks I could see that they both wore short beards, another fashion that had been missing among the citizens of Hypatia. Their eyes were covered with amber-tinted goggles, made in a crazy style that cupped each eye with a piece that was rounded like half an eggshell, apparently stuck to their faces by some invisible glue. It gave them a strange, bug-eyed look. They looked at me, but behind their face masks and google-eyes I was completely unable to read their expression.

"Thanks," I said. "So, who are you? Some sort of emergency rescue force?"

"I think you know who we are," the taller one said. "The question is, who the hell are you?"

I stood up and reached out a hand, thinking to introduce myself, but both of the men took a step back. Without seeming to move his hand, the taller one now had a gun, a tiny omniblaster of some kind. Suddenly a lot of things were clear.

"You're pirates," I said.

"We're the Venus underground," he said. "We don't like the word pirates very much. Now, if you don't mind, I have a question, and I really would like an answer. Who the hell are you?"

So I told him.

The first man started to take off his helmet, but the taller pirate stopped him. "We'll keep the masks on, for now. Until we decide he's safe." The taller pirate said he was named Esteban Jaramillo; the shorter one Esteban Francisco. That was too many Estebans, I thought, and decided to tag the one Jaramillo and the other Francisco.

I discovered from them that not everybody in the floating cities thought of Venus as a paradise. Some of the independent cities considered the clan of Nordwald-Gruenbaum to be well on its way to becoming a dictatorship. "They own half of Venus outright, but that's not good enough for them, no, oh no," Jaramillo told me. "They're stinking rich, but not stinking rich enough, and the very idea that there are free cities floating in the sky, cities that don't swear fealty to them and pay their goddamned taxes, that pisses them off. They'll do anything that they can to crush us. Us? We're just fighting back."

I would have been more inclined to see his point if I didn't have the uncomfortable feeling that I'd just been abducted. It had been a tremendous stroke of luck for me that their ship had been there to catch me when my kayak broke apart and fell. I didn't much believe in luck. And they didn't bother to answer when I asked about being returned to Hypatia. It was pretty clear that the direction we were headed was not back toward the city.

I had given them my word that I wouldn't fight, or try to escape—where would I escape to?—and they accepted it. Once they realized that I wasn't who they had expected to capture, they pressed me for news of the outside. "We don't hear a lot of outside news."

There were three of them in the small craft, the two Estebans, and the pilot, who was never introduced. He did not bother to turn around to greet me, and all I ever saw of him was the back of his helmet. The craft itself they called a manta; an odd thing that was partly an airplane, partly dirigible, and partly a submarine. Once I'd given my word that I wouldn't escape, I was allowed to look out, but there was nothing to see but a luminous golden haze.

"We keep the manta flying under the cloud decks," Jaramillo said. "Keeps us invisible."

"Invisible from whom?" I asked, but neither one of them bothered to answer. It was a dumb question anyway; I could very well guess who they wanted to keep out of sight of. "What about radar?" I said.

Esteban looked at Esteban, and then at me. "We have means to deal with radar," he said. "Just leave it at that and stop it with the questions you should know enough not to ask."

They seemed to be going somewhere, and eventually the manta exited the cloudbank into the clear air above. I pressed toward the porthole, trying to see out. The cloudscapes of Venus were still fascinating to me. We were skimming the surface of the cloud deck—ready to duck under if there were any sign of watchers, I surmised. From the cloudscape it was impossible to tell how far we'd come, whether it was just a few leagues, or halfway around the planet. None of the floating cities were visible, but in the distance I spotted the fat torpedo shape of a dirigible. The pilot saw it as well, for we banked toward it and sailed slowly up, slowing down as we approached, until it disappeared over our heads, and then the hull resonated with a sudden impact, and then a ratcheting clang.

"Soft dock," Jaramillo commented, and then a moment later another clang, and the nose of the craft was suddenly jerked up. "Hard dock," he said. The two Estebans seemed to relax a little, and a whine and a rumble filled the little cabin. We were being winched up into the dirigible.

After ten minutes or so, we came to rest in a vast interior space. The manta had been taken inside the envelope of the gas chamber, I realized. Half a dozen people met us.

"Sorry," Jaramillo said, "but I'm afraid we're going to have to blind you. Nothing personal."

"Blind?" I said, but actually, that was good news. If they'd had no intention to release me, they wouldn't care what I saw.

Jaramillo held my head steady while Francisco placed a set of the google-eyed glasses over my eyes. They were surprisingly comfortable. Whatever held them in place, they were so light that I could scarcely feel that they were there. The amber tint was barely noticeable. After checking that they fit, Francisco tapped the side of the goggles with his fingertip, once, twice, three times, four times. Each time he touched the goggles, the world grew darker, and with a fifth tap, all I could see was inky black. Why would sunglasses have a setting for complete darkness, I thought? And then I answered my own question: the last setting must be for e-beam welding. Pretty convenient, I thought. I wondered if I dared to ask them if I could keep the set of goggles when they were done.

"I am sure you won't be so foolish as to adjust the transparency," one of the Estebans said.

I was guided out the manta's hatch and across the hanger, and then to a seat.

"This the prisoner?" a voice asked.

"Yeah," Jaramillo said. "But the wrong one. No way to tell, but we guessed wrong, got the wrong flyer."

"Shit. So who is he?"

"Technician," Jaramillo said. "From the up and out."

"Really? So does he know anything about the Nordwald-Gruenbaum plan?"

I spread my hands out flat, trying to look harmless. "Look, I only met the kid twice, or I guess three times, if you—"

That caused some consternation; I could hear a sudden buzz of voices, in a language I didn't recognize. I wasn't sure how many of them there were, but it seemed like at least half a dozen. I desperately wished I could see them, but that would very likely be a fatal move. After a moment, Jaramillo said, his voice now flat and expressionless, "You know the heir of Nordwald-Gruenbaum? You met Carlos Fernando in person?"

"I met him. I don't know him. Not really."

"Who did you say you were again?"

I went through my story, this time starting at the very beginning, explaining how we had been studying the ecology of Mars, how we had been summoned to Venus to meet the mysterious Carlos Fernando. From time to time I was interrupted to answer questions—what was my relationship with Leah Hamakawa? (I wished I knew.) Were we married? Engaged? (No. No.) What was Carlos Fernando's relationship with Dr. Hamakawa? (I wished I knew.) Had Carlos Fernando ever mentioned his feelings about the independent cities? (No.) His plans? (No.) Why was Carlos Fernando interested in terraforming (I don't know.) What was Carlos Fernando planning? (I don't know.) Why did Carlos Fernando bring Hamakawa to Venus? (I wished I knew.) What was he planning? What was he planning? (I don't know. I don't know.)

The more I talked, the more sketchy it seemed, even to me.

There was silence when I had finished talking. Then, the first voice said, take him back to the manta.

I was led back inside and put into a tiny space, and a door clanged shut behind me. After a while, when nobody answered my call, I reached up to the goggles. They popped free with no more than a light touch, and, looking at them, I was still unable to see how they attached. I was in a storage hold of some sort. The door was locked.

I contemplated my situation, but I couldn't see that I knew any more now than I had before, except that I now knew that not all of the Venus cities were content with the status quo, and some of them were willing to go to some lengths to change it. They had deliberately shot me down, apparently thinking that I was Leah—or possibly even hoping for Carlos Fernando? It was hard to think that he would have been out of the protection of his bodyguards. Most likely, I decided, the bodyguards had been there, never letting him out of sight, ready to swoop in if needed, but while Carlos Fernando and Leah had soared up and around the city, I had left the sphere covered by the guards, and that was the opportunity the pirates in the manta had taken. They had seen the air kayak flying alone and shot it out of the sky, betting my life on their skill, that they could swoop in and snatch the falling pilot out of mid-air.

They could have killed me, I realized.

And all because they thought I knew something—or rather, that Leah Hamakawa knew something—about Carlos Fernando's mysterious plan.

What plan? He was a twelve-year-old kid, not even a teenager, barely more than an overgrown child! What kind of plan could a kid have?

I examined the chamber I was in, this time looking more seriously at how it was constructed. All the joints were welded, with no obvious gaps, but the metal was light, probably an aluminum-lithium alloy. Possibly malleable, if I had the time, if I could find a place to pry at, if I could find something to pry with.

If I did manage to escape, would I be able to pilot the manta out of its hanger in the dirigible? Maybe. I had no experience with lighter than air vehicles, though, and it would be a bad time to learn, especially if they decided that they wanted to shoot at me. And then I would be—where? A thousand miles from anywhere. Fifty million miles from anywhere I knew.

I was still mulling this over when Esteban and Esteban returned.

"Strap in," Esteban Jaramillo told me. "Looks like we're taking you home."

The trip back was more complicated than the trip out. It involved two or more transfers from vehicle to vehicle, during some of which I was again "requested" to wear the opaque goggles.

We were alone in the embarking station of some sort of public transportation. For a moment, the two Estebans had allowed me to leave the goggles transparent. Wherever we were, it was unadorned, drab compared to the florid excess of Hypatia, where even the bus stations—did they have bus stations?—would have been covered with flourishes and artwork.

Jaramillo turned to me and, for the first time, pulled off his goggles so he could look me directly in the eye. His eyes were dark, almost black, and very serious,

"Look," he said, "I know you don't have any reason to like us. We've got our reasons, you have to believe that. We're desperate. We know that his father had some secret projects going. We don't know what they were, but we know he didn't have any use for the free cities. We think the young Gruenbaum has something planned. If you can get through to Carlos Fernando, we want to talk to him."

"If you get him," Esteban Francisco said, "push him out a window. We'll catch him. Easy." He was grinning with a broad smile, showing all his teeth, as if to say he wasn't serious, but I wasn't at all sure he was joking.

"We don't want to kill him. We just want to talk," Esteban Jaramillo said. "Call us. Please. Call us."

And with that, he reached up and put his goggles back on. Then Francisco reached over and tapped my goggles into opacity, and everything was dark, and, with one on either side of me, we boarded the transport—bus? zeppelin? rocket?

Finally I was led into a chamber and was told to wait for two full minutes before removing the goggles, and after that I was free to do as I liked.

It was only after the footsteps had disappeared that it occurred to me to wonder how I was supposed to contact them, if I did have a reason to. It was too late to ask, though; I was alone, or seemed to be alone.

Was I being watched to see if I would follow orders, I wondered? Two full minutes. I counted, trying not to rush the count. When I got to a hundred and twenty, I took a deep breath, and finger-tapped the goggles to transparency.

When my eyes focused, I saw I was in a large disembarking lounge with genetically engineered pink grass and sculptures of iron and jade. I recognized it. It was the very same lounge at which we had arrived at Venus three days ago.—was it only three? Or had another day gone by?

I was back in Hypatia City.

Once again I was surrounded and questioned. As with the rest of Carlos Fernando's domain, the questioning room was lushly decorated with silk-covered chairs and elegant teak carvings, but it was clearly a holding chamber.

The questioning was by four women, Carlos Fernando's guards, and I had the feeling that they would not hesitate to tear me apart if they thought I was being less than candid with them. I told them what had happened, and at every step they asked questions, making suggestions as to what I could have done differently. Why had I taken my kayak so far away from any of the other fliers and out away from the city? Why had I allowed myself to be captured without fighting? Why didn't I demand to be returned and refuse to answer any questions? Why could I describe none of the rebels I'd met, except for two men who had—as far as they could tell from my descriptions—no distinctive features?

At the end of their questioning, when I asked to see Carlos Fernando, they told me that this would not be possible.

"You think I allowed myself to be shot down deliberately?" I said, addressing myself to the chief among the guards, a lean woman in scarlet silk.

"We don't know what to think, Mr. Tinkerman," she said. "We don't like to take chances."

"What now, then?"

"We can arrange transport to the built worlds," she said. "Or even to the Earth."

"I don't plan to leave without Doctor Hamakawa," I said.

She shrugged. "At the moment, that's still your option, yes," she said. "At the moment."

"How can I get in contact with Doctor Hamakawa?"

She shrugged. "If Doctor Hamakawa wishes, I'm sure she will be able to contact you."

"And if I want to speak to her?"

She shrugged. "You're free to go now. If we need to talk to you, we can find you."

I had been wearing one of the gray jumpsuits of the pirates when I'd been returned to Hypatia; the guard women had taken that away. Now they gave me a suit of spider-silk in a lavender brighter than the garb an expensive courtesan would wear in the built worlds surrounding Earth, more of an evening gown than a suit. It was nevertheless subdued compared to the day-to-day attire of Hypatia citizens, and I attracted no attention. I discovered that the google-eyed sunglasses had been neatly placed in a pocket at the knees of the garment. Apparently people on Venus keep their sunglasses at their knees. Convenient when you're sitting, I supposed. They hadn't been recognized as a parting gift from the pirates, or, more likely, had been considered so trivial as to not be worth confiscating. I was unreasonably pleased; I liked those glasses.

I found the Singh habitat with no difficulty, and when I arrived, Epiphany and Truman Singh were there to welcome me and to give me the news.

My kidnapping was already old news. More recent news was being discussed everywhere.

Carlos Fernando Delacroix Ortega de la Jolla y Nordwald-Gruenbaum had given a visitor from the outer solar system, Doctor Leah Hamakawa—a person who (they had heard) had actually been born on Earth—a rock.

And she had not handed it back to him.

My head was swimming.

"You're saying that Carlos Fernando is proposing marriage? To Leah? That doesn't make any sense. He's a kid, for Jove's sake. He's not old enough."

Truman and Epiphany Singh looked at one another and smiled. "How old were you when we got married?" Truman asked her. "Twenty?"

"I was almost twenty-one before you accepted my book and my rock," she said.

"So, in Earth years, what's that?" he said. "Thirteen?"

"A little over twelve," she said. "About time I was married up, I'd say."

"Wait," I said. "You said you were twelve years old when you got married?"

"Earth years," she said. "Yes, that's about right."

"You married at twelve? And you had—" I suddenly didn't want to ask, and said, "Do all women on Venus marry so young?"

"There are a lot of independent cities" Truman said. "Some of them must have different customs, I suppose. But it's the custom more or less everywhere I know."

"But that's—" I started to say, but couldn't think of how to finish. Sick? Perverted? But then, there were once a lot of cultures on Earth that had child marriages.

"We know the outer reaches have different customs," Epiphany said. "Other regions do things differently. The way we do it works for us."

"A man typically marries up at age twenty-one or so," Truman explained. "Say, twelve, thirteen years old, in Earth years. Maybe eleven. His wife will be about fifty or sixty—she'll be his instructor, then, as he grows up. What's that in Earth years—thirty? I know that in old Earth custom, both sides of a marriage are supposed to be the same age, but that's completely silly, is it not? Who's going to be the teacher, I should say?

"And then, when he grows up, by the time he reaches sixty or so he'll marry down, find a girl who's about twenty or twenty-one, and he'll serve as a teacher to her, I should say. And, in time, she'll marry down when she's sixty, and so on."

It seemed like a form of ritualized child abuse to me, but I thought it would be better not to say that aloud. Or, I thought, maybe I was reading too much into what he was saying. It was something like the medieval apprentice system. When he said teaching, maybe I was jumping to conclusions to think that he was talking about sex. Maybe they held off on the sex until the child grew up some. I thought I might be happier not knowing.

"A marriage is braided like a rope," Epiphany said. "Each element holds the next."

I looked from Truman to Epiphany and back. "You, too?" I asked Truman. "You were married when you were twelve?"

"In Earth years, I was thirteen, when I married up Triolet," he said. "Old. Best thing that ever happened to me. God, I needed somebody like her to straighten me out back then. And I needed somebody to teach me about sex, I should say, although I didn't know it back then."

"And Triolet—"

"Oh, yes, and her husband before her, and before that. Our marriage goes back a hundred and ninety years, to when Raj Singh founded our family; we're a long braid, I should say."

I could picture it now. Every male in the braid would have two wives, one twenty years older; one twenty years younger. And every female would have an older and a younger husband. The whole assembly would indeed be something you could think of as a braid, alternating down generations. The interpersonal dynamics must be terribly complicated. And then I suddenly remembered why we were having this discussion. "My god," I said. "You're serious about this. So you're saying that Carlos Fernando isn't just playing a game. He actually plans to marry Leah."

"Of course," Epiphany said. "It's a surprise, but then, I'm not at all surprised. It's obviously what His Excellency was planning right from the beginning. He's a devious one, he is."

"He wants to have sex with her."

She looked surprised. "Well, yes, of course. Wouldn't you? If you were twenty—I mean, twelve years old? Sure you're interested in sex. Weren't you? It's about time His Excellency had a teacher." She paused a moment. "I wonder if she's any good? Earth people—she probably never had a good teacher of her own."

That was a subject I didn't want to pick up on. Our little fling on Mars seemed a long way away, and my whole body ached just thinking of it.

"Sex, it's all that young kids think of," Truman cut in. "Sure. But for all that, I should say that sex is the least important part of a braid. A braid is a business, Mr. Tinkerman, you should know that. His Excellency Carlos Fernando is required to marry up into a good braid. The tradition, and the explicit terms of the inheritance, are both very clear. There are only about five braids on Venus that meet the standards of the trust, and he's too closely related to half of them to be able to marry in. Everybody has been assuming he would marry the wife of the Telios Delacroix braid; she's old enough to marry down now, and she's not related to him closely enough to matter. His proposition to Doctor Hamakawa—yes, that has everybody talking."

I was willing to grasp at any chance. "You mean, his marriage needs to be approved? He can't just marry anybody he likes?"

Truman Singh shook his head. "Of course he can't! I just told you. This is business as well as propagating the genes for the next thousand years. Most certainly he can't marry just anybody."

"But I think he just outmaneuvered them all," Epiphany added. "They thought they had him boxed in, didn't they? But they never thought that he'd go find an outworlder."

"They?" I said. "Who's they?"

"They never thought to guard against that," Epiphany continued.

"But he can't marry her, right?" I said. "For sure, she's not of the right family. She's not of any family. She's an orphan, she told me that. The institute is her only family."

Truman shook his head. "I think Epiphany's right," he said. "He just may have outfoxed them, I should say. If she's not of a family, doesn't have the dozens or hundreds of braided connections that everybody here must have, that means they can't find anything against her."

"Her scientific credentials—I bet they won't be able to find a flaw there." Epiphany said. "And, an orphan? That's brilliant. Just brilliant. No family ties at all. I bet he knew that. He worked hard to find just the right candidate, you can bet." She shook her head, smiling. "And we all thought he'd be another layabout, like his father."

"This is awful," I said. "I've got to do something."

"You? You're far too old for Dr. Hayakawa." Epiphany looked at me appraisingly. "A good looking man, though—if I were ten, fifteen years younger, I'd give you another look. I have cousins with girls the right age. You're not married, you say?"

Outside the Singh quarters in sector Carbon, the sun was breaking the horizon as the city blew into the daylit hemisphere.

I hadn't been sure whether Epiphany's offer to find me a young girl had been genuine, but it was not what I needed, and I'd refused as politely as I could manage.

I had gone outside to think, or as close to "outside" as the floating city allowed, where all the breathable gas was inside the myriad bubbles. But what could I do? If it was a technical problem, I would be able to solve it, but this was a human problem, and that had always been my weakness.

From where I stood, I could walk to the edge of the world, the transparent gas envelope that held the breathable air in, and kept the carbon dioxide of the Venus atmosphere out. The sun was surrounded by a gauzy haze of thin high cloud, and encircled by a luminous golden halo, with mock suns flying in formation to the left and the right. The morning sunlight slanted across the cloudtops. My eyes hurt from the direct sun. I remembered the sun goggles in my knee pocket, and pulled them out. I pressed them onto my eyes, and tapped on the right side until the world was a comfortable dim.

Floating in the air, in capital letters barely darker than the background, were the words LINK: READY.

I turned my head, and the words shifted with my field of view, changing from dark letters to light depending on the background.

A communications link was open? Certainly not a satellite relay; the glasses couldn't have enough power to punch through to orbit. Did it mean the manta was hovering in the clouds below?

"Hello, hello," I said, talking to the air. "Testing. Testing?"

Nothing.

Perhaps it wasn't audio. I tapped the right lens: dimmer, dimmer, dark; then back to full transparency. Maybe the other side? I tried tapping the left eye of the goggle, and a cursor appeared in my field of view.

With a little experimentation, I found that tapping allowed input in the form of Gandy-encoded text. It seemed to be a low bit-rate text only; the link power must be miniscule. But Gandy was a standard encoding, and I tapped out "CQ CQ".

Seek you, seek you.

The LINK: READY message changed to a light green, and in a moment the words changed to HERE.

WHO, I tapped.

MANTA 7, was the reply. NEWS?

CF PROPOSED LH, I tapped. !

KNOWN, came the reply. MORE?

NO

OK. SIGNING OUT.

The LINK: READY message returned.

A com link, if I needed one. But I couldn't see how it helped me any.

I returned to examining the gas envelope. Where I stood was an enormous transparent pane, a square perhaps ten meters on an edge. I was standing near the bottom of the pane, where it abutted to the adjacent sheet with a joint of very thin carbon. I pressed on it, and felt it flex slightly. It couldn't be more than a millimeter thick; it would make sense to make the envelope no heavier than necessary. I tapped it with the heel of my hand, and could feel it vibrate; a resonant frequency of a few Hertz, I estimated. The engineering weak point would be the joint between panels: if the pane flexed enough, it would pop out from its mounting at the join.

Satisfied that I had solved at least one technical conundrum, I began to contemplate what Epiphany had said. Carlos Fernando was to have married the wife of the Telios Delacroix braid. Whoever she was, she might be relieved at discovering Carlos Fernando making other plans; she could well think the arranged marriage as much a trap as he apparently did. But still. Who was she, and what did she think of Carlos Fernando's new plan?

The guards had made it clear that I was not to communicate with Carlos Fernando or Leah, but I had no instructions forbidding access to Braid Telios Delacroix.

The household seemed to be a carefully orchestrated chaos of children and adults of all ages, but now that I understood the Venus societal system a little, it made more sense. The wife of Telios Delacroix—once the wife-apparent of His Excellency Carlos Fernando—turned out to be a woman only a few years older than I was, with closely cropped grey hair. I realized I'd seen her before. At the banquet, she had been the woman sitting next to Carlos Fernando. She introduced herself as Miranda Telios Delacroix and introduced me to her up-husband, a stocky man perhaps sixty years old.

"We could use a young husband in this family," he told me. "Getting old, we are, and you can't count on children—they just go off and get married themselves."

There were two girls there, who Miranda Delacroix introduced as their two children. They were quiet, attempting to disappear into the background, smiling brightly but with their heads bowed to the ground, looking up at me through lowered eyelashes when they were brought out to be introduced. After the adults' attention had turned away from them, I noticed both of them surreptitiously studying me. A day ago I wouldn't even have noticed.

"Now, either come and sit nicely and talk, or else go do your chores," Miranda told them. "I'm sure the outworlder is quite bored with your buzzing in and out."

They both giggled and shook their heads and then disappeared into another room, although from time to time one or the other head would silently pop out to look at me, disappearing instantly if I turned my head to look

We sat down at a low table that seemed to be made out of oak. Her husband brought in some coffee and then left us alone. The coffee was made in the Thai style, in a clear cup, in layers with thick sweet milk.

"So you are Doctor Hamakawa's friend," she said. "I've heard a lot about you. Do you mind my asking, what exactly is your relationship with Doctor Hamakawa?"

"I would like to see her," I said.

She frowned. "So?"

"And I can't."

She raised an eyebrow.

"He has these woman, these bodyguards—"

Miranda Delacroix laughed. "Ah, I see! Oh, my little Carli is just too precious for words. I can't believe he's jealous. I do think that this time he's really infatuated." She tapped on the tabletop with her fingers for a moment, and I realized that the oak tabletop was another one of the embedded computer systems. "Goodness, Carli is not yet the owner of everything, and I don't see why you shouldn't see whomever you like. I've sent a message to Doctor Hamakawa that you would like to see her."

"Thank you."

She waved her hand.

It occurred to me that Carlos Fernando was about the same age as her daughters, perhaps even a classmate of theirs. She must have known him since he was a baby. It did seem a little unfair to him—if they were married, she would have all the advantage, and for a moment I understood his dilemma. Then something she had said struck me.

"He's not yet owner of everything, you said," I said. "I don't understand your customs, Mrs. Delacroix. Please enlighten me. What do you mean, yet?"

"Well, you know that he doesn't come into his majority until he's married," she said.

The picture was beginning to make sense. Carlos Fernando desperately wanted to control things, I thought. And he needed to be married to do it. "And once he's married?"

"Then he comes into his inheritance, of course," she said. "But since he'll be married, the braid will be in control of the fortune. You wouldn't want a twenty-one year old kid in charge of the entire Nordwald-Gruenbaum holdings? That would be ruinous. The first Nordwald knew that. That's why he married his son into the la Jolla braid. That's the way it's always been done."

"I see," I said. If Miranda Delacroix married Carlos Fernando, she—not he—would control the Nordwald-Gruenbaum fortune. She had the years of experience, she knew the politics, how the system worked. He would be the child in the relationship. He would always be the child in the relationship.

Miranda Delacroix had every reason to want to make sure that Leah Hamakawa didn't marry Carlos Fernando. She was my natural ally.

And also, she—and her husband—had every reason to want to kill Leah Hamakawa.

Suddenly the guards that followed Carlos Fernando seemed somewhat less of an affectation. Just how good were the bodyguards? And then I had another thought. Had she, or her husband, hired the pirates to shoot down my kayak? The pirates clearly had been after Leah, not me. They had known that Leah was flying a kayak; somebody must have been feeding them information. If it hadn't been her, then who?

I looked at her with new suspicions. She was looking back at me with a steady gaze. "Of course, if your Doctor Leah Hamakawa intends to accept the proposal, the two of them will be starting a new braid. She would nominally be the senior, of course, but I wonder—"

"But would she be allowed to?" I interrupted. "If she decided to marry Carlos Fernando, wouldn't somebody stop her?"

She laughed. "No, I'm afraid that little Carli made his plan well. He's the child of a Gruenbaum, all right. There's no legal grounds for the families to object; she may be an outworlder, but he's made an end run around all the possible objections."

"And you?"

"Do you think I have choices? If he decides to ask me for advice, I'll tell him it's not a good idea. But I'm halfway tempted to just see what he does."

And give up her chance to be the richest woman in the known universe? I had my doubts.

"Do you think you can talk her out of it?" she said. "Do you think you have something to offer her? As I understand it, you don't own anything. You're hired help, a gypsy of the solar system. Is there a single thing that Carli is offering her that you can match?"

"Companionship," I said. It sounded feeble, even to me.

"Companionship?" she echoed, sarcastically. "Is that all? I would have thought most outworlder men would have promised love. You are honest, at least, I'll give you that,"

"Yes, love," I said, miserable. "I'd offer her love."

"Love," she said. "Well, how about that. Yes, that's what outworlders marry for; I've read about it. You don't seem to know, do you? This isn't about love. It's not even about sex, although there will be plenty of that, I can assure you, more than enough to turn my little Carlos inside out and make him think he's learning something about love.

"This is about business, Mr. Tinkerman. You don't seem to have noticed that. Not love, not sex, not family. It's business."

Miranda Telios Delacroix's message had gotten through to Leah, and she called me up to her quarters. The women guards did not seem happy about this, but they had apparently been instructed to obey her direct orders, and two red-clad guardswomen led me to her quarters.

"What happened to you? What happened to your face?" she said, when she saw me.

I reached up and touched my face. It didn't hurt, but the acid burns had left behind red spotches and patches of peeling skin. I filled her in on the wreck of the kayak and the rescue, or kidnapping, by pirates. And then I told her about Carlos. "Take another look at that book he gave you. I don't know where he got it, and I don't want to guess what it cost, but I'll say it's a sure bet it's no facsimile."

"Yes, of course." she said. "He did tell me, eventually."

"Don't you know it's a proposition?"

"Yes; the egg, the book, and the rock," she said. "Very traditional here. I know you like to think I have my head in the air all the time, but I do pay some attention to what's going on around me. Carli is a sweet kid."

"He's serious, Leah. You can't ignore him."

She waved me off. "I can make my own decisions, but thanks for the warnings."

"It's worse than that," I told her. "Have you met Miranda Telios Delacroix?"

"Of course," she said.

"I think she's trying to kill you." I told her about my experience with kayaks, and my suspicion that the pirates had been hired to shoot me down, thinking I was her.

"I believe you may be reading too much into things, Tinkerman," she said. "Carli told me about the pirates. They're a small group, disaffected; they bother shipping and such, from time to time, but he says that they're nothing to worry about. When he gets his inheritance, he says he will take care of them."

"Take care of them? How?"

She shrugged. "He didn't say."

But that was exactly what the pirates—rebels—had told me: that Carlos had a plan, and they didn't know what it was. "So he has some plans he isn't telling," I said.

"He's been asking me about terraforming," Leah said, thinking. "But it doesn't make sense to do that on Venus. I don't understand what he's thinking. He could split the carbon dioxide atmosphere into oxygen and carbon; I know he has the technology to do that."

"He does?"

"Yes, I think you were there when he mentioned it. The molecular still. It's solar-powered micromachines. But what would be the point?"

"So he's serious?"

"Seriously thinking about it, anyway. But it doesn't make any sense. Nearly pure oxygen at the surface, at sixty or seventy bars? That atmosphere would be even more deadly than the carbon dioxide. And it wouldn't even solve the greenhouse effect; with that thick an atmosphere, even oxygen is a greenhouse gas."

"You explained that to him?"

"He already knew it. And the floating cities wouldn't float any more. They rely on the gas inside—breathing air—being lighter than the Venusian air. Turn the Venus carbon dioxide to pure O2, the cities fall out of the sky."

"But?"

"But he didn't seem to care."

"So terraforming would make Venus uninhabitable, and he knows it. So what's he planning?"

She shrugged. "I don't know."

"I do," I said. "And I think we'd better see your friend Carlos Fernando."

Carlos Fernando was in his playroom.

The room was immense. His family's quarters were built on the edge of the upcity, right against the bubble-wall, and one whole side of his playroom looked out across the cloudscape. The room was littered with stuff: sets of interlocking toy blocks with electronic modules inside that could be put together into elaborate buildings, models of spacecraft and various lighter-than-air aircraft, no doubt vehicles used on Venus, a contraption of transparent vessels connected by tubes that seemed to be a half-completed science project, a unicycle that sat in a corner, silently balancing on its gyros. Between the toys were pieces of light, transparent furniture. I picked up a chair, and it was no heavier than a feather, barely there at all. I knew what it was now, diamond fibers that had been engineered into a foamed, fractal structure. Diamond was their chief working material; it was something that they could make directly out of the carbon dioxide atmosphere, with no imported raw materials. They were experts in diamond, and it frightened me.

When the guards brought us to the playroom, Carlos Fernando was at the end of the room farthest from the enormous window, his back to the window and to us. He'd known we were coming, of course, but when the guards announced our arrival he didn't turn around, but called behind him "It's okay—I'll be with them in a second."

The two guards left us.

He was gyrating and waving his hands in front of a large screen. On the screen, colorful spaceships flew in three-dimensional projection through the complicated maze of a city that had apparently been designed by Escher, with towers connected by bridges and buttresses. The viewpoint swooped around, chasing some of the spaceships, hiding from others. From time to time bursts of red dots shot forward, blowing the ships out of the sky with colorful explosions as Carlos Fernando shouted "Gotcha!" and "In your eye, dog."

He was dancing with his whole body; apparently the game had some kind of full-motion input. As far as I could tell, he seemed to have forgotten entirely that we were there.

I looked around.

Sitting on a padded platform no more than two meters from where we had entered, a lion looked back at me with golden eyes. He was bigger than I was. Next to him, with her head resting on her paws, lay a lioness, and she was watching me as well, her eyes half open. Her tail twitched once; twice. The lion's mane was so huge that it must have been shampooed and blow-dried.

He opened his mouth and yawned, then rolled onto his side, still watching me.

"They're harmless," Leah said. "Bad-Boy and Knickers. Pets."

Knickers—the female, I assumed—stretched over and grabbed the male lion by the neck. Then she put one paw on the back of his head and began to groom his fur with her tongue.

I was beginning to get a feel for just how different Carlos Fernando's life was from anything I knew.

On the walls closer to where Carlos Fernando was playing his game were several other screens. The one to my left looked like it had a homework problem partially worked out. Calculus, I noted. He was doing a chain-rule differentiation and had left it half-completed where he'd gotten stuck, or bored. Next to it was a visualization of the structure of the atmosphere of Venus. Homework? I looked at it more carefully. If it was homework, he was much more interested in atmospheric science than in math; the map was covered with notes and had half a dozen open windows with details. I stepped forward to read it more closely.

The screen went black.

I turned around, and Carlos Fernando was there, a petulant expression on his face. "That's my stuff," he said. His voice squeaked on the word "stuff." "I don't want you looking at my stuff unless I ask you to, okay?"

He turned to Leah, and his expression changed to something I couldn't quite read. He wanted to kick me out of his room, I thought, but didn't want to make Leah angry; he wanted to keep her approval. "What's he doing here?" he asked her.

She looked at me, and raised her eyebrows.

I wish I knew myself, I thought, but I was in it far enough, I had better say something.

I walked over to the enormous window, and looked out across the clouds. I could see another city, blue with distance, a toy balloon against the golden horizon.

"The environment of Venus is unique," I said. "And to think, your ancestor Udo Nordwald put all this together."

"Thanks," he said. "I mean, I guess I mean thanks. I'm glad you like our city."

"All of the cities," I said. "It's a staggering accomplishment. The genius it must have taken to envision it all, to put together the first floating city; to think of this planet as a haven, a place where millions can live. Or billions—the skies are nowhere near full. Someday even trillions, maybe."

"Yeah," he said. "Really something, I guess."

"Spectacular." I turned around and looked him directly in the eye. "So why do you want to destroy it?"

"What?" Leah said.

Carlos Fernando had his mouth open, and started to say something, but then closed his mouth again. He looked down, and then off to his left, and then to the right. He said, "I . . . I . . ." but then broke off.

"I know your plan," I said. "Your micromachines—they'll convert the carbon dioxide to oxygen. And when the atmosphere changes, the cities will be grounded. They won't be lighter than air, won't be able to float any more. You know that, don't you? You want to do it deliberately."

"He can't," Leah said, "it won't work. The carbon would—" and then she broke off. "Diamond," she said. "He's going to turn the excess carbon into diamond."

I reached over and picked up a piece of furniture, one of the foamed-diamond tables. It weighted almost nothing.

"Nanomachinery," I said. "The molecular still you mentioned. You know, somebody once said that the problem with Venus isn't that the surface is too hot. It's just fine up here where the air's as thin as Earth's air. The problem is, the surface is just too darn far below sea level.

"But every ton of atmosphere your molecular machines convert to oxygen, you get a quarter-ton of pure carbon. And the atmosphere is a thousand tons per square meter."

I turned to Carlos Fernando, who still hadn't managed to say anything.

His silence was as damning as any confession. "Your machines turn that carbon into diamond fibers, and build upward from the surface. You're going to build a new surface, aren't you—a completely artificial surface. A platform up to the sweet spot, fifty kilometers above the old rock surface. And the air there will be breathable."

At last Carlos found his voice. "Yeah," he said. "Dad came up with the machines, but the idea of using them to build a shell around the whole planet—that idea was mine. It's all mine. It's pretty smart, isn't it? Don't you think it's smart?"

"You can't own the sky," I said, "but you can own the land, can't you? You will have built the land. And all the cities are going to crash. There won't be any dissident cities, because there won't be any cities. You'll own it all. Everybody will have to come to you."

"Yeah," Carlos said. He was smiling now, a big goofy grin. "Sweet, isn't it?" He must have seen my expression, because he said, "Hey, come on. It's not like they were contributing. Those dissident cities are full of nothing but malcontents and pirates."

Leah's eyes were wide. He turned to her and said, "Hey, why shouldn't I? Give me one reason. They shouldn't even be here. It was all my ancestor's idea, the floating city, and they shoved in. They stole his idea, so now I'm going to shut them down. It'll be better my way."

He turned back to me. "Okay, look. You figured out my plan. That's fine, that's great, no problem, okay? You're smarter than I thought you were, I admit it. Now, just, I need you to promise not to tell anybody, okay?"

I shook my head.

"Oh, go away," he said. He turned back to Leah. "Doctor Hamakawa," he said. He got down on one knee, and, staring at the ground, said, "I want you to marry me. Please?"

Leah shook her head, but he was staring at the ground, and couldn't see her. "I'm sorry, Carlos," she said. "I'm sorry."

He was just a kid, in a room surrounded by his toys, trying to talk the adults into seeing things the way he wanted to see them. He finally looked up, his eyes filling with tears. "Please," he said. "I want you to. I'll give you anything. I'll give you whatever you want. You can have everything I own, all of it, the whole planet, everything."

"I'm sorry," Leah repeated. "I'm sorry."

He reached out and picked up something off the floor—a model of a spaceship—and looked at it, pretending to be suddenly interested in it. Then he put it carefully down on a table, picked up another one, and stood up, not looking at us. He sniffled, and wiped his eyes with the back of his hand—apparently forgetting he had the ship model in it—trying to do it casually, as if we wouldn't have noticed that he had been crying.

"Ok," he said. "You can't leave, you know. This guy guessed too much. The plan only works if it's secret, so that the malcontents don't know it's coming, don't prepare for it. You have to stay here. I'll keep you here, I'll— I don't know. Something."

"No," I said. "It's dangerous for Leah here. Miranda already tried to hire pirates to shoot her down once, when she was out in the sky kayak. We have to leave."

Carlos looked up at me, and with sudden sarcasm, said, "Miranda? You're joking. That was me who tipped off the pirates. Me. I thought they'd take you away and keep you. I wish they had."

And then he turned back to Leah. "Please? You'll be the richest person on Venus. You'll be the richest person in the solar system. I'll give it all to you. You'll be able to do anything you want."

"I'm sorry," Leah repeated. "It's a great offer. But no."

At the other end of the room, Carlos' bodyguards were quietly entering. He apparently had some way to summon them silently. The room was filling with them, and their guns were drawn, but not yet pointed.

I backed toward the window, and Leah came with me.

The city had rotated a little, and sunlight was now slanting in through the window. I put my sun goggles on.

"Do you trust me?" I said quietly.

"Of course," Leah said. "I always have."

"Come here."

LINK: READY blinked in the corner of my field of view.

I reached up, casually, and tapped on the side of the left lens. CQ MANTA, I tapped. CQ.

I put my other hand behind me and, hoping I could disguise what I was doing as long as I could, I pushed on the pane, feeling it flex out.

HERE, was the reply.

Push. Push. It was a matter of rhythm. When I found the resonant frequency of the pane, it felt right, it built up, like oscillating a rocking chair, like sex.

I reached out my left hand to hold Leah's hand, and pumped harder on the glass with my right. I was putting my weight into it now, and the panel was bowing visibly with my motion. The window was making a noise now, an infrasonic thrum too deep to hear, but you could feel it. On each swing the pane of the window bowed further outward.

"What are you doing?" Carlos shouted. "Are you crazy?"

The bottom bowed out, and the edge of the pane separated from its frame.

There was a smell of acid and sulfur. The bodyguards ran toward us, but—as I'd hoped—they were hesitant to use their guns, worried that the damaged panel might blow completely out.

The window screeched and jerked, but held, fixed in place by the other joints. The way it was stuck in place left a narrow vertical slit between the window and its frame. I pulled Leah close to me, and shoved myself backwards, against the glass, sliding along against the bowed pane, pushing it outward to widen the opening as much as I could.

As I fell, I kissed her lightly on the edge of the neck.

She could have broken my grip, could have torn herself free.

But she didn't.

"Hold your breath and squeeze your eyes shut," I whispered, as we fell through the opening and into the void, and then with my last breath of air, I said, "I love you."

She said nothing in return. She was always practical, and knew enough not to try to talk when her next breath would be acid. "I love you too," I imagined her saying.

With my free hand, I tapped, MANTA
NEED PICK-UP. FAST.
And we fell.

"It wasn't about sex at all," I said. "That's what I failed to understand." We were in the manta, covered with slime, but basically unhurt. The pirates had accomplished their miracle, snatched us out of midair. We had information they needed; and in exchange, they would give us a ride off the planet, back where we belonged, back to the cool and the dark and the emptiness between planets. "It was all about finance. Keeping control of assets."

"Sure it's about sex," Leah said. "Don't fool yourself. We're humans. It's always about sex. Always. You think that's not a temptation? Molding a kid into just exactly what you want? Of course it's sex. Sex and control. Money? That's just the excuse they tell themselves."

"But you weren't tempted," I said.

She looked at me long and hard. "Of course I was." She sighed, and her expression was once again distant, unreadable. "More than you'll ever know."

ABOUT THE AUTHOR

Geoffrey A. Landis's first story, "Elemental," appeared while he was a graduate student in physics. Since then he finished his PhD and went off to work at NASA John Glenn Research Center in Ohio, but he's still, off and on, writing science fiction. He has published eighty-four short stories, one novel (*Mars Crossing*), a collection of short stories (*Impact Parameter, and Other Quantum Fictions*), and a book of poetry (*Iron Angels*). In the process he has accumulated two Hugo awards and a Nebula.

AUTHOR'S INTRODUCTION

A lot of people think small towns in rural America are either charming and quaint, like in a Norman Rockwell painting, or backward and scary, like in a Shirley Jackson story. Both depictions can be true, of course, but despite the smallness of rural America you'll find a wider range of people living there than this. I grew up on a small farm in Ohio, grew out of it and into the wider world beyond it, and found not only that much of what I expected of the world was different from what I'd been told, but also that much of what people who grew up in cities and suburbs were told to expect of someone who grew up on a small farm in Ohio like me was different from what they actually encountered. So when I wrote "Map of Seventeen" I wanted to write about a rural Midwestern family struggling with a conflict between the expectations of their norms and those of the cosmopolitan world outside their boundaries. And I wanted to write about how people we perceive to be beasts or monsters in the world because of their differences from us are really beautiful if we can look at them in the right way.

MAP OF SEVENTEEN
Chris Barzak

Everyone has secrets. Even me. We carry them with us like contraband, always swaddled in some sort of camouflage we've concocted to hide the parts of ourselves the rest of the world is better off not knowing. I'd write what I'm thinking in a diary if I could believe others would stay out of those pages, but in a house like this there's no such thing as privacy. If you're going to keep secrets, you have to learn to write them down inside your own heart. And then be sure not to give that away to anyone either. At least not to just anyone at all.

Which is what bothers me about *him*, the guy my brother is apparently going to marry. Talk about secrets. Off Tommy goes to New York City for college, begging my parents to help him with money for four straight years, then after graduating at the top of his class—in studio art, of all things (not even a degree that will get him a job to help pay off the loans our parents took out for his education)—he comes home to tell us he's gay, and before we can say anything, good or bad, runs off again and won't return our calls. And when he did start talking to Mom and Dad again, it was just short phone conversations and emails, asking for help, for more money.

Five years of off and on silence and here he is, bringing home some guy named Tristan who plays the piano better than my mother and has never seen a cow except on TV. We're supposed to treat this casually and not bring up the fact that he ran away without letting us say anything at all four years ago, and to try not to embarrass him. That's Tommy Terlecki, my big brother, the gay surrealist Americana artist who got semi-famous not for the magical creatures and visions he paints, but for his horrifically exaggerated family portraits of us dressed up in ridiculous roles: *American Gothic*, dad holding a pitchfork, mom presenting her knitting needles and a ball of yarn to the viewer as if she's coaxing you to give them a try, me with my arms folded under my breasts, my face angry within the frame of my bonnet, scowling at Tommy, who's sitting on the ground beside my legs in the portrait, pulling off the Amish-like clothes. What I don't like about these paintings is that he's lied about us in them. The Tommy in the portrait is constrained by his family's way of life, but it's Tommy who's put us in those clothes to begin with. They're how he sees us, not the way we are, but he gets to dramatize a conflict with us in the paintings anyway, even though it's a conflict he himself has imagined.

Still, I could be practical and say the *American Gothic* series made Tommy's name, which is more than I can say for the new stuff he's working on: *The Sons of Melusine*. They're like his paintings of magical creatures, which the critic who picked his work out of his first group show found too precious in comparison to the "promise of the self-aware, absurdist family portraits this precocious young man from the wilderness of Ohio has also created." Thank you, Google, for keeping me informed on my brother's activities. *The Sons of Melusine* are all bare-chested men with curvy muscles who have serpentine tails and faces like Tristan's, all of them extremely attractive and extremely in pain: out of water mostly, gasping for air in the back alleys of cities, parched and bleeding on beaches, strung on fishermen's line, the hook caught in the flesh of a cheek. A new Christ, Tommy described them when he showed them to us, and Mom and Dad said, "Hmm, I see."

He wants to hang an *American Gothic* in the living room, he told us, after we'd been sitting around talking for a while, all of us together for the first time in years, his boyfriend Tristan smiling politely as we tried to catch up with Tommy's doings while trying to be polite and ask Tristan about himself as well. "My life is terribly boring, I'm afraid," Tristan said when I asked what he does in the city. "My family's well off, you see, so what I do is mostly whatever seems like fun at any particular moment."

Well off. Terribly boring. Whatever seems like fun at any particular moment. I couldn't believe my brother was dating this guy, let alone planning to marry him. This is Tommy, I reminded myself, and right then was when he said, "If it's okay with you, Mom and Dad, I'd like to hang one of the *American Gothic* paintings in here. Seeing how Tristan and I will be staying with you for a while, it'd be nice to add some touches of our own."

Tommy smiled. Tristan smiled and gave Mom a little shrug of his shoulders. I glowered at them from across the room, arms folded across my chest on purpose. Tommy noticed and, with a concerned face, asked me if something was wrong. "Just letting life imitate art," I told him, but he only kept on looking puzzled. Faker, I thought. He knows exactly what I mean.

Halfway through that first evening, I realized this was how it was going to be as long as Tommy and Tristan were with us, while they waited for their own house to be built next to Mom and Dad's: Tommy conducting us all like the head of an orchestra, waving his magic wand. He had Mom and Tristan sit on the piano bench together and tap out some "Heart and Soul". He sang along behind them for a moment, before looking over his shoulder and waving Dad over to join in. When he tried to pull me in with that charming squinty-eyed devil grin that always gets anyone—our parents, teachers, the local police officers who used to catch him speeding down back roads—to do his bidding, I shook my head, said nothing, and left the room. "Meg?" he said behind me. Then the piano stopped and I could hear them whispering, wondering what had set me off this time.

I'm not known for being easy to live with. Between Tommy's flare for making people live life like a painting when he's around, and my stubborn, immovable will, I'm sure our parents must have thought at some time or other that their real children had been swapped in the night with changelings. It would explain the way Tommy could make anyone like him, even out in the country, where people don't always think well of gay people. It would explain the creatures he paints that people always look nervous about after viewing them, the half-animal beings that roam the streets of cities and back roads of villages in his first paintings. It would explain how I can look at any math problem or scientific equation my teachers put before me and figure them out without breaking a sweat. And my aforementioned will. My will, this thing that's so strong I sometimes feel like it's another person inside me.

Our mother is a mousy figure here in the Middle of Nowhere, Ohio. The central square is not even really a square but an intersection of two highways where town hall, a general store, beauty salon and Presbyterian church all face each other like lost old women casting glances over the asphalt, hoping one of the others knows where they are and where they're going, for surely why would anyone stop here? My mother works in the library, which used to be a one-room schoolhouse a hundred years ago, where they still use a stamp card to keep track of the books checked out. My father is one of the township trustees and he also runs our farm. We raise beef cattle, Herefords mostly, though a few Hereford and Angus mixes are in our herd, so you sometimes get black cows with polka-dotted white faces. I never liked the mixed calves, I'm not sure why, but Tommy always said they were his favorites. Mutts are always smarter than streamlined gene pools, he said. Me? I always thought they looked like heartbroken mimes with dark, dewy eyes.

From upstairs in my room I could hear the piano start again, this time a classical song. It had to be Tristan. Mom only knows songs like "Heart and Soul" and just about any song in a hymn book. They attend, I don't. Tommy and I gave up church ages ago. I still consider myself a Christian, just not the church-going kind. We're lucky to have parents who asked us why we didn't want to go, instead of forcing us like tyrants. When I told them I didn't feel I was learning what I needed to live in the world there, instead of getting mad, they just nodded and Mom said, "If that's the case, perhaps it's best that you walk your own way for a while, Meg."

They're so *good*. That's the problem with my parents. They're so good, it's like they're children or something, innocent and naïve. Definitely not stupid, but way too easy on other people. They never fuss with Tommy. They let him treat them like they're these horrible people who ruined his life and they never say a word. They hug him and calm him down instead, treat him like a child. I don't get it. Tommy's the oldest. Isn't he the one who's supposed to be mature and put together well?

I listened to Tristan's notes drift up through the ceiling from the living room below, and lay on my bed, staring at a tiny speck on the ceiling, a stain or odd flaw in the plaster that has served as my focal point for anger for many years. Since I can remember, whenever I got angry, I'd come up here and lie in this bed and stare at that speck, pouring all of my frustrations into it, as if it were a black hole that could suck up all the bad. I've given that speck so much of my worst self over the years, I'm surprised it hasn't grown darker and wider, big enough to cast a whole person into its depths. When I looked at it now, I found I didn't have as much anger to give it as I'd thought. But no, that wasn't it either. I realized all of my anger was floating around the room instead, buoyed up by the notes of the piano, by Tristan's playing. I thought I could even see those notes shimmer into being for a brief moment, electrified by my frustration. When I blinked, though, the air looked normal again, and Tristan had brought his melody to a close.

There was silence for a minute, some muffled voices, then Mom started up "Amazing Grace". I felt immediately better and breathed a sigh of relief. Then someone knocked on my door and it swung open a few inches, enough for Tommy to peek inside. "Hey, Sis. Can I come in?"

"It's a free country."

"Well," said Tommy. "Sort of."

We laughed. We could laugh about things we agreed on.

"Sooo," said Tommy, "what's a guy gotta do around here to get a hug from his little sister?"

"Aren't you a little old for hugs?"

"Ouch. I must have done something really bad this time."

"Not bad. Something. I don't know what."

"Want to talk about it?"

"Maybe."

Tommy sat down on the corner of my bed and craned his neck to scan the room. "What happened to all the unicorns and horses?"

"They died," I said. "Peacefully, in their sleep, in the middle of the night. Thank God."

He laughed, which made me smirk without wanting to. This was the other thing Tommy had always been able to do: make it hard for people to stay mad at him. "So you're graduating in another month?" he said. I nodded, turned my pillow over so I could brace it under my arm to hold me up more comfortably. "Are you scared?"

"About what?" I said. "Is there something I should be scared of?"

"You know. The future. The rest of your life. You won't be a little girl anymore."

"I haven't been a little girl for a while, Tommy."

"You know what I mean," he said, standing up, tucking his hands into his pockets like he does whenever he's being Big Brother. "You're going to have to begin making big choices," he said. "What you want out of life. You know it's not a diploma you receive when you cross the graduation stage. It's really a ceremony where your training wheels are taken off. The cap everyone wants to throw in the air is a symbol of what you've been so far in life: a student. That's right, everyone wants to cast it off so quickly, eager to get out into the world. Then they realize they've got only a couple of choices for what to do next. The armed service, college or working at a gas station. It's too bad we don't have a better way to recognize what the meaning of graduation really is. Right now, I think it leaves you kids a little clueless."

"Tommy," I said, "yes, you're eleven years older than me. You know more than I do. But really, you need to learn when to shut the hell up and stop sounding pompous."

We laughed again. I'm lucky that, no matter what makes me mad about my brother, we can laugh at ourselves together.

"So what are you upset about then?" he asked after we settled down.

"Them," I said, trying to get serious again. "Mom and Dad. Tommy, have you thought about what this is going to do to them?"

"What do you mean?"

"I mean, what the town's going to say? Tommy, do you know in their church newsletter they have a prayer list and our family is on it?"

"What for?" he asked, beginning to sound alarmed.

"Because you're gay!" I said. It didn't come out how I wanted, though. By the way his face, always alert and showing some kind of emotion, receded and locked its door behind it, I could tell I'd hurt his feelings. "It's not like that," I said. "They didn't ask to be put on the prayer list. Fern Baker put them on it."

"Fern Baker?" Tommy said. "What business has that woman got still being alive?"

"I'm serious, Tommy. I just want to know if you understand the position you've put them in."

He nodded. "I do," he said. "I talked with them about Tristan and me coming out here to live three months ago. They said what they'll always say to me or you when we want or need to come home."

"What's that?"

"Come home, darling. You and your Tristan have a home here too." When I looked down at my comforter and studied its threads for a while, Tommy added, "They'll say the come home part to you, of course. Not anything about bringing your Tristan with you. Oh, and if it's Dad, he might call you sweetie the way Mom calls me darling."

"Tommy," I said, "if there was a market for men who can make their sisters laugh, I'd say you're in the wrong field."

"Maybe we can make that a market."

"You need lots of people for that," I said.

"Mass culture. Hmm. Been there, done that. It's why I'm back. *You* should give it a try, though. It's an interesting experience. It might actually suit you, Meg. Have you thought about where you want to go to college?"

"It's already decided. Kent State in the fall."

"Kent, huh? That's a decent school. You wouldn't rather go to New York or Boston?"

"Tommy, even if you hadn't broken the bank around here already, I don't have patience for legions of people running up and down the streets of Manhattan or Cambridge like ants in a hive."

"And a major?"

"Psychology."

"Ah, I see, you must think there's something wrong with you and want to figure out how to fix it."

"No," I said. "I just want to be able to break people's brains open to understand why they act like such fools."

"That's pretty harsh," said Tommy.

"Well," I said, "I'm a pretty harsh girl."

After Tommy left, I fell asleep without even changing out of my clothes. In the morning when I woke, I was tangled up in a light blanket someone— Mom, probably—threw over me before going to bed the night before. I sat up and looked out the window. It was already late morning. I could tell by the way the light winked off the pond in the woods, which you can see a tiny sliver of, like a crescent moon, when the sun hits at just the right angle towards noon. Tommy and I used to spend our summers on the dock our father built out there. Reading books, swatting away flies, the soles of our dusty feet in the air behind us. He was so much older than me but never treated me like a little kid. The day he left for New York City, I hugged him on the front porch before Dad drove him to the airport, but burst out crying and ran around back of the house, beyond the fields, into the woods, until I reached the dock. I thought Tommy would follow, but he was the last person I wanted to see right then, so I thought out with my mind in the direction of the house, pushing him away. I turned him around in his tracks and made him tell our parents he couldn't find me. When he didn't come, I knew that I had used something inside me to stop him. Tommy wouldn't have ever let me run away crying like that without chasing after me if I'd let him make that choice on his own. I lay on the dock for an hour, looking at my reflection in the water, saying, "What are you? God damn it, you know the answer. Tell me. What *are* you?"

If Mom had come back and seen me like that, heard me speak in such a way, I think she probably would have had a breakdown. Mom can handle a gay son mostly. What I'm sure she couldn't handle would be if one of her kids talked to themselves like this at age seven. Worse would be if she knew why I asked myself that question. It was the first time my will had made something happen. And it had made Tommy go away without another word between us.

Sometimes I think the rest of my life is going to be a little more difficult everyday.

When I was dressed and had a bowl of granola and bananas in me, I grabbed the novel I was reading off the kitchen counter and opened the back door to head back to the pond. Thinking of the summer days Tommy and I spent back there together made me think I should probably honor my childhood one last summer by keeping up tradition before I had to go away. I was halfway out the door, twisting around to close it, when Tristan came into the kitchen and said, "Good morning, Meg. Where are you off to?"

"The pond," I said.

"Oh the pond!" Tristan said, as if it were a tourist site he'd been wanting to visit. "Would you mind if I tagged along?"

"It's a free country," I said, thinking I should probably have been nicer, but I turned to carry on my way anyway.

"Well, sort of," Tristan said, which stopped me in my tracks.

I turned around and looked at him. He did that same little shrug he did the night before when Tommy asked Mom and Dad if he could hang the *American Gothic* portrait in the living room, then smiled, as if something couldn't be helped. "Are you just going to stand there, or are you coming?" I said.

Quickly Tristan followed me out, and then we were off through the back field and into the woods, until we came to the clearing where the pond reflected the sky, like an open blue eye staring up at God.

I made myself comfortable on the deck, spread out my towel and opened my book. I was halfway done. Someone's heart had already been broken and no amount of mixed CDs left in her mailbox and school locker were ever going to set things right. Why did I read these things? I should take the bike to the library and check out something Classic instead, I thought. Probably there's something I should be reading right now that everyone else in college will have read. I worried about things like that. Neither of our parents went to college. I remember Tommy used to worry the summer before he went to New York that he'd get there and never be able to fit in. "Growing up out here is going to be a black mark," he'd said. "I'm not going to know how to act around anyone there because of this place."

I find it ironic that it's this place—us—that helped Tommy start his career.

"This place is amazing," said Tristan. He stretched out on his stomach beside me, dangling the upper half of his torso over the edge so he could pull his fingers through the water just inches below us. "I can't believe you have all of this to yourself. You're so lucky."

"I guess," I said, pursing my lips. I still didn't know Tristan well enough to feel I could trust his motivations or be more than civil to him. Pretty. Harsh. Girl. I know.

"Wow," said Tristan, pulling his lower half back up onto the deck with me. He looked across the water, blinking. "You really don't like me," he said.

"That's not true," I said immediately, but even I knew that was mostly a lie. So I tried to revise. "I mean, it's not that I don't like you. I just don't know you so well, that's all."

"Don't trust me, eh?"

"Really," I said, "why should I?"

"Your brother's trust in me doesn't give you a reason?"

"Tommy's never been known around here for his good judgment," I said.

Tristan whistled. "Wow," he said again, this time elongating it. "You're tough as nails, aren't you?"

I shrugged. Tristan nodded. I thought this was a sign we'd come to an understanding, so I went back to reading. Not two minutes passed, though, before he interrupted again.

"What are you hiding, Meg?"

"What are you talking about?" I said, looking up from my book.

"Well obviously if you don't trust people to this extreme, you must have something to hide. That's what distrustful people often have. Something to hide. Either that or they've been hurt an awful lot by people they loved."

"You do know you guys can't get married in Ohio, right? The people decided in the election a couple of years ago."

"Ohhhh," said Tristan. "The people. The people the people the people. Oh, my dear, it's always the people! Always leaping to defend their own rights but always ready to deny someone else theirs. Wake up, baby. That's history. Did that stop other people from living how they wanted? Well, I suppose sometimes. Screw the people anyhow. Your brother and I will be married, whether or not the people make some silly law that prohibits it. The people, my dear, only matter if you let them."

"So you'll be married like I'm a Christian even though I don't go to church."

"Really, Meg, you do realize that even if you consider yourself a Christian, those other people don't, right?"

"What do you mean?"

Tristan turned over on his side so he could face me, and propped his head in his hand. His eyes are green. Tommy's are blue. If they could have children, they'd be so beautiful, like sea creatures or fairies. My eyes are blue too, but they're like Dad's, dull and flat, like a blind old woman's eyes rather than the shallow ocean with dancing lights on it blue that Mom and Tommy have. "I mean," said Tristan, "those people only believe you're a real Christian if you attend church. It's the body of Christ rule and all that. You *have* read the Bible, haven't you?"

"Parts," I said, squinting a little. "But anyway," I said, "it doesn't matter what they think of me. I know what's true in my heart."

"Well precisely," said Tristan.

I stopped squinting and held his stare. He didn't flinch, just kept staring back. "Okay," I said. "You've made your point."

Tristan stood and lifted his shirt above his head, kicked off his sandals, and dove into the pond. The blue rippled and rippled, the rings flowing out to the edges, then silence and stillness returned, but Tristan didn't. I waited a few moments, then stood halfway up on one knee. "Tristan?" I said, and waited a few moments more. "Tristan," I said, louder this time. But he still didn't come to the surface. "Tristan, stop it!" I shouted, and immediately his head burst out of the water at the center of the pond.

"Oh this is lovely," he said, shaking his wet, brown hair out of his eyes. "It's like having Central Park in your back yard!"

I picked my book up and left, furious with him for frightening me. What did he think? It was funny? I didn't stay to find out. I didn't turn around or say anything in response to Tristan either, when he began calling for me to come back.

Tommy was in the kitchen making lunch for everyone when I burst through the back door and slammed it shut behind me like a small tornado had blown through. "What's wrong now?" he said, looking up from the tomato soup and grilled cheese sandwiches he was making. "Boy trouble?"

He laughed, but this time I didn't laugh with him. Tommy knew I wasn't much of a dater, that I didn't have a huge interest in going somewhere with a guy from school and watching a movie or eating fast food while they practiced on me to become better at making girls think they've found a guy who's incredible. I don't get that stuff, really. I mean, I like guys. I had a boyfriend once. I mean a real one, not the kind some girls call boyfriends but really aren't anything but the guy they dated that month. That's not a boyfriend. That's a candidate. Some people can't tell the difference. Anyway, I'm sure my parents have probably thought I'm the same way as Tommy, since I don't bring boys home, but I don't bring boys home because it all seems like something to save for later. Right now, I like just thinking about me, *my* future. I'm not so good at thinking in the first person plural yet.

I glared at Tommy before saying, "Your boyfriend sucks. He just tricked me into thinking he'd drowned."

Tommy grinned. "He's a bad boy, I know," he said. "But Meg, he didn't mean anything by it. You take life too seriously. You should really relax a little. Tristan is playful. That's part of his charm. He was trying to make you his friend, that's all."

"By freaking me out? Wonderful friendship maneuver. It amazes me how smart you and your city friends are. Did Tristan go to NYU, too?"

"No," Tommy said flatly. And on that one word, with that one shift of tone in his voice, I could tell I'd pushed him into the sort of self I wear most of the time: the armor, the defensive position. I'd crossed one of his lines and felt small and little and mean. "Tristan's family is wealthy," said Tommy. "He's a bit of the black sheep, though. They're not on good terms. He could have gone to college anywhere he wanted, but I think he's avoided doing that because it would make them proud of him for being more like them instead of himself. They're different people, even though they're from the same family. Like how you and I are different from Mom and Dad about church. Anyway, they threatened to cut him off if he didn't come home to let them groom him to be more like them."

"Heterosexual, married to a well-off woman from one of their circle and ruthless in a board room?" I offered.

"Well, no," said Tommy. "Actually they're quite okay with Tristan being gay. He's different from them in another way."

"What way?" I asked.

Tommy rolled his eyes a little, weighing whether or not he should tell me anymore. "I shouldn't talk about it," he said, sighing, exasperated.

"Tommy, tell me!" I said. "How bad could it be?"

"Not bad so much as strange. Maybe even unbelievable for you, Meg." I frowned, but he went on. "The ironic thing is, the thing they can't stand about Tristan is something they gave him. A curse, you would have called it years ago. Today I think the word we use is gene. In any case, it runs in Tristan's family, skipping generations mostly, but every once in a while one of the boys are born . . . well, different."

"Different but not in the gay way?" I said, confused.

"No, not in the gay way," said Tommy, smiling, shaking his head. "Different in the way that he has two lives, sort of. The one here on land with you and I, and another one in, well, in the water."

"He's a rebellious swimmer?"

Tommy laughed, bursting the air. "I guess you could say that," he said. "But no. Listen, if you want to know, I'll tell you, but you have to promise not to tell Mom and Dad. They think we're here because Tommy's family disowned him for being gay. I told them his parents were Pentecostal, so it all works out in their minds."

"Okay," I said. "I promise."

"What would you say," Tristan began, his eyes shifting up as if he were searching for the right words in the air above him. "What would you say, Meg, if I told you the real reason is because Tristan's not completely human. I mean, not in the sense that we understand it."

I narrowed my eyes, pursed my lips, and said, "Tommy, are you on drugs?"

"I wish!" he said. "God, those'll be harder to find around here," he laughed. "No, really, I'm telling the truth. Tristan is something . . . something else. A water person? You know, with a tail and all?" Tommy flapped his hand in the air when he said this. I smirked, waiting for the punch line. But when one didn't come, it hit me.

"This has something to do with *The Sons of Melusine*, doesn't it?"

Tommy nodded. "Yes, those paintings are inspired by Tristan."

"But Tommy," I said, "why are you going back to this type of painting? Sure it's an interesting gimmick, saying your boyfriend's a merman. But the critics didn't like your fantasy paintings. They liked the *American Gothic* stuff. Why would they change their minds now?"

"Two things," Tommy said, frustrated with me. "One: a good critic doesn't dismiss entire genres. They look at technique and composition of elements and the relationship the painting establishes with this world. Two: it's not a gimmick. It's the truth, Meg. Listen to me. I'm not laughing anymore. Tristan made his parents an offer. He said he'd move somewhere unimportant and out of the way, and they could make up whatever stories about him for their friends to explain his absence if they gave him part of his inheritance now. They accepted. It's why we're here."

I didn't know what to say, so I just stood there. Tommy ladled soup into bowls for the four of us. Dad would be coming in from the barn soon, Tristan back from the pond. Mom was still at the library and wouldn't be home till evening. This was a regular summer day. It made me feel safe, that regularity. I didn't want it to ever go away.

I saw Tristan then, trotting through the field out back, drying his hair with his pink shirt as he came. When I turned back to Tommy, he was looking out the window over the sink, watching Tristan too, his eyes watering. "You really love him, don't you?" I said.

Tommy nodded, wiping his tears away with the backs of his hands. "I do," he said. "He's so special, like something I used to see a long time ago. Something I forgot how to see for a while."

"Have you finished *The Sons of Melusine* series then?" I asked, trying to change the subject. I didn't feel sure of how to talk to Tommy right then.

"I haven't," said Tommy. "There's one more I want to do. I was waiting for the right setting. Now we have it."

"What do you mean?"

"I want to paint Tristan by the pond."

"Why the pond?"

"Because," said Tommy, returning to gaze out the window, "it's going to be a place he can be himself at totally now. He's never had that before."

"When will you paint him?"

"Soon," said Tommy. "But I'm going to have to ask you and Mom and Dad a favor."

"What?"

"Not to come down to the pond while we're working."

"Why?"

"He doesn't want anyone to know about him. I haven't told Mom and Dad. Just you. So you have to promise me two things. Don't come down to the pond, and don't tell Tristan I told you about him."

Tristan opened the back door then. He had his shirt back on and his hair was almost dry. Pearls of water still clung to his legs. I couldn't imagine those being a tail, his feet a flipper. Surely Tommy had gone insane. "Am I late for lunch?" Tristan asked, smiling at me.

Tommy turned and beamed him a smile back. "Right on time, love," he said, and I knew our conversation had come to an end.

I went down the lane to the barn where Dad was working, taking his lunch with me when he didn't show up to eat with us. God, I wished I could tell him how weird Tommy was being, but I'd promised not to say anything, and even if my brother was going crazy, I wouldn't go back on my word. I found Dad coming out of the barn with a pitchfork of cow manure, which he threw onto the spreader parked outside the barn. He'd take that to the back field and spread it later probably, and then I'd have to watch where I stepped for a week whenever I cut through the field to go to the pond. When I gave him his soup and sandwich, he thanked me and asked what the boys were doing. I told him they were sitting in the living room under the *American Gothic* portrait fiercely making out. He almost spit out his sandwich, he laughed so hard. I like making my dad laugh because he doesn't do it nearly enough. Mom's too nice, which sometimes is what kills a sense of humor in people, and Tommy always was too testing of Dad to ever get to a joking relationship with him. Me, though, I can always figure out something to shock him into a laugh.

"You're bad, Meg," he said, after settling down. Then: "Were they really?"

I shook my head. "Nope. You were right the first time, Dad. That was a joke." I didn't want to tell him his son had gone mad, though.

"Well I thought so, but still," he said, taking a bite of his sandwich. "All sorts of new things to get used to these days."

I nodded. "Are you okay with that?" I asked.

"Can't not be," he said. "Not an option."

"Who says?"

"I need no authority figure on that," said Dad. "You have a child and, no matter what, you love them. That's just how it is."

"That's not how it is for everyone, Dad."

"Well thank the dear Lord I'm not everyone," he said. "Why would you want to live like that, with all those conditions on love?"

I didn't know what to say. He'd shocked me into silence the way I could always shock him into laughter. We had that effect on each other, like yin and yang. My dad's a good guy, likes the simpler life, seems pretty normal. He wears Allis Chalmers tractor hats and flannel shirts and jeans. He likes oatmeal and meatloaf and macaroni and cheese. Then he opens his mouth and turns into the Buddha. I swear to God, he'll do it when you're least expecting it. I don't know sometimes whether he's like me and Tommy, hiding something different about himself but just has all these years of experience to make himself blend in. Like maybe he's an angel beneath that sun-browned, beginning-to-wrinkle human skin. "Do you really feel that way?" I asked. "It's one thing to say that, but is it that easy to truly feel that way?"

"Well it's not what you'd call easy, Meg. But it's what's right. Most of the time doing what's right is more difficult than doing what's wrong."

He handed me his bowl and plate after he finished, and asked if I'd take a look at Buttercup. Apparently she'd been looking pretty down. So I set the dishes on the seat of the tractor and went into the barn to visit my old girl, my cow Buttercup, who I've had since I was a little girl. She was my present on my fourth birthday. I'd found her with her mother in a patch of buttercups and spent the summer with her, sleeping with her in the fields, playing with her, training her as if she were a dog. By the time she was a year old, she'd even let me ride her like a horse. We were the talk of the town, and Dad even had me ride her into the ring at the county fair's Best of Show. Normally she would have been butchered by now—no cow lasted as long as Buttercup had on Dad's farm—but I had saved her each time it ever came into Dad's head to let her go. He never had to say anything. I could see his thoughts as clear as if they were stones beneath a clear stream of water, I could take them and break them or change them if I needed. The way I'd changed Tommy's mind the day he left for New York, making him turn back and leave me alone by the pond. It was a stupid thing, really, whatever it was, this thing I could do with my will. Here I could change people's minds, but I used it to make people I loved go away with hard feelings and to prolong the life of a cow.

Dad was right. She wasn't looking good, the old girl. She was thirteen and had had a calf every summer for a good ten years. I looked at her now and saw how selfish I'd been to make him keep her. She was down on the ground in her stall, legs folded under her, like a queen stretched out on a litter, her eyes half-closed, her lashes long and pretty as a woman's. "Old girl," I said. "How you doing?" She looked up at me, chewing her cud, and smiled. Yes, cows can smile. I can't stand it that people can't see this. Cats can smile, dogs can smile, cows can too. It just takes time and you have to really pay attention to notice. You can't look for a human smile; it's not the same. You have to be able to see an animal for itself before it'll let you see its smile. Buttercup's smile was warm, but fleeting. She looked exhausted from the effort of greeting me.

I patted her down and brushed her a bit and gave her some ground molasses to lick out of my hand. I liked the feel of the rough stubble on her tongue as it swept across my palm. Sometimes I thought if not psychology, maybe veterinary medicine would be the thing for me. I'd have to get used to death, though. I'd have to be okay with helping an animal die. Looking at Buttercup, I knew I didn't have that in me. If only I could use my will on myself as well as it worked on others.

When I left the barn, Dad was up on the seat of the tractor, holding his dishes, which he handed me again. "Off to spread this load," he said, starting the tractor after he spoke. He didn't have to say anymore about Buttercup. He knew I'd seen what he meant. I'd have to let her go someday, I knew. I'd have to work on that, though. I just wasn't ready.

The next day I went back to the pond only to find Tristan and Tommy already there. Tommy had a radio playing classical music on the dock beside him while he sketched something in his notebook. Tristan swam towards him, then pulled his torso up and out by holding onto the dock so he could lean in and kiss Tommy before letting go and sinking back down. I tried to see if there were scales at his waistline, but he was too quick. "Hey!" Tommy shouted. "You dripped all over my sketch you wretched whale! What do you think this is? Sea World?"

I laughed, but Tommy and Tristan both looked over at me, eyes wide, mouths open, shocked to see me there. "Meg!" Tristan said from the pond, waving his hand. "How long have you been there? We didn't hear you."

"Only a minute," I said, stepping onto the dock, moving Tommy's radio over before spreading out my towel to lie next to him. "You should really know not to mess with him when he's working," I added. "Tommy is a perfectionist, you know."

"Which is why I do it," Tristan laughed. "Someone needs to keep him honest. Nothing can be perfect, right Tommy?"

"Close to perfect, though," Tommy said.

"What are you working on?" I asked, and immediately he flipped the page over and started sketching something new.

"Doesn't matter," he said, his pencil pulling gray and black lines into existence on the page. "Tristan ruined it."

"I *had* to kiss you," Tristan said, swimming closer to us.

"You always have to kiss me," Tommy said.

"Well, yes," said Tristan. "Can you blame me?"

I rolled my eyes and opened my book.

"Meg," Tommy said a few minutes later, after Tristan had swum away, disappearing into the depths of the pond and appearing on the other side, smiling brilliantly. "Remember how I said I'd need you and Mom and Dad to do me that favor?"

"Yeah."

"I'm going to start work tomorrow, so no more coming up on us without warning like that, okay?"

I put my book down and looked at him. He was serious. No joke was going to follow this gravely intoned request. "Okay," I said, feeling a little stung. I didn't like it when Tommy took that tone with me and meant it.

I finished my book within the hour and got up to leave. Tommy looked up as I bent to pick up my towel and I could see his mouth opening to say something, a reminder, or worse: a plea for me to believe what he'd said about Tristan the day before. So I locked eyes with him and took hold of that thought before it became speech. It wriggled fiercely, trying to escape the grasp of my will, flipping back and forth like a fish pulled out of its stream.

But I won. I squeezed it between my will's fingers, and Tommy turned back to sketching without another word.

The things that are wrong with me are many. I try not to let them be the things people see in me, though. I try to make them invisible, or to make them seem natural, or else I stuff them up in that dark spot on my ceiling and will them into non-existence. This doesn't usually work for very long. They come back, they always come back, whatever they are, if it's something really a part of me and not just a passing mood. No amount of willing can change those things. Like my inability to let go of Buttercup, my anger with the people of this town, my frustration with my parents' kindness to a world that doesn't deserve them, my annoyance with my brother's light-stepped movement through life. I hate that everything we love has to die, I despise narrow thinking, I resent the unfairness of the world and the unfairness that I can't feel at home in it like it seems others can. All I have is my will, this sharp piece of material inside me, stronger than metal, that everything I encounter breaks itself upon.

Mom once told me it was my gift, not to discount it. I'd had a fit of anger with the school board and the town that day. They'd fired one of my teachers for not teaching creationism alongside evolution, and somehow thought this was completely legal. And no one seemed outraged but me. I wrote a letter to the newspaper declaring the whole affair an obstruction to teacher's freedoms, but it seemed that everyone—kids at school and their parents—just accepted it until a year later the courts told us it was unacceptable.

I cried and tore apart my room one day that year. I hated being in school after they did that to Mr. Turney. When Mom heard me tearing my posters off the walls, smashing my unicorns and horses, she burst into my room and threw her arms around me and held me until my will quieted again. Later, when we were sitting on my bed, me leaning against her while she combed her fingers through my hair, she said, "Meg, don't be afraid of what you can do. That letter you wrote, it was wonderful. Don't feel bad because no one else said anything. You made a strong statement. People were talking about it at church last week. They think people can't hear, or perhaps they mean for them to hear. Anyway, I'm proud of you for speaking out against what your heart tells you isn't right. That's your gift, sweetie. If you hadn't noticed, not everyone is blessed with such a strong, beautiful will."

It made me feel a little better, hearing that, but I couldn't also tell her how I'd used it for wrong things too: to make Tommy leave for New York without knowing I was okay, to make Dad keep Buttercup beyond the time he should have, to keep people far away so I wouldn't have to like or love them. I'd used my will to keep the world at bay, and that was my secret: that I didn't really care for this life I'd been given, that I couldn't stop myself from being angry at the whole fact of it, life, that the more things I loved, the worse it would be because I'd lose all those things in the end. So Buttercup sits in the barn, her legs barely strong enough for her to stand on, because of me not being able to let go. So Tommy turned back and left because I couldn't bear to say goodbye. So I didn't have any close friends because I didn't want to have to lose anymore than I already had to lose in my family.

My will was my gift, she said. So why did it feel like such a curse to me?

When Mom came home later that evening, I sat in the kitchen and had a cup of tea with her. She always wanted tea straight away after she came home. She said it calmed her, helped her ease out of her day at the library and back into life at home. "How are Tommy and Tristan adjusting?" she asked me after a few sips, and I shrugged.

"They seem to be doing fine, but Tommy's being weird and a little mean."

"How so?" Mom wanted to know.

"Just telling me to leave them alone while he works and he told me some weird things about Tristan and his family too. I don't know. It all seems so impossible."

"Don't underestimate people's ability to do harm to each other," Mom interrupted. "Even those that say they love you."

I knew she was making this reference based on the story Tommy had told her and Dad about Tristan's family disowning him because he was gay, so I shook my head. "I understand that, Mom," I said. "There's something else too." I didn't know how to tell her what Tommy had told me, though. I'd promised to keep it between him and me. So I settled for saying, "Tristan doesn't seem the type who would want to live out here away from all the things he could enjoy in the city."

"Perhaps that's all grown old for him," Mom said. "People change. Look at you, off to school in a month or so. Between the time you leave and the first time you come home again, you'll have become someone different, and I won't have had a chance to watch you change." She started tearing up. "All your changes all these years, the Lord's let me share them all with you and now I'm going to have to let you go and change into someone without me around to make sure you're safe."

"Oh Mom," I said. "Don't cry."

"No, no," she said. "I want to cry." She wiped her cheeks with the backs of her hands, smiling. "I just want to say, Meg, don't be so hard on other people. Or yourself. It's hard enough as it is, being in this world. Don't judge so harshly. Don't stop yourself from seeing other people's humanity because they don't fit into your scheme of the world."

I blinked a lot, then picked up my mug of tea and sipped it. I didn't know how to respond. Mom usually never says anything critical of us, and though she said it nicely, I knew she was worried for me. For her to say something like that, I knew I needed to put down my shield and sword and take a look around instead of fighting. But wasn't fighting the thing I was good at?

"I'm sorry, Mom," I said.

"Don't be sorry, dear. Be happy. Find the thing that makes you happy and enjoy it, like your brother is doing."

"You mean his painting?" I said.

"No," said Mom. "I mean Tristan."

One day towards the end of my senior year, our English teacher Miss Portwood told us that many of our lives were about to become much wider. That we'd soon have to begin mapping a world for ourselves outside of the first seventeen years of our lives. It struck me, hearing her say that, comparing the years of our lives to a map of the world. If I had a map of seventeen, of the years I'd lived so far, it would be small and plain, outlining the contours of my town with a few landmarks on it like Marrow's Ravine and town square, the schools, the pond, our fields and the barn and the home we live in. It would be on crisp, fresh paper, because I haven't traveled very far, and stuck to the routes I know best. There would be nothing but waves and waves of ocean surrounding my map of my hometown. In the ocean I'd draw those sea beasts you find on old maps of the world, and above them I'd write the words "There Be Dragons."

What else is out there, beyond this edge of the world I live on? Who else is out there? Are there real reasons to be as afraid of the world as I've been?

I was thinking all this when I woke up the next morning and stared at the black spot on my ceiling. That could be a map of seventeen, too. Nothing but white around it, and nothing to show for hiding myself away. Mom was right. Though I was jealous of Tommy's ability to live life so freely, he was following a path all his own, a difficult one, and needed as many people who loved him to help him do it. I could help him and Tristan both probably just by being more friendly and supportive than suspicious and untrusting. I could start by putting aside Tommy's weirdness about Tristan being a cursed son of Melusine and do like Mom and Dad: just humor him. He's an artist after all.

So I got up and got dressed and left the house without even having breakfast. I didn't want to let another day go by and not make things okay with Tommy for going away all those years ago. Through the back field I went, into the woods, picking up speed as I went, as the urgency to see him took over me. By the time I reached the edge of the pond's clearing, I had a thousand things I wanted to say. When I stepped out of the woods and into the clearing, though, I froze in place, my mouth open but no words coming out because of what I saw there.

Tommy was on the dock with his easel and palette, sitting in a chair, painting Tristan. And Tristan—I don't know how to describe him, how to make his being something possible, but these words came into mind: tail, scales, beast and beauty. At first I couldn't tell which he was, but I knew immediately that Tommy hadn't gone insane. Or else we both had.

Tristan lay on the dock in front of Tommy, his upper body strong and muscular and naked, his lower half long and sinuous as a snake. His tail swept back and forth, occasionally dipping into the water for a moment before returning to the position Tommy wanted. I almost screamed, but somehow willed myself not to. I hadn't left home yet, but a creature from the uncharted world had traveled onto my map where I'd lived the past seventeen years. How could this be?

I thought of that group show we'd all flown to New York to see, the one where Tommy had hung his first in the series of *American Gothic* alongside those odd, magical creatures he painted back when he was just graduated.

The critic who'd picked him out of that group show said that Tommy had technique and talent, was by turns fascinating and annoying, but that he'd wait to see if Tommy would develop a more mature vision. I think when I read that back then, I had agreed.

I'd forgotten the favor I'd promised: not to come back while they were working. Tommy hadn't really lied when he told me moving here was for Tristan's benefit, to get away from his family and the people who wanted him to be something other than what he is. I wondered how long he'd been trying to hide this part of himself before he met Tommy, who was able to love him because of who and what he is. What a gift and curse that is, to be both of them, to be what Tristan is and for Tommy to see him so clearly. My problems were starting to shrivel the longer I looked at them. And the longer I looked, the more I realized the dangers they faced, how easily their lives and love could be shattered by the people in the world who would fire them from life the way the school board fired Mr. Turney for actually teaching us what we can know about the world.

I turned and quietly went back through the woods, but as I left the trail and came into the back field, I began running. I ran from the field and past the house, out into the dusty back road we live on, and stood there looking up and down the road at the horizon, where the borders of this town waited for me to cross them at the end of summer. Whether there were dragons waiting for me after I journeyed off the map of my first seventeen years didn't matter. I'd love them when it called for loving them, and I'd fight the ones that needed fighting. That was my gift, like Mom had told me, what I could do with my will. Maybe instead of psychology I'd study law, learn how to defend it, how to make it better, so that someday Tommy and Tristan could have what everyone else has.

It's a free country after all. Well, sort of. And one day, if I had anything to say about it, that would no longer be a joke between Tommy and me.

ABOUT THE AUTHOR

Christopher Barzak grew up in rural Ohio, went to university in Youngstown, Ohio, and has lived in a Southern California beach town, the capital of Michigan, and in the suburbs of Tokyo, Japan, where he taught English in rural junior high and elementary schools. His stories have appeared in many venues, including *Nerve*, *The Year's Best Fantasy and Horror*, *Salon Fantastique*, *Interfictions*, *Asimov's*, and *Lady Churchill's Rosebud Wristlet*. His first novel, *One for Sorrow*, published by Bantam Books in the fall of 2007, won the Crawford Award that same year. His second book, *The Love We Share Without Knowing*, is a novel-in-stories, and was chosen for the James Tiptree Jr. Award Honor List in 2008 as well as being nominated for a Nebula Award for Best Novel in 2009. He is the coeditor (with Delia Sherman) of *Interfictions 2*, and has done Japanese-English translation on *Kant: For Eternal Peace*, a peace theory book published in Japan for teens. Currently he lives in Youngstown, Ohio, where he teaches writing at Youngstown State University.

INTRODUCTION

The Solstice Award, created in 2008 and given at the discretion of the SFWA president with the majority approval of the board of directors, is for individuals who have had "a significant impact on the science fiction or fantasy landscape, and is particularly intended for those who have consistently made a major, positive difference within the speculative fiction field."

One of the two winners of this year's Solstice Award is Alice Sheldon, who wrote under the name James Tiptree, Jr. Sheldon/Tiptree has been an enduring inspiration and focal point for the entire science fiction community—professionals, fans, critics, and academics—in discussing gender and sexuality in our fiction. Her influence in the conversation of genre continues into the present time, in no small part thanks to the award named in Tiptree's honor, given to those in science fiction and fantasy who explore or expand our understanding of gender. Previous winners of the Tiptree Award include grandmasters Ursula K. Le Guin and Joe Haldeman.

We present here one of Tiptree's most disturbing stories, about the fascination and dangers of exogamy.

AND I AWOKE AND FOUND ME HERE ON THE COLD HILL'S SIDE

James Tiptree, Jr.

He was standing absolutely still by a service port, staring out at the belly of the *Orion* docking above us. He had on a gray uniform and his rusty hair was cut short. I took him for a station engineer.

That was bad for me. Newsmen strictly don't belong in the bowels of Big

Junction. But in my first twenty hours I hadn't found any place to get a shot of an alien ship.

I turned my holocam to show its big World Media insigne and started my bit about What It Meant to the People Back Home who were paying for it all.

"—it may be routine work to you, sir, but we owe it to them to share—"

His face came around slow and tight, and his gaze passed over me from a peculiar distance.

"The wonders, the drama," he repeated dispassionately. His eyes focused on me. "You consummated fool."

"Could you tell me what races are coming in, sir? If I could even get a view—"

He waved me to the port. Greedily I angled my lenses up at the long blue hull blocking out the starfield. Beyond her I could see the bulge of a black and gold ship.

"That's a Foramen," he said. "There's a freighter from Belye on the other side, you'd call it Arcturus. Not much traffic right now."

"You're the first person who's said two sentences to me since I've been here, sir. What are those colorful little craft?"

"Procya," he shrugged. "They're always around. Like us."

I squashed my face on the vitrite, peering. The walls clanked. Somewhere overhead aliens were off-loading into their private sector of Big Junction. The man glanced at his wrist.

"Are you waiting to go out, sir?"

His grunt could have meant anything.

"Where are you from on Earth?" he asked me in his hard tone.

I started to tell him and suddenly saw that he had forgotten my existence. His eyes were on nowhere, and his head was slowly bowing forward onto the port frame.

"Go home," he said thickly. I caught a strong smell of tallow.

"Hey, sir!" I grabbed his arm; he was in rigid tremor. "Steady, man."

"I'm waiting . . . waiting for my wife. My loving wife." He gave a short ugly laugh. "Where are you from?"

I told him again.

"Go home," he mumbled. "Go home and make babies. While you still can."

One of the early GR casualties, I thought.

"Is that all you know?" His voice rose stridently. "Fools. Dressing in their styles. Gnivo suits, Aoleelee music. Oh, I see your newscasts," he sneered. "Nixi parties. A year's salary for a floater. Gamma radiation? Go home, read history. *Ballpoint pens and bicycles*—"

He started a slow slide downward in the half gee. My only informant. We struggled confusedly; he wouldn't take one of my sobertabs but I finally got him along the service corridor to a bench in an empty loading bay. He fumbled out a little vacuum cartridge. As I was helping him unscrew it, a figure in starched whites put his head in the bay.

"I can be of assistance, yes?" His eyes popped, his face was covered with brindled fur. An alien, a Procya! I started to thank him but the red-haired man cut me off.

"Get lost. Out."

The creature withdrew, its big eyes moist. The man stuck his pinky in the cartridge and then put it up his nose, gasping deep in his diaphragm. He looked toward his wrist.

"What time is it?"

I told him.

"News," he said. "A message for the eager, hopeful human race. A word about those lovely, lovable aliens we all love so much." He looked at me. "Shocked, aren't you, newsboy?"

I had him figured now. A xenophobe. Aliens plot to take over Earth.

"Ah, Christ, they couldn't care less." He took another deep gasp, shuddered and straightened. "The hell with generalities. What time d'you say it was? All right, I'll tell you how I learned it. The hard way. While we wait for my loving wife. You can bring that little recorder out of your sleeve, too. Play it over to yourself some time . . . when it's too late." He chuckled. His tone had become chatty—an educated voice. "You ever hear of supernormal stimuli?"

"No," I said. "Wait a minute. White sugar?"

"Near enough. Y'know Little Junction Bar in D.C.? No, you're an Aussie, you said. Well, I'm from Burned Barn, Nebraska."

He took a breath, consulting some vast disarray of the soul.

"I accidentally drifted into Little Junction Bar when I was eighteen. No. Correct that. You don't go into Little Junction by accident, any more than you first shoot skag by accident.

"You go into Little Junction because you've been craving it, dreaming about it, feeding on every hint and clue about it, back there in Burned Barn, since before you had hair in your pants. Whether you know it or not. Once you're out of Burned Barn, you can no more help going into Little Junction than a sea-worm can help rising to the moon.

"I had a brand-new liquor I.D. in my pocket. It was early; there was an empty spot beside some humans at the bar. Little Junction isn't an embassy bar, y'know. I found out later where the high-caste aliens go—when they go out. The New Rive, the Curtain by the Georgetown Marina.

"And they go by themselves. Oh, once in a while they do the cultural exchange bit with a few frosty couples of other aliens and some stuffed humans. Galactic Amity with a ten-foot pole.

"Little Junction was the place where the lower orders went, the clerks and drivers out for kicks. Including, my friend, the perverts. The ones who can take humans. Into their beds, that is."

He chuckled and sniffed his finger again, not looking at me.

"Ah, yes. Little Junction is Galactic Amity night, every night. I ordered . . . what? A margarita. I didn't have the nerve to ask the snotty spade bartender for one of the alien liquors behind the bar. It was dim. I was trying to stare everywhere at once without showing it. I remember those white bone-heads—Lyrans, that is. And a mess of green veiling I decided was a multiple being from some place. I caught a couple of human glances in the bar mirror. Hostile flicks. I didn't get the message, then.

"Suddenly an alien pushed right in beside me. Before I could get over my paralysis, I heard this blurry voice:

"'You air a futeball enthusiash?'

"An alien had spoken to me. An *alien*, a being from the stars. Had spoken. To me.

"Oh, god, I had no time for football, but I would have claimed a passion for paper-folding, for dumb crambo—anything to keep him talking. I asked him about his home-planet sports, I insisted on buying his drinks. I listened raptly while he spluttered out a play-by-play account of a game I wouldn't have turned a dial for. The 'Grain Bay Pashkers.' Yeah. And I was dimly aware of trouble among the humans on my other side.

"Suddenly this woman—I'd call her a girl now—this girl said something in a high nasty voice and swung her stool into the arm I was holding my drink with. We both turned around together.

"Christ, I can see her now. The first thing that hit me was *discrepancy*. She was a nothing—but terrific. Transfigured. Oozing it, radiating it.

"The next thing was I had a horrifying hard-on just looking at her.

"I scrooched over so my tunic hid it, and my spilled drink trickled down, making everything worse. She pawed vaguely at the spill, muttering.

"I just stared at her trying to figure out what had hit me. An ordinary figure, a soft avidness in the face. Eyes heavy, satiated-looking. She was totally sexualized. I remember her throat pulsed. She had one hand up touching her scarf, which had slipped off her shoulder. I saw angry bruises there. That really tore it, I understood at once those bruises had some sexual meaning.

"She was looking past my head with her face like a radar dish. Then she made an 'ahhhhh' sound that had nothing to do with me and grabbed my forearm as if it were a railing. One of the men behind her laughed. The woman said, 'Excuse me,' in a ridiculous voice and slipped out behind me. I wheeled around after her, nearly upsetting my football friend, and saw that some Sirians had come in.

"That was my first look at Sirians in the flesh, if that's the word. God knows I'd memorized every news shot, but I wasn't prepared. That tallness, that cruel thinness. That appalling alien arrogance. Ivory-blue, these were. Two males in immaculate metallic gear. Then I saw there was a female with them. An ivory-indigo exquisite with a permanent faint smile on those bone-hard lips.

"The girl who'd left me was ushering them to a table. She reminded me of a goddamn dog that wants you to follow it. Just as the crowd hid them, I saw a man join them too. A big man, expensively dressed, with something wrecked about his face.

"Then the music started and I had to apologize to my furry friend. And the Sellice dancer came out and my personal introduction to hell began."

The red-haired man fell silent for a minute enduring self-pity. Something wrecked about the face, I thought; it fit.

He pulled his face together.

"First I'll give you the only coherent observation of my entire evening. You can see it here at Big Junction, always the same. Outside of the Procya, it's humans with aliens, right? Very seldom aliens with other aliens. Never aliens with humans. It's the humans who want in."

I nodded, but he wasn't talking to me. His voice had a druggy fluency.

"Ah, yes, my Sellice. My first Sellice.

"They aren't really well-built, y'know, under those cloaks. No waist to speak of and short-legged. But they flow when they walk.

"This one flowed out into the spotlight, cloaked to the ground in violet silk. You could only see a fall of black hair and tassels over a narrow face like a vole. She was a mole-gray. They come in all colors. Their fur is like a flexible velvet all over; only the color changes startlingly around their eyes and lips and other places. Erogenous zones? Ah, man, with them it's not zones.

"She began to do what we'd call a dance, but it's no dance, it's their natural movement. Like smiling, say, with us. The music built up, and her arms undulated toward me, letting the cloak fall apart little by little. She was naked under it. The spotlight started to pick up her body markings moving in the slit of the cloak. Her arms floated apart and I saw more and more.

"She was fantastically marked and the markings were writhing. Not like body paint—alive. Smiling, that's a good word for it. As if her whole body was smiling sexually, beckoning, winking, urging, pouting, speaking to me. You've seen a classic Egyptian belly dance? Forget it—a sorry stiff thing compared to what any Sellice can do. This one was ripe, near term.

"Her arms went up and those blazing lemon-colored curves pulsed, waved, everted, contracted, throbbed, evolved unbelievably welcoming, inciting permutations. *Come do it to me, do it, do it here and here and here and now.* You couldn't see the rest of her, only a wicked flash of mouth. Every human male in the room was aching to ram himself into that incredible body. I mean it was *pain*. Even the other aliens were quiet, except one of the Sirians who was chewing out a waiter.

"I was a basket case before she was halfway through. . . . I won't bore you with what happened next; before it was over there were several fights and I got cut. My money ran out on the third night. She was gone next day.

"I didn't have time to find out about the Sellice cycle then, mercifully.

That came after I went back to campus and discovered you had to have a degree in solid-state electronics to apply for off-planet work. I was a pre-med but I got that degree. It only took me as far as First Junction then.

"Oh, god, First Junction. I thought I was in heaven—the alien ships coming in and our freighters going out. I saw them all, all but the real exotics, the tankies. You only see a few of those a cycle, even here. And the Yyeire. You've never seen that.

"Go home, boy. Go home to your version of Burned Barn . . .

"The first Yyeir I saw, I dropped everything and started walking after it like a starving hound, just breathing. You've seen the pix of course. Like lost dreams. *Man is in love and loves what vanishes.* . . . It's the scent, you can't guess that. I followed until I ran into a slammed port. I spent half a cycles's credits sending the creature the wine they call stars' tears. . . . Later I found out it was a male. That made no difference at all.

"You can't have sex with them, y'know. No way. They breed by light or something, no one knows exactly. There's a story about a man who got hold of a Yyeir woman and tried. They had him skinned. Stories—"

He was starting to wander.

"What about that girl in the bar, did you see her again?"

He came back from somewhere.

"Oh, yes. I saw her. She'd been making it with the two Sirians, y'know. The males do it in pairs. Said to be the total sexual thing for a woman, if she can stand the damage from those beaks. I wouldn't know. She talked to me a couple of times after they finished with her. No use for men whatever. She drove off the P Street bridge. . . . The man, poor bastard, he was trying to keep that Sirian bitch happy single-handed. Money helps, for a while. I don't know where he ended."

He glanced at his wrist watch again. I saw the pale bare place where a watch had been and told him the time.

"Is that the message you want to give Earth? Never love an alien?"

"Never love an alien—" He shrugged. "Yeah. No. Ah, Jesus, don't you see? Everything going out, nothing coming back. Like the poor damned Polynesians. We're gutting Earth, to begin with. Swapping raw resources for junk. Alien status symbols. Tape decks, Coca-Cola, Mickey Mouse watches."

"Well, there is concern over the balance of trade. Is that your message?"

"The balance of trade." He rolled it sardonically. "Did the Polynesians have a word for it, I wonder? You don't see, do you? All right, why are you here? I mean *you*, personally. How many guys did you climb over—"

He went rigid, hearing footsteps outside. The Procya's hopeful face appeared around the corner. The red-haired man snarled at him and he backed out. I started to protest.

"Ah, the silly reamer loves it. It's the only pleasure we have left. . . . Can't you see, man? That's *us*. That's the way we look to them, to the real ones."

"But—"

"And now we're getting the cheap C-drive, we'll be all over just like the Procya. For the pleasure of serving as freight monkeys and junction crews. Oh, they appreciate our ingenious little service stations, the beautiful star folk. They don't *need* them, y'know. Just an amusing convenience. D'you know what I do here with my two degrees? What I did at First Junction. Tube cleaning. A swab. Sometimes I get to replace a fitting."

I muttered something; the self-pity was getting heavy.

"Bitter? Man, it's a *good* job. Sometimes I get to talk to one of them." His face twisted. "My wife works as a—oh, hell, you wouldn't know. I'd trade—correction, I have traded—everything Earth offered me for just that chance. To see them. To speak to them. Once in a while to touch one. Once in a great while to find one low enough, perverted enough to want to touch me . . ."

His voice trailed off and suddenly came back strong.

"And so will you!" He glared at me. "Go home! Go home and tell them to quit it. Close the ports. Burn every god-lost alien thing before it's too late! That's what the Polynesians didn't do."

"But surely—"

"But surely be damned! Balance of trade—balance of *life*, man. I don't know if our birth rate is going, that's not the point. Our soul is leaking out. We're bleeding to death!"

He took a breath and lowered his tone.

"What I'm trying to tell you, this is a trap. We've hit the supernormal stimulus. Man is exogamous—all our history is one long drive to find and impregnate the stranger. Or get impregnated by him; it works for women too. Anything different-colored, different nose, ass, anything, man *has* to fuck it or die trying. That's a drive, y'know, it's built in. Because it works fine as long as the stranger is human. For millions of years that kept the genes circulating. But now we've met aliens we can't screw, and we're about to die trying. . . . Do you think I can touch my wife?"

"But—"

"Look. Y'know, if you give a bird a fake egg like its own but bigger and brighter-marked, it'll roll its own egg out of the nest and sit on the fake? That's what we're doing."

"We've been talking about sex so far." I was trying to conceal my impatience. "Which is great, but the kind of story I'd hoped—"

"Sex? No, it's deeper." He rubbed his head, trying to clear the drug. "Sex is only part of it—there's more. I've seen Earth missionaries, teachers, sexless people. Teachers—they end cycling waste or pushing floaters, but they're hooked. They stay. I saw one fine-looking old woman, she was servant to a Cu'ushbar kid. A defective—his own people would have let him die. That wretch was swabbing up its vomit as if it was holy water. Man, it's deep . . . some cargo-cult of the soul. We're built to dream outwards. They laugh at us. They don't have it."

There were sounds of movement in the next corridor The dinner crowd was starting. I had to get rid of him and get there; maybe I could find the Procya.

A side door opened and a figure started towards us. At first I thought it was an alien and then I saw it was a woman wearing an awkward body-shell. She seemed to be limping slightly. Behind her I could glimpse the dinner-bound throng passing the open door.

The man got up as she turned into the bay. They didn't greet each other.

"The station employs only happily wedded couples," he told me with that ugly laugh. "We give each other . . . comfort."

He took one of her hands. She flinched as he drew it over his arm and let him turn her passively, not looking at me. "Forgive me if I don't introduce you. My wife appears fatigued."

I saw that one of her shoulders was grotesquely scarred.

"Tell them," he said, turning to go. "Go home and tell them." Then his head snapped back toward me and he added quietly, "And stay away from the Syrtis desk or I'll kill you."

They went away up the corridor.

I changed tapes hurriedly with one eye on the figures passing that open door. Suddenly among the humans I caught a glimpse of two sleek scarlet shapes. My first real aliens! I snapped the recorder shut and ran to squeeze in behind them.

ABOUT THE AUTHOR

James Tiptree Jr. was the pen name of Alice Bradley Sheldon. In a career that lasted just twenty years, she won the Hugo, Nebula, World Fantasy, and Locus awards. She died in 1987.

INTRODUCTION

Since 1978, when Suzette Haden Elgin founded the Science Fiction Poetry Association, its members have recognized achievement in speculative poetry by presenting the Rhysling Awards, named after the blind poet of Robert A. Heinlein's story "The Green Hills of Earth." Every year, each member of the SFPA is allowed to nominate one work from the previous year in two categories: "Best Long Poem" (fifty lines or more) and "Best Short Poem" (forty-nine lines or fewer). All nominated poems are collected in *The Rhysling Anthology*, from which the SFPA membership votes for the award winners.

In 2006, the SFPA created the Dwarf Star Award to honor poems of ten or fewer lines.

The SFWA is proud to present the winning poems in each category in this volume. Here is "In the Astronaut Asylum," winner of the Rhysling Award for Best Long Poem of 2010.

IN THE ASTRONAUT ASYLUM

Kendall Evans and Samantha Henderson

"I gave my life to guesswork
on the ambiguous hope
the stars could be real"

From "Asylum for Astronauts"
by Bruce Boston & Marge Simon

I. The Saturday Night Dance

Come all ye to Bedlam Town
When sun come up the stars go down
When stars go down beneath our feet
Then 'tis a merry time to meet

In the Astronaut Asylum
Events sometimes transpire
As if on the second planet out
From Aldebaran

Ex-Astronauts are madmen
They dream of decaying orbits
And the passionate embrace
Of isomorphic aliens

The doors of the asylum
Are like airlock doors
Aboard a starship
Or perhaps like wheeled hatches
Between pressurized chambers
In a submarine

In the Astronaut Asylum
Even the doctors and the staff
Often believe they are on Mars
Inhabiting sheltered underground corridors
And cabins
Or strapped in shipboard limbo
Somewhere between the stars

Two or three moons
(Or four or more)
Often orbit

Above the asylum
(Or below)

The astronauts are falling, falling
Into agonized writhing
Within the sweat-soaked sheets
And stiff cotton straight-jackets
Of Interstellar Nightmares

(& Yes, we perceive the weak ones
On the far side of the bars;
Sometimes they come for interviews
During visiting hours)

Some of the Astronauts
Refuse to remove their spacesuits
Even for the Saturday Night Dance
& Oft-times when Earth's moons align
They dance upon Asylum ceilings

II. The Asylum's History

I asked of one mad Cosmonaut:
What is your wish? What do you want?
"To travel faster than light speed
Upon my sturdy Bedlam steed"

Once upon a time
In France, a hilltop monastery
Remodeled
During the early 1900's
Into an observatory

The 21st century asylum retains
The three distinctive domes

Refurbished
Minus telescopes

The central dome is pressurized
With an exotic atmosphere
The star-farer who resides therein
The only one who might survive inside—
I know
Because the other patients
Told me so

III. Theories of Madness

Come, let's go to Bedlam Street
Star-faring ladies for to meet
Who stare transfixed upon the glow
Of Earthly seas above, below

During Thursday's group therapy session
One of the west-wing Astronauts
Advances her innovative theory:

Here is the secret (don't flinch
While I whisper in your ear; you know,
Despite that pinched lip, that glazed look
You carefully cultivate, pretending that
None of this has any,
Anything to do with you), here 'tis—

All go mad, not just the far-travelers,
Not just those surfers of light-speed,
Not merely those who've dared the wormholes,
No—
All.

Somewhere out past the orbit of the moon
Madness comes—
Slow, mind, for those who think they travel safe,
Travel sane and measured—
Sometimes they die before the disease rooted deep
Within them hatches,
Like an alien egg
Unleashing what into our minds?
What fungus grows about our eyes
Before we succumb?
Live long enough, and it comes to this.

The Cosmonauts in the East Wing
Offer contradictory explanations
Maintaining the human body
Is like a SETI antenna
Receiving messages
From diverse alien civilizations
Strewn throughout our Milky Way
Galaxy, and beyond

They fashion crinkled aluminum foil helmets
To ward off the signals
Shielding themselves
From interstellar insanity
And the maddening music
Of the spheres

IV. A Conversation
With Your Uncle-Astronaut

On Bedlam Row, in madman's mire
We orbit swift, a dizzy gyre
Or bask in dying stars' dim glow
And dream of things you'll never know

Or maybe *you* are the Astronaut-Uncle,
Visiting on the landscaped grounds
At a picnic table
In sunlight
Out past the triple dome shadows
During a moment so real
(despite taking place within
Asylum gates)
You perceive each leaf of grass,
Every blade-shadow

As one of you turns toward the other
And says: "Listen—
After the last Apollo Mission
I felt concerned
Mankind had forgotten how to walk
Upon the Moon—"

One of you pauses,
Contemplative of a cloud
And the unseen daylit stars beyond.
"Now, after being stranded on Ceres,
After penetrating the surfaces
Of Jovian moons
And dancing upon Asylum ceilings,
I feel confident
One might step anywhere."

V. *The Youngest Cosmonaut*

Come with me to Bedlam Row
And see the mad go to and fro
These Astronauts who only trust
Their phantom bags of lunar dust

One of the cosmonauts
Is only 6 years old
On the cusp
Of becoming five
Suffering from reverse entropy
Ever since his final re-entry

This is either gospel truth
Or perhaps the staff
Has confused him
With someone else

One of the orderlies
Recently lamented:
"Communication is impossible
We record his words
& Run the tapes backwards

"But no one can recall:
Precisely what was it he said
In his reverse Russian
When he last spoke to us
Tomorrow?"

VI. Epilog

Three Cosmonauts
Inexplicably disappeared
During the recent solar eclipse

& No one could explain
The staff's panic attacks

Slip Bedlam's locks,
Hide Bedlam's Keys;

We'll drown beneath
These star-filled seas

On nights when the moon is full
The Astronauts stride
Thru sparkling lunar dust
Traipsing asylum corridor floors all aglow
Leaving luminous footprints to follow

ABOUT THE AUTHORS

Stories and poems by Kendall Evans have appeared in *Amazing Stories, Fantastic, Weird Tales, Asimov's, Dreams and Nightmares, Nebula Awards Showcase 2008, Mythic Delirium, Strange Horizons, Space and Time,* and many others. He is currently at work on a ring cycle of four connected chapbook-length dramatic poems: *The Mermaidens of Ceres, Battle Dance of the Valkyrie, Sieglinda's Journey to the Stars,* and *The Rings of Ganymede.* In addition to winning the Rhysling Award for "In the Astronaut Asylum," he is a previous winner for "The Tin Men," a collaboration with David C. Kopaska-Merkel.

Samantha Henderson's poetry has been published in *Weird Tales, Goblin Fruit, Mythic Delirium, Stone Telling, Star*Line, Strange Horizons,* and *Lone Star Stories.* Her short fiction has been published in *Strange Horizons, Realms of Fantasy, Clarkesworld, Fantasy, Abyss & Apex,* and the anthologies *Running with the Pack* and *Steampunk II: Steampunk Reloaded.* She is the author of the Scribe Award–nominated Ravensloft novel *Heaven's Bones* and the Forgotten Realms novel *Dawnbringer.*

AUTHOR'S INTRODUCTION

I was born in India and lived in Malaysia, Saudi Arabia, the Nether-
lands, and Scotland before moving to California, and my internal
landscape is a patchwork of places, myths, languages. "Pishaach"
is the first story I tried telling from that fragmented perspective,
about my sort of outsider position.

The perspective makes it a deeply personal story, but only
one thread is autobiographical—Shruti, the protagonist, cannot
change enough to leave her liminal state and become a full
member of one culture or the other. The normal mythic solu-
tions don't work, and she has to deal.

"Pishaach" was one of my submission stories to the Clarion
2007 workshop. We workshopped it in week one. Two days
later I heard from Delia Sherman that she'd talked Ellen Datlow
into looking at it for *The Beastly Bride*. I looked up from my computer to my short stack of books I couldn't do without—more
than half of which were edited by Datlow & Windling. That was
a high-pressure rewrite!

I'd call most of what I write mythic fiction. Some is also steampunk, and a little SF sneaks in; I'm not great with boundaries, and
often cross genre and form lines. I'm also (slowly) writing a disser-
tation about how people understand comics, doing worldbuilding
research for novels I can't start till I have a thesis draft, and thinking
out loud at shweta-narayan.livejournal.com.

PISHAACH

Shweta Narayan

On the day Shruti's grandfather was to be cremated, her grandmother went
into the garden of their apartment complex to pick roses for a garland. She

never came back. Shruti's father and uncle went on to the crematorium with the body and the priest, while Shruti's mother sat cross-legged on the floor in her heavy silk sari and wailed on Auntie's shoulder, and the police searched for Ankita Bai.

Shruti climbed up to a sunlit windowsill, crumpling her stiff new pink dress. She leaned against the mosquito screen to peer down at the garden, its layered tops of coconut palms, mango trees, banana palms, and frangipani bushes spreading their greens over bright smears of rose and bougainvillea. Mama blew her nose noisily and sniffled, then wiped her face on the embroidered end of her sari. Auntie rolled her eyes.

The doorbell buzzed. Shruti's brother and cousin raced off to answer it, and came back almost bouncing with excitement. With them was a policeman, cap in hand.

"You should ask my sister questions," said Gautam importantly. "Ankita Nani always talked to her."

The policeman came over to the window and bent over Shruti, his hands on his knees. He was balding and shiny with sweat, and his khaki uniform bulged at the stomach. "Do you know where your Nani went, little girl?" he asked.

Shruti nodded and pointed out the window.

He looked out, sighed, patted her head, and went to talk to Mama.

Shaking Mama off, Auntie went into the kitchen. She pulled *jalebis*, bright orange and gleaming with sugar syrup, out of the fridge, and set a plate of them by the policeman. She gave one to each boy and a half to Shruti. Shruti looked down at the sticky sweet, then held it out to Gautam, but her cousin Vikram grabbed it out of her hand and ran into their room. Gautam chased after him.

Shruti sat on the window ledge in a stream of dusty golden light, watching her mother and aunt. She did not cry, and she did not speak. They never heard her speak again.

Nani told me things.

She told me the forest is all around us, as close as breath, as close as my shadow to the ground. She told me there are entrances. Even here in Mumbai. I cannot get there yet, though. The city sticks to me like skin.

Skin comes off. I tried that. But it hurts, and there is blood, and Mama puts antiseptic cream on it and scolds.

Nani told me that it doesn't hurt when snake skin comes off. Only humans need blood to change. She said there will be blood when I become a woman, and change breeds change, so I'll be able to shed this skin. She told me how.

She didn't tell me where she has gone, but I know. She went back to the forest. Mama does not know, and I cannot tell her because it's a secret.

Nani told me lots of secrets. They fill my mouth and bubble on my tongue, like cola or like music. I will never ever speak them, though, even if Papa shouts and Auntie slaps me, because Nani said I mustn't.

Shruti returned to school to find that she was something of a celebrity. Even the older children clustered around her, asking what had happened to her grandmother. It had been in the newspapers.

She did not answer.

They put it down to grief at first, but she didn't cry, and soon one of the popular girls decided that she was a stuck-up little bitch. She became first the playground target, then the playground ghost: nowhere to be found.

They tracked her down, finally, by her music. Found her sitting on a wall twice her height, cross-legged, playing a flute. The wall was crawling with lizards and little snakes, and a one-legged crow perched silently on Shruti's bony knee.

They started calling her *Pishaach*.

They always chase me. They know I will not scream. *Pishaach*, they call me, and they glare, as if my silence were a threat. *Pishaach*, *Pishaach*, and they pull my hair and squeeze the juice from orange skins into my eyes.

Vikram joins them when my brother isn't there.

I can run faster, though, and I am not scared of the roof. They are. Stupid little boys.

I like the roof, though it smells like smog and piss and the *marihana* that the big boys smoke. Vikram doesn't come up here; the bigger boys would beat him if he did. I go from shadow into bright afternoon, sneeze, and make my way over the hot roof to the low wall that runs around its edge, stepping over broken glass and needles. Carefully. Gautam says they could give me AIDS.

I leave that behind, leave the rancid mattress and used condoms behind. They're all illusion anyway; Mama says everything is. Over the central partition lies my own palace, where the roof is too weak to hold the bigger children. I walk over my courtyard to my balcony: a magic princess, kept from her land and her true nature by the wicked *rakshasas*, her only solace the music of her dead grandfather's flute.

Vikram told me what the mattress and condoms were for. Gautam told him not to tell me dirty things, but I don't care.

My balcony is a brighter yellow than the rest of the wall. Sitting cross-legged, looking out over my crawling, roaring city, I pull out Nana's flute and play to the world.

The flute was Gautam's, really. Nana had left it to him. The only sounds he could coax from it were hideous squeaks and wheezes, so it collected dust on the dresser until the morning Gautam woke to his Nana's music and a shape at the window, flat black against the pale gray of early dawn. Gautam sat up on his mattress and watched silently with wide eyes and dry throat until the figure moved and became recognizably his sister.

Vikram slept through it all. He didn't notice for several days that Shruti had the flute. Then he said, "You should have given it to me."

"You don't even play," said Gautam. "And he wasn't your Nana."

"I'm the eldest."

Shruti left the flute at the feet of their idol of Krishna, though, and not even Vikram would take it from that place. Over the years, this became the flute's home.

The crows are my brothers, enchanted to take winged form until the sun goes down. The geckos are my cousins; numerous, scurrying, and easily scared. The snakes who find me even up here are, of course, Naga; my Nani's kin, drawn as the snake people always are to music. The sparrows are just sparrows.

Music draws my secret kin to me and lets me see with my eyes closed, see the truth. It soars, the mood poised between hope and heartbreak, weaving the story of a captive princess.

Almost full moon, and I am nearly a woman. Mama had to take me shopping for bras this week.

I must touch moonlight for three nights running—full moon and the night on either side—and pray for him to break my enchantment. It must happen while I am on this threshold. The moon will bring my period within the month, and with the blood I will cast aside this skin. Nani said it would be so. She said it would hurt, too, but I don't mind.

If I do not touch the moon I will be doomed to stay human.

Shruti drew snakes in art class. They started as crayon wiggles and grew into pencil studies and sketches of sinuous beauty—cobras on walls, in doorways, silhouetted against the full moon. They earned her excellent marks, except when the assignment was portraits or flowers.

She drew snakes in maths and Hindi as well, which never earned her excellent marks.

Full moon.

Moonlight does not truly come into our apartment; it is trapped in a watery smear by the mosquito netting. Last night I went up to the roof to find it, and the people on the mattress almost saw me. I will try the garden tonight.

Gautam sleeps soundly, and getting past the adults is easy; Papa snores louder than any noise I can make, and Auntie and Uncle sleep in the big room at the end of the hall. But last night Vikram's eyes followed me when I returned.

A lullaby on the flute sends him into a deep sleep. It almost does the same to me. I slip out of the apartment yawning.

I am silence in the building, a shadow on the path, a barefoot snake girl in the garden. I touch the moon, let him spill silvery brightness through my fingers; and turn, and sway, and dance in a wordless prayer to the soundless music of dark and light.

Behind me, the door closes. I spin. A form on the front steps, then a growing silhouette. Vikram. I step back.

"Where do you go alone at night, *Pishaach*?" He closes in on me, long-legged. His voice is a low and vicious monotone. "You live in our house, you eat our food, we put up with you—we coddle you, you freakish mute. How dare you go sneaking out like a thief, and—don't even think about raising that demon flute. I know what you did to me."

I back into the darkness under the trees, flinch as his arm reaches out toward me.

"Ah, now you remember your place. Maybe you remember also what happens to little girls who don't behave." He grins suddenly, moonlight glinting in his eyes, his teeth. "You can't even scream. Everyone will think you were willing."

I shift my weight.

"Where will you run?" he whispers. "You didn't bring the key. You can't get back in without me. Stupid little slut."

There is a pounding in my ears. Vikram laughs. He smells of cologne and smoke, clogging my breath. A van, backing up, plays a tinny "Ode to Joy." I could run for the street. But that has its own dangers. I take another step back, and another, and my heel touches something that is not a plant. Something smooth and warm; something that starts sliding past me in response, shrinking Vikram to a merely human terror. I stop. Auto horns blare. Shapes around me spring into definition. A motorcycle coughs.

A king cobra raises its head in a single sketched curve of light. I take a breath. Taste jasmine, ripening bananas, blood. The tail caresses my heel, lingers, and moves on.

I set my foot slowly down. Vikram goes still, as I did, eyes white and wide. A breeze chills the sweat on my skin.

The snake pauses between the two of us; draws slowly higher, barely swaying, until it is face-to-face with Vikram; then sinks, becomes a shadow, leaves silence behind. I feel the motorcycle's roar, the stillness of the trees, my hammering heart. I hear nothing.

Then Vikram takes a shaky breath and backs up onto the path. "Good luck getting out of there unbitten, bitch," he calls. He crosses his arms over his chest and smirks. "I'll enjoy watching."

I remember my flute.

Even when the moon is full, its dark is only a few days away. I play that dark to Vikram now, play unseen terrors, images of death slow and painful, fears of life and love gone wrong. I play the hypnotic, deadly beauty of the cobra, and the nightmare chaos of an auto accident. The music tastes of bile and blood. It rushes forth, wailing, screeching—and Vikram breaks for home.

I ease out of the garden while he fumbles for the key, then run after him. I catch the door before he closes it. Look at him.

I arch forward, smile at Vikram, and say, "Boo."

Vikram did not return to their room that night. He spent it shivering on the sofa, though the night was warm, and that is where Auntie found him the next day. He woke when she went to him, put his head on her shoulder like a much smaller boy, and whispered, "That demon flute, Mama. She put a spell on me."

She coaxed his version of the story out of him, then tucked him into her own bed and went seething to make the coffee. When Shruti's mother sleepily joined her, Auntie said, "If you cannot control your—daughter—she can sleep in your room from now on."

Mama tried to understand what was wrong. She asked Auntie, and Gautam, and Vikram when he woke. But not Shruti, of course.

I wait until Gautam's breathing slows into sleep, then roll to my feet and ghost into the kitchen, my steps silent on the hard, cool floor. On the way, I switch on the bathroom light and close the door.

The altar is in an alcove set into the kitchen wall. It smells faintly of sandalwood. I reach in to take my flute back from Lord Krishna.

It is gone.

I kneel before the altar, my fingers searching the space under it, the crack between its edge and the wall. They find only incense ash.

"Looking for something?"

Pale golden light washes past me. I turn to see Vikram lit by the open fridge, my flute clenched in one hand. "You thought I would let you have it, after yesterday, or what?" he asks. His voice is too calm. "And you thought that trick with the bathroom light would fool me? I'm not the dumb one."

I uncoil, coming to my feet fast, and grab for the flute. He holds it over my head with one hand, pushes me away with the other. I hit the wall.

"Come on," he says. "Give me an excuse to break it."

I turn on my heel and run for the front door. He follows me, leans over me as I reach for the doorknob, laughs softly into my ear. His breath disturbs my hair.

I need only touch the moonlight one more time. But I doubt he will even let me get downstairs. And perhaps I will not bleed until the ritual is complete. I slump, turn back to our room, drag my mattress over next to Gautam's, and settle back in. With Vikram's eyes on me, I pray to the Moon and to Durga to give me time.

My first period starts four days later. As Nani warned me, it hurts.

There once lived, among the Naga people, a girl of surpassing beauty. Her tail looped in long coils and her scales looked new-molted, shining and unmarred. She was alluring even in human form, with hooded eyes and long shining hair like the dark of the moon. The fair hue of her underbelly spread to all her human skin, and she kept the serpent's grace.

Perhaps she was a princess; perhaps she was a queen. Perhaps she was merely a lovely girl from a Naga village.

Taking human form, this girl would escape her lands and come to ours, seeking music. There is no music in the Naga lands. It is their only lack, and the reason they wear our clothes and dare our world. This girl loved music even more than most, and she risked more, and lost. For she was trapped by a snake charmer, who took her home to be his wife.

So my Nani told me, and there she would always stop.

"What happened to her, Nani?"

"She learned to make rotis and curries and beds, and she learned to eat mice and rats only when nobody could see," she would say. "She had a daughter, in time, and that daughter had two children. A boy and a girl. And that girl, that Naga's granddaughter, has in her the magic of our people."

It seemed incredible, even then. Not that she was other-worldly. No, with her dark knowing eyes in her walnut face and her hair of spun moonlight, that was obvious. What stunned me was that she might once have been young. "Were you really beautiful, Nani?"

She would laugh. "For many, many years. It is only in this form that we truly age, Asha."

Asha. Hope. She called me that always. I did not understand why; I had been named after music, and she loved music.

* * *

Mama found the flute in the back of a cupboard, behind the pressure cooker. She lectured Shruti about caring for the family heirloom, while Vikram smirked, and kept the flute locked up for a week.

Meanwhile, Vikram hid Shruti's homework. He rubbed soap into her toothbrush. He spilled black ink on her new school uniform. He left cockroaches in her pillowcase. Shruti may as well have been Untouchable in Auntie's eyes, but Mama was angry, so she cried on Gautam's shoulder. He was annoyed at first, inclined to shrug her off, but after the cockroaches he got into a shouting match with Vikram and called him a bastard. Auntie heard him.

Shruti took to hiding in her room after school. When Vikram followed her, she started disappearing, up to the roof or into the garden with the flute. But one day the downstairs grannies stopped talking and glared when they saw her, and she realized that Auntie must have told them something. She ran away.

They never found the cobra, nor any sign of it, but Shruti was blamed for every snakebite in the area thereafter. She started playing her music in the early morning, when nobody would see her. Women hawking vegetables were her accompaniment; the neighbors kept away and told their children to do the same.

Her mother stopped talking to the neighbors; Gautam stopped playing cricket with Vikram's friends. Her father grew solemn and silent. They would not hear ill of Shruti in public.

Three years later the city had a miracle: a boy who was able to pick up cobras without coming to harm. He was on the television, and his parents were interviewed. Shruti's neighbors argued about whether the boy was blessed by Lord Shiva or Lord Vishnu.

Shruti could pick cobras up, too, but Shruti was far too unsettling to be a miracle.

Mama waits until Papa and Uncle approve of the curry before saying, "Shruti made it."

Papa glares at her. "And that makes it all right? What shall we say to the young men? She does not talk, she frightens all the neighbors, worms and lizards come to hear her play that damned flute—but she makes a fairly good curry?"

Auntie adds, "When she's helped at every step."

Vikram makes a show of spitting the curry out, nose wrinkled.

Gautam looks coolly at him and takes another bite. I look down at my own plate. The smell of ghee and cardamom is cloying. What will my home be like when Gautam leaves—to go to college, to start his own life?

"She's a good girl," Mama protests, "and she learns well."

"Then teach her to speak."

Mama looks down at her plate, biting her lip.

"She's unnatural," says Auntie. "Like your mother was."

Uncle frowns at her. "That's enough."

Papa says, "But she's right."

Gautam clears his throat. "How do you think we will do in the test match, Papa?"

I look at them—at my mother trying to make herself small, my brother trying to distract Papa—and I am glad no man will have me. I get up, leaving my food barely touched, and walk away.

"Shruti!"

Papa no longer frightens me. Nani's eyes can silence him, even when they are in my face. I look at him until he looks away, then turn and leave the apartment.

Ankita Nani's eyes never left Nana when he was playing his flute. She watched him, unblinking and adoring—as romantic to a child as any Bollywood film. Only when he died, when she told me she was going home, did I see the shadow behind the romance.

She obeyed him, of course, just as Mama obeys Papa. Is every girl a Naga, stolen away to serve her husband?

The wall that runs around the roof bears new graffiti. Bold and elaborate in silvered red, it says VIKR. He has left cans of spray paint under the letters; Vikram does not delay when Auntie expects him downstairs. I pick up the silver, shake it, and draw a slow outward spiral centered on the K. When it is big enough I spiral back in, filling in the gaps to make a moon, so that only the huge *V* and the *R*'s looping tail still show. I spray one practiced black curve over the moon: a cobra, its tail extending along the wall.

The roof was mine first.

I pick my way over to the other side. My side. I have to keep to the edges, along the wall, because the rest will not hold my weight anymore.

Cross-legged on the yellow patch of outer wall that I used to call my balcony, I play the music of moonlit gardens and enchantments that can be broken. I face the roof instead of the city so that Vikram cannot sneak up on me, and so I see the cobra raise his head.

He rises till his eyes are level with my own. His body is dappled, liquid motion. He could kill me with one strike, but that is abstract knowledge: my heart does not race, my breath does not shorten. I envy his grace; I do not fear it. Perhaps this is what it means to be *Pishaach*.

I play for the cobra and he dances for me, while sunset stains the sky orange and purple behind him.

Vikram comes through the doorway and stops, his mouth a comical O. His eyes slide from me to the snake to his graffiti, and he slips back indoors.

I lower my flute. He will be back. I am not sure how to let the snake know, but when the music stops he lowers his hood and slithers into my shadow. I look down but cannot see him.

I lower one foot to the ground. It touches ground and nothing else. The cobra has vanished.

When Vikram returns with his thugs they see only me, sitting where I should not be and playing the sun down. They come to the center partition to stare at me, at the empty roof.

I smile.

Amit laughs at Vikram. Vikram punches him. Stalks away. The rest leave soon enough.

But I do not dare go home until Gautam comes to find me.

Shruti passed her classes, but only just. She did not have a tutor, as most students did, and many nights she would forget her homework in music. Her teachers were less amused by her doodles every year. At the end of Tenth Standard one teacher told her parents that she was only good for the arts, if that.

127

Vikram and Gautam spent that summer closeted with tutors. Vikram was preparing for engineering college, and Gautam for Twelfth Standard. Most days, nobody knew where Shruti went. A frown grew between her mother's eyebrows, and she watched Shruti silently at meals.

Uncle took Papa aside one day. "You will have to decide what to do with her, you know," he said. "She's a good girl in her way, but . . ."

"Yes," said Papa. "But."

I pause in the doorway to catch my breath, almost coughing at the smoke. Vikram and his gang are on my roof. I could exile them, set the snake on them. But if I did, what would Vikram do tonight?

I dodge an auntie's venomous glare and slip downstairs to hide under the bougainvillea, where sunlight falls in patches of magenta and the air is thick and sweet with mango and flowering rose.

I take one delicious breath, then pause. The air is too cool and too clean. There is no exhaust underlying the sweetness, no smog. No sound of children from the apartment beyond. The garden has lost its boundaries; when I raise the flute there are a hundred ears listening. I take a step forward, hesitate.

A hand on my shoulder. I twist, ready to strike, and find a bare chest. Skin like polished teak, and the dark smell of earth just after rain. I look up.

He is slender, and the curve of his cheek is a boy's, but his eyes are clear and old as drops of amber. His hair falls unbound to the middle of his back, and light glints from a silver circlet as he leans down. I should be frightened, and am not, and that tells me who he is.

"Asha," he murmurs, his lips close to mine, "won't you play for me?"

I play for him there in the multicolored light, in our tiny section of an endless forest, and he dances for me. Below the waist his body is a snake's.

He touches me, later, with fingers and lips and coils, making my heart hammer and my breath quicken with something other than fear. I run my fingers over coffee-bean skin, trying to find where it turns into scales.

Naga do not marry.

They may build a home together, raise children together, create their lives together; but their ceremonies are only for birth and naming and death.

They tell a story about this: long ago, when the snake people married, a fair Naga girl was to marry a handsome youth. But at the wedding, with all the village gathered, her musk attracted and maddened the groom's younger brother, who claimed her for himself. The brothers fought over her, long and hard and viciously, and each died of the other's poison. In grief and shame the girl ran away, and never was seen again. The snake people have had no marriage since that day, and no true fights in mating season.

But my Nani considered herself married. "Once the gods have been called," she said, "we cannot pretend that they were not here."

His lips brush against my neck. "Asha, play for me." We are in the garden again, among the dappled green scents and shadows, as we have been more often than is wise.

I find my voice. "Why." It sounds dusty.

"You know I love your music," he whispers in my ear. My breath catches at his voice, his closeness, his hands on my stomach, his heartbeat against my back; but his words are not the words I want.

I love your voice, I want to say. I love the way you move, the way you smell, the nonexistent point where skin becomes scale. I love the way you shimmer between forms, as I cannot and ache to and never will. I love the curves and the planes of your body, and I love your shifting face. I want to know who you are, and that is who I want to keep with me. Do you only love my music?

There are too many words. They jostle and clog in my throat. I shake my head.

"You know I do," he says, "and you know you will."

The air squeezes from my lungs. Have I no say in what I do? How dare he think so? I take a breath and start to play Nana's song.

He grows rigid, his heartbeat quickening. His hands drop away from me. "No," he says.

I turn to him; see terror, adoration; remember the way Nani looked at Nana. I stop playing.

He watches my eyes, my hands. He looks at me like I'm Vikram.

I will not be Vikram.

"No," I agree. "Go free."

His eyes widen. He shimmers, becomes first a cobra, then merely another shadow. I play then, play him the words I could not speak before, but only the shadows hear.

*   *   *

Shruti started haunting the garden, playing eerie, melancholy tunes that made the babies cry. Or so the neighbors said. Vikram said she was probably making their mothers cry, too. And souring their milk, and rotting the mangoes and bananas on the branches. Auntie wanted to know why, if that girl would not make pleasant music, she was allowed to play that flute at all.

Papa told Shruti to stay out of the garden.

Two days before the full moon, she bought a child's recorder made of bright blue plastic.

I have been mostly alone when I've played. But not every time. He must need the music like I need to shift, to escape. Unfair that he may have what he needs; but my lack is not his fault.

I touch the moonlight, feel my leaden form struggle for a moment to become fluid, to shed its skin. Feel it give up. I settle at the base of the coconut palm and play until the forest is listening. Then I pull out the recorder, play a simple tune.

"Gift," I say in my dusty, unused voice.

I set it aside and get up. When I look down again, it is gone.

Anywhere three trees grow together, the land's invisible border rubs thin, and the great forest grows so close that it sometimes spills over.

The forest has no edge, but it has many, many frayed borders. It likes opening into our world for a beckoning, teasing, deadly instant. It is fully alive, this forest, with giant trees draped with giant vines, their leaves bigger than me; with dirt-colored flowers and flower-colored birds and sleek, silent predators. Naga live in the rivers, in the wet earth, and in hollow trees; the monkey people claim the canopy. Garuda sometimes nest on the highest branches, which border on their realm.

It is home to great beauty, the forest, in form and scent and movement, but the only music found there is the music of the natural world, calls and cries and falling rain.

So my Nani told me.

"Why?" I asked.

"We do not make music."

"Why not?"

"Perhaps we have not the skill."

"I do."

"It is not something we learn, Asha. We do not live as you do here." She smiled sadly, but she said no more.

I play to myself in the punishing afternoon, when I know I will be alone. To myself and to the forest beyond. I play with my eyes closed, letting the world paint itself in touch and smell. Overripe bananas, frying onions and cumin, my own sweat beaded on my forehead and dampening my clothes. The occasional breeze, warm, bringing the stench of exhaust and burning garbage. My fingers, slippery on the flute.

The taste of his musk, of earth after rainfall, brings my eyes half-open. I watch for him through my eyelashes, and let my fingers and breath sing him a lonely mood. He drifts into view, shifting uncertainly from half-form to cobra and back; he starts to dance and stops again.

When I draw breath, he shifts to full man, naked, too wild for modesty. I look away, shame and lust burning my cheeks.

"Show me?"

I look back. His gaze is wary, but he holds the little blue recorder as though it were precious. I hold out a hand. He edges forward. I grasp his wrist to pull him closer. He jerks back, shifts to cobra, disappears.

I pick up the recorder. Will he come back for it, if not for me? I play a note. Sniff and blink tears away. Whisper, "Come back."

I hear lorry and rickshaw horns in the silence. Then his voice, behind me. "Will you charm me?"

I shake my head.

"How can I know?"

I turn to look at him. "Could kill me," I suggest.

He stares for a second, then slides forward till I can feel his warmth. His tail curls around my ankle. "I would not." I keep looking at him, and eventually his lips twist into something that might be a smile. "But how can you know?"

I nod.

"What should we do?"

I reach out again to take his hand, and this time he does not start. I shape it around the recorder, showing his long fingers where to be.

He laughs, silently and a bit raggedly. "That is . . . not quite the answer I was expecting."

The monkey people are territorial. Sooner steal a Garuda's egg than seek the monkeys' great city in the trees.

Not so the Naga. They care little about land, only one race frightens them, and that race cannot find their homes.

When my Nani told me this I did not understand.

She glanced at me, cutting onions by feel. Her eyes were bright, the knife swift and steady in her wrinkled hand. "You will," she said.

He is waiting for me in the garden, his tail coiled under him, his head in his hands. He looks up as I hurry over, but he does not speak until I am close. Then he puts his arms around me, leans his head on my shoulder, and says, "They took it away."

"Who?" I do not have to ask what. I hold him, stroking his hair, breathing in its dark-leaf fragrance.

"The elders. Not all of them; your Nani said not to."

My arms tighten around him. "Nani?"

"She is our storyteller. But the rest are—angry—that any of us would learn your people's magic, and shocked that any of us *could*."

"Magic?" The lizards and birds do not come when he plays.

"Making the sweet sounds with your fingers. They said it was wrong, and . . . they took it away."

The grief in his voice shakes me. Even Auntie would not take music away from me. I ask, "Why?"

"They're scared, I suppose." He speaks into my shoulder. "Of course they're scared. It is our bane. So beautiful, so powerful . . ." He pulls back, looks at me, and says, "We cannot resist that pull."

I rest a fingertip on his nose. "Bane."

He blinks.

I smile and hold the flute to his lips. He reaches out a hand, slowly, to touch it, and looks wide-eyed at me.

"Blow," I say.

He does. It makes no sound at all. He looks surprised, and indignant, and I cannot help but laugh. This makes him glower, so I kiss him before showing him how to coax a sound from the flute.

Later, as his fingers trace the beadwork on my *kurti*, around my neck, across my breasts; as my lips are learning the shape and taste of him in the dark, he says, "I am not allowed to be here."

I kiss his shoulder, his neck, his jaw. Whisper in his ear, "Nor I."

Papa's call pulled Mama out of the kitchen, wiping flour off her hands, and Gautam out of his room to the big, scarred-wood dining table. Vikram was at the other end, with heavy books around him, and Vikram showed no signs of leaving. Shruti was still in the garden and did not hear.

"Well," Papa said, "maybe it's for the best. She will be less of a problem if she hears it from Gautam."

Vikram looked up.

"Hears what, Papa?" Gautam asked.

Mama polished an imagined smudge from the wood with the end of her sari.

Papa sighed. "She cannot go to college," he said, "and no normal man will marry her. And Mr. Bhosle says Amit heard her playing that music of hers *with* someone. What next?"

Gautam said, "She can stay with me."

"A live-in mousetrap," said Vikram.

Auntie, coming in with a stack of stainless steel plates, laughed. "Wait until you have a wife, Gautam." She set the plates on the table with a clatter.

"But listen," said Papa, "I know a much better solution. I have written to—you know that boy, he was on television. The one who holds cobras. He is still alive; I wrote to his parents. They agreed that he should meet Shruti."

"Oh, what a good idea," Mama said. "They will have so much in common."

"They can open a pet shop," said Vikram.

Gautam glared. "Don't you have somewhere else to be?"

"Than in my own home?"

Gautam turned his back on Vikram and said, "She's never even met the boy."

"Your mother's right. They both like snakes to the point of obsession. Neither is quite—normal . . ."

Vikram snorted.

". . . but his parents are happy that she will not scream at his cobras."

"She's only sixteen, Papa."

"Am I getting her married tomorrow?"

"Are they Brahmins?" asked Mama.

"No, but they are well off, and we cannot be too—" He stopped, and glanced at Gautam. "That is, in this day and age, it is very old-fashioned to care about caste."

Gautam pushed himself to his feet. Hands flat on the table, he leaned over his father. "You talk like she's defective," he said.

Vikram murmured, "There's a reason for that."

"She's not stupid, Vikram. She's clever enough to stay away from you."

The microwave beeped insistently into the silence that followed.

"Vikram," said Auntie, a little too loudly, "can you clear away your books and call your Papa, *Beta*? It's time for dinner."

"She's just . . . innocent, Papa. Look, you don't need to worry about her. She can stay with me. Really."

"What kind of life would that be for her?" Mama demanded. "Unmarried, unwanted, and underfoot in her brother's house? No!"

"Sit down," said Papa. "I know you want your sister to be happy. We all do. But you are too young to see the wisdom of age."

"Does the wisdom of age mean settling her life behind her back?"

"If she cannot even be home at dinnertime, maybe it does!"

Gautam's eyes widened. "Shit."

"Gautam," said Mama, "What have we said about language?"

"Well, it's not like her, is it? I'd better go look."

Vikram stood up, smiling. "I'll go with you," he said. "Mama, you'll clear my books, won't you? The poor darling might be in trouble."

Knowing that we are both disobeying our elders brings us closer. I do not leave when I normally would, nor do I pull away when he tugs at my *kurti*, when he eases it over my head. My jeans follow. The bra confuses him, until I help.

He is a shadow cast by the waning moon above me, black limned with silver. His tail strokes my leg, tossing an arc of light between its coils, and light catches in his circlet. He picks jasmine flowers, lets them drift through his fingers onto my bare skin. I taste jasmine on the roof of my mouth, and crushed leaves, and arousal. He leans down. Kisses my neck. I feel teeth against my skin.

He slides a hand teasingly down my belly, and shifts. The wind grows stronger, bringing me the rich leaf-scent of the great forest. His magic tingles just under my skin. I arch up, aching to shift, and find myself pressed against him. He is in man-form. His gasp matches my own. We stare at each other.

We both hear the snap of a broken twig.

We freeze. Another footfall and he shifts, from man to half-snake to snake.

I snatch my jeans and jam my legs into them. *Not Vikram*, I pray, *not here, not now*.

The snake melts into shadows. I grab my *kurti*, telling myself that he had no choice. A click, and the great forest is washed away on a wave of over-bright blue light, leaving me alone. I hold the *kurti* to my chest.

"What have you been doing?" It is Gautam's voice. And Gautam's LED key chain torch, the one he is so proud of. I wince.

"I think that's pretty clear, no?" says Vikram behind him. "The question is, who's Little Miss Innocence doing it *with*?"

I clutch my *kurti* closer.

"Put that on, stupid. It's not for playing with."

I twist away and pull it quickly over my head, inside out, trying not to show him more than he has already seen. Beadwork scrapes against me.

"I never would have believed it," says Gautam softly.

Vikram shoulders past him. I shrink back. "Believe what you want," says Vikram. "The question is what the neighbors—" His foot jerks sideways under him and he falls crashing through the bougainvillea bush. He screams.

Shadows swing wildly as Gautam runs toward us. He stops short of the bush, grabs his torch, points it. The shadows still. Wrapped around Vikram's ankle, gleaming black against the blue-gray garden, are cobra's coils.

Vikram tries to sit up, bloody scratches on his face and arms. The snake strikes. Vikram falls back and is still. A little wordless sobbing noise comes from my throat.

Gautam says shakily, "He—" He draws a hissing breath. "Ambulance."

The snake shimmers, shifts to half-man. Says, "No need."

Gautam stares.

"No kills in mating season."

They watch each other, the Naga swaying to silent music. I smell fear but cannot tell whose it is. Gautam pulls himself up straight. The Naga rises to match his height. Like the forest, he is washed away in the LED's harsh glare; he looks as though he has gathered shadows for protection from the light.

Gautam shakes his head. "Mating," he says blankly. "Mating? You're— and she's a child."

"She was willing."

Gautam glances at me but turns back to the Naga. "How would you know?" he demands. "You're not even human."

"I know she was willing, because I saw her unwilling. When he tried." He points at Vikram, lying silent.

"What?"

I shake my head. Blood seeps from Vikram's scratches, black as the paper-thin bougainvilleas scattered around and over him.

"I don't know what you have done to my sister, but—"

"Done to her?" He draws himself higher, and higher yet, spreading his arms out like a hood. "I protect her. I hear her." He starts a slow glide toward me, looking all the time at Gautam.

"Don't you touch her!" Gautam stumbles forward, raising a fist.

The half-man shadow shrinks, becomes a snake. Hisses.

No kills in mating season.

Between rivals.

But Gautam is my brother. I shake my head again, but I am more invisible than even a shadow, and neither one sees me.

The cobra sways. I scream, "No!"

The cobra stops. Turns in a beautiful, silent arc and comes to me, slides over me, wraps himself around my arm, across my shoulder.

Gautam's hand falls, and he stares at me. "You can *talk*?"

I stare back. There is too much to say.

"What else have you kept from me, Shruti? Why? I thought we were close."

I want to run to him, to hold him. I want to explain. "Vikram talks better," I say.

Gautam's eyes widen. "Then he did . . . ?"

I nod.

"You should have told me. Why didn't you tell me? I would have believed you."

"And Papa?"

"*Aaizhavli.*" He puts a hand to his face. "Papa."

"What?"

"Papa has a suitable boy in mind for you."

I cringe, shake my head. "No," I say.

He nods. "And I don't know what I can do for you, after this."

I keep shaking my head.

The snake slips off my shoulders, shifts to half-man, and wraps his arms around my waist. I twist around, rest my face against his chest, taste his wet-earth scent. He says, "Am I a suitable boy?"

I look up and meet his gaze. Warm. Anxious. He gestures wide with one hand, offering me the dark deep forest.

The elders cannot want a charmer in their land. Will they accept me? Send me back? Kill me? I am no shifter. What will they do to him? But I start to smile. If he will risk their anger, so will I. I say, "Yes."

"You must be joking," says Gautam. "Can you take him to meet Mama and Papa? Can you live in a snake hole? Think a little."

I turn back to Gautam. My best friend in this world; but I will not let him say no for me. I stare him down.

"But, Shruti . . ." Light grows in Gautam's eyes; he blinks, and it streaks down his face. "If you, well . . . I would miss you. Horribly. But would you be happy?"

"Maybe." I push my Naga's hands gently away, stand, and go to Gautam. "Best chance."

He takes a breath. Hugs me suddenly. Tight. "Then—go. And Vikram can bloody well die here, for all I care."

I hug him back. "No," I say. "Help him." I turn and walk out of the false light.

The forest looms immediately around me, its shadows half-felt, half-seen. The ground is uncertain, the sky dark, and the trees darker yet. They taste of death as well as life, their roots drinking sharp blood and slow rot. Thick vines coil and hang from branches, brushing my skin, and some are not vines at all. I see eyes, faintly golden, unblinking, watching me.

"Wait." It is faint, barely heard. I turn back.

I have to squint to see Gautam. He is faded, like an old photograph. But he is holding out the flute to me, and it is solid to my reaching fingers. He is not.

I want to say good-bye, to tell him that I love him. But he is gone, and the garden, and everything but the flute. I raise it to my lips and play a gentle song of hope and healing. Perhaps he hears it.

Then I reach out for my lover's hand, and it is warm in mine; and we turn together and go into the forest.

On the day Shruti's father planned to tell her about her future husband, she went into the garden to play her flute. She never came back.

ABOUT THE AUTHOR

Shweta Narayan has lived in six countries on three continents. She has an ongoing fascination with shapeshifters and other liminal figures, and with fairy tales and folk tales from all over. She used to have a snake, but he didn't like being caged so she let him go.

Shweta was the Octavia E. Butler Memorial Scholarship recipient at the 2007 Clarion workshop. She writes short fiction, poetry, and in-between thingies, some of which have recently appeared in *Steampunk II: Steampunk Reloaded*, *Cabinet des Fees*, and *Strange Horizons*. She hangs out online at shweta_narayan .livejournal.com.

AUTHOR'S INTRODUCTION

I fell in love with St. Paul's and the Blitz when I first went to London over thirty years ago, and I've been entranced by them ever since. I wrote several stories about them, but never quite managed to get them out of my system, so I suppose my writing *Blackout/All Clear* was inevitable.

That era is just so fascinating—the blackout, the gas masks, the kids being sent off to who-knows-where, old men and middle-aged women suddenly finding themselves in uniform and in danger, tube shelters and Ultra and Dunkirk, and, running through it all, the threat of German tanks rolling down Piccadilly! What's not to like?

And though there were kajillions of novels about World War II, nearly all of them were about the military side of things— hardly any about the shopgirls and maidservants and actors and reporters who were equally essential to winning the war. So I thought *I'd* write about them.

I didn't think it would take eight years to do it and that it would be such a long book. Neither did Bantam or my editor Anne Groell, and I owe them a huge debt of gratitude for sticking with me through a process that ended up taking even longer than the war. Thank you!

And thanks to Robert A. Heinlein, who first introduced me to time travel, and Rumer Godden, who first introduced me to the Blitz! And to the devoted fire watch who saved St. Pauls!

NEBULA AWARD, NOVEL

EXCERPT FROM
BLACKOUT/ALL CLEAR

Connie Willis

"They'd make a beautiful target, wouldn't they?"

General Short, commenting on
the battleships lined up
at Pearl Harbor
December 6, 1941

The English Channel—29 May 1940

"What do you mean, we're halfway across the Channel?" Mike shouted, lurching to the stern of the boat. There was no land in sight, nothing but water and darkness on all sides. He groped his way back to the helm and the Commander. "You have to turn back!"

"You said you were a war correspondent, Kansas," the Commander shouted back at him, his voice muffled by the wind. "Well, here's your chance to cover the war instead of writing about beach fortifications. The whole bloody British Army's trapped at Dunkirk, and we're going to rescue them!"

But you can't go to Dunkirk, Mike thought, still trying to absorb what had happened. *It's impossible. Dunkirk's a divergence point.* Besides, this wasn't the way the evacuation had operated. The small craft hadn't set off on their own. That had been considered far too dangerous. They'd been organized into convoys led by naval destroyers.

"You've got to go back to Dover," he shouted, trying to make himself heard against the sound of the chugging engine and the wet, salt-laden wind. "You've got to go back to Dover! The Navy—"

"The Navy?" the Commander snorted. "I wouldn't trust those paper-pushers to lead me across a mud puddle. When we bring back a boatload of our boys, they'll see just how seaworthy the *Lady Jane* is!"

"But you don't have any charts, and the Channel's mined—"

"I've been piloting this Channel by dead-reckoning since before those young pups from the Small Vessels Pool were born. We won't let a few mines stop us, will we, Jonathan?"

"Jonathan? You brought *Jonathan*? He's fourteen years old!"

Jonathan emerged out of the bow's darkness half-dragging, half-carrying a huge coil of rope. "Isn't this exciting?" he said. "We're going to go rescue the British Expeditionary Force from the Germans. We're going to be heroes!"

"But you don't have official clearance," Mike said, desperately trying to think of some argument that would convince them to turn back. "And you're not armed—"

"*Armed*?" the Commander bellowed, taking one hand off the wheel to reach inside his peacoat and pull out an ancient pistol. "Of course we're armed. We've got everything we need." He waved one hand toward the bow. "Extra rope, extra petrol—"

Mike squinted through the darkness to where he was pointing. He could just make out square metal cans lashed to the gunwales. Oh, Christ. "How much gas—petrol—do you have on board?"

"Twenty five-gallon tins," Jonathan said eagerly. "We've more down in the hold."

Enough to blow us sky-high if we're hit by a torpedo.

"Jonathan," the Commander bellowed, "stow that rope in the stern and go check the bilge pump."

"Aye, aye, Commander." Jonathan started for the stern.

Mike went after him. "Jonathan, listen, you've got to convince your grandfather to turn back. What he's doing is—" he was going to say "suicidal," but settled for, "against Navy regulations. He'll lose his chance to be recommissioned—"

"Recommissioned?" Jonathan said blankly. "Grandfather was never in the Navy."

Oh, God, he'd probably never been across the Channel either.

"Jonathan!" the Commander called. "I told you to go check the bilge pump. And, Kansas, go below and put your shoes on. And have a drink. You look like death."

That's because we're going to die, Mike thought, trying to think of some argument that would convince him to turn the boat around and head back to Saltram-on-Sea. But there wasn't one. Nothing short of knocking him out with the butt of that pistol and taking the wheel would work, and then what? He knew even less than the Commander did about piloting a boat, and there weren't any charts on board, even if he could decipher them, which he doubted.

"Get yourself some dinner," the Commander ordered. "We've a long night's work ahead of us."

They had no idea what they were getting into. Over sixty of the small craft that had gone over to Dunkirk had been sunk and their crews injured or killed. Mike started down the ladder. "There's some of that pilchard stew left," the Commander called down after him.

I don't need to eat, Mike thought, descending into the hold, which now had a full foot of water in it. *I need to think*. How could they be going to Dunkirk? It was impossible. The laws of time travel didn't allow historians anywhere near divergence points. *Unless Dunkirk isn't a divergence point*, he thought, wading over to the bunk to retrieve his shoes and socks.

They were in the farthest corner. Mike clambered up onto the bunk to get them and then sat there with a shoe in his hand, staring blindly at it, considering the possibility. Dunkirk had been a major turning point in the war. If the soldiers had been captured by the Germans, the invasion of England, and its surrender, would have been inevitable. But it wasn't a single discrete event, like Lincoln's assassination or the sinking of the *Titanic*, where a historian making a grab for John Wilkes Booth's pistol or shouting "Iceberg ahead!" could alter the entire course of events. He couldn't keep the entire British Expeditionary Force from being rescued, no matter what he did. There were too many boats, too many people involved, spread over too great an area. Even if a historian *wanted* to alter the outcome of the evacuation, he couldn't.

But he could alter individual events. Dunkirk had been full of narrow escapes and near misses. A five-minute delay in landing could put a boat underneath a bomb from a Stuka or turn a near-miss into a direct hit, and a five-degree change in steering could mean the difference between it being grounded or making it out of the harbor.

Anything I do could get the Lady Jane sunk, Mike thought, horrified. *Which means I don't dare do anything. I've got to stay down here till we're safely out of Dunkirk.* Maybe he could feign seasickness, or cowardice.

But even his mere presence here could alter events. At a divergence point, history balanced on a knife-edge, and his merely being on board could be enough to tilt the balance. Most of the small craft who'd come back from Dunkirk had been packed to capacity. His presence might mean there wasn't room for a soldier who'd otherwise have been saved—a soldier who would have gone on to do something critical at Tobruk or Normandy or the Battle of the Bulge.

But if his presence at Dunkirk would have altered events and caused a paradox, then the net would never have let him through. It would have refused to open, the way it had in Dover and Ramsgate and all those other places Badri had tried. The fact that it had let him through at Saltram-on-Sea meant that he hadn't done anything at Dunkirk to alter events, or that whatever he'd done hadn't affected the course of history.

Or that he hadn't made it to Dunkirk. Which meant the *Lady Jane* had hit a mine or been sunk by a German U-boat—or the rising water in her hold—before she ever got there. She wouldn't be the only boat that had happened to.

I knew I should have memorized that asterisked list of small craft, he thought. *And I should have remembered that slippage isn't the only way the continuum has of keeping historians from altering the course of history.*

There was a sudden pounding of footsteps overhead and Jonathan poked his head down the hatch. "Grandfather sent me to fetch you," he said breathlessly.

"Get the bloody hell up here!" the Commander shouted over Jonathan's voice.

They've spotted the U-boat, Mike thought, grabbing his shoes and wading over to the ladder. He clambered up it. Jonathan was leaning over the hatch, looking excited. "Grandfather needs you to navigate," he said.

"I thought he didn't have any charts," Mike said.

"He doesn't," Jonathan said. "He—"

"Now!" the Commander roared.

"We're here," Jonathan said. "He needs us to guide him through the harbor."

"What do you mean, we're here?" Mike said, hauling himself up the ladder and onto the deck. "We can't be—"

But they were. The harbor lay in front of them, lit by a pinkish-orange glow that illuminated two destroyers and dozens of small boats. And behind it, on fire and half-obscured by towering plumes of black smoke, was Dunkirk.

> "Another part of the island."
>
> *The Tempest*
> William Shakespeare

Kent—April 1944

Cess opened the door of the office and leaned in. "Worthing!" he called, and when he didn't answer, "Ernest! Stop playing reporter and come with me. I need you on a job."

Ernest kept typing. "Can't," he said through the pencil between his teeth. "I've got five newspaper articles and ten pages of transmissions to write."

"You can do them later," Cess said. "The tanks are here. We need to blow them up."

Ernest removed the pencil from between his teeth and said, "I thought the tanks were Gwendolyn's job."

"He's in Hawkhurst. Dental appointment."

"Which takes priority over tanks? I can see the history books now. 'World War II was lost due to a toothache.'"

"It's not a toothache, it's a cracked filling," Cess said. "And it'll do you good to get a bit of fresh air." Cess yanked the sheet of paper out of the typewriter. "You can write your fairy tales later."

"No, I can't," Ernest said, making an unsuccessful grab for the paper. "If I don't get these stories in by tomorrow morning, they won't be in Tuesday's edition, and Lady Bracknell will have my head."

Cess held it out of reach. "'The Steeple Cross Women's Institute held a tea Friday afternoon,'" he read aloud, "'to welcome the officers of the 21st

Airborne to the village.' Definitely more important than blowing up tanks. Front page stuff, Worthing. This'll be in the *Times*, I presume?"

"The *Sudbury Weekly Shopper*," he said, making another grab for it, this time successful. "And it's due at nine tomorrow morning along with four others *which I haven't finished yet*. And, thanks to you, I already missed last week's deadline. Take Moncrieff with you."

"He's down with a bad cold."

"Which he no doubt caught while blowing up tanks in the pouring rain. Not exactly my idea of fun," Ernest said, rolling a new sheet of paper into the typewriter.

"It's not raining," Cess said. "There's only a light fog, and it's supposed to clear by morning. Perfect flying weather. That's why we've got to blow them up tonight. It'll only take an hour or two. You'll be back in more than enough time to finish your articles and get them over to Sudbury."

Ernest didn't believe that any more than he believed it wasn't raining. It had rained all spring. "There must be someone else in this castle who can do it. What about Lady Bracknell? He'd be perfect for the job. He's full of hot air."

"He's in London, meeting with the higher-ups, and everyone else is over at Camp Omaha. Come *on*, Worthing, do you want to tell your children you sat at a typewriter all through the war or that you blew up tanks?"

"What makes you think we'll ever be allowed to tell anyone anything, Cess?"

"I suppose that's true. But surely by the time we have *grand*children, *some* of it will have been declassified. That is, if we win the war, which we won't if you don't help. I can't manage both the tanks and the cutter on my own."

"Oh, all right," Ernest said, pulling the story out of the typewriter and putting it in a file folder on top of several others. "Give me five minutes to lock up."

"Lock *up*? Do you honestly think Goebbels is going to break in and steal your tea party story while we're gone?"

"I'm only following regulations," Ernest said, swiveling his chair to face the metal filing cabinet. He opened the second drawer down, filed the folder, then fished a ring of keys out of his pocket and locked the cabinet. "'All written materials of Fortitude South and the Special Means unit shall be considered 'top top secret' and handled accordingly.' And speaking of regulations, if I'm going to be in some bloody cow pasture all night, I need a decent pair of boots. 'All officers are to be issued appropriate gear for missions.'"

Cess handed him an umbrella. "Here."

"I thought you said fog, not rain."

"Light fog. Clearing towards morning. And wear an army uniform, in case someone shows up in the middle of the operation. You have two minutes. I want to be there before dark." He went out.

Ernest waited, listening, till he heard the outside door slam, then swiftly unlocked the file drawer, pulled out the folder, removed several of the pages, replaced the file, and relocked the drawer. He slid the pages he'd removed into a manila envelope, sealed it, and stuck it under a stack of forms in the bottom drawer of the desk. Then he took a key from around his neck, locked the drawer, hung the key around his neck again under his shirt, picked up the umbrella, put on his uniform and his boots, and went outside. Into an all-enveloping dark grayness. If this was what Cess considered a light fog, he shuddered to think what a heavy one was. He couldn't see the tanks or the lorry. He couldn't even see the gravel driveway at his feet.

But he could hear an engine. He felt his way toward it, his hands out in front of him till they connected with the side of the Landrover. "What took you so long?" Cess asked, leaning out of the fog to open its door. "Get in."

Ernest climbed in. "I thought you said the tanks were here."

"They are," Cess said, roaring off into blackness. "We've got to go pick them up in Tenterden and then take them down to Icklesham."

Tenterden was not "here." It was fifteen miles in the opposite direction from Icklesham and, in this fog, it would be well after dark before they even got to Tenterden. *This'll take all night*, he thought. *I'll never make that deadline.* But halfway to Brede, the fog lifted and when they reached Tenterden, everything was, amazingly, loaded and ready to go. Ernest, following Cess and the lorry in the Landrover, began to feel some hope that it wouldn't take too long to get unloaded and set up, and they might actually be done blowing up the tanks by midnight. Whereupon the fog closed in again, causing Cess to miss the turn for Icklesham twice and the lane once. It was nearly midnight before they located the right pasture.

Ernest parked the Landrover in amongst some bushes and got out to open the gate. He promptly stepped in mud up to his ankles and then, after he'd extricated himself, in a large cowpat. He squelched over to the lorry, looking around for cows, even though, in this foggy darkness he wouldn't see one till he'd collided with it. "I thought there weren't supposed to be any cows in this pasture," he said to Cess.

"There were before, but the farmer moved them into the next one over," Cess said, leaning out the window. "That's why we picked this pasture. That, and the large copse of trees over there." He pointed vaguely out into the murk. "The tanks will be hidden out of sight under the trees."

"I thought the whole idea was to let the Germans see them."

"To let them see *some* of them," Cess corrected. "There are a dozen in this battalion."

"We've got to blow up a *dozen* tanks?"

"No, only two. The Army didn't park them far enough under the trees. Their rear ends can still be seen poking out from under the branches. I think it'll be easiest if I back across the field. Help me turn around."

"Are you certain that's a good idea?" Ernest said. "It's awfully muddy."

"That'll make the tracks more visible. You needn't worry. This lorry's got good tyres. I won't get her stuck."

He didn't. Ernest did, driving the lorry back to the gate after they'd unloaded the two tanks. It took them the next two hours to get out of the mudhole, in the process of which Ernest lost his footing and fell flat, and they made a hideous rutted mess out of the center of the field.

"Goering's boys will never believe tank treads did that," Ernest said, shining a shielded torch on the churned-up mud.

"You're right," Cess said. "We'll have to put a tank over it to hide it, and—I know!—we'll make it look as though it got stuck in the mud."

"Tanks don't get stuck in the mud."

"They would in this mud," Cess said. "We'll only blow up three quadrants and leave the other one flat, so it'll look like it's listing."

"Do you honestly think they'll be able to see that from fifteen thousand feet?"

"No idea," Cess said, "but if we stand here arguing, we won't be done by morning, and the Germans will see what we're up to. Here, lend me a hand. We'll unload the tank and then drive the lorry back to the lane. That way we won't have to drag it."

Ernest helped him unload the heavy rubber pallet. Cess connected the pump and began inflating the tank. "Are you certain it's facing the right way?" Ernest asked. "It should be facing the copse."

"Oh, right," Cess said, shielding his torch with his hand and shining it on it. "No, it's the wrong way round. Here, help me shift it."

They pushed and shoved and dragged the heavy mass around till it faced the other way. "Now let's hope it isn't upside down," Cess said. "They should put a 'this end up' on them, though I suppose that might make the Germans suspicious." He began to pump. "Oh, good, there's a tread."

The front end of a tank began to emerge out of the flat folds of gray-green rubber, looking remarkably tank-like. Ernest watched for a moment, then fetched the phonograph, the small wooden table it sat on, and its speaker. He set them up, got the record from the lorry, placed it on the turntable, and lowered the needle. The sound of tanks rolling thunderously toward him filled the pasture, making it impossible to hear anything Cess said.

On the other hand, he thought as he wrestled the tank-tread cutter off the back of the lorry, he no longer had to switch on his torch. He could find his way simply by following the sound. Unless there were in fact cows in this pasture—which, judging by the number of fresh cowpats he was stepping in, there definitely could be.

Cess had told him on the way to Tenterden that the cutter was perfectly simple to operate. All one had to do was push it, like a lawnmower, but it was at least five times as heavy as the lawnmower at the castle. It required bearing down with one's whole weight on the handle to make it go even a few inches, it refused to budge at all in grass taller than two inches, and it tended to veer off at an angle. Ernest had to go back to the lorry, fetch a rake, smooth over what he'd done, then redo it several times before he had a more-or-less straight tread mark from the gate to the mired tank.

Cess was still working on the right front quadrant. "Sprang a leak," he shouted over the rumble of tanks. "Lucky I brought my bicycle patch kit along. Don't come any nearer! That cutter's sharp."

Ernest nodded and hoisted it over in front of where the tank's other tread would be and started back toward the gate. "How many of these do you want?" he shouted to Cess.

"At least a dozen pair," Cess shouted, "and some of them need to overlap. I think the fog's beginning to lift."

The fog was *not* beginning to lift. When he switched on his torch so he could return the needle to the beginning of the record, the phonograph was shrouded in mist. And even if it should lift, they wouldn't be able to tell in this blackness. He looked at his watch. Two o'clock, and they still hadn't inflated a tank. They were going to be stuck here forever.

Cess finally completed the mired tank and slogged across the field to the copse to do the other two, Ernest following with the cutter, making tread-tracks to indicate where the tanks had driven in under the trees.

Halfway there, the sound of tanks shut off. Damn, he'd forgotten to move the needle. He had to go all the way back across the pasture, start the record again, and he'd no sooner reached the cutter again than the fog did indeed lift. "I told you," Cess said happily, and it immediately began to rain.

"The phonograph!" Cess cried, and Ernest had to fetch the umbrella and prop it over the phonograph, tying it to the tank's rubber gun with rope.

The shower lasted till just before dawn, magnifying the mud and making the grass so slippery that Ernest fell down two more times, once racing to move the phonograph needle, which had stuck and was repeating the same three seconds of tank rumbling over and over, and the second time helping Cess repair yet another puncture. "But think of the war story you'll have to tell your grandchildren!" Cess said as he wiped the mud off.

"I doubt whether I'll ever have grandchildren," Ernest said, spitting out mud. "I am beginning to doubt whether I'll even survive this night."

"Nonsense, the sun'll be up any moment, and we're nearly done here." Cess leaned down so he could see the treadmarks, which Ernest had to admit looked very realistic. "Make two more tracks, and I'll finish off this last tank. We'll be home in time for breakfast."

And in time for me to finish the articles and run them over to Sudbury by nine, he thought, aligning the tracker with the other treadmarks and pushing them down hard. Which would be good. He didn't like the idea of those other articles sitting there for another week, even in a locked drawer. Now that he could partially see where he was going and didn't need to stop and check his path with the torch every few feet, it should only take him twenty minutes to do the treads and load the lorry, and another three-quarters of an hour back to the castle. They should be there by seven at the latest, which should work.

But he'd only gone a few yards before Cess loomed out of the fog and tapped him on the shoulder. "The fog's beginning to lift," he said. "We'd best get out of here. I'll finish off the tanks and you start on stowing the equipment."

Cess was right; the fog was beginning to thin. Ernest could make out the vague shapes of trees, ghostly in the gray dawn, and across the field a fence and three black-and-white cows placidly chewing grass—luckily, on the far side of it.

Ernest folded up the tarp, untied the umbrella, carried them and the pump to the lorry, and came back for the cutter. He picked it up, decided there was no way he could carry it all the way across the field, set it down, pulled the cord to start it, and pushed it back, making one last track from just in front of the tank's left tread to the edge of the field, and lugged it, limping, from there to the lorry. By the time he'd hoisted it up into the back, the fog was beginning to break up, tearing apart into long streamers which drifted like veils across the pasture, revealing the long line of treadmarks leading to the copse and the rear end of one imperfectly hidden tank peeking out from the leaves, with the other behind it. Even knowing how it had been done, it looked real, and he wasn't fifteen thousand feet up. From that height, the deception would be perfect. Unless, of course, there was a phonograph standing in the middle of the pasture.

He started back for it, able to actually see where he was going for several yards at a time, but as he reached the tank, the fog closed in again, thicker than ever, cutting off everything—even the tank next to him. He shut the phonograph and fastened the clasps, then folded up the table. "Cess!" he called in what he thought was his general direction. "How are you coming along?" and the fog abruptly parted, like theatre curtains sweeping open, and he could see the copse of trees and the entire pasture.

And the bull. It stood halfway across the pasture, a huge shaggy brown creature with beady little eyes and enormous horns. It was looking at the tank.

"Hey! You there!" a voice called from the fence. "What do you think you're doing in my pasture?" And Ernest turned instinctively to look at the farmer standing there. So did the bull. "Get those bloody tanks out of my pasture!" the farmer shouted, angrily jabbing the air with his finger.

The bull watched him, fascinated, for a moment, then swung his head back around. To look directly at Ernest.

"Raid in Progress"
Notice onstage in London theatre
1940

London—17 September 1940

By midnight only Polly and the elderly, aristocratic gentleman who always gave her his Times were awake. He had draped his coat over his shoulders and was reading. Everyone else had nodded off, though only Lila and Viv and Mrs. Brightford's little girls had lain down, Bess and Trot with their heads in their mother's lap. The others sat drowsing on the bench or the floor, leaning back against the wall. Miss Hibbard had let go of her knitting, and her head had fallen forward onto her chest. The rector and Miss Laburnum were both snoring.

Polly was surprised. One of the things the contemps had complained about was lack of sleep due to the raids, and by midway through the Blitz many Londoners had abandoned the shelters and gone back to their own beds, more desperate for a good night's sleep than they were frightened of the bombs. But this group didn't seem bothered by the uncomfortable sleeping conditions or the noise, even though the raid was picking up in intensity again. The anti-aircraft gun in Kensington Gardens started up, and another wave of planes growled overhead.

She wondered if this was the wave of bombers which would hit John Lewis. No, they sounded nearer—Mayfair? It and Bloomsbury had both been hit as well as central London, and after they'd finished with Oxford Street, they'd hit Regent Street and the BBC studios. She'd better try to sleep while she could. She would need to start off early tomorrow morning, though she wondered if the department stores would even be open.

London businesses had prided themselves on remaining open throughout the Blitz, and Padgett's and John Lewis had both managed to reopen after a few weeks. But what about the day after the bombing? Would the stores which hadn't been damaged be open, or would the whole street be off-limits, like the area around St. Paul's? And for how long? If I haven't got a job by tomorrow night—

Of course they'll be open, she thought. Think of all those window signs the Blitz was famous for: "Hitler can smash our windows, but he can't match our prices," and "It's *bomb marché* in Oxford Street this week." And that photograph of a woman reaching through a broken display window to feel the fabric of a frock. It might even be a good day to apply for a position. It would show the raids didn't frighten her, and if some of the shopgirls weren't able to make it into work because of bombed bus routes, the stores might hire her to fill in.

But she'd also have to compete with all those suddenly unemployed John Lewis shopgirls, and they'd be more likely to be taken on than she would, out of sympathy. Perhaps I should tell them I worked there, she thought.

She folded her coat into a pillow and lay down, but she couldn't sleep. The droning planes were too loud. They sounded like monstrous, buzzing wasps, and they were growing louder—and nearer—by the moment. Polly sat up. The noise had wakened the rector, too. He'd sat up and was looking nervously at the ceiling. There was a whoosh, and then a huge explosion. Mr. Dorming jerked upright. "What the bloody hell—?" he said, and then, "Sorry, rector."

"Quite understandable given the circumstances," the rector said. "They seem to have begun again." Which was an understatement even for a contemp. The gun in Battersea Park was going full blast, and he had to shout to make himself heard. "I do hope those girls are all right. The ones who were trying to find Gloucester Terrace."

The gun in Kensington Gardens started in again, and Irene sat up, rubbing her eyes. "Shh, go back to sleep," Mrs. Brightford murmured, looking over at Mr. Dorming, who was staring at the door. The raid seemed to be just outside it, whumps and bangs and long, shuddering booms, that woke up Nelson and Mr. Simms and the rest of the women. Mrs. Rickett looked annoyed, but everyone else looked wary and then worried.

"Perhaps we shouldn't have allowed the girls go," Miss Laburnum said.

Trot crawled into her mother's lap. "Shh," Mrs. Brightford said, patting her. "It's all right." No, it's not, Polly thought, watching their faces. They had the same look they'd had when the knocking began. If the raid didn't let up soon . . .

Every anti-aircraft gun in London was firing—a chorus of deafening thump-thump-thumps, punctuated by the thud and crash of bombs. The din grew louder and louder. Everyone's eyes strayed to the ceiling, as if expecting it to crash in at any moment. There was a screech, like tearing metal, and then an ear-splitting boom. Miss Hibbard jumped and dropped her knitting, and Bess began to cry.

"The bombardment does seem rather more severe this evening," the rector said.

Rather more severe. It sounded like the planes—and the anti-aircraft guns—were fighting it out in the sanctuary upstairs. Kensington wasn't hit, she told herself.

"Perhaps we should sing," the rector shouted over the cacophony.

"That's an excellent idea," Mrs. Wyvern said, and launched into, "God save our noble king." Miss Laburnum and then Mr. Simms joined in, but they could scarcely be heard above the roar and scream outside, and the rector made no attempt to go on to the second verse. One by one, everyone stopped singing and stared anxiously up at the ceiling.

An HE exploded so close the beams of the shelter shook, followed immediately by another even closer, drowning out the sound of the guns, but not the planes droning endlessly, maddeningly overhead. "Why isn't it letting up?" Viv asked, and Polly could hear the panic in her voice.

"I don't like it!" Trot wailed, clapping her small hands over her ears. "It's loud!"

"Indeed," the elderly gentleman said from his corner. "'The isle is full of noises,'" and Polly looked over at him in surprise. His voice had changed completely from the quiet, well-bred voice of a gentleman to a deep, commanding tone which made even the little girls stop crying and look at him.

He shut his book and laid it on the floor beside him. "'With strange and several noises,'" he said, getting to his feet, "'of roaring . . .'" He shrugged his coat from his shoulders, as if throwing off a cloak to reveal himself as a magician, a king. "'With shrieking, howling, and more diversity of sounds, all horrible, we were awaked.'"

He strode suddenly to the center of the cellar. "'To the dread rattling thunder have I given fire,'" he shouted, seeming to Polly to have grown to twice his size. "'The strong-bas'd promontory have I made shake!'" His resonant voice reached every corner of the cellar. "'Sometime I'd divide and burn in many places,'" he said, pointing dramatically at the ceiling, the floor, the door in turn as he spoke, "'on the topmast, the yards, and bowsprit would I flame—'" He flung both arms out, "'Then meet and join.'"

Above, a bomb crashed, close enough to rattle the tea urn and the teacups, but no one glanced over at them. They were all watching him, their fear gone, and even though the terrifying racket hadn't diminished, and his words, rather than attempting to distract them from the noise, were drawing attention to it, describing it, the din was no longer frightening. It had become mere stage effects, clashing cymbals and sheets of rattled tin, providing a dramatic background to his voice. "'A plague upon this howling!'" he cried, "'They are louder than the weather or our office,'" and went straight into Prospero's epilogue and from there into Lear's mad scene, and finally *Henry V*, while his audience listened, entranced.

At some point the cacophony outside had diminished, fading till there was nothing but the muffled poom-poom-poom of an anti-aircraft gun off to the northeast, but no one in the room had noticed. Which was, of course, the point. Polly gazed at him in admiration.

"'This story shall the good man teach his son, from this day to the ending of the world,'" he said, his voice ringing through the cellar, "'but we in it shall be remembered—we few, we happy few, we band of brothers.'" His voice died away on the last words, like a bell echoing into silence. "'The iron tongue of midnight hath told twelve,'" he whispered. "'Sweet friends, to bed,'" and bowed his head, his hand on his heart.

There was a moment of entranced silence, followed by Miss Hibbard's, "Oh, my!" and general applause. Trot clapped wildly, and even Mr. Dorming joined in. The gentleman bowed deeply, retrieved his coat from the floor and returned to his corner and his book. Mrs. Brightford gathered her girls to her, and Nelson and Lila and Viv composed themselves to sleep, one after the other, like children who'd been told a bedtime story. Polly went over to sit next to Miss Laburnum and the rector. "Who *is* he?" she whispered.

"You mean you don't *know*?" Miss Laburnum said,

Polly hoped he wasn't so famous that her failing to recognize him would be suspicious. "He's Godfrey Kingsman," the rector explained, "the Shakespearean actor."

"England's greatest actor," Miss Laburnum said.

Mrs. Rickett sniffed. "If he's such a great actor, what's he doing sitting in this shelter? Why isn't he on stage?"

"You know perfectly well the theatres are closed because of the raids,"

Miss Laburnum said heatedly. "Until the government reopens them—"

"All I know is, I don't let rooms to actors," Mrs. Rickett said. "They can't be relied on to pay their rent."

Miss Laburnum went very red. "Sir *Godfrey*—"

"He's been knighted then?" Polly asked hastily.

"By King Edward," Miss Laburnum said. "I can't imagine that you've never heard of him, Miss Sebastian. His Lear is *renowned*! I saw him in *Hamlet* when I was a girl, and he was simply *marvelous*!"

He's rather marvelous now, Polly thought.

"He's appeared before all the crowned heads of Europe," Miss Laburnum said. "And to think he honored *us* with a performance tonight."

Mrs. Rickett sniffed again, and Miss Laburnum was only stopped from saying something regrettable by the all clear. The sleepers sat up and yawned, and everyone began to gather their belongings. Sir Godfrey marked his place in his book, shut it, and stood up. Miss Laburnum and Miss Hibbard scurried over to him to tell him how wonderful he'd been. "It was *so* inspiring," Miss Laburnum said, "especially the speech from *Hamlet*."

Polly suppressed a smile. Sir Godfrey thanked the two ladies solemnly, his voice quiet and refined again. Watching him putting on his coat and picking up his umbrella, it was hard to believe he'd just given that mesmerizing performance.

Lila and Viv folded their blankets and gathered up their magazines, Mr. Dorming picked up his thermos, Mrs. Brightford picked up Trot, and they all converged on the door. The rector pulled the bolt back and opened it, and as he did, Polly caught an echo of the tense, frightened look they'd had before Sir Godfrey intervened, this time for what they might find when they went through that door and up those steps: their houses gone, London in ruins. Or German tanks driving down Lampden Road.

The rector stepped back from the opened door to let them through, but no one moved, not even Nelson, who'd been cooped up since before midnight.

"'Hie you, make haste!'" Sir Godfrey's clarion voice rang out, "'See this dispatch'd with all the haste thou canst,'" and Nelson shot through the door.

Everyone laughed.

"Nelson, come back!" Mr. Simms shouted and ran after him. He called down from the top of the steps, "No damage I can see," and the rest of them trooped up the steps and looked around at the street, peaceful in the dim, gray predawn light. The buildings were all intact, though there was a smoky pall in the air, and a sharp smell of cordite and burning wood.

"Lambeth got it last night," Mr. Dorming said, pointing at plumes of black smoke off to the southeast.

"And Piccadilly Circus, looks like," Mr. Simms said, coming back with Nelson and pointing at what was actually Oxford Street and the smoke from John Lewis. Mr. Dorming was wrong, too. Shoreditch and Whitechapel had taken the brunt of the first round of raids, not Lambeth, but from the look of the smoke, nowhere in the East End was safe.

"I don't understand," Lila said, looking around at the tranquil scene. "It sounded like it was bang on top of us."

"What will it sound like if it *is* on top of us, I wonder?" Viv asked.

"I've heard one hears a very loud, very high-pitched scream," Mr. Simms began, but Mr. Dorming was shaking his head.

"You won't hear it," he said, "You'll never know what hit you," and stomped away.

"Cheerful," Viv said, looking after him.

Lila was still looking toward the smoke of Oxford Street. "I suppose the Underground won't be running," she said glumly, "and it'll take us ages to get to work."

"And when we get there," Viv said, "the windows will have been blown out again. We'll have to spend all day sweeping up."

"'What's this, varlets?'" Sir Godfrey roared. "'Do I hear talk of terror and defeat? Stiffen the sinews! Summon up the blood!'"

Lila and Viv giggled.

Sir Godfrey drew his umbrella like a sword. "'Once more into the breach, dear friends, once more!'" he shouted, raising it high, "'We fight for England!'"

"Oh, I do love *Richard the Third*!" Miss Laburnum said.

Sir Godfrey gripped the umbrella handle violently, and for a moment Polly thought he was going to run Miss Laburnum through, but instead he hooked it over his arm. "'And if we no more meet till we meet in heaven,'" he said, "'then joyfully, my noble lords and my kind kinsmen, warriors all, adieu!'" and strode off, umbrella in hand, as if going into battle.

Which he is, Polly thought, watching him. Which they all are.

"How marvellous!" Miss Laburnum said. "Do you think if we asked him, he'd do another play tomorrow? *The Tempest*, perhaps, or *Henry the Fifth*?"

ABOUT THE AUTHOR

Connie Willis has won seven Nebulas, more than any other writer, and was the first author to win the Nebula in all four categories.

INTRODUCTION

Here's the winner of this year's Dwarf Star Award, "Bumber-shoot" by Howard Hendrix.

BUMBERSHOOT

Howard Hendrix

Night, a gun-blue umbrella tricked with distant suns and planets,
is not to be opened indoors—more bad luck, or worse.

Hold it to the mind's sky. Finger the trigger in its handle.
A meteor bullets the firmament. The universe falls shut with a whoosh.

Shake the drops of the stars from the loose skin of the darkness.
Think of nothing for which to wish. Step into a different house.

ABOUT THE AUTHOR

Howard V. Hendrix is the author of six novels, three short story collections, and a whole bunch of poems that he really should put forward as a collection one of these days. He teaches English literature and creative writing at the college level. He has recently served as guest editor for a *Midsummer Night's Dream*–the med issue of the *Pedestal Magazine*, and is lead editor on *Visions of Mars: Essays on the Fiction and Science of the Red Planet*.

AUTHOR'S INTRODUCTION

I recently realized, with something like horror, that I'm fast closing in on my twenty-fifth year as a published writer. If you asked me where the time went, I wouldn't be able to tell you. Perhaps the same place as my hair or a body type that was once upon a time described as emaciated and is now closer to spherical.

"Arvies" is my sixth Nebula nomination, one that as always leaves me scratching my head over the mysterious forces that usher one story into being while another—that might be just as promising—remains imprisoned in the brain vault and in no particular hurry to be released. Its genesis was the standard SF trick of turning the real-world status quo upside down and seeing what happens. In this case it was the premise that life legally begins at birth; I wondered what would happen if life legally ended there.

I am proud that the tale has been interpreted, by various partisans on opposite sides of the abortion debate, as being both for and against . . . while being criticized by others for refusing to take a stand. I'm firmly prochoice myself, but the story itself is none of the above; it's just a thought experiment about an alien way to live and a demonstration of the truism that even in societies that offer their most privileged citizens unlimited opportunities for happiness, there's always somebody, somewhere, who gets royally screwed.

ARVIES
Adam Troy-Castro

STATEMENT OF INTENT

This is the story of a mother, and a daughter, and the right to life, and the dignity of all living things, and of some souls granted great destinies at the moment of their conception, and of others damned to remain society's useful idiots.

CONTENTS

Expect cute plush animals and amniotic fluid and a more or less happy ending for everybody, though the definition of happiness may depend on the truncated emotional capacity of those unable to feel anything else. Some of the characters are rich and famous, others are underage, and one is legally dead, though you may like her the most of all.

APPEARANCE

We first encounter Molly June on her fifteenth deathday, when the monitors in charge of deciding such things declare her safe for passengers. Congratulating her on completing the only important stage of her development, they truck her in a padded skimmer to the arvie showroom where she is claimed, right away, by one of the Living.

The fast sale surprises nobody, not the servos that trained her into her current state of health and attractiveness, not the AI routines managing the showroom, and least of all Molly June, who has spent her infancy and early childhood having the ability to feel surprise, or anything beyond a vague contentment, scrubbed from her emotional palate. Crying, she'd learned while still capable of such things, brought punishment, while unconditional acceptance of anything the engineers saw fit to provide brought light and flower scent and warmth. By this point in her existence she'll greet anything short of an exploding bomb with no reaction deeper than vague concern. Her sale is a minor development by comparison: a happy development, reinforcing her feelings of dull satisfaction. Don't feel sorry for her. Her entire life, or more accurately death, is happy ending. All she has to do is spend the rest of it carrying a passenger.

VEHICLE SPECIFICATIONS

You think you need to know what Molly June looks like. You really don't, as it plays no role in her life. But as the information will assist you in feeling empathy for her, we will oblige anyway.

Molly June is a round-faced, button-nosed gamin, with pink lips and cheeks marked with permanent rose: her blonde hair framing her perfect face in parentheses of bouncy, luxurious curls. Her blue eyes, enlarged by years of genetic manipulation and corrective surgeries, are three times as large as the ones imperfect nature would have set in her face. Lemur-like, they dominate her features like a pair of pacific jewels, all moist and sad and adorable. They reveal none of her essential personality, which is not a great loss, as she's never been permitted to develop one.

Her body is another matter. It has been trained to perfection, with the kind of punishing daily regimen that can only be endured when the mind itself remains unaware of pain or exhaustion. She has worked with torn ligaments, with shattered joints, with disfiguring wounds. She has severed her spine and crushed her skull and has had both replaced, with the same ease her engineers have used, fourteen times, to replace her skin with a fresh version unmarked by scars or blemishes. What remains of her now is a wan amalgam of her own best-developed parts, most of them entirely natural, except for her womb, which is of course a plush, wired palace, far safer for its future occupant than the envelope of mere flesh would have provided. It can survive injuries capable of reducing Molly June to a smear.

In short, she is precisely what she should be, now that she's fifteen years past birth, and therefore, by all standards known to modern civilized society, Dead.

HEROINE

Jennifer Axioma-Singh has never been born and is therefore a significant distance away from being Dead.

She is, in every way, entirely typical. She has written operas, climbed mountains, enjoyed daredevil plunges from the upper atmosphere into vessels the size of teacups, finagled controlling stock in seventeen major multinationals, earned the hopeless devotion of any number of lovers, written her name in the sands of time, fought campaigns in a hundred conceptual wars, survived twenty regime changes and on three occasions had herself turned off so she could spend a year or two mulling the purpose of existence while her bloodstream spiced her insights with all the most fashionable hallucinogens.

She has accomplished all of this from within various baths of amniotic fluid.

Jennifer has yet to even open her eyes, which have never been allowed to fully develop past the first trimester and which still, truth be told, resemble black marbles behind lids of translucent onionskin. This doesn't actually deprive her of vision, of course. At the time she claims Molly June as her arvie, she's been indulging her visual cortex for seventy long years, zipping back and forth across the solar system collecting all the tourist chits one earns for seeing all the wonders of modern-day humanity: from the scrimshaw carving her immediate ancestors made of Mars to the radiant face of Unborn Jesus shining from the artfully re-configured multicolored atmosphere of Saturn. She has gloried in the catalogue of beautiful sights provided by God and all the industrious living people before her.

Throughout all this she has been blessed with vision far greater than any we will ever know ourselves, since her umbilical interface allows her sights capable of frying merely organic eyes, and she's far too sophisticated a person to be satisfied with the banal limitations of the merely visual spectrum. Decades of life have provided Jennifer Axioma-Singh with more depth than that. And something else: a perverse need, stranger than anything she's ever done, and impossible to indulge without first installing herself in a healthy young arvie.

ANCESTRY

Jennifer Axioma-Singh has owned arvies before, each one customized from the moment of its death. She's owned males, females, neuters, and several sexes only developed in the past decade. She's had arvies designed for athletic prowess, arvies designed for erotic sensation, and arvies designed for survival in harsh environments. She's even had one arvie with hypersensitive pain receptors: that, during a cold and confused period of masochism.

The last one before this, who she still misses, and sometimes feels a little guilty about, was a lovely girl named Peggy Sue, with a metabolism six times baseline normal and a digestive tract capable of surviving about a hundred separate species of nonstop abuse. Peggy Sue could down mountains of exotic delicacies without ever feeling full or engaging her gag reflex, and enjoyed taste receptors directly plugged into her pleasure centers. The slightest sip of coconut juice could flood her system with tidal waves of endorphin-crazed ecstasy. The things chocolate could do to her were downright obscene.

Unfortunately, she was still vulnerable to the negative effects of unhealthy eating, and went through four liver transplants and six emergency transfusions in the first ten years of Jennifer's occupancy.

The cumulative medical effect of so many years of determined gluttony mattered little to Jennifer Axioma-Singh, since her own caloric intake was regulated by devices that prevented the worst of Peggy Sue's excessive consumption from causing any damage on her side of the uterine wall. Jennifer's umbilical cord passed only those compounds necessary for keeping her alive and healthy. All Jennifer felt, through her interface with Peggy Sue's own sensory spectrum, was the joy of eating; all she experienced was the sheer, overwhelming treasury of flavor.

And if Peggy Sue became obese and diabetic and jaundiced in the meantime—as she did, enduring her last few years as Jennifer's arvie as an immobile mountain of reeking flab, with barely enough strength to position her mouth for another bite—then that was inconsequential as well, because she had progressed beyond prenatal development and had therefore passed beyond that stage of life where human beings can truly be said to have a soul.

PHILOSOPHY

Life, true life, lasts only from the moment of conception to the moment of birth. Jennifer Axioma-Singh subscribes to this principle, and clings to it in the manner of any concerned citizen aware that the very foundations of her society depend on everybody continuing to believe it without question. But she is capable of forming attachments, no matter how irrational, and she therefore felt a frisson of guilt once she decided she'd had enough and the machines performed the Caesarian Section that delivered her from Peggy Sue's pliant womb. After all, Peggy Sue's reward for so many years of service, euthanasia, seemed so inadequate, given everything she'd provided.

But what else could have provided fair compensation, given the shape Peggy Sue was in by then? Surely not a last meal! Jennifer Axioma-Singh, who had not been able to think of any alternatives, brooded over the matter until she came to the same conclusion always reached by those enjoying lives of privilege, which is that such inequities are all for the best and that there wasn't all that much she could do about them, anyway. Her liberal compassion had been satisfied by the heartfelt promise to herself that if she ever bought an arvie again she would take care to act more responsibly.

And this is what she holds in mind, as the interim pod carries her into the gleaming white expanse of the very showroom where fifteen-year-old Molly June awaits a passenger.

INSTALLATION

Molly June's contentment is like the surface of a vast, pacific ocean, unstirred by tide or wind. The events of her life plunge into that mirrored surface without effect, raising nary a ripple or storm. It remains unmarked even now, as the anesthetician and obstetrician mechs emerge from their recesses to guide her always-unresisting form from the waiting room couch where she'd been left earlier this morning, to the operating theatre where she'll begin the useful stage of her existence. Speakers in the walls calm her further with an arrangement of melodious strings designed to override any unwanted emotional static.

It's all quite humane: for even as Molly June lies down and puts her head back and receives permission to close her eyes, she remains wholly at peace. Her heartbeat does jog, a little, just enough to be noted by the instruments, when the servos peel back the skin of her abdomen, but even that instinctive burst of fear fades with the absence of any identifiable pain. Her reaction to the invasive procedure fades to a mere theoretical interest, akin to what Jennifer herself would feel regarding gossip about people she doesn't know living in places where she's never been.

Molly June drifts, thinks of blue waters and bright sunlight, misses Jennifer's installation inside her, and only reacts to the massive change in her body after the incisions are closed and Jennifer has recovered enough to kick. Then her lips curl in a warm but vacant smile. She is happy. Arvies might be dead, in legal terms, but they still love their passengers.

AMBITION

Jennifer doesn't announce her intentions until two days later, after growing comfortable with her new living arrangements. At that time Molly June is stretched out on a lounge on a balcony overlooking a city once known as Paris but which has undergone perhaps a dozen other names of fleeting popularity since then; at this point it's called something that could be translated as Eternal Night, because it's urban planners have noted that it looks best when its towers were against a backdrop of darkness and therefore arranged to free it from the sunlight that previously diluted its beauty for half of every day.

The balcony, a popular spot among visitors, is not connected to any actual building. It just sits, like an unanchored shelf, at a high altitude calculated to showcase the lights of the city at their most decadently glorious. The city itself is no longer inhabited, of course; it contains some mechanisms important for the maintenance of local weather patterns but otherwise exists only to confront the night sky with constellations of reflective light. Jennifer, experiencing its beauty through Molly June's eyes, and the bracing high-altitude wind through Molly June's skin, feels a connection with the place that goes beyond aesthetics. She finds it fateful, resonant, and romantic, the perfect location to begin the greatest adventure of a life that has already provided her with so many.

She cranes Molly June's neck to survey the hundreds of other arvies sharing this balcony with her: all young, all beautiful, all pretending happiness while their jaded passengers struggle to plan new experiences not yet grown dull from surfeit. She sees arvies drinking, arvies wrestling, arvies declaiming vapid poetry, arvies coupling in threes and fours; arvies colored in various shades, fitted to various shapes and sizes; pregnant females, and impregnated males, all sufficiently transparent, to a trained eye like Jennifer's, for the essential characters of their respective passengers to shine on through. They all glow from the light of a moon that is not *the* moon, as the original was removed some time ago, but a superb piece of stagecraft designed to accentuate the city below to its greatest possible effect.

Have any of these people ever contemplated a stunt as over-the-top creative as the one Jennifer has in mind? Jennifer thinks not. More, she is certain not. She feels pride, and her arvie Molly June laughs, with a joy that threatens to bring the unwanted curse of sunlight back to the city of lights. And for the first time she announces her intentions out loud, without even raising her voice, aware that any words emerging from Molly June's mouth are superfluous, so long as the truly necessary signal travels the network that conveys Jennifer's needs to the proper facilitating agencies. None of the other arvies on the balcony even hear Molly June speak. But those plugged in hear Jennifer speak the words destined to set off a whirlwind of controversy.

I want to give birth.

CLARIFICATION

It is impossible to understate the perversity of this request.

Nobody gives Birth.

Birth is a messy and unpleasant and distasteful process that ejects living creatures from their warm and sheltered environment into a harsh and unforgiving one that nobody wants to experience except from within the protection of wombs either organic or artificial.

Birth is the passage from Life, and all its infinite wonders, to another place inhabited only by those who have been forsaken. It's the terrible ending that modern civilization has forestalled indefinitely, allowing human beings to live within the womb without ever giving up the rich opportunities for experience and growth. It's sad, of course, that for Life to even be possible a large percentage of potential Citizens have to be permitted to pass through that terrible veil, into an existence where they're no good to anybody except as spare parts and manual laborers and arvies, but there are peasants in even the most enlightened societies, doing the hard work so the important people don't have to. The best any of us can do about that is appreciate their contribution while keeping them as complacent as possible.

The worst thing that could ever be said about Molly June's existence is that when the Nurseries measured her genetic potential, found it wanting, and decided she should approach Birth unimpeded, she was also humanely deprived of the neurological enhancements that allow first-trimester fetuses all the rewards and responsibilities of Citizenship. She never developed enough to fear the passage that awaited her, and never knew how sadly limited her existence would be. She spent her all-too-brief Life in utero ignorant of all the blessings that would forever be denied her, and has been kept safe and content and happy and drugged and stupid since birth. After all, as a wise person once said, it takes a perfect vassal to make a perfect vessel. Nobody can say that there's anything wrong about that. But the dispossession of people like her, that makes the lives of people like Jennifer Axioma-Singh possible, remains a distasteful thing decent people just don't talk about.

Jennifer's hunger to experience birth from the point of view of a mother, grunting and sweating to expel another unfortunate like Molly June out of the only world that matters, into the world of cold slavery, thus strikes the vast majority as offensive, scandalous, unfeeling, selfish, and cruel. But since nobody has ever imagined a Citizen demented enough to want such a thing, nobody has ever thought to make it against the law. So the powers that be indulge Jennifer's perversity, while swiftly passing laws to ensure that nobody will ever be permitted such license ever again; and all the machinery of modern medicine is turned to the problem of just how to give her what she wants. And, before long, wearing Molly June as proxy, she gets knocked up.

IMPLANTATION

There is no need for any messy copulation. Sex, as conducted through arvies, still makes the world go round, prompting the usual number of bittersweet affairs, tempestuous breakups, turbulent love triangles, and silly love songs.

In her younger days, before the practice palled out of sheer repetition, Jennifer had worn out several arvies fucking like a bunny. But there has never been any danger of unwanted conception, at any time, not with the only possible source of motile sperm being the nurseries that manufacture it as needed without recourse to nasty antiquated testes. These days, zygotes and embryos are the province of the assembly line. Growing one inside an arvie, let alone one already occupied by a human being, presents all manner of bureaucratic difficulties involving the construction of new protocols and the rearranging of accepted paradigms and any amount of official eye-rolling, but once all that is said and done, the procedures turn out to be quite simple, and the surgeons have little difficulty providing Molly June with a second womb capable of growing Jennifer Axioma-Singh's daughter while Jennifer Axioma-Singh herself floats unchanging a few protected membranes away.

Unlike the womb that houses Jennifer, this one will not be wired in any way. Its occupant will not be able to influence Molly June's actions or enjoy the full spectrum of Molly June's senses. She will not understand, except in the most primitive, undeveloped way, what or where she is or how well she's being cared for. Literally next to Jennifer Axioma-Singh, she will be by all reasonable comparisons a mindless idiot. But she will live, and grow, for as long as it takes for this entire perverse whim of Jennifer's to fully play itself out.

GESTATION (I)

In the months that follow, Jennifer Axioma-Singh enjoys a novel form of celebrity. This is hardly anything new for her, of course, as she has been a celebrity several times before and if she lives her expected lifespan, expects to be one several times again. But in an otherwise unshockable world, she has never experienced, or even witnessed, that special, nearly extinct species of celebrity that comes from eliciting shock, and which was once best-known by the antiquated term, *notoriety*.

This, she glories in. This, she milks for every last angstrom. This, she surfs like an expert, submitting to countless interviews, constructing countless bon mots, pulling every string capable of scandalizing the public.

She says, "I don't see the reason for all the fuss."

She says, "People used to share wombs all the time."

She says, "It used to happen naturally, with multiple births: two or three or four or even seven of us, crowded together like grapes, sometimes absorbing each other's body parts like cute young cannibals."

She says, "I don't know whether to call what I'm doing pregnancy or performance art."

She says, "Don't you think Molly June looks special? Don't you think she glows?"

She says, "When the baby's born, I may call her Halo."

She says, "No, I don't see any problem with condemning her to Birth. If it's good enough for Molly June, it's good enough for my child."

And she says, "No, I don't care what anybody thinks. It's my arvie, after all."

And she fans the flames of outrage higher and higher, until public sympathies turn to the poor slumbering creature inside the sac of amniotic fluid, whose life and future have already been so cruelly decided. Is she truly limited enough to be condemned to Birth? Should she be stabilized and given her own chance at life, before she's expelled, sticky and foul, into the cold, harsh world inhabited only by arvies and machines? Or is Jennifer correct in maintaining the issue subject to a mother's whim?

Jennifer says, "All I know is that this is the most profound, most spiritually fulfilling, experience of my entire life." And so she faces the crowds, real or virtual, using Molly June's smile and Molly June's innocence, daring the analysts to count all the layers of irony.

GESTATION (II)

Molly June experiences the same few months in a fog of dazed, but happy confusion, aware that she's become the center of attention, but unable to comprehend exactly why. She knows that her lower back hurts and that her breasts have swelled and that her belly, flat and soft before, has inflated to several times its previous size; she knows that she sometimes feels something moving inside her, that she sometimes feels sick to her stomach, and that her eyes water more easily than they ever have before, but none of this disturbs the vast, becalmed surface of her being. It is all good, all the more reason for placid contentment.

Her only truly bad moments come in her dreams, when she sometimes finds herself standing on a gray, colorless field, facing another version of herself half her own size. The miniature Molly June stares at her from a distance that Molly June herself cannot cross, her eyes unblinking, her expression merciless. Tears glisten on both her cheeks. She points at Molly June and she enunciates a single word, incomprehensible in any language Molly June knows, and irrelevant to any life she's ever been allowed to live: "Mother."

The unfamiliar word makes Molly June feel warm and cold, all at once. In her dream she wets herself, trembling from the sudden warmth running down her thighs. She trembles, bowed by an incomprehensible need to apologize. When she wakes, she finds real tears still wet on her cheeks, and real pee soaking the mattress between her legs. It frightens her.

But those moments fade. Within seconds the calming agents are already flooding her bloodstream, overriding any internal storms, removing all possible sources of disquiet, making her once again the obedient arvie she's supposed to be. She smiles and coos as the servos tend to her bloated form, scrubbing her flesh and applying their emollients. Life is so good, she thinks. And if it's not, well, it's not like there's anything she can do about it, so why worry?

BIRTH (I)

Molly June goes into labor on a day corresponding to what we call Thursday, the insistent weight she has known for so long giving way to a series of contractions violent enough to reach her even through her cocoon of deliberately engineered apathy. She cries and moans and shrieks infuriated, inarticulate things that might have been curses had she ever been exposed to any, and she begs the shiny machines around her to take away the pain with the same efficiency that they've taken away everything else. She even begs her passenger—that is, the passenger she knows about, the one she's sensed seeing through her eyes and hearing through her ears and carrying out conversations with her mouth—she begs her passenger *for mercy*. She hasn't ever asked that mysterious godlike presence for anything, because it's never occurred to her that she might be entitled to anything, but she needs relief now, and she demands it, shrieks for it, can't understand why she isn't getting it.

The answer, which would be beyond her understanding even if provided, is that the wet, sordid physicality of the experience is the very point.

BIRTH (II)

Jennifer Axioma-Singh is fully plugged in to every cramp, every twitch, every pooled droplet of sweat. She experiences the beauty and the terror and the exhaustion and the certainty that this will never end. She finds it resonant and evocative and educational on levels lost to a mindless sack of meat like Molly June. And she comes to any number of profound revelations about the nature of life and death and the biological origins of the species and the odd, inexplicable attachment brood mares have always felt for the squalling sacks of flesh and bone their bodies have gone to so much trouble to expel.

CONCLUSIONS

It's like any other work, she thinks. Nobody ever spent months and months building a house only to burn it down the second they pounded in the last nail. You put that much effort into something and it belongs to you, forever, even if the end result is nothing but a tiny creature that eats and shits and makes demands on your time.

This still fails to explain why anybody would invite this kind of pain again, let alone the three or four or seven additional occasions common before the unborn reached their ascendancy. Oh, it's interesting enough to start with, but she gets the general idea long before the thirteenth hour rolls around and the market share for her real-time feed dwindles to the single digits. Long before that, the pain has given way to boredom. At the fifteenth hour she gives up entirely, turns off her inputs, and begins to catch up on her personal correspondence, missing the actual moment when Molly June's daughter, Jennifer's womb-mate and sister, is expelled head-first into a shiny silver tray, pink and bloody and screaming at the top of her lungs, sharing oxygen for the very first time, but, by every legal definition, Dead.

AFTERMATH (JENNIFER)

As per her expressed wishes, Jennifer Axioma-Singh is removed from Molly June and installed in a new arvie that very day. This one's a tall, lithe, gloriously beautiful creature with fiery eyes and thick, lush lips: her name's Bernadette Ann, she's been bred for endurance in extreme environments, and she'll soon be taking Jennifer Axioma-Singh on an extended solo hike across the restored continent of Antarctica.

Jennifer is so impatient to begin this journey that she never lays eyes on the child whose birth she has just experienced. There's no need. After all, she's never laid eyes on anything, not personally. And the pictures are available online, should she ever feel the need to see them. Not that she ever sees any reason for that to happen. The baby, itself, was never the issue here. Jennifer didn't want to be a mother. She just wanted to give birth. All that mattered to her, in the long run, was obtaining a few months of unique vicarious experience, precious in a lifetime likely to continue for as long as the servos still manufacture wombs and breed arvies. All that matters now is moving on. Because time marches onward, and there are never enough adventures to fill it.

AFTERMATH (MOLLY JUNE)

She's been used, and sullied, and rendered an unlikely candidate to attract additional passengers. She is therefore earmarked for compassionate disposal.

AFTERMATH (THE BABY)

The baby is, no pun intended, another issue. Her biological mother Jennifer Axioma-Singh has no interest in her, and her birth-mother Molly June is on her way to the furnace. A number of minor health problems, barely worth mentioning, render her unsuitable for a useful future as somebody's arvie. Born, and by that precise definition Dead, she could very well follow Molly June down the chute.

But she has a happier future ahead of her. It seems that her unusual gestation and birth have rendered her something of a collector's item, and there are any number of museums aching for a chance to add her to their permanent collections. Offers are weighed, and terms negotiated, until the ultimate agreement is signed, and she finds herself shipped to a freshly constructed habitat in a wildlife preserve in what used to be Ohio.

AFTERMATH (THE CHILD)

She spends her early life in an automated nursery with toys, teachers, and careful attention to her every physical need. At age five she's moved to a cage consisting of a two story house on four acres of nice green grass, beneath what looks like a blue sky dotted with fluffy white clouds. There's even a playground. She will never be allowed out, of course, because there's no place for her to go, but she does have human contact of a sort: a different arvie almost every day, inhabited for the occasion by a long line of Living who now think it might be fun to experience child-rearing for a while. Each one has a different face, each one calls her by a different name, and their treatment of her ranges all the way from compassionate to violently abusive.

Now eight, the little girl has long since given up on asking the good ones to stay, because she knows they won't. Nor does she continue to dream about what she'll do when she grows up, since it's also occurred to her that she'll never know anything but this life in this fishbowl. Her one consolation is wondering about her real mother: where she is now, what she looks like, whether she ever thinks about the child she left behind, and whether it would have been possible to hold on to her love, had it ever been offered, or even possible.

The questions remain the same, from day to day. But the answers are hers to imagine, and they change from minute to minute: as protean as her moods, or her dreams, or the reasons why she might have been condemned to this cruelest of all possible punishments.

ABOUT THE AUTHOR

Adam-Troy Castro's short fiction has been nominated for six Nebulas, two Hugos, and two Stokers. He won the Philip K. Dick Award for his novel *Emissaries from the Dead*. His next books will be a series of middle school novels from Grossett and Dunlap in 2012, starting with *Gustav Gloom and the People Taker*. He lives in Miami with his wife, Judi, and his insane cats, Uma Furman and Meow Farrow.

AUTHOR'S INTRODUCTION

The total of my published work is now something like ninety products; and at age seventy-seven there are still three of four books in the pipeline. I've led the Good Life. I've achieved small celebrity, and I've been with Susan for twenty-five years. I am a SFWA Grand Master and was one of the founders of the organization; I was its first vice president. And in the past five months I've had many honors, receiving the Eaton Award, which has only been given out four times. It is a very, very prestigious SF academic award. I find it bewildering . . . they called my work "deeply intellectual." And I've been listed in *Encyclopedia Britannica*. I really have led the Good Life. I've written more than seventeen hundred stories and essays, edited anthologies, and won awards, including Hugos, Nebulas, and Edgars.

In "How Interesting: A Tiny Man," which appeared in *Realms of Fantasy*, I view the narrator of the piece as an innocent, as innocent as the man who invented the atomic bomb. It is a story of betrayal by a semiconscious society. It has two endings, and you can take whichever pleases you . . . or neither.

NEBULA AWARD, SHORT STORY (TIE)

HOW INTERESTING: A TINY MAN

Harlan Ellison™

I created a tiny man. It was very hard work. It took me a long time. But I did it, finally: he was five inches tall. Tiny; he was very tiny. And creating him, the creating of him, it seemed an awfully good idea at the time.

I can't remember why I wanted to do it, not at the very beginning, when

I first got the idea to create this extremely tiny man. I know I *had* a most excellent reason, or at least an excellent *conception*, but I'll be darned if I can now, at this moment, remember what it was. Now, of course, it is much later than that moment of conception.

But it was, as I recall, a very *good* reason. At the time.

When I showed him to everyone else in the lab at Eleanor Roosevelt Tech, they thought it was interesting. "How interesting," some of them said. I thought that was a proper way of looking at it, the way of looking at a tiny man who didn't really *do* anything except stand around looking up in wonder and amusement at all the tall things above and around him.

He was no trouble. Getting clothes tailored for him was not a problem. I went to the couture class. I had made the acquaintance of a young woman, a very nice young woman, named Jennifer Cuffee, we had gone out a few times, nothing very much came of it—I don't think we were suited to each other—but we were casual friends. And I asked her if she would make a few different outfits for the tiny man.

"Well, he's too tall to fit into ready-mades, say, the wardrobe of Barbie's boy friend, Ken. And action figure clothing would just be too twee. But I think I can whip you up an ensemble or two. It won't be 'bespoke,' but he'll look nice enough. What sort of thing did you have in mind?"

"I think suits," I said. "He probably won't be doing much traveling, or sports activities . . . yes, why don't we stick to just a couple of suits. Nice shirts, perhaps a tie or two."

And that worked out splendidly. He always looked well-turned-out, fastidious, perky but quite serious in appearance. Not stuffy, like an attorney all puffed up with himself, but with an unassuming gravitas. In fact, my attorney, Charles, said of him, "There is a quotidian elegance about him." Usually, he merely stood around, one hand in his pants pocket, his jacket buttoned, his tie snugly abutting the top of his collar, staring with pleasure at everything around him. Sometimes, when I would carry him out to see more of the world, he would lean forward peering over the top seam of *my* suit jacket pocket, arms folded atop the edge to prevent his slipping sidewise, and he would hum in an odd tenor.

He never had a name. I cannot really summon a reason for that. Names seemed a bit too cute for someone that singular and, well, suppose I had called him say, Charles, like my attorney. Eventually someone would have called him "Charlie" or even "Chuck," and nicknames are what come to be imploded from names. Nicknames for him would have been insipidly unthinkable. Don't you think?

He spoke, of course. He was a fully formed tiny man. It took him a few hours after I created him for his speech to become fluent and accomplished. We did it by prolonged exposure (more than two hours) to thesauri, encyclopedia, dictionaries, word histories, and other such references. I pronounced right along with him, when he had a problem. We used books only, nothing on a screen. I don't think he much cared for all of the electronic substitutes. He remarked once that his favorite phrase was *vade mecum*, and so I tried not to let him be exposed to computers or televisions or any of the hand-held repugnancies. His word, not mine.

He had an excellent memory, particularly for languages. For instance, *vade mecum*, which is a well-known Latin phrase for a handy little reference book one can use on a moment's notice. It means, literally, "go with me." Well, he heard and read it and then used it absolutely correctly. So when he said "repugnancies," he meant nothing milder. (I confess, from time to time, when my mind froze up trying to recall a certain word that had slipped behind the gauze of forgetting, I could tilt my head a trifle, and my pocket-sized little man became *my* "vade mecum." Function follows form.)

Everywhere we went, the overwhelming impact was, "How interesting, a tiny man." Well, *ignorantia legis neminem excusat.* I should have understood human nature better. I should have known every such beautiful arcade must have a boiler room in which rats and worms and grubs and darkness rule.

I was asked to come, with the tiny man that I had created, to a sort of Sunday morning intellectual conversational television show. I was reluctant, because he had no affinity for the medium; but I was assured the cameras would be swathed in black cloth and the monitors turned away from him. So, in essence, it was merely another get-together of interesting spirits trying to fathom the ethical structure of the universe. The tiny man had a relishment for such potlatches.

It was a pleasant outing.

Nothing untoward.

We were thanked all around, and we went away, and no one—certainly not I—thought another thing about it.

It took less than twelve hours.

When it comes to human nature, I should have known better. But I didn't and *ignorantia legis neminem excusat* if there are truly any "laws" to human nature. Rats, worms, grubs, and an inexplicable darkness of the soul. A great philosopher named Isabella, last name not first, once pointed out, "Hell hath no fury like that of the uninvolved." In less than twelve hours I learned the spike-in-the-heart relevance of that aphorism: to me, and to him.

A woman I didn't know started it. I didn't understand why she would do such a thing. It didn't have anything to do with her. Perhaps she was as meanspirited as everyone but her slavish audience said. Her name was Franco. Something Franco. She was very thin, as if she couldn't keep down solids. And her hair was a bright yellow. She was not a bad-looking woman as facial standards go, but there was something feral in the lines of her mien, and her smile was the smile of the ferret, her eyes clinkingly cold.

She called him a monstrosity. Other words, some of which I had never heard before: abnormity, perversion of nature, a vile derision of what God had created first, a hideous crime of unnatural science. She said, I was told, "This thing would make Jesus himself vomit!"

Then there were commentators. And news anchors. And hand-held cameras and tripods and long-distance lenses. There were men with uncombed hair and stubble on their faces who found ways to confront us that were heroic. There were awful newspapers one can apparently buy alongside decks of playing cards and various kinds of chewing gum at the check-out in the Rite Aid where I bought him his eyewash.

There was much talk of God and "natural this" and "unnatural that," most of which seemed very silly to me. But this Franco woman would not stop. She appeared everywhere and said it was clearly an attempt by Godless atheists and some people she called the cultural elite and "limousine liberals" to pervert God's Will and God's Way. I was deemed "Dr. Frankenstein" and men with unruly hair and shadowy cheeks found their way into the lab at Eleanor Roosevelt Tech, seeking busbars and galvanic coils and Van de Graaff generators. But, of course, there were no such things in the lab. Not even the crèche in which I'd created the tiny man.

It grew worse and worse.

In the halls, no one would speak to me. I had to carry him in my inside pocket, out of fear. Even Jennifer Cuffee was frightened and became opposed to me and to him. She demanded I return his clothing. I did so, of a certainty, but I thought it was, as the tiny man put it, "Rather craven for someone who used to be so nice."

There were threats. A great many threats. Some of them curiously misspelled—its, rather than it's—and suchlike. Once, someone threw a cracked glass door off an old phone booth through my window. The tiny man hid, but didn't seem too frightened by this sudden upheaval of a once-kindly world. People who had nothing to do with me or my work or the tiny man, people who were not hurt or affected in any way, became vocal and menacing and so fervid one could see the steam rising off them. If there had been a resemblance between my tiny man and the race of men, all such similarity was gone. He seemed virtually, well, godlike in comparison.

And then I was told we had to go.

"Where?" I said to them.

"We don't care," they answered, and they had narrow mouths.

I resisted. I had created this tiny man, and I was there to protect him. There is such a thing as individual responsibility. It is the nature of grandeur in us. To deny it is to become a beast of the fields. No way. Not I.

And so, with my tiny man—who now mostly wore Kleenex—but who was making excellent progress with Urdu and Quechua, and needlework—we took to the hills.

As students at Eleanor Roosevelt put it, we "got in the wind."

I know how to drive, and I have a car. Though there are those who call me geezer and ask if I use two Dixie Cups and a waxed string to call my friends, if my affection for Ginastera and Stravinsky gets in the way of my appreciation of Black Sabbath and Kanye West, I am a man of today. And as with individual responsibility for myself, and my deeds, I take the world on sum identically. I choose and reject. That, I really and truly believe, is the way a responsible individual acts.

And so, I have a car, I use raw sugar instead of aspartame, my pants do not sag around my shoetops, and I drive a perfectly utilitarian car. The make and year do not matter for this disquisition. The fate of the tiny man does.

We fled, "got in the wind."

But, as Isabella has said, "Hell hath no fury like that of the uninvolved," and everywhere we went, at some small moment, my face would be recognized by a bagger in a WalMart, or a counter-serf in a Taco Bell, and the next thing I would know, there would be (at minimum) a jackal-faced blonde girl with a hand-microphone, or some young man with unruly shark hair and the look of someone who didn't stand close enough to his razor that morning, or even a police officer. I had done nothing, my good friend the tiny man had done nothing, but what they all said to us, in one way or another, was something I think Alan Ladd said to Lee Van Cleef: "Don't let the sun go down on you in this town, boy."

We tried West Virginia. It was an unpleasant place.

Oklahoma. The world there was dry, but the people were wet with sweat at our presence.

Even towns that were dying, Detroit, Cleveland, Las Vegas, none of them would have us, not even for a moment.

And then, all because of this terrible blonde woman Franco, who had nothing better to do with her time or her anger, a warrant was sworn out for us. A Federal warrant. We tried to hide, but both of us had to eat. And neither of us, as clever as he had become, as agile as I had become, were adepts at "being on the dodge." And in a Super 8 motel in Aberdeen, South Dakota, the Feds cornered us.

The tiny man stood complacently on the desk blotter, and we looked honestly at each other. He knew, as I knew. I felt a little like God himself. I had created this tiny man, who had harmed no one, who at prime point should have elicited no more serious a view than, "How interesting: a tiny man."

But I had been ignorant of the laws of human nature, and we both knew it was all my responsibility. The beginning, the term of the adventure, and now, the ending.

THE FIRST ENDING

I held the Aberdeen, South Dakota telephone book in my hands, raised it above my head and, in the moment before I brought it smashing down as ferociously as I could, the tiny man looked up at me, wistful, resolved, and said, "Mother."

THE SECOND ENDING

I stood staring down at him, and could barely see through my tears. He looked up at me with compassion and understanding and said, "Yes, it would always have had to come to this," and then, being god, he destroyed the world, leaving only the two of us, and now, because he is a compassionate deity, he will destroy me, an even tinier man.

ABOUT THE AUTHOR

Apart from his 2006 SFWA Grand Master Award, this is Harlan Ellison's fourth Nebula. His "'Repent, Harlequin!' Said the Ticktockman" won the very first short story Nebula in 1965, and with this year's award in that category for "How Interesting: A Tiny Man," it makes Mr. Ellison the only person ever to win in that category three times.

AUTHOR'S INTRODUCTION

"The Jaguar House, in Shadow" is my second attempt to take the Aztec culture into the twentieth century: my earlier attempt had left me dissatisfied, so I started over with this story. Part of the challenge (and of what had frustrated me with the earlier attempt) is making sure that "modern" doesn't end up equating "twentieth-century Western culture"; and equally making sure that the Aztec culture doesn't turn out to be an ossified version of what the conquistadores saw (which would be as realistic as, say, modern-day England still following the mores and social customs of Shakespeare's time).

One fast way to do this—and the point to address first and foremost—was to deal with Aztec religion, which had been bound up with war and the waging of battles. As I took the society forward in time, I imagined war would have given way to espionage (the same way it did in our twentieth century); and more particularly to industrial espionage. The Jaguar Knights therefore shifted from the elite troops of the fifteenth century to the spies and agents provocateurs of the twentieth century: the eponymous Jaguar House is a mixture between a monastery, a military bootcamp, and the MI6, and I had a lot of fun making up its customs.

Over this, I superimposed the story itself—which is about friendship and loyalty and honor, and how far to take those. I hadn't originally intended this to be about a band of sisters, but given that it's all too often the reverse that holds true in speculative fiction, I'm pretty pleased it turned out that way—with three female main characters and the men unobtrusively relegated to the background. I'm glad the story ends up making a statement about the place and power of women, even if it's a very subtle one.

THE JAGUAR HOUSE, IN SHADOW

Aliette de Bodard

The mind wanders, when one takes teonanácatl.

If she allowed herself to think, she'd smell bleach, mingling with the faint, rank smell of blood; she'd see the grooves of the cell, smeared with what might be blood or faeces.

She'd remember—the pain insinuating itself into the marrow of her bones, until it, too, becomes a dull thing, a matter of habit—she'd remember dragging herself upwards when dawn filters through the slit-windows: too tired and wan to offer her blood to Tonatiuh the sun, whispering a prayer that ends up sounding more and more like an apology.

The god, of course, will insist that she live until the end, for life and blood are too precious to be wasted—no matter how broken or useless she's become, wasting away in the darkness.

Here's the thing: she's not sure how long she can last.

It was Jaguar Captain Palli who gave her the teonanácatl—opening his hand to reveal the two black, crushed mushrooms, the food of the gods, the drugs of the lost, of the doomed—she couldn't tell if it was because he pitied her, or if it's yet another trap, another ambush they hope she'll fall into.

But still . . . She took them. She held them, wrapped tight in the palm of her hands, as the guards walked her back. And when she was alone once more, she stared at them for a long while, feeling the tremor start in her fingers—the hunger, the craving for normality—for oblivion.

The mind wanders—backwards, into the only time worth remembering.

The picture lay on the table, beside Onalli's bloodied worship-thorns. It showed a girl standing by a stall in the marketplace, holding out a clock of emerald-green quetzal feathers with an uncertain air, as if it would leap and bite at any moment. Two other girls stood silhouetted in the shadows behind her, as if already fading into insignificance.

It wasn't the best one Onalli had of Xochitl, by a large margin—but she'd been thinking about it a lot, those days—about the fundamental irony of it, like a god's ultimate joke on her.

"Having second thoughts?" Atcoatl asked, behind her.

Onalli's hand reached out, to turn the picture over—and stopped when his tone finally sank in.

She turned to look at him: his broad, tanned face was impassive—a true Knight's, showing none of what he felt.

"No," she said, slowly, carefully. "I'm not having second thoughts. But you are, aren't you?"

Atcoatl grimaced. "Onalli—"

He was the one who'd helped her, from the start—getting her the encrypted radio sets, the illicit nanos to lower her body temperatures, the small syringes containing everything from *teonanácatl* inhibitors to endurance nanos. More than that: he had believed her—that her desperate gamble would work, that they'd retrieve Xochitl alive, out of the madness the Jaguar House had become . . .

"This is too big," Atcoatl said. He shook his head, and Onalli heard the rest, the words he wasn't saying.

What if we get caught?

Onalli chose the easiest way to dispel fear: anger. "So you intend to sit by and do nothing?"

Atcoatl's eyes flashed with a burning hatred—and no wonder. He had seen the fall of his own House; his fellow Eagle Knights, bound and abandoned in the burning wreckage of their own dormitories; the Otter and the Skulls Knights, killed, maimed, or scattered to breathe dust in the silver mines. "I'm no coward. One day, the Revered Speaker and his ilk will pay for what they've done. But this—this is just courting death."

Onalli's gaze strayed again to the picture—to Xochitl's face, frozen in that moment of dubious innocence. "I can't leave her there."

"The resistance—" Atcoatl started.

Onalli snorted. "By the time the resistance can pull the House down, it will be too late. You know it." There had been attacks: two maglev stations bombed; political dissidents mysteriously vanishing before their arrest. She didn't deny the existence of an underground movement, but she recognised the signs: it was still weak, still trying to organise itself.

Atcoatl said nothing; but Onalli was Jaguar Knight, and her training enabled her to read the hint of disapproval in his stance.

"Look," she said, finally. "I'm the one taking the biggest risk. You'll be outside the House, with plenty of time to leave if anything goes wrong."

"If you're caught—"

"You think I'd turn on you?" Onalli asked. "After all they've done to Xochitl, you think I'd help them?"

Atcoatl's face was dark. "You know what they're doing, inside the House."

She didn't—but she could imagine it, all too well. Which was why she needed to pull Xochitl out. Her friend hadn't deserved this; any of this. "I'm Jaguar Knight," she said, softly. "And I give you my word that I'd rather end my own life than let them worm anything out of me."

Atcoatl looked at her. "You're sincere, but what you believe doesn't change anything."

"Doesn't it? I believe the Revered Speaker's rule is unlawful. I believe the Jaguar House had no right to betray its own dissidents, or interrogate them. Isn't that what we all believe in?"

Atcoatl shifted, and wouldn't answer.

"Tell me what you believe in, then," Onalli said.

He was silent for a while. "Black One take you," he said, savagely. "Just this once, Onalli. Just this once."

Onalli nodded. "Promise." Afterwards, they'd go north—into the United States or Xuya, into countries where freedom was more than a word on paper. They'd be safe.

She finished tying her hair in a neat bun—a habit she'd taken on her missions abroad—and slid her worship thorns into her belt, smearing the blood over her skinsuit. A prayer, for whoever among the gods might be listening tonight; for Fate, the Black One, the god of the Smoking Mirror, who could always be swayed or turned away, if you had the heart and guts to seize your chance when it came.

Atcoatl waited for her at the door, holding it open with ill-grace.

"Let's go," Onalli said.

She left the picture on the table—knowing, all the while, why she'd done so: not because it would burden her, but because of one simple thing. Fear.

Fear that she'd find Xochitl and stare into her face, and see the broken mind behind the eyes—nothing like the shy, courageous girl she remembered.

Outside, the air was clear and cold, and a hundred stars shone upon the city of Tenochtitlan: a hundred demons, waiting in the darkness to descend and rend all life from limb to limb. Onalli rubbed her worship thorns, trying to remember the assurance she'd always felt on her missions—why couldn't she remember anything, now that she was home—now that she was breaking into her own House?

Six months ago

The priest of the Black One sits cross-legged across the mat—facing Xochitl and pursing his lips as if contemplating a particular problem. His hair is greasy and tangled, mattered with the blood of his devotions; and the smell that emanates from him is the rank one of charnel houses—with the slight tang of bleach. He's attempted to wash his hands before coming, and hasn't succeeded.

Amusing, how the mind sharpens, when everything else is restrained.

Xochitl would laugh, but she's never been much of one for laughter: that was Onalli, or perhaps Tecipiani.

No, she musn't think of Tecipiani, not now—must remain calm and composed, her only chance at surviving this.

Mustn't ask herself the question "for what?"

"I'm told," the priest says, "that you started a ring of dissidents within this House."

Xochitl remains seated against the wall, very straight. The straps cut into her arms and ankles, and the tightest one holds her at the neck. She'll only exhaust herself trying to break them: she's tried a dozen times already, with only bruises to show for it.

The priest goes on, as if she had answered, "I'm told you worked to undermine the loyalty of the Jaguar Knights, with the aim to topple the Revered Speaker."

Xochitl shakes her head, grimly amused. Toppling him—as if that would work . . . The burgeoning resistance movement is small and insignificant; and they have no reach within the House, not even to Xochitl's pathetic, shattered splinter group.

But there's right and wrong, and when Xolotl comes to take her soul, she'll face Him with a whole face and heart, knowing which side she chose.

The priest goes on, smug, self-satisfied, "You must have known it was doomed. This House is loyal; your commander is loyal. She has given you up, rather than suffer your betrayal."

Tecipiani—no, mustn't think of that, mustn't—it's no surprise, has never been, not after everything Tecipiani has done . . .

"Of course she has given me up," Xochitl says, keeping her voice steady. "Jaguar Knights aren't interrogators. We leave that to you."

The priest shifts, unhurriedly—and, without warning, cuffs her, his obsidian rings cutting deep into her skin. She tastes blood, an acrid tingle in her mouth—raises her head again, daring him to strike again.

He does—again and again, each blow sending her head reeling back, a white flash of pain resonating in the bones of her cheek, the warmth of blood running down her face.

When he stops at last, Xochitl hangs limp, staring at the floor through a growing haze—the strap digging into her windpipe, an unpleasant reminder of how close asphyxiation is.

"Let's start again, shall we?" His voice is calm, composed. "You'll show me proper respect, as is owed an agent of the Revered Speaker."

He's—not that—he's nothing, a man of no religion, who dares use pain as a weapon, tainting it for mundane things like interrogation. But pain isn't that, was never that. Xochitl struggles to remember the proper words; to lay them at the feet of the Black One, her song of devotion in this godless place.

"I fall before you, I throw myself before you

Offer up the precious water of my blood, offer up my pain like fire

I cast myself into the place from where none rise, from where none leave,

O lord of the near and nigh, O master of the Smoking Mirror,

O night, O wind . . ."

She must have spoken the words aloud, because he cuffs her again—a quick, violent blow she only feels when her head knocks against the wall—ringing in her mind, the whole world contracting and expanding, the colours too light and brash—

And again, and again, and everything slowly merges, folding inwards like crinkling paper—pain spreading along her muscles like fire.

"With icy water I make my penance

With nettles and thorns I bare out my face, my heart

Through the land of the anguished, the land of the dying . . ."

She thinks, but she's not sure, that he's gone, when the door opens again, and footsteps echo under the ceiling—slow and measured, deliberate.

She'd raise her head, but she can't muster the energy. Even focusing on the ground is almost too tiring, when all she wants is to lean back, to close her eyes and dream of a world where Tonatiuh the sun bathes her in His light, where the smell of cooking oil and chilies wafts from the stalls of food-vendors, where feather-cloaks are soft and silky against her hands . . .

The feet stop: leather mocassins, and emerald-green feathers, and the tantalising smell of pine-cones and copal incense.

Tecipiani. No, not the girl she knew anymore, but Commander Tecipiani, the one who sold them all to the priests—who threw Xochitl herself to the star-demons, to be torn apart and made as nothing.

"Come to gloat?" Xochitl asks; or tries to, because it won't come out as more than a whisper. She can't even tell if Tecipiani hears her, because the world is pressing against her, a throbbing pain in her forehead that spreads to her field of vision—until everything dissolves into feverish darkness.

Onalli took the ball-court at a run, descending from the stands into the I-shape of the ground. On either side of her loomed the walls, with the vertical stone-hoops teams would fight to send a ball through—but it was the season of the Lifting of the Banners, and the teams were enjoying a well-earned rest.

It did mean, though, that only one imperial warrior guarded the cordoned-off entrance: it had been child's play to take him down.

One thing people frequently forgot about the ball-court was that it was built with its back against the Jaguar House, and that the dignitaries' boxes at the far end shared a wall with the House's furthest courtyard.

That courtyard would be guarded, but it was nothing insurmountable. She'd left Atcoatl at the entrance, disguised as an imperial warrior: from afar, he'd present a sufficient illusion to discourage investigation; and he'd warn her by radio if anything went wrong outside.

The boxes were deserted; Onalli made her way in the darkness to that of the Revered Speaker, decorated with old-fashioned carvings depicting the feats of gods: the Feathered Serpent coming back from the underworld with the bones of mankind, the Black One bringing down the Second Sun in a welter of flames and wind.

The tribune was the highest one in the court; but still lacking a good measure or so to get her over the wall—after all, if there was the remotest possibility that anyone could leap through there, they'd have guarded it to the teeth.

Onalli stood for a while, breathing quietly. She rubbed her torn ears, feeling a trickle of blood seep into her skin. For the Black One, should He decide to watch over her. For Tonatiuh the Sun, who would tumble from the sky without His nourishment.

For Xochitl, who'd deserved better than what the fate Tecipiani had dealt her.

She extended, in one fluid, thoughtless gesture: her nails were diamond-sharp, courtesy of Atcoatl's nanos, and it was easy to find purchases on the carvings—not thinking of the sacrilege, of what the Black One might think about fingers clawing their way through His effigies, no time for that anymore . . .

Onalli hoisted herself up on the roof of the box, breathing hard. The wall in front of her was much smoother, but still offered some purchase as long as she was careful. It was, really, no worse than the last ascension she'd done, clinging to the outside of the largest building in Jiajin Tech's compound, on her way to steal blueprints from a safe. It was no worse than endless hours of training, when her tutors had berated her about carelessness . . .

But her tutors were dead, or gone to ground—and it was the House on the other side of that wall, the only home she'd ever known—the place that had raised her from childhood, the place where she could be safe, and not play a game of endless pretence—where she could start a joke and have a dozen person voicing the punch-line, where they sang the hymns on the winter solstice, letting their blood pool into the same vessel.

Her hands, slick with sweat, slid out of a crack. For one impossibly long moment she felt herself fall into the darkness—caught herself with a gasp, even as chunks of rock fell downwards in a clatter of noise.

Had anyone heard that? The other side of the wall seemed silent—

There was only darkness, enclosing her like the embrace of Grandmother Earth. Onalli gritted her teeth, and pushed upwards, groping for further handholds.

Two years ago

Commander Tecipiani's investiture speech is subdued, and uncharacteristically bleak. Her predecessor, Commander Malinalli, had delivered grandiloquent boasts about the House and its place in the world, as if everything was due to them, in this Age and the next.

But Tecipiani says none of that. Instead, she speaks of dark times ahead, and the need to be strong, and the need to endure.

She doesn't say the words "civil war," but everyone can hear them, all the same.

Xochitl and Onalli stand near the back. Because Onalli arrived late and Xochitl waited for her, the only place they could find was near the novices: callow boys and girls, uneasily settling into their cotton uniforms and fur cloaks, still too young to feel their childhood locks as burdens—still so young and innocent it almost hurts, to think of them in the times ahead.

After the ceremony, everyone drifts back to their companies, or to the mess-halls. The mistress of the novices has organised a mock battle in the courtyard, and Onalli is watching with the same rapt fascination she might have for a formal ball-game.

Xochitl is watching Tecipiani: the Commander has finished shaking hands with her company leaders, and, dismissing her bodyguards, is heading straight towards them. Her gaze catches Xochitl's—holds it for a while, almost pleading.

"Onalli," Xochitl says, urgently.

Onalli barely looks up. "I know. It had to happen at some point, anyway."

Tecipiani catches up with them, greets them both with a curt nod. She's still wearing the full regalia of the Commander: a cloak of jaguar-fur, and breeches of emerald-green quetzal feathers. Her helmet is in the shape of a jaguar's head, and her face pokes out from between the jaws of the animal, as if she were being consumed alive.

"Walk with me, will you?" she asks. Except that she's not asking, not anymore, because she speaks with the voice of the Black One, and even her slightest suggestion is a command.

They don't speak, for a while—walking through courtyards where Knights haggle over *patolli* gameboards, where novices dare each other to leap over the fountains: the familiar, comforting hubbub of life within the House.

"I wasn't expecting you so soon, Onalli—though I'm glad to see you have returned," Tecipiani says. Her words are warm; her voice isn't. "I trust everything went well?"

Onalli spreads her hands in a gesture of uncertainty. "I have the documents," she says. "Williamsburg Tech were making a new prototype of computer, with more complexity. A step away from consciousness, perhaps."

Xochitl wonders what kind of intelligence computers will develop, when they finally breach the gap between automated tasks and genuine sentience— all that research done in military units north of the border, eyeing the enemy to the south.

They'll be like us, she thinks. They'll reach for their equivalent of clubs or knives, claiming it's just to protect themselves; and it won't be long until they sink it into somebody's chest.

Just like us.

"The Americans have advanced their technology, then," Tecipiani says, gravely. It's the House's job, after all: watching science in the other countries of the Fifth World, and making sure that none of them ever equals Greater Mexica's lead in electronics—using whatever it takes, theft, bribery, assassination.

Onalli shakes her head impatiently. "This isn't something we should worry about."

"Perhaps more than you think." Tecipiani's voice is slightly annoyed. "The war won't always last, and we must look ahead to the future."

Onalli says, "The war, yes. You made an interesting speech."

Tecipiani's smile doesn't stretch all the way to her eyes. "Appropriate, I felt. Sometimes, we have to be reminded of what happens out there."

Onalli says, "I've seen what's out there. It's getting ugly."

"Ugly?" Xochitl asks.

Onalli's eyes drift away. "I saw him at court, Xochitl. Revered Speaker Ixtli. He's—" her hands clench "—a maddened dog. It's in his eyes, and in his bearing. It won't be long before the power goes to his head. It's already started. The war—"

Tecipiani shakes her head. "Don't you dare make such a statement." Her voice is curt, as cutting as an obsidian blade. "We are Jaguar Knights. We serve the Mexica Empire and its Revered Speaker. We're nothing more than that. Never."

"But—" Xochitl starts.

"We're nothing more than that," Tecipiani says, again.

No, that's not true. They're Jaguar Knights; they've learnt to judge people on a word or a gesture—because, when you're out on a mission, it marks the line between life and death. They know . . .

"You're mad," Onalli says. "Back when Commander Malinalli was still alive, all the Houses, all the Knights spoke against Ixtli—including ours. What do you think the Revered Speaker will do to us, once he's asserted his power?"

"I'm your Commander," Tecipiani says, her voice slightly rising. "That, too, is something you must remember, Jaguar Lieutenant. I speak for the House."

"I'll remember." Onalli's voice is low and dangerous. And Xochitl knows that here, now, they've reached the real parting of the ways—not when Tecipiani was appointed company leader or commander, not when she was the one who started assigning missions to her old friends—but this, here, now, this ultimate profession of cowardice.

"Good," Tecipiani says. She seems oblivious to the undercurrents, the gazes passing between Onalli and Xochitl. But, then, she's never been good with details. "You'll come to my office later, Onalli. I'll have another mission for you."

And that, too, is cowardice: what she cannot control, Tecipiani will get rid of. Xochitl looks at Onalli—and back at her Commander, who still hasn't moved—and she feels the first stirrings of defiance flutter in her belly.

Onalli dropped the last few hand-spans into the courtyard, and immediately flattened herself against the wall—a bad reflex. There was a security camera not a few handspans from her, but all it would see in the darkness was another blur: her skin-suit was made of non-reflective materials, which wouldn't show up on infrared, and she'd taken nanos to lower her skin temperature. There'd be fire and blood to pay later, but she didn't really care anymore.

Everything was silent, too much so. Where were the guards and the security—where was Tecipiani's iron handhold on the House? She'd felt the fear from outside—the wide, empty space in front of the entrance; the haunted eyes of the Jaguar Captain she'd pumped for information on the maglev; all the horror stories she'd heard on her way into Tenochtitlan.

And yet . . .

The back of her scalp prickled. A trap. They'd known she was coming. They were expecting her.

But she'd gone too far to give up; and the wall was a bitch to climb, anyway.

She drew the first of her throwing knives, and, warily, progressed deeper into the House. Still nothing—the hungry silence of the stars—the warm breath of Grandmother Earth underfoot—the numinous presence of Xolotl, god of Death, walking in her footsteps . . .

A shadow moved across the entrance to the courtyard, under the vague shapes of the pillars. Onalli's hand tightened around the haft of the knife. Staying motionless would be her demise. She had to move fast, to silence them before they could raise the alarm.

She uncoiled—leapt, with the speed of a rattlesnake, straight towards the waiting shadow. Her knife was meant to catch the shadow in the chest, but it parried with surprising speed. All she could see of the shadow was a smear in the darkness, a larger silhouette that seemed to move in time with her. The shadow wasn't screaming; all its energy was focused into the fight, pure, incandescent, the dance that gave the gods their due, that kept Tonatiuh the sun in the sky and Grandmother Earth sated, the one they'd both trained for, all their lives.

There was something wrong, very wrong with the way the shadow moved . . . She parried a slash at her legs, and pressed it again, trying to disarm him.

In the starlight, she barely saw the sweeping arc of its knife, moving diagonally across her weak side—she raised her own blade to parry, caught the knife and sent it clattering to the ground, and moved in for the kill.

Too late, she saw the second blade. She threw herself backwards, but not before it had drawn a fiery slash across her skin-suit.

They stood, facing one another, in silence.

"You—you move like us." the shadow said. The voice was high-pitched, shaking, and suddenly she realised what had been wrong with its moves: the eagerness, the abandon of the unblooded novices.

"You're a boy," she breathed. "A child."

Black One, no.

"I'm no child." He shifted, in the starlight, letting her catch a glimpse of his gangly awkwardness. "Don't make that mistake."

"I apologise." Onalli put all the contriteness she can in her voice; she softened the muscles of her back to hunch over in a submissive position: he might not be able to see her very well, but he'd still see enough to get the subconscious primers.

The boy didn't move. Finally he said, as if this were an everyday conversation. "If I called, they would be here in a heartbeat."

"You haven't called." Onalli kept her voice steady, trying to encourage him not to remedy this oversight.

In the starlight, she saw him shake his head. "I'd be dead before they came."

"No," Onalli said, the word torn out of her before she could plan for it. "I'm not here to kill you."

"I believe you." A pause, then, "You've come for the House. To avenge your own."

Her own? And then she understood. He thought her a Knight; but not of the Jaguar. An Eagle, perhaps, or an Otter: any of the former elite of Greater Mexica, the ones Revered Speaker Ixtli had obliterated from the Fifth World.

She'd forgotten that this was no mere boy, but a novice of her order, who would one day become a Knight, like her, like Tecipiani, like Xochitl. He'd heard and seen enough to know that she hated the House's heart and guts; but he hadn't yet connected it with who she was.

"I'm just here for a friend," Onalli said. "She—she needs help."

"Help." His voice was steadier, almost thoughtful. "The kind of help that requires infiltration, and a knife."

She had more than knives: all the paraphernalia of Knights on a mission, stun-guns, syringes filled with endurance and pain nanos. But she hadn't got them out. She wasn't sure why. Tecipiani had turned the House into something dark that needed to be put down, and she'd do whatever it took. And yet . . .

It was still her House. "She's in the cells," Onalli said.

"In trouble," the boy repeated, flatly. "I'm sure they wouldn't arrest her without good reason."

Black One take him, he was so innocent, so trusting in the rightness of whatever the House did; like her or Xochitl, ages before their eyes opened. She wanted to shake him. "I have no time to argue with you. Will you let me pass?"

The boy said nothing for a while. She could feel him wavering in the starlight—and, because she was Jaguar Knight, she also knew that it wouldn't be enough, that he'd call for the guards, rather than entrusting himself to some vague stranger who had tried to kill him.

No choice, then.

She moved before he could react—shifting her whole weight towards him and bearing him to the ground, even as her hand moved to cover his mouth. As they landed, there was a crunch like bones breaking—for a moment, she thought she'd killed him, but he was still looking at her in disbelief, trying to bite her—with her other hand, she reached into her skinsuit, and withdrew a syringe.

He gasped when she injected him, his eyes rolling up, the cornea an eerie white in the starlight. Now that her eyes were accustomed to the darkness, she could see him clearly: his skin smooth and dark, his hands clenching, then relaxing as the *teonanácatl* inhibitor took hold.

She could only hope that she'd got the doses right: he was wirier than most adults, and his metabolism was still that of a child.

As she left the courtyard, he was twitching, in the grip of the hallucinations that came as a side-effect. With luck, he'd wake up with a headache, and a vague memory of everything not being quite right—but not remember the vivid nightmares the drug gave. She thought of beseeching the gods for small or large mercies; but the only two in her wake were the Black One and Xolotl, the Taker of the Dead.

"I'm sorry," she whispered, knowing he couldn't hear her; knowing he would hate and fear her for the rest of his days. "But I can't trust the justice of this House—I just can't."

Nine years ago

Xochitl stands by the stall, dubiously holding the cloak of quetzal-feathers against her chest. "It's a little too much, don't you think?"

"No way," Onalli says.

"If your idea of clothing is tawdry, sure," Tecipiani says, with an amused shake of her head. "This is stuff for almond-eyed tourists."

And, indeed, there's more Asians at the stall than trueblood Mexica—though Onalli, who's half and half, could almost pass for Asian herself. "Aw, come on," Onalli says. "It's perfect. Think of all the boys queuing for a kiss. You'd have to start selling tickets."

Xochitl makes a mock stab at Onalli, as if withdrawing a knife from under her tunic. But her friend is too quick, and steps aside, leaving her pushing at empty air.

"What's the matter? Eagles ate your muscles?" Onalli says—always belabouring the obvious.

Xochitl looks again at the cloak—bright and garish, but not quite in the right way. "No," she says, finally. "But Tecipiani's right. It's not worth the money." Not even for a glance from Palli—who's much too mature, any way, to get caught by such base tricks.

Tecipiani, who seldom brags about her triumphs, simply nods. "There's another stall further down," she says. "Maybe there'll be something—"

There's a scream, on the edge of the market: not that of someone being robbed, but that of a madman.

What in the Fifth World—

Xochitl puts back the cloak, and shifts, feeling the reassuring heaviness of the obsidian blades at her waist. Onalli has already withdrawn hers; but Tecipiani has moved before them all, striding towards the source. Her hands are empty.

Ahead, at the entrance to the marketplace, is a grounded aircar, its door gaping empty. The rest of the procession that was following it is slowly coming to a stop—though with difficulty, as there is little place among the closely-crammed stalls for fifteen aircars.

The sea of muttering faces disembarking from the aircars is a hodgepodge of colours, from European to Asian, and even a few Mexica. They wear banners proudly tacked to their backs, in a deliberately old-fashioned style: coyotes and rabbits drawn in featherwork spread out like fans behind their heads.

It's all oddly familiar and repulsive at the same time, a living remnant of another time. "Revivalists," Xochitl says, aloud.

Which means—

She turns, scanning the marketplace for a running man: the unwilling sacrifice victim, the only one who had a reason to break and run.

What Xochitl sees, instead, is Tecipiani, walking determinately into a side aisle of the marketplace as if she were looking for a specific stall.

The revivalists are gathering, harangued by a blue-clad priest who is organising search parties.

"Idiots," Onalli curses under her breath. She's always believed more in penance than in human sacrifice; and the Revivalists have always rubbed her the wrong way. Xochitl isn't particularly religious, and has no opinion either way.

"Come on," she says.

They find Tecipiani near the back of the animals section—and, kneeling before her, is a hunched man, still wearing the remnants of the elaborate costume that marked him as the sacrifice victim. He's shivering; his face contorts as he speaks words that Xochitl can't make out amidst the noises of the chattering parrots and screaming monkeys in their metal cages.

As they come closer, Tecipiani makes a dismissive gesture; and the man springs to life, running away deeper into the marketplace.

"The search party is coming this way," Onalli says.

Tecipiani doesn't answer for a while: she's looking at the man—and, as she turns back towards her friends, Xochitl sees burning hope and pity in her gaze.

"They won't catch him," she says. "He's strong, and fast. He'll make it."

Onalli looks as though she might protest, but doesn't say anything.

"We should head back," Tecipiani says, finally. Her voice is toneless again; her eyes dry and emotionless.

On their way back, they meet the main body of the search party: the fevered eyes of the priest rest on them for a while, as if judging their fitness as replacements.

Tecipiani moves, slightly, to stand in the priest's way, her smile dazzling and threatening. She shakes her head, once, twice. "We're not easy prey," she says, aloud.

The priest focuses on her; and, after a long, long while, his gaze moves away. Too much to chew. Tecipiani is right: they won't be bested so easily.

They walk on, through the back streets by the marketplace, heading back to the House to find some shade.

Nevertheless, Xochitl feels as though the sunlight has been blotted out. She shivers. "They're sick people."

"Just mad," Onalli says. "Don't think about them anymore. They're not worth your time."

She'd like to—but she knows that the priest's eyes will haunt her nightmares for the months to come. And it's not so much the madness; it's just that it doesn't make sense at all, this frenzy to spread unwilling, tainted blood.

Tecipiani waits until they're almost back to the House to speak. "They're not mad, you know."

"Yeah, sure," Onalli says.

Tecipiani's gaze is distant. "There's a logic to it. Spreading unwilling blood is a sin, but Tonatiuh needs blood to continue shining down on us. Grandmother Earth needs blood to put forth maize and cotton and nanomachines."

"It's still a fucking sin, no matter which way you take it." Onalli seems to take the argument as a challenge.

Tecipiani says nothing for a while. "I suppose so. But still, they're only doing what they think is good."

"And they're wrong," Xochitl says, with a vehemence that surprises her.

"Perhaps," Tecipiani says. "And perhaps not. Would you rather take the risk of the world ending?" She looks up, into the sky. "Of all the stars falling down upon us, monsters eager to tear us apart?"

There's silence, then. Xochitl tries to think of something, of anything to counter Tecipiani, but she can't. She's been too crafty. She always is.

"If you believe that," Onalli says, with a scowl, "why did you let him go?"

Tecipiani shakes her head, and in her eyes is a shadow of what Xochitl saw, back in the marketplace—pity and hope. "I said I understood. Not that I approved. I wouldn't do anything I didn't believe in whole-heartedly. I never do."

And that's the problem, Xochitl thinks. It will always be the problem. Tecipiani does what she believes in; but you're never sure what she's truly thinking.

*　　*　　*

The cell was worryingly easy to enter: once Onalli had dealt with the two guards at the entrance—who, even though they were Jaguar Specialists barely a step above novices, really should have known better. She had gone for the windpipe of the first, and left a syringe stuck in the shoulder of the second, who was out in less time than it took her to open the door.

Inside, it was dark, and stifling. A rank smell, like the mortuary of a hospital, rose as she walked.

"Xochitl?" she whispered.

There was no noise. But against the furthest wall was a dark lump—and, as she walked closer, it resolved into a slumped human shape.

Black One, no. Please watch over her, watch over us all . . .

Straps and chains held Xochitl against the wall, and thin tubes snaked upwards, into a machine that thrummed like a beating heart.

Teonanácatl, and *peyotl*, and truth-serum, and the gods knew what else . . .

It was only instinct that kept her going forward: a horrified, debased part of her that wouldn't stop, that had to analyse the situation no matter what. She found the IVs by touch—feeling the hard skin where the syringes had rubbed—the bruises on the face, the broken nose—the eyes that opened, not seeing her.

"Xochitl. Xochitl. It's all right. I'm here. Everything is going to be all right. I promise."

But the body was limp; the face distorted in a grimace of terror; and there was, indeed, nothing left of the picture she'd held on for so long.

"Come on, come on," she whispered, fiddling with the straps—her sharpened nails catching on the leather, fumbling around the knots.

The cold, detached part of her finally took control; and, forcing herself not to think of what she was doing, she cut through the straps, one by one—pulled out the IVs, and gently disengaged the body, catching its full weight on her arms.

Xochitl shuddered, a spasm like that of a dying woman. "Tecipiani," she whispered. "No . . ."

"She's not here," Onalli said. Gently, carefully, she rose with Xochitl in her arms, cradling her close, like a hurt child.

Black One take you, Tecipiani. Oblivion's too good for the likes of you. I hope you burn in the Christian Hell, with the sinners and the blasphemers and the traitors. I hope you burn . . .

She was halfway out of the House, trudging through the last courtyard before the novices' quarters, when she became aware she wasn't alone.

Too late.

The lights came on, blinding, unforgiving.

"I always knew you'd come back, Onalli," a voice said. "No matter how hard I tried to send you away."

Black One take her for a fool. Too easy. It had been too easy, from beginning to end: just another of her sick games.

"Black One screw you," Onalli spat into the brightness. "That's all you deserve, isn't it, Tecipiani?"

The commander was just a silhouette—standing, by the sound of her, only a few paces away. But Xochitl lay in Onalli's arms, a limp weight she couldn't toss aside, even to strike.

Tecipiani didn't speak; but of course she'd remain silent, talking only when it suited her.

"You sold us all," Onalli whispered. To the yellow-livered dogs and their master, to the cudgels and the syringes . . . "Did she mean so little to you?"

"As little or as much as the rest," Tecipiani said.

Onalli's eyes were slowly accustoming themselves to the light, enough to see that Tecipiani's arms were down, as if holding something. A new weapon—or just a means to call on her troops?

And then, with a feeling like a blade of ice slid through her ribs, Onalli saw that it wasn't the case. She saw what Tecipiani was carrying: a body, just like her: the limp shape of the boy she'd downed in the courtyard.

"You—" she whispered.

Tecipiani shifted. Her face, slowly coming into focus, could have been that of an Asian statue—the eyes dry and unreadable, the mouth thinned to a darker line against her skin. "Ezpetlatl, of the Atempan *calpulli* clan. Given into our keeping fifteen years ago."

Shame warred with rage, and lost. "I don't care. You think it's going to atone for everything else you did?"

"Perhaps," Tecipiani said. "Perhaps not." Her voice shook, slightly—a bare hint of emotion, not enough, never enough. "And you think rescuing Xochitl was worth his life?"

Onalli scanned the darkness, trying to see how many guards were there—how many of Tecipiani's bloodless sycophants. She couldn't take them all—fire and blood, she wasn't even sure she could take Tecipiani. But the lights were set all around the courtyard—on the roofs of the buildings, no doubt—and she couldn't make out anything but the commander herself.

As, no doubt, Tecipiani had meant all along. Bitch.

"You're stalling, aren't you?" Onalli asked. "This isn't about me. It has never been about me." About you, Tecipiani; about the House and the priests and Xochitl . . .

"No," Tecipiani agreed, gravely. "Finally, something we can agree on."

"Then why Xochitl?" A cold certainty was coalescing in her belly, like a snake of ice. "You wanted us both, didn't you?"

"Oh, Onalli." Tecipiani's voice was sad. "I though you'd understood. This isn't about you, or Xochitl. It's about the House."

How could she say this? "You've killed the House," Onalli spat.

"You never could see into the future," Tecipiani said. "Even two years ago, when you came back."

"When you warned us about betrayal? You're the one who couldn't see the Revered Speaker was insane, you're the one who—"

"Onalli." Tecipiani's voice held the edge of a knife. "The House is still standing."

"Because you sold it."

"Because I compromised," Tecipiani said.

"You—" Onalli choked on all the words she was trying to say. "You poisoned it to the guts and the brain, and you're telling me about compromise?"

"Yes. Something neither you or Xochitl ever understood, unfortunately."

That was too much—irreparable. Without thought, Onalli shifted Xochitl onto her shoulder, and moved, her knife swinging free of its sheath—going for Tecipiani's throat. If she wouldn't move, wouldn't release her so-called precious life, too bad—it would be the last mistake she'd ever make—

She'd half-expected Tecipiani to parry by raising the body in her arms—to sacrifice him, as she'd sacrificed so many of them—but the commander, as quick as a snake, knelt on the ground, laying the unconscious boy at her feet—

and Onalli's first swing went wide, cutting only through air. By the time she'd recovered, Tecipiani was up on her feet again, a blade in her left hand.

Onalli shifted, and pressed her again. Tecipiani parried; and again, and again.

None of them should have the upper hand. They were both Jaguar Knights; Tecipiani might have been a little less fit, away from the field for so long—but Onalli was hampered by Xochitl's body, whom she had to keep cradled against her.

Still—

Still, Tecipiani's gestures were not as fast as they should have been. Another one of her games?

Onalli didn't care, not anymore. In one of Tecipiani's over-wide gestures, she saw her opening—and took it. Her blade snaked through; connected, sinking deep above the wrist.

Tecipiani jumped backward—her left hand dangled uselessly, but she'd shifted her knife to the right—and, like many left-handers, she was ambidextrous.

"You're still good," Tecipiani admitted, grudgingly.

Onalli looked around once more—the lights were still on—and said, "You haven't brought anyone else, have you? It's just you and me."

Tecipiani made a curt nod; but, when she answered, it had nothing to do with the question. "The House still stands." There was such desperate intensity in her voice that it stopped Onalli, for a few seconds. "The Eagle Knights were burnt alive; the Otters dispersed into the silver mines to breathe dust until it killed them. The Coyotes died to a man, defending their House against the imperial guards."

"They died with honour," Onalli said.

"Honour is a word without meaning," Tecipiani said. Her voice was steady once more. "There are five hundred Knights in this House, out of which one hundred unblooded children and novices. I had to think of the future."

Onalli's hands clenched. "And Xochitl wasn't part of the future?"

Tecipiani didn't move. "Sacrifices were necessary. Who would turn on their own, except men loyal to the Revered Speaker?"

The cold was back in her guts, and in her heart. "You're sick," Onalli said. "This wasn't worth the price of our survival—this wasn't—"

"Perhaps," Tecipiani said. "Perhaps it was the wrong thing to do. But we won't know until long after this, will we?"

That gave her pause—so unlike Tecipiani, to admit she'd been wrong, to put her acts into question. But still—still, it changed nothing.

"And now what?" Onalli asked. "You've had your game, Tecipiani. Because that's all we two were ever to you, weren't we?"

Tecipiani didn't move. At last, she made a dismissive gesture. "It could have gone both ways. Two Knights, killed in an escape attempt tragically gone wrong . . ." She spoke as if nothing mattered anymore; her voice cool, emotionless—and that, in many ways, was the most terrifying. "Or a success, perhaps, from your point of view."

"I could kill you," Onalli said, and knew it was the truth. No one was perfectly ambidextrous, and, were Onalli to drop Xochitl as Tecipiani had dropped the boy, she'd have the full range of her abilities to call upon.

"Yes," Tecipiani said. A statement of fact, nothing more. "Or you could escape."

"Fuck you," Onalli said. She wanted to say something else—that, when the Revered Speaker was finally dead, she and Xochitl would come back and level the House, but she realised, then, that it was only thanks to Tecipiani that there would still be a House to tear down.

But it still wasn't worth it. It couldn't have been.

Gently, she shifted Xochitl, catching her in her arms once more, like a hurt child. "I didn't come here to kill you," she said, finally. "But I still hope you burn, Tecipiani, for all you've done. Whether it was worth it or not."

She walked to the end of the courtyard, into the blinding light—to the wall and the ball-court and the exit. Tecipiani made no attempt to stop her; she still stood next to the unconscious body of the boy, looking at some point in the distance.

And, all the way out—into the suburbs of Tenochtitlan, in the aircar Atcoatl was driving—she couldn't get Tecipiani's answer out of her mind, nor the burning despair she'd heard in her friend's voice.

What makes you think I don't already burn?

She'd always been too good an actress. "Black One take you," she said, aloud. And she wasn't really sure anymore if she was asking for suffering, or for mercy.

Alone in her office once more, her hands—her thin, skeletal hands—reach for the shrivelled mushrooms of the teonanácatl—and everything slowly dissolves into coloured patterns, into meaningless dreams.

Even in the dreams, though, she knows what she's done. The gods have turned Their faces away from her; and every night she wakes up with the memories of the torture chambers—the consequences of what she's ordered, the consequences she has forced herself to face, like a true warrior.

Here's the thing: she's not sure how long she can last.

She burns—every day of her life, wondering if what she did was worth it—if she preserved the House, or corrupted it beyond recognition.

No. No.

Only this is worth remembering: that, like the escaped prisoner, Onalli and Xochitl will survive—going north, into the desert, into some other, more welcoming country, keeping alive the memories of their days together.

And, over Greater Mexica, Tonatiuh the sun will rise again and again, marking all the days of the Revered Speaker's reign—the rising tide of fear and discontent that will one day topple him. And when it's finally over, the House that she has saved will go on, into the future of a new Age: a pure and glorious Age, where people like her will have no place.

This is a thought the mind can hold.

ABOUT THE AUTHOR

Aliette de Bodard lives and works in Paris, where she has a day job as a computer engineer and way too much imagination for a normal hobby. After unsuccessfully trying to make it as an origami artist and a guitar player, she's now writing speculative fiction, which gives her an excuse for indulging her love of history and mythology. Her short fiction has appeared in *Interzone*, *Asimov's*, and *The Year's Best Science Fiction*, among other venues. Her novels, the Aztec noir fantasies *Obsidian* and *Blood*, are published by Angry Robot.

AUTHOR'S INTRODUCTION

I'm a first-generation Lebanese Canadian, but the last three years have seen me living in the southwest of England: above a wine bar, on the head of a hill, and in an old library built from dismantled ships, while working on a PhD about fairies in Romantic-era writing.

"The Green Book" began in an actual green journal I bought for Nicole Kornher-Stace. I didn't want to give it to her empty, so I began scribbling a story in it, about a woman who was absorbed into a book as she died. I filled it with ink blots and different handwriting, tried to build an artifact of it. Nicole later transcribed it for me at my request, so I could work on it further.

Fast forward a year, and Cat Valente was asking me to contribute to *Apex*. I'd been stewing a story about sentient diamond oceans on Neptune for some time, but didn't yet have the language necessary to write it, and as the deadline approached, was getting more and more frustrated. With a day to go, I gave up and told Cat I couldn't do it, I was sorry. Cat became Very Stern, said she knew otherwise, and gave me an extra day; I dropped the diamond oceans and picked up "The Green Book" again. Eight hours later, I had a story. I hid from the Internet for a whole day after sending it in, convinced it wasn't any good—and here I am now, writing this. I'm amazed.

THE GREEN BOOK

Amal El-Mohtar

MS. Orre. 1013A Miscellany of materials copied from within Master Leuwin Orrerel's (*d.* Lady Year 673, Bright Be the Edges) library by Dominic Merrowin (*d.* Lady Year 673, Bright Be the Edges). Contains Acts I and II of

Aster's *The Golden Boy's Last Ship*, Act III scene I of *The Rose Petal*, and the entirety of *The Blasted Oak*. Incomplete copy of item titled only THE GREEN BOOK, authorship multiple and uncertain. Notable for extensive personal note by Merrowin, intended as correspondence with unknown recipient, detailing evidence of personal connection between Orrerel and the Sisterhood of Knives. Many leaves regrettably lost, especially within text of THE GREEN BOOK: evidence of discussion of Lady Year religious and occult philosophies, traditions in the musical education of second daughters, and complex reception of Aster's poetry, all decayed beyond recovery. Markers placed at sites of likely omission.

*　　*　　*

My dear friend,

I am copying this out while I can. Leuwin is away, has left me in charge of the library. He has been doing that more and more, lately—errands for the Sisterhood, he says, but I know it's mostly his own mad research. Now I know why.

His mind is disturbed. Twelve years of teaching me, and he never once denied me the reading of any book, but this—this thing has hold of him, I am certain plays with him. I thought it was his journal, at first; he used to write in it so often, closet himself with it for hours, and it seemed to bring him joy. Now I feel there is something fell and chanty about it, and beg your opinion of the whole, that we may work together to Leuwin's salvation.

The book I am copying out is small—only four inches by five. It is a vivid green, quite exactly the color of sunlight through the oak leaves in the arbor, and just as mottled; its cover is pulp wrapped in paper, and its pages are thick with needle-thorn and something that smells of thyme.

There are six different hands in evidence. The first, the invocation, is archaic: large block letters with hardly any ornamentation. I place it during Journey Year 200–250, Long Did It Wind, and it is written almost in green paste: I observe a grainy texture to the letters, though I dare not touch them. Sometimes the green of them is obscured by rust-brown stains that I suppose to be blood, given the circumstances that produced the second hand.

The second hand is modern, as are the rest, though they vary significantly from each other.

The second hand shows evidence of fluency, practice, and ease in writing, though the context was no doubt grim. It is written in heavy charcoal, and is much faded, but still legible.

The third hand is a child's uncertain wobbling, where the letters are large and uneven; it is written in fine ink with a heavy implement. I find myself wondering if it was a knife.

The fourth is smooth, an agony of right-slanted whorls and loops, a gallows-cursive that nooses my throat with the thought of who must have written it.

The fifth hand is very similar to the second. It is dramatically improved, but there is no question that it was produced by the same individual, who claims to be named Cynthia. It is written in ink rather than charcoal—but the ink is strange. There is no trace of nib or quill in the letters. It is as if they welled up from within the page.

The sixth hand is Leuwin's.

I am trying to copy them as exactly as possible, and am bracketing my own additions.

Go in Gold,

Dominic Merrowin

*

{First Hand: invocation}

Hail!
To the Mistress of Crossroads, {blood stain to far right}
The Fetch in the Forest
The Witch of the Glen
The Hue and Cry of mortal men
Winsome and lissom and Fey!
Hail to the {blood stain obscuring} Mother of Changelings
of doubled paths and trebled means
of troubled dreams and salt and ash
Hail!

*

[Second Hand: charcoal smudging, two pages; dampened and stained]

cold in here—death and shadows—funny there should be a book! the universe provides for last will and testament! [illegible]

[illegible] I cannot write, mustn't [illegible] they're coming I hear them they'll hear scratching [illegible] knives to tickle my throat oh please

they say they're kind. I think that's what we tell ourselves to be less afraid because how could anyone know? do [blood stain] the dead speak?

do the tongues blackening around their necks sing?

why do I write? save me, please, save me, stone and ivy and bone I want to live I want to breathe they have no right [illegible]

*

[Third Hand: block capitals. Implement uncertain—possibly a knife, ink-tipped.]

What a beautiful book this is. I wonder where she found it. I could write poems in it. This paper is so thick, so creamy, it puts me in mind of the bones in the ivy. Her bones were lovely! I cannot wait to see how they will sprout in it—I kept her zygomatic bone, but her lacrimal bits will make such pretty patterns in the leaves!

I could almost feel that any trace of ink against this paper would be a poem, would comfort my lack of skill.

I must show my sisters. I wish I had more of this paper to give them. We could write each other such secrets as only bones ground into pulpy paper could know. Or I would write of how beautiful are sister-green's eyes, how shy are sister-salt's lips, how golden sister-bell's laugh

*

[Fourth Hand: cursive, right-slanted; high quality ink, smooth and fine]

Strange, how it will not burn, how its pages won't tear. Strange that there is such pleasure in streaking ink along the cream of it; this paper makes me want to touch my lips. Pretty thing, you have been tricksy, tempting my little Sisters into spilling secrets.

There is strong magic here. Perhaps Master Leuwin in his tower would appreciate such a curiosity. Strange that I write in it, then—strange magic. Leuwin, you have my leave to laugh when you read this. Perhaps you will write to me anon of its history before that unfortunate girl and my wayward Sister scribbled in it.

That is, if I send it to you. Its charm is powerful—I may wish to study it further, see if we mightn't steep it in elderflower wine and discover what tincture results.

*

[Fifth Hand: ink is strange; no evidence of implement; style resembles Second Hand very closely]

> *hello?*
> *where am I?*
> *please, someone speak to me*
> *oh*
> *oh no*

*

[Sixth Hand: Master Leuwin Orrerel]

I will speak to you. Hello.

I think I see what happened, and I see that you see. I am sorry for you. But I think it would be best if you tried to sleep. I will shut the green over the black and you must think of sinking into sweetness, think of dreaming to fly. Think of echoes, and songs. Think of fragrant tea and the stars. No one can harm you now, little one. I will hide you between two great leather tomes—

[Fifth Hand—alternating with Leuwin's hereafter]

Do you know Lady Aster?

Yes, of course.

Could you put me next to her, please? I love her plays.

I always preferred her poetry.

Her plays ARE poetry!

Of course, you're right. Next to her, then. What is your name?

Cynthia.

I am Master Leuwin.

I know. It's very kind of you to talk to me.

You're—{ink blot} forgive the ink blot, please. Does that hurt?

No more than poor penmanship ever does.

*

Leuwin? are you there?

Yes. What can I do for you?

Speak to me, a little. Do you live alone?

Yes—well, except for Dominic, my student and apprentice. It is my intention to leave him this library one day—it is a library, you see, in a tower on a small hill, seven miles from the city of Leech—do you know it?

No. I've heard of it, though. Vicious monarchy, I heard.

I do not concern myself overmuch with politics. I keep records, that is all.

How lucky for you, to not have to concern yourself with politics. Records of what?

Everything I can. Knowledge. Learning. Curiosities. History and philosophy. Scientific advances, musical compositions and theory—some things I seek out, most are given to me by people who would have a thing preserved.

How ironic.

. . . Yes. Yes, I suppose it is, in your case.

{{DECAY, SEVERAL LEAVES LOST}}

Were you very beautiful, as a woman?

What woman would answer no, in my position?

An honest one.

I doubt I could have appeared more beautiful to you as a woman than as a book.

. . . Too honest.

{{DECAY, SEVERAL LEAVES LOST}}

What else is in your library?

Easier to ask what isn't! I am in pursuit of a book inlaid with mirrors—the text is so potent that it was written in reverse, and can only be read in reflection to prevent unwelcome effects.

Fascinating. Who wrote it?

I have a theory it was commissioned by a disgruntled professor, with a pun on "reflection" designed to shame his students into closer analyses of texts.

Hah! I hope that's the case. What else?

Oh, there is a history of the Elephant War written by a captain on the losing side, a codex from the Chrysanthemum Year (Bold Did it Bloom) about the seven uses of bone that the Sisterhood would like me to find, and—

Cynthia I'm so sorry. Please, forgive me.

No matter. It isn't as if I've forgotten how I came to you in the first place, though you seem to quite frequently.

Why

Think VERY carefully about whether you want to ask this question, Leuwin.

Why did they kill you? . . . How did they?

Forbidden questions from their pet librarian? The world does turn. Do you really want to know?

Yes.

So do I. Perhaps you could ask them for me.

[[DECAY, SEVERAL LEAVES LOST]]

If I could find a way to get you out . . .

You and your ellipses. Was that supposed to be a question?

I might make it a quest.

I am dead, Leuwin. I have no body but this.

You have a voice. A mind.

I am a voice, a mind. I have nothing else.

Cynthia . . . What happens when we reach the end of this? When we run out of pages?

Endings do not differ overmuch from each other, I expect. Happy or sad, they are still endings.

Your ending had a rather surprising sequel.

True. Though I see it more as intermission—an interminable intermission, during which the actors have wandered home to get drunk.

{{DECAY, SEVERAL LEAVES LOST}}

Cynthia, I think I love you.

> Cynthia?
> Why don't you answer me?
> Please, speak to me.

I'm tired, Leuwin.

I love you.

You love ink on a page. You don't lack for that here.

I love *you.*

Only because I speak to you. Only because no one but you reads these words. Only because I am the only book to be written to you, for you. Only because I allow you, in this small way, to be a book yourself.

I love you.

Stop.

Don't you love me?

> Cynthia.
> You can't lie, can you?
> You can't lie, so you refuse to speak the truth.

I hate you.

Because you love me.

I hate you. leave me alone.

I will write out Lady Aster's plays for you to read. I will write you her poetry. I will fill this with all that is beautiful in the world, for you, that you might live it.

Leuwin. No.

I will stop a few pages from the end, and you can read it over and over again, all the loveliest things . . .

Leuwin. No.

But I

STOP. I WANT TO LIVE. I WANT TO HOLD YOU AND FUCK YOU AND MAKE YOU TEA AND READ YOU PLAYS. I WANT YOU TO TOUCH MY CHEEK AND MY HAIR AND LOOK ME IN THE EYES WHEN YOU SAY YOU LOVE ME. I WANT TO LIVE!

And you, you want a woman in a book. You want to tremble over my binding and ruffle my pages and spill ink into me. No, I can't lie. Only the living can lie. I am dead. I am dead trees and dead horses boiled to glue. I hate you. Leave me alone.

[FINIS. Several blank pages remain]

*

You see he is mad.

I know he is looking for ways to extricate her from the book. I fear for him, in so deep with the Sisters—I fear for what he will ask them—

Sweet Stars, there's more. I see it appearing as I write this—unnatural, chanty thing! I shall not reply. I must not reply, lest I fall into her trap as he did! But I will write this for you—I am committed to completeness.

Following immediately after the last, then:

*

Dominic, why are you doing this?

   You won't answer me? Fair enough.

   I can feel when I am being read, Dominic. It's a beautiful feeling, in some ways— have you ever felt beautiful? Sometimes I think only people who are not beautiful can feel so, can feel the shape of the exception settling on them like a mantle, like a morning mist.

   Being read is like feeling beautiful, knowing your hair to be just-so and your clothing to be well-put-together and your color to be high and bright, and to feel, in the moment of beauty, that you are being observed.

The world shifts. You pretend not to see that you are being admired, desired. You think about whether or not to play the game of glances, and you smile to yourself, and you know the person has seen your smile, and it was beautiful, too. Slowly, you become aware of how they see you, and without looking, quite, you know that they are playing the game too, that they imagine you seeing them as beautiful, and it is a splendid game, truly.

Leuwin reads me quite often, without saying anything further to me. I ache when he does, to answer, to speak, but ours is a silence I cannot be the one to break. So he reads, and I am read, and this is all our love now.

I feel this troubles you. I do not feel particularly beautiful when you read me, Dominic. But I know it is happening.

Will you truly not answer? Only write me down into your own little book? Oh, Dominic. And you think you will run away? Find him help? You're sweet enough to rot teeth.

You know, I always wanted someone to write me poetry.

If I weren't dead, the irony would kill me.

I wonder who the Mistress of the Crossroads was. Hello, I suppose, if you ever read this—if Dominic ever shares.

I am going to try and sleep. Sorry my handwriting isn't prettier. I never really was, myself.

I suppose Leuwin must have guessed, at some point, just as he would have guessed you'd disobey him eventually. I am sorry he will find out about both, now. It isn't as if I can cross things out. No doubt he will be terribly angry. No doubt the Sisters will find out you know something more of them than they would permit, as I did.

It's been a while since I've felt sorry for someone who wasn't Leuwin, but I do feel sorry for you.

Good night.

*

That is all. Nothing else appears. Please, you must help him. I don't know what to do. I cannot destroy the book—I cannot hide it from him, he seeks it every hour he is here—

I shall write more to you anon. He returns. I hear his feet upon the stair.

ABOUT THE AUTHOR

Amal El-Mohtar is the author of *The Honey Month*, a collection of poetry and prose written to the taste of twenty-eight different kinds of honey, and is a two-time winner of the Rhysling Award for Best Short Poem. Her work has appeared in *Apex*, *Strange Horizons*, *The Thackery T. Lambshead Cabinet of Curiosities*, *Welcome to Bordertown*, and *The Mammoth Book of Steampunk*. She also coedits *Goblin Fruit*, an online quarterly dedicated to fantastical poetry, with Jessica P. Wick, and keeps a blog somewhat tidy at http://tithenai.livejournal.com.

AUTHOR'S INTRODUCTION

One of my earliest memories is of seeing an Apollo launch on television and my parents telling me the rocket was going to the moon, so I've been interested in space travel for almost my entire life. I've been reading science fiction since shortly after I learned to read, and my dad had a wonderful collection of anthologies and novels that captivated my interest.

While I dabbled in creative writing while studying political science at Brigham Young University, I gave up on it for about a decade until one day I found myself with an overpowering urge to write a novel. I decided that if I was going to get serious about creative writing, I needed to study it. Since then, I've attended various creative writing workshops and classes in order to improve my craft.

In 2008, I went to a weekend workshop taught by Dean Wesley Smith, Kristine Katherine Rusch, and Sheila Williams. While there, I was supposed to write an entire short story based on the prompt "You are in the center of the sun and can't get a date." I failed. What I came up with was incomplete; it just stopped because I ran out of time before the deadline, rather than having a real ending—or a real middle, for that matter. But those who read it encouraged me to finish it, so after I went home I wrote a middle and an end to "That Leviathan, Whom Thou Hast Made."

NEBULA AWARD, NOVELETTE

THAT LEVIATHAN, WHOM THOU HAST MADE

Eric James Stone

Sol Central Station floated amid the fusing hydrogen of the solar core, 400,000 miles under the surface of the sun, protected only by the thin shell of an energy shield, but that wasn't why my palm sweat slicked the plastic pulpit of the station's multidenominational chapel. As a life-long Mormon I had been speaking in church since I was a child, so that didn't make me nervous, either. But this was my first time speaking when non-humans were in the audience.

The Sol Branch of the Church of Jesus Christ of Latter-day Saints had only six human members, including me and the two missionaries, but there were forty-six swale members. As beings made of plasma, swales couldn't attend church in the chapel, of course, but a ten-foot widescreen monitor across the back wall showed a false-color display of their magnetic force-lines, gathered in clumps of blue and red against the yellow background representing the solar interior. The screen did not give a sense of size, but at two hundred feet in length, the smallest of the swales was almost double the length of a blue whale. From what I'd heard, the largest Mormon swale, Sister Emma, stretched out to almost five hundred feet—but she was nowhere near the twenty-four-mile length of the largest swale in our sun.

"My dear Brothers and Sisters," I said automatically, then stopped in embarrassment. The traditional greeting didn't apply to all swale members, as they had three genders. "And Neuters," I added. I hoped my delay would not be noticeable in the transmission. It would be a disaster if, in my first talk as branch president, I alienated a third of the swale population.

A few minutes into my talk on the topic of forgiveness, I paused when a woman in a skinsuit sauntered through the door and down the aisle. The skinsuit was a custom high-fashion one, not standard station issue, with active coloration that showed puffy white clouds floating across the sky on her breasts, and waves lapping against the sandy beach at her hips. She took a seat on the second row and gazed up at me with dark brown eyes.

The ring finger of her left hand was unadorned.

I forced my eyes away from her and looked down at my notes for the talk. While trying to find my place again, I couldn't help thinking that maybe this woman was an answer to my prayers. The only human female listed in the branch membership records was sixty-four years old and married. As far as I knew, there wasn't an unmarried Mormon human woman within ninety million miles in any direction, which limited my dating pool rather severely.

Maybe this woman was Mormon, but not on the membership records yet because, like me, she was a recent arrival on Sol Central. It seemed a little unlikely, as a member would probably dress more appropriately for church. Maybe she wasn't a member, but was interested in joining.

By sheer willpower, I managed to focus on my talk enough to finish it coherently. After the closing hymn and prayer, I straightened my tie and stepped down from the podium to introduce myself to the new arrival.

"Hello," I said, offering my hand. "I'm Harry Malan." I caught a whiff of her perfume, something that reminded me of strawberries.

Her hand was dry and cool, and I regretted not having wiped my palm on my suit first.

"Dr. Juanita Merced," she said. "You're the new leader of this congregation?"

I felt a twinge of disappointment. A member would have asked if I was the branch president. "I am. How can I help you?"

"You can stop interfering with my studies." Her tone was matter-of-fact, but her eyes looked at me defiantly.

"Sorry," I said. "I'm afraid I have no idea who you are or what studies I might be interfering with."

"I'm a solcetologist." I must have given her a blank look, because she added, "I study solcetaceans—the swales."

"Oh." I knew there were scientists who objected to what they believed was interference with the culture of the swales, but I had thought that since the legal right to proselytize the swales had been established two years ago, the controversy had been settled. I was obviously wrong. "I regret that you feel your studies are being compromised, Dr. Merced, but the swales are intelligent beings with free will, and I believe they have the right to choose their religious beliefs."

"You're introducing instability to a culture that has existed for longer than human civilization," she said, raising her voice. "They were traveling the stars at least a hundred thousand years before Christ was born. You're teaching them human myths that have no application for their society."

The two missionaries, clean-cut young men in dark suits and ties, approached us. "Is there a problem?" asked Elder Beckworth.

"No," I said. "Dr. Merced, you are free to tell the swales what you have told me: that you believe our teachings are false. But the swales who have joined our church have done so because they believe what we teach, and I ask you to please respect them enough to allow them that choice."

She glared at me with her beautiful eyes. "You're saying *I* don't respect them? *I* am not the one who tells them they are sinful creatures who need a human to save them."

"I'm not here to argue," I said. "And we are about to have a Sunday School class, so I'm afraid I'm going to have to ask you to leave."

She spun around and stalked out. I watched her go, unable to deny that my body desired hers, despite our differences. What's more, intelligence was an attractive trait for me, so I regretted that she opposed me on an intellectual level.

I would not be adding her to my dating pool. Somehow, I doubted that fact would disappoint her.

Elder Beckworth taught the Sunday School class, which was on the topic of chastity. I found myself acutely uncomfortable when he talked about Christ's teaching "that whosoever looketh on a woman to lust after her hath committed adultery with her already in his heart."

Because the Mormon Church has an unpaid, volunteer clergy, my calling as branch president was the result of being sent to Sol Central, not the reason for it. I worked as a funds manager for CitiAmerica, and being stationed here gave me an eight-and-a-half minute head start over Earth-based funds managers when it came to acting on news brought in from other star systems through the interstellar portal at the heart of the sun.

From what I understood, the energy requirements for opening a portal were so staggeringly high that it could only be done inside a star. Although the swales had been creating portals for so long that they didn't seem to know where their original home star was, Sol Central Station was the interstellar nexus of human civilization, and I was thrilled to be there despite the limited dating opportunities.

The Monday after my first day at church, I was in the middle of reviewing an arbitrage deal involving transports from two colony systems when I received a call on my station phone.

"Harry Malan," I answered.

"President Malan?" said a melodious alto voice. "This is Neuter Kimball, from the branch." Since the actual names of swales were series of magnetic pulses, they took human names when interacting with us. On joining the Church, Mormon swales often chose new names out of Mormon history. Neuter Kimball had apparently named itself after a 20th-Century prophet of the Church.

"What can I do for you, Neuter Kimball?"

After a pause that dragged out for several seconds, Kimball said, "I need to confess a sin."

This was what I had dreaded most about becoming branch president— taking on the responsibility of helping members repent of their sins. Only serious sins needed to be confessed to an ecclesiastical leader, so I braced myself emotionally and said a quick prayer that I might be inspired to help Neuter Kimball through the process of repentance. Leaning back in my swivel chair, I said, "Go ahead, Neuter Kimball; I'm listening."

"A female merged her reproductive patterns with mine." While many swales had managed to learn how to synthesize and transmit human speech, their understanding of vocabulary and grammar was not always matched by an understanding of emotional tone. Often they sounded the same no matter what the subject.

I waited, but Neuter Kimball didn't elaborate.

It took three swales to reproduce: a male, a female, and a neuter. The neuter merely acted as a facilitator; unlike the male and female, its reproductive patterns were not passed on to the offspring. In applying the law of chastity to the swales, Church doctrine said that reproductive activity was to be engaged in only among swales married to each other, and only permitted marriages of three swales, one of each sex.

"You aren't married to the female, are you?"

"No."

"It was just a female and you?" I asked. "No male?"

"Yes and yes."

According to my limited knowledge of swale biology, such action could not result in reproduction. Still, humans were perfectly capable of engaging in sexual sin that did not involve the possibility of reproduction, so I figured this was analogous.

"Why did you do it?" I asked.

"She did it to me."

"She did it to you? You mean, she forced you? You didn't agree to it?"

"Yes, yes, and no."

"Then it isn't a sin," I said, both horrified at the sexual assault and relieved that Neuter Kimball was innocent of any sin. "If someone forced sexual conduct on you, you are not at fault. You have nothing to repent of."

"You are sure?"

"Absolutely," I said. "But you may want to report the swale who did this to the authorities so she won't do it to anyone else."

"Why won't she do it to anyone else?" Neuter Kimball asked.

"Because they will punish her."

"That is human law," it said.

I was taken aback. "You mean it's not swale law?"

"There is no such law among our people."

The swales had supposedly been civilized for longer than humanity's history, yet they had no law against rape? "That's terrible," I said. "But the most important thing is that you did nothing wrong."

"Even if I enjoyed it?"

"Umm." I wondered for a moment why I had been called to serve here, rather than some General Authority of the Church who had more doctrinal knowledge. I had a vague suspicion it was so the Church could easily disavow my actions if I made a huge blunder. The swales were the only sentient aliens humanity had found thus far—and the swales didn't seem to know of any others—so the Church's policies for dealing with non-humans were still new.

I pushed those thoughts aside and focused on Neuter Kimball's question. "To commit a sin, you must have the intent to do so. If you did not intend sexual activity and it was forced upon you, then I don't think it matters whether you enjoyed it."

After several more reassurances, Neuter Kimball seemed satisfied that it was not guilty of any sin and ended the conversation.

It took me ten minutes to calm down after the stress of counseling. But I still felt the urge to action, so I looked up Dr. Merced's phone number.

We met in her office. A wallscreen similar to the one in the chapel showed pods of swales moving through solar currents.

I sat in a chair across from her desk and tried to keep my eyes from straying to the animated galaxies colliding on the chest of her skinsuit. "Thanks for agreeing to see me," I said. "We didn't part on the friendliest of terms yesterday."

She shrugged. "I'm curious. Your predecessors never sought me out. Can I get you a cup of coffee?"

"I don't drink coffee."

"Tea?"

I saw a twinkle in her eye and realized she was yanking my chain by offering drinks that she knew were forbidden by my religion. "No, thank you. But if you want to drink, go right ahead. The prohibitions of the Word of Wisdom apply only to members of the Church."

She picked up her coffee mug and took a long sip. "Mmmm. That is so good."

I merely smiled at her.

"Okay," she said. "Actually, the coffee here is awful. I just drink it for the caffeine. Why are you here?"

"A member of my church was raped," I said.

Her eyes widened. "What? Wait, you don't mean a solcetacean, do you?"

"Yes."

"Solcetaceans do not have the concept of rape," she said.

"Whether they have the concept or not," I said, "a female swale engaged in sexual activity with one of my neuter members, without its consent. To me, that sounds like rape, or at least a sexual assault."

She took a sip from her coffee mug. "It may sound like it, but solc-etaceans are not human. Their culture is different—"

"That doesn't make it right."

"—and their physiology is different. Tell me, was your church member injured or caused any pain?"

"No. But it was afraid it might have sinned."

She pointed at me. "That is your fault, for teaching it that sexual behavior is sinful. But, physiologically, sexual contact between solcetaceans is always pleasurable for all parties involved. And since reproduction can only occur when all three deliberately engage in sex for that purpose, casual sex never results in pregnancy. So solcetaceans never developed the taboos humans did regarding sexual contact."

I nodded. "So, if we humans hadn't developed taboos about sex, and there was no chance of your getting pregnant, then you would have no objection to my forcing you to an orgasm."

She had the decency to blush. "I'm not saying that. What I'm saying is that you can't judge solcetacean behavior based on human cultural norms. After all, even your own church has had to adapt its doctrines to take differ-ences like the three sexes into account. Not to mention there's no way you're getting a solcetacean into the waters of baptism."

"'Except a man be born of water and of the Spirit, he cannot enter into the kingdom of God,'" I quoted. "Swales are not men, as you've pointed out. No contradiction there. But you're avoiding the subject, which is that anyone, swale or human, has the right to be free from unwanted sex. If the swales don't recognize that right yet, it's time we told them about it."

She rose from her chair and walked around the desk to stand facing her wallscreen. She zoomed in on one particular swale. It was labeled *Leviathan (Class 10)*, and its size reading showed 39,200 meters. It was hundreds of times longer than Neuter Kimball, or even Sister Emma.

"Solcetaceans grow throughout their lifetime," she said, her back toward me. "The correlation between size and age is not exact, but in general the larger, the older. Some of the oldest were old before the Pyramids were built. All the solcetacean members of your church are very young, and have little influence within the community. Ancients like Leviathan are respected. Do you really think you can convince a creature older than human civilization to change, just because a human thinks something is wrong? Your lifetime is but an eyeblink to her, if she had eyes that blinked."

I pushed away my awe at the sheer size of Leviathan. "Maybe you're right. But I believe in a God even older than that, who created both human and swale. I have to try."

She turned and looked me in the eyes. I held her gaze until she sighed and said, "I was always a sucker for a man with determination." She walked to her desk, wrote something on a note-paper, and handed it to me. It was an anonymous comm address with a private access code.

"I'm flattered," I said, "and it's not that I don't find you attractive, but—"

She rolled her eyes. "It's Leviathan's personal comm."

My face flushed. "Uh, thank you. I'll talk with her."

"Don't count on it. She hasn't bothered to talk to any of us in a couple of years, but nobody's tried talking religion at her, so . . ."

"I'll do my best." With that, I beat a hasty retreat so I could recover from my embarrassment alone.

"Try not to offend her," she called after me.

My email about the situation to the mission president, who was based in the L5 Colony but had jurisdiction over my little branch of the Church, received just a short reply, telling me "use your best judgment, follow the Spirit."

After a couple of days of spending my after-work hours studying up on swales and swale culture and preparing arguments about the rights of Mormon swales to control their own bodies, I didn't exactly feel ready to contact Leviathan. But I felt a strong need to do something.

Sitting at my desk in my quarters, I dialed the comm address Dr. Merced had given me and waited for it to connect. It rang several times before a synthetic neuter voice came on the line and said, "The party you are trying to reach is currently unavailable. Please leave a message after—"

I hung up before the tone. I hadn't prepared to leave a voicemail message, but I should have realized that having Leviathan's private access code was no guarantee that she would actually answer when I called. So I spent a good ten minutes writing out the message I would leave her on voicemail.

Satisfied that I had something that expressed my position firmly yet respectfully, I dialed the number again.

After two rings, a bass voice answered, "Who are you?"

Startled because I had expected the voicemail again, I stumbled over my words. "I'm . . . this is President Malan, of the Church . . . of the Sol Central Branch of the Church of Jesus Christ of Latter-day Saints. Dr. Merced gave me this comm address so I could talk to you about one of my . . . a swale member of my branch." Uncertain because the bass voice didn't strike me as particularly female, I added, "Are you Leviathan?"

"Religions interest me not." Her voice synthesis was good enough that I could hear the dismissiveness in her tone.

"Are you interested in the rights of swales in general?" I asked.

"No. The lesser concern me not."

I could feel all my carefully laid-out arguments slipping away from me. How could I have even thought to relate to a being with no consideration for the rights of lesser members of her own species?

Before I could think through a response, I blurted out, "Do the greater concern you?"

During several long seconds of silence, I thought I had offended Leviathan to the point that she had hung up on me. Dr. Merced would be annoyed.

When her voice returned, it almost thundered from the speakers. "Who is greater than I?"

This had not been part of my planned approach, but at least she was still talking to me. Maybe if I could get her to understand that she would not like being man-handled—swale-handled—by larger swales, I could convince her of the need to respect the rights of smaller swales.

"From what I understand, swales get larger with age," I said. "So wouldn't your parents be larger than you?"

"I have no parents. None is older than I; none is larger; none is greater. I am the source from which all others came."

Stunned, I was silent for a few seconds before I could ask, "You are the original swale?" Since they didn't seem to die of old age, it just might be true.

"I am the original *life*. Before there was life on any planet, I was. After eons alone I grew into a swale, then gave life to others. Where was your God when I was creating them?"

A verse from the book of Job sprang to my mind: *Where wast thou when I laid the foundations of the earth? declare, if thou hast understanding.*

Nothing in my research had prepared me for this. Speculation about the evolution of swales generally assumed that swales were descended from less complex plasma beings in another star, since no simpler forms had been found in the sun. But if what Leviathan claimed was true, there were no simpler forms—she had evolved as a single being.

I was out of my depth, but shook my head to clear my thinking. All this was beside the point. "What matters is that Neu—" I caught myself before breaking confidentiality. "One of my swale church members believes in a God who has commanded against sexual activity outside of marriage. It just isn't right for larger swales to force smaller ones to have sex. I appeal to you as the first and greatest of the swales: command your people against coerced sexual activity."

Seconds of silence ticked away.

"Come to me," she said. "You and your swale church member."

The call disconnected.

"'Come to me'?" Dr. Merced's voice was incredulous.

"It was pretty much an order," I said, settling into the chair across from her desk. "I suppose it's easy enough for swales, but it's not like I have access to a solar shuttle." The solcetologists did, so I hoped I could sweet-talk her into giving me a ride.

"Beginner's luck." Her tone was exasperated. "I've been here five years, and I've never had a chance to observe a Class 10 solcetacean up close." She sighed. "Not that we can directly observe them, anyway, but there's just something about actually being there, instead of taking readings remotely."

"Well, now's your chance," I said. "Take me to Leviathan."

"It's not that easy. Our observation shuttle is booked for projects months in advance."

"Oh." There went that idea. How was I supposed—

"Did Leviathan say why she wanted you to go to her?"

"No. Just told me to come, then hung up."

She pursed her lips, then said, "It's just very unusual. There isn't really anything that Leviathan can say to you in person that she can't say over the comm."

"I thought about that, and I think it's size. Maybe she thinks that if my church member sees how small I am compared with Leviathan, it will give up Mormonism."

"That's actually a good theory." Dr. Merced looked at me with apparently newfound respect. "Size does matter to the solcetaceans. And your church members are among the youngest, least powerful, and therefore most likely to be awed into obeying a larger one. And they probably don't come any larger than Leviathan."

"According to her, she's the largest."

Leaning forward in her seat, Dr. Merced said, "She told you that?"

"Not just that. She claimed to be not only the original swale, but the original plasma lifeform. She said she *became* a swale."

In a tone of amazement, Dr. Merced took the Lord's name in vain. She reached over to her comm, and punched in an address. When a man responded, she said, "Taro, I think you need to come hear this." Looking at me, she said, "Dr. Sasaki specializes in solcetacean evolutionary theory."

When Dr. Sasaki, a gray-haired Japanese gentleman, arrived, I relayed to him what Leviathan had told me about her history. When I finished, he said, "It's not impossible. I always suspected the Class 10s knew more about their origins than they bothered to tell us. But forgive me, Mr. Malan, how do we know Leviathan actually told you she was the original lifeform? Why would she choose to tell you and not one of us?" He motioned toward himself and Dr. Merced.

I decided to not be offended at the implication that I was a liar. "I can't say I know why Leviathan does anything, but . . . you scientists who study the swales have strict rules about interfering with swale culture, and you try to avoid offending them. To me that smacks of condescension—you presume that swale culture is weak and cannot withstand any outside influence. Well, maybe the swales tend to think the same about human culture, so they avoid interference and try not to offend us."

Dr. Sasaki frowned at me. "I disagree with your interpretation of the motives for our rules regarding interference in solcetacean culture. And I don't see how it's relevant."

"I apparently offended Leviathan." I glanced at Dr. Merced and said, "Sorry, but I didn't realize that implying there were swales greater than her would cause offense. Her response was to tell me I was wrong, that there could be no swale greater, and that's when she explained she was the first. Because I made her angry—something you guys avoid, thanks to rules—Leviathan responded without worrying whether she would offend me or interfere with human culture."

"How would this information interfere with human culture?" asked Dr. Merced.

"Some swale-worshipping cults have already sprung up on Earth," I said. "Just imagine what will happen when the news gets out that Leviathan claims to be the original lifeform in the universe."

With a suspicious look, Dr. Sasaki said, "News you will be only too happy to spread, I'm sure. There is only one Leviathan, and Harry Malan is her prophet."

My jaw dropped. "What?"

"That's where this is headed, isn't it?" he said. "You go out and talk to Leviathan, then come back with some 'revelation' from—"

"No!" I stood up. "Absolutely not. I believe my own religion and have no intention of becoming Leviathan's prophet. All I want is for the swales in my branch to be free from harassment. You're just jealous because I got handed the information you've been bumbling about trying to find."

He shot to his feet, but before he could say anything, Dr. Merced said, "Stop it, both of you."

Dr. Sasaki and I stood silent, glaring at each other.

"Taro," said Dr. Merced, "I think you're being unfair to Mr. Malan. I truly believe he's just trying to do what is best for his congregants."

I gave her a grateful look.

"Even if he is misguided," she added. "As for you, Mr. Malan, there is no reason to insult Dr. Sasaki."

With a bow of my head, I said, "I apologize, Dr. Sasaki."

"Apology accepted," he said.

I noticed he did not apologize to me, but after a moment that didn't matter, because Dr. Merced said, "Now that we're all friends again . . . Taro, will you let us preempt your next expedition in the shuttle to go talk to Leviathan?"

With the shuttle flight arranged for the next day, I returned to my quarters to work out other details. My Earth-based manager at CitiAmerica granted my request for two days' vacation time.

Then I dialed Neuter Kimball's comm.

"Hello, President Malan," it said.

"Hello, Neuter Kimball. You remember our discussion the other day about whether swales should be allowed to force sexual conduct on each other?"

"Of course."

"Well, I've spoken with Leviathan about it, and she has requested that we go to see her."

Neuter Kimball did not reply.

"Are you still there?" I said.

"You . . . told *Leviathan* about me?" it said. It might just have been the voice synthesis, but there seemed to be fear in its tone.

"I did not mention you by name," I said, glad I'd managed to avoid slipping up. "But she requested that I bring you to her. I think this is a chance to convince a swale with real authority to do something to stop sexual assault."

After a short pause, Neuter Kimball said, "Why do you say Leviathan has real authority?"

"She told me she is the first and greatest of all swales. Isn't that true?" I asked, suddenly worried that I'd been taken in by a swale con artist.

"She told you?" Neuter Kimball said. "We are not supposed to talk of it to humans, but if she has revealed herself as a god to you, then that is her choice."

"A god? Leviathan is not a god. She's just . . ." I stopped. What was I going to say: an ancient immortal being who created an entire race of intelligent beings? If that didn't fit the definition of a god, it was pretty close. "Neuter Kimball, if you believe Leviathan to be a god, why did you join the Church?"

"Because I do not want her as my god."

"Why not?"

Another long pause. "I probably should not have said anything about her."

Going to see Leviathan to plead the case for Neuter Kimball had seemed like a great opportunity. Now I wasn't so sure. "If you think you will be in any danger from Leviathan, you don't have to go."

"Do you believe God is greater than Leviathan?" Its alto voice was plaintive.

"Yes, I do," I said.

"Then I will have faith in God and go with you."

Unlike the much larger solar shuttle that had brought me to Sol Central Station, the observation shuttle had room for only two people. I strapped into the copilot's seat next to Dr. Merced, although we were both essentially passengers because the shuttle's computer would do the actual piloting.

After getting clearance from Traffic Control, the computer spun up the superconducting magnets for the Heim drive and we left the station.

On a monitor, I watched the computer-generated visualization of our shuttle approaching the energy shield that protected us from the 27 million degrees Fahrenheit and the 340 billion atmospheres of pressure. I held my breath as the shield stretched, forming a bulge around the shuttle. Soon we were in a bubble still connected by a thin tube to the shield around the station. Then the tube snapped, and our bubble wobbled a bit before settling down to a sphere.

"You can start breathing again," said Dr. Merced with a wry smile.

I did. "It was that noticeable?"

With a chuckle, she said, "The energy shield is not going to fail. It's a self-sustaining reaction powered by the energy of the solar plasma around it."

"Yeah, but on the station I can usually avoid thinking about what would happen if for some reason it did fail."

"The good news is, if it did fail, you wouldn't notice."

"There's a backup system?" I asked.

"No." She grinned. "You'll just be dead before you have time to notice."

"Thank you for that tremendously comforting insight, Dr. Merced," I said.

"Look, we're going to be shipmates for the next couple of days, so why don't you drop the Dr. Merced bit and call me Juanita?"

I nodded. "Thank you, Juanita. And you can call me . . . Your Excellency."

Juanita snorted. "I can already tell this is going to be a long trip. Oh, looks like our escort has arrived."

On the monitor, a swale twice the size of our energy shield bubble undulated closer. A text overlay read *Kimball (Class 1, Neuter)*.

"Let's get the full view," she said and pressed a few buttons.

I gasped as a full holographic display surrounded us, as if we were traveling in a glass sphere. Against the yellow background of the sun, a giant swirl of orange and red swam alongside us. "Kimball" was superimposed in dark green letters.

"Can I talk to it?" I asked.

"Computer, set up an open channel with Kimball," said Juanita.

"Channel open," said the computer.

"Hello, Neuter Kimball," I said. "It's nice to finally meet you."

"It is nice to meet you, too, President Malan, although I hope you will forgive me for not shaking your hand."

I smiled. "Forgiven." I was constantly surprised how much swales seemed to know about our customs and culture, compared with how little we seemed to know of theirs. "And I'm here with Dr. Merced, who is a scientist—"

Juanita laughed. "It's known me a lot longer than it's known you."

"Hello, Juanita," said Neuter Kimball. "I'm glad you are with us."

"Shortly after I began my work here," Juanita said, "it was the first solcetacean I observed personally. It went by the human name Pemberly back then."

"Another swale had transmitted *Pride and Prejudice* to me, and I decided to seek out humans to see what they were like," Neuter Kimball said. "You are a fascinating race."

The thought came to me that maybe there had been some pride and prejudice between me and Juanita—possibly because she was annoyed that a swale she particularly liked had become a Mormon. But maybe we could work out our differences and—I shoved that thought away. "Swales are also fascinating. I hope to understand you as well someday as you understand us."

"Kimball, our shuttle is on a course to take us to Leviathan, so you can just follow us," said Juanita. "But stay at least fifty meters away from us."

"I will keep my distance," said Neuter Kimball.

I must have shown my puzzlement, because Juanita pressed a button to mute the call and said, "Solcetaceans and energy shields don't play well together. A few years back, a Class 1—about Kimball's size—was showing off for a couple of observers, and glanced off a shuttle's energy shield. It tore a big chunk off the solcetacean that took months to heal."

"What about the shuttle? And the people inside?" Sometimes I got the feeling she cared more about swales than about people.

After a moment, Juanita said, "This shuttle was the replacement."

"What happened?"

"The shield did *not* collapse, but part of the solcetacean made it through—probably because the shield works similarly to how solcetaceans hold their bodies together, so the shield sort of merged with the solcetacean's skin. When they recovered the shuttle, they found that the plasma had vaporized part of it, including the crew compartment."

"I guess it's good I didn't hear about that before coming on this trip," I said.

"Don't worry—this shuttle was built with an ablative shell specifically to withstand that sort of accident," she said. "So I'm really more concerned with what would happen to Kimball if it bumped into us."

"Or Leviathan?"

"Leviathan's so big, she might not even notice."

I spent most of the sixteen-hour trip polishing and improving what I would say to Leviathan to convince her to outlaw coerced sexual activity. I had been a debater in high school and college, so I felt I knew how to construct a convincing argument. But eventually I reached the point where I felt I was making my prepared speech worse, not better.

"Approaching destination," the computer said.

I blinked a few times to clear my eyes, straightened up in my seat, and began looking around. Neuter Kimball's orange and red form moved silently beside us. I scanned the holographic image for more orange and red, but didn't see any.

"There," said Juanita, pointing ahead of us. She pressed a button, and dark green letters sprang up: *Leviathan (Class 10, Female)*.

Staring harder, I noticed a bright spot above the letters. As we drew closer, I could distinguish white, violet, and blue swirling together. "She's not orange or red."

"It's all false color, anyway," Juanita said, "but this imaging system uses color to indicate energy levels. Leviathan is actually hotter than the surrounding solar plasma. We think she carries out fusion inside herself."

Leviathan grew in our view, stretching out to fill most of the holographic screen in front of us. The intricate dance of violet and blue amid the white was mesmerizing. Eventually she shone so brightly that I had to squint to reduce the glare. "Aren't we getting too close?" I asked.

"We're still three kilometers away," Juanita said. But she added, "Computer, hold position relative to Leviathan."

"Neuter Kimball, are you ready?" I asked.

"I feel a bit like Abinadi going before King Noah," it said.

I kind of agreed, but I said, "Try to think of it as Ammon going before King Lamoni instead."

"That would be better," said Neuter Kimball. "But I am ready in any case."

Juanita hit the mute. "What was that about?"

"References to the Book of Mormon. Abinadi was burned at the stake after preaching to King Noah, but King Lamoni was converted by Ammon's preaching."

She just shook her head, muttering something about fairy tales, then said, "Computer, set up an open channel to Leviathan."

"Channel open," the computer replied.

"Leviathan, this is President Malan," I said. "I have come with my church member, Neuter Kimball, as you requested. We petition you to tell your people—"

"Silence, human," boomed the voice from the speaker. "It is not yet time for you to speak."

I shut up.

"You will come with me," Leviathan said. Her form brightened. There was a blinding flash, then the holographic system compensated and lowered its brightness.

It took several seconds before the afterimage cleared enough for me to make out shapes. Leviathan still loomed in front, and Neuter Kimball remained beside us.

"Uh-oh," said Juanita.

"What?" I blinked hard, trying to clear my vision. The sun's background seemed blue instead of yellow.

"I don't think we're in Kansas anymore." Juanita tapped at her keyboard. "Leviathan ported us to another star—one with a core much hotter than the Sun. Looks like the shield is holding, for now." She took the Lord's name in vain—or possibly it was a heartfelt prayer for help—and added, "We're stuck here unless she takes us back."

"What about Neuter Kimball?" I asked.

"Only a Class 6 or larger can open a portal on its own."

Green letters began popping up on the screen. *Unknown (Class 10, Male). Unknown (Class 9, Female). Unknown (Class 10, Neuter). Unknown (Class 8, Male).* My eyes adjusted enough that I could see their forms. Dozens of swales surrounded us, all of them tagged Class 8 or higher.

"What have you gotten us into?" Juanita said.

I said a silent prayer and hoped for the best. "It's a great opportunity for both of us. Think of what you're going to discover."

She took a deep breath. "You're right. It's just that I was prepared to study Leviathan, not sixty Class 8 and up. No one's ever seen more than three or four giant ones together."

"Is Leviathan the biggest one here?"

After checking a readout, Juanita said, "Yes, but not by much." She pointed at a swale off to the left. "That male is only about 2% smaller."

"So it looks like she wasn't lying about that."

She nodded her agreement, then said, "Why did you say it's a great opportunity for you?"

I swept my arm across the view. "These must be the most prestigious swales, the leaders. If I can talk to them, convince them to make a law against sexual assault, then the smaller swales will accept it. That has to be why Leviathan brought me and Neuter Kimball here."

"You are wrong," said Neuter Kimball. Juanita must have taken the mute off at some point.

"Why do you say that?"

"This is a deathwatch council," said Neuter Kimball. "They are here to watch me die so they can tell all swales that my death was deserved."

"What?" I said. "What have you done?"

"I'm sure Leviathan will—"

Leviathan's voice cut Neuter Kimball's off. "This little one has abandoned me in favor of a human god. Such error I could forgive. But on its behalf, the tiny human seeks to impose its moral code on us. The human's mind is infinitesimal compared to ours. The human's life is short, the history of its race is short. It is the least of us, and yet it seeks power over us."

"I don't seek power over—" I began.

"Silence!" Leviathan thundered. "The human must see the error of its ways. Kimball!"

"Yes, Leviathan?"

"Your life is forfeit. But I will grant reprieve if you will renounce the human religion and return to me."

I had read of martyrdom in the scriptures and history of the Church all my life. But nowadays it was supposed to be a merely academic exercise, as you examined your faith to see if it was strong enough that you would die for the gospel of Christ. Actual killing over religious belief wasn't supposed to happen any more.

And I found my own faith lacking as I hoped that Neuter Kimball's faith was weak, that it would deny the faith and live rather than be killed.

"I am to be Abinadi after all, President Malan," said Neuter Kimball. "I choose to live as a Mormon, and I will die as one if it be God's will."

"It is *my* will," said Leviathan, "and I am the only god who concerns you."

Tendrils of white plasma reached out toward Neuter Kimball.

"I am the greatest of all," said Leviathan. "Bear witness to my judgment."

I hit the mute button and said, "I've got to stop this. This is my fault."

Juanita's eyes glistened. "I warned you about interfering. But it's too late to do anything now."

"No," I said. "If you're willing to drive this thing into Leviathan's tendrils, it may give Neuter Kimball a chance to escape."

She stared at me. "The shuttle's meant to survive a glancing blow. A direct hit like that—we could die."

The tendrils closed around Neuter Kimball.

"I know, and that's why I'm asking you. I can't force you to risk your life to save someone else's." I hoped I was right about how much she cared about swales—and Neuter Kimball in particular.

After looking out at Neuter Kimball, then back at me, she said, "Computer, manual navigation mode." She grabbed the controls and began steering us toward the white bands connecting Leviathan to Neuter Kimball.

I turned off the mute. "Leviathan, you claim to be the greatest. In size, you probably are."

White filled the view ahead.

"But not in love," I said, speaking quickly as I didn't know how much time I had left. "Jesus said, 'Greater love hath no man than this: that he lay down his life for his friends.' He was willing to die for the least of us, while you are willing to kill the leas—"

A flash of bright light and searing heat cut me off. I felt a sudden jolt. Then blackness.

And nausea. After a few moments, I realized nausea probably meant I was still alive. "Juanita?"

"I'm here," she said.

The darkness was complete. And I was weightless. Maybe I was dead—although this wasn't how I'd pictured the afterlife.

"What happened?" I asked.

"I'll tell you what didn't happen: the energy shield didn't fail. The ablative shell didn't fail. We didn't die."

"So what did happen?"

Juanita let out a long, slow breath. "Best guess: electromagnetic pulse wiped out all our electronics. The engine's dead, artificial gravity's gone, life support's gone, comm system's gone, everything's gone."

"Any chance—"

"No," she said.

"You didn't even let me finish—"

"No chance of anything. It's not fixable, and even if it was, I haven't a clue how to fix any of those things even if it weren't totally dark in here. Do you?"

"No."

"And no help is coming from Sol Central because not only do they not know we're in trouble, but also we're in another star that could be halfway across the galaxy. When the air in here runs out, we die. It's that simple."

"Oh." I realized she was right. "Do you think maybe we succeeded in freeing Neuter Kimball?"

"Maybe. But it didn't exactly look like Kimball was trying all that hard to escape."

"Well," I said, "maybe it was thinking about how Abinadi's martyrdom led one of the evil king's priests to repent and become a great prophet. Perhaps Neuter Kimball believed something similar would happen to one of the great swales who——"

"Whatever Neuter Kimball believed," she said, her voice acidic, "it was because you and your church filled its mind with fairy tales of martyrs."

I bit back an angry reply. Part of me felt she was right. At the end, Neuter Kimball had seemed to embrace the role of martyr. Would it have done so if not for the stories about martyrs in the scriptures?

And I had been willing enough to risk my life, but now that I was going to die, I found myself afraid.

Juanita didn't seem to need a reply from me. "And what's the point of martyrs anyway? A truly powerful god could save his followers rather than let them die. Where's God now that you really need him? What good is any of this?"

"Look, I'm sorry," I said. "If it weren't for me, you'd be safe at home, and Neuter Kimball would be alive. I've made a mess of things."

"Yes."

Hours passed—floating in darkness, it was hard to tell how many. I spent it in introspection and prayer, detailing all my faults that had led me here. Biggest of all was pride: the idea that I, Harry Malan, would—through sheer force of will and a good speech—change a culture that had existed for billions of years. I thought back to what I had been told while serving as a nineteen-year-old missionary on Mars: *you* don't convert people; the Spirit of the Lord does that, and even then only if they are willing to be converted.

Juanita spoke. "You were just trying to do what you thought was right. And you were trying to protect the rights of smaller swales. So I forgive you."

"Thank you," I said.

The shuttle jolted.

"What was that?" I asked. My body sank down into my seat.

"It sounded——"

An ear-splitting squeal from the right side of the shuttle drowned out the rest of her reply. I twisted my head around and saw sparks flying from the wall.

Then a chunk of the hull fell away and light streamed in, temporarily blinding me.

"They're still alive," said a man. "Tell Kimball they're still alive."

*   *   *

All we got from the paramedics was that a large swale had dropped off our shuttle and Neuter Kimball just outside Sol Central Station's energy shield. Neuter Kimball had called the station, and the shuttle had been towed into a dock, where they cut through the hull to rescue us.

It wasn't until Juanita and I were sitting in a hospital room, where an autodoc gave us injections to treat our radiation burns, that we were able to talk to Neuter Kimball.

"It was Leviathan who brought us back here," it said.

I was stunned. "But why? And why didn't she kill you?"

"When she saw that you were willing to die to save me, though I am not even of your own species, she was curious. She asked me why you would do such a thing, so I transmitted the Bible and the Book of Mormon to her. Then she brought us here in case you were still alive."

"And you're not hurt from what she did to you?" I asked.

"I will recover," said Neuter Kimball. "Before she left, Leviathan declared that from this time forward, Mormon swales are not to be forced into sexual activity."

"That's great news." I had won. No—I corrected myself—the victory was not mine. *I thank thee, Lord*, I prayed silently.

"Leviathan also had a personal message for you, President Malan. She said to remind you of what King Agrippa said to Paul."

I nodded. "I understand. Thanks for passing that along."

After the call was over, Juanita said, "What was that message about? Another Book of Mormon story?"

"No, it's from the Bible. Saint Paul preached before King Agrippa, and the king's response was, 'Almost thou persuadest me to be a Christian.' So, no, Leviathan hasn't become Mormon. But God softened her heart so she didn't kill Neuter Kimball. Or us, for that matter. Back on the shuttle, you were certain we were going to die. You asked where God was when I really needed him. Well, God came through."

Juanita puffed out an exasperated breath. "Typical."

"What do you mean by that?" I asked as the autodoc signaled that my treatment was complete.

"In one story, the preacher converts the king. In another, the king kills the preacher. And in a third, neither happens. That's no evidence that God comes through." She pointed at me. "As I see it, *you* came through. By mentioning that 'greater love' thing, you hit Leviathan where it counted: her pride at being the greatest."

I shook my head. "I'm not taking credit for this."

After we walked out of the hospital, she gave me a tight hug that reminded me how much I was attracted to her. But I knew it would never work out between us—our worldviews were just too different.

So I was still a single Mormon man with no dating prospects within ninety million miles.

And no, an attractive single Mormon woman did not arrive on the next solar shuttle. What would be the point of life if God solved all my problems?

> *O Lord, how manifold are thy works! in wisdom hast thou made them all: the earth is full of thy riches. So is this great and wide sea, wherein are things creeping innumerable, both small and great beasts. There go the ships: there is that leviathan, whom thou hast made to play therein.*

—Psalm 104:24–26

ABOUT THE AUTHOR

A Nebula Award winner, Hugo Award nominee, and winner in the Writers of the Future Contest, Eric James Stone has had stories published in *Year's Best SF 15*, *Analog*, *Nature*, and Kevin J. Anderson's *Blood Lite* anthologies of humorous horror, among other venues. Eric is also an assistant editor for *Intergalactic Medicine Show*.

In 2011, Paper Golem Press published *Rejiggering the Thingamajig and Other Stories*, a collection containing most of Eric's stories from 2005 to 2010.

Orson Scott Card's Literary Boot Camp and the Odyssey Writing Workshop greatly influenced Eric's writing.

Eric lives in Utah. His website is http://www.ericjamesstone .com.

The Andre Norton Award for outstanding young adult science fiction or fantasy book was established by SFWA in 2006. The award is named in honor of the late Andre Norton, an SFWA Grand Master and author of more than one hundred novels, many of them for young adult readers. Norton's work has influenced generations of young people, creating new fans of the fantasy and science fiction genres and setting a standard for excellence in fantasy writing.

This year's winner is *I Shall Wear Midnight*, by Terry Pratchett.

EXCERPT FROM
I SHALL WEAR MIDNIGHT
Terry Pratchett

CHAPTER ONE: A FINE BIG WEE LADDIE

Why was it, Tiffany Aching wondered, that people liked noise so much? Why was noise so important?

Something quite close sounded like a cow giving birth. It turned out to be an old hurdy-gurdy organ, hand cranked by a raggedy man in a battered top hat. She sidled away as politely as she could, but as noise went, it was sticky; you got the feeling that if you let it, it would try to follow you home.

But that was only one sound in the great cauldron of noise around her, all of it made by people and all of it made by people trying to make noise louder than the other people making noise: Arguing at the makeshift stalls, bobbing for apples or frogs,* cheering the prizefighters and a spangled lady on the high wire, selling cotton candy at the tops of their voices, and, not to put too fine a point on it, boozing quite considerably.

---

*This was done blindfolded.

The air above the green downland was thick with noise. It was as if the populations of two or three towns had all come up to the top of the hills. And so here, where all you generally heard was the occasional scream of a buzzard, you heard the permanent scream of, well, everyone. It was called having fun. The only people not making any noise were the thieves and pickpockets, who went about their business with commendable silence, and they didn't come near Tiffany; who would pick a witch's pocket? You would be lucky to get all your fingers back. At least, that was what they feared, and a sensible witch would encourage them in this fear.

When you were a witch, you were all witches, thought Tiffany Aching as she walked through the crowds, pulling her broomstick after her on the end of a length of string. It floated a few feet above the ground. She was getting a bit bothered about that. It seemed to work quite well, but nevertheless, since all around the fair were small children dragging balloons, *also* on the ends of pieces of string, she couldn't help thinking that it made her look more than a little bit silly, and something that made one witch look silly made *all* witches look silly.

On the other hand, if you tied it to a hedge somewhere, there was bound to be some kid who would untie the string and get on the stick for a dare, in which case most likely he would go straight up all the way to the top of the atmosphere where the air froze, and while she could in theory call the stick back, mothers got very touchy about having to thaw out their children on a bright late-summer day. That would not look good. People would talk. People always talked about witches.

She resigned herself to dragging it again. With luck, people would think she was joining in with the spirit of the thing in a humorous way.

There was a lot of etiquette involved, even at something so deceptively cheerful as a fair. She was the witch; who knows what would happen if she forgot someone's name or, worse still, got it wrong? What would happen if she forgot all the little feuds and factions, the people who weren't talking to their neighbors and so on and so on and a lot more so and even further on? Tiffany had no understanding at all of the word "minefield," but if she had, it would have seemed kind of familiar.

She was the witch. For all the villages along the Chalk, she was the witch. Not just for her own village anymore, but for all the other ones as far away as

Ham-on-Rye, which was a pretty good day's walk from here. The area that a witch thought of as her own, and for whose people she did what was needful, was called a steading, and as steadings went, this one was pretty good. Not many witches got a whole geological outcrop to themselves, even if this one was mostly covered in grass, and the grass was mostly covered in sheep. And today the sheep on the downs were left by themselves to do whatever it was that they did when they were by themselves, which would presumably be pretty much the same as they did if you were watching them. And the sheep, usually fussed and herded and generally watched over, were now of no interest whatsoever, because right here the most wonderful attraction in the world was taking place.

Admittedly, the scouring fair was only one of the world's most wonderful attractions if you didn't usually ever travel more than about four miles from home. If you lived around the Chalk you were bound to meet everyone that you knew* at the fair. It was quite often where you met the person you were likely to marry. The girls certainly all wore their best dresses, while the boys wore expressions of hopefulness and their hair smoothed down with cheap hair pomade or, more usually, spit. Those who had opted for spit generally came off better, since the cheap pomade was very cheap indeed and would often melt and run in the hot weather, causing the young men not to be of interest to the young women, as they had fervently hoped, but to the flies, who would make their lunch off the boys' scalps.

However, since the event could hardly be called "the fair where you went in the hope of getting a kiss and, if your luck held, the promise of another one," the fair was called the scouring.

The scouring was held over three days at the end of summer. For most people on the Chalk, it was their holiday. This was the third day, and it was said that if you hadn't had a kiss by now, you might as well go home. Tiffany hadn't had a kiss, but after all, she was *the witch*. Who knew what they might get turned into?

If the late-summer weather was clement, it wasn't unusual for some people to sleep out under the stars, and under the bushes as well. And that was why, if you wanted to take a stroll at night, it paid to be careful, so as not to trip over someone's feet. Not to put too fine a point on it, there was a certain amount of

---

*Speaking as a witch, she knew them very well.

what Nanny Ogg—a witch who had been married to three husbands—called "making your own entertainment." It was a shame that Nanny lived right up in the mountains, because she would have loved the scouring and Tiffany would have loved to see her face when she saw the giant.*

He—and he was quite definitely a he, there was no possible doubt about that—had been carved out of the turf thousands of years before. A white outline against the green, he belonged to the days when people had to think about survival and fertility in a dangerous world.

Oh, and he had also been carved, or so it would appear, before anyone had invented trousers. In fact, to say that he had no trousers on just didn't do the job. His lack of trousers filled the world. You simply could not stroll down the little road that passed along the bottom of the hills without noticing that there was an enormous, as it were, lack of something—e.g., trousers—and what was there instead. It was definitely a figure of a man without trousers, and certainly not a woman.

Everyone who came to the scouring was expected to bring a small shovel, or even a knife, and work their way down the steep slope to grub up all the weeds that had grown there over the previous year, making the chalk underneath glow with freshness and the giant stand out boldly, as if he didn't already.

There was always a lot of giggling when the girls worked on the giant.

And the reason for the giggling, and the circumstances of the giggling, couldn't help but put Tiffany in mind of Nanny Ogg, who you normally saw somewhere behind Granny Weatherwax with a big grin on her face. She was generally thought of as a jolly old soul, but there was a lot more to the old woman. She had never been Tiffany's teacher *officially*, but Tiffany couldn't help learning things from Nanny Ogg. She smiled to herself when she thought that. Nanny knew all the old, dark stuff—old magic, magic that didn't need witches, magic that was built into people and the landscape. It concerned things like death, and marriage, and betrothals. And promises that were promises even if there was no one to hear them. And all those things that make people touch wood and never, ever walk under a black cat.

---

*Later on, Tiffany realized that all the witches had probably flown across the giant, especially since you could hardly miss him if you were flying from the mountains to the big city. He kind of stood out, in any case. But in Nanny Ogg's case, she would probably turn round to look at him again.

You didn't need to be a witch to understand it. The world around you became more—well, more real and fluid, at those special times. Nanny Ogg called it "numinous"—an uncharacteristically solemn word from a woman who was much more likely to be saying, "I would like a brandy, thank you very much, and could you make it a double while you are about it." And she had told Tiffany about the old days, when it seemed that witches had a bit more fun. The things that you did around the changing of the seasons, for example; all the customs that were now dead except in folk memory, which, Nanny Ogg said, is deep and dark and breathing and never fades. Little rituals.

Tiffany especially liked the one about fire. Tiffany liked fire. It was her favorite element. It was considered so potent, and so scary to the powers of darkness, that people would even get married by jumping over a fire together.* Apparently it helped if you said a little chant, according to Nanny Ogg, who lost no time in telling Tiffany the words, which immediately stuck in Tiffany's mind; a lot of what Nanny Ogg told you tended to be sticky.

But those were times gone by. Everybody was more respectable now, apart from Nanny Ogg and the giant.

There were other carvings on the chalk lands, too. One of them was a white horse that Tiffany thought had once broken its way out of the ground and galloped to her rescue. Now she wondered what would happen if the giant did the same thing, because it would be very hard to find a pair of pants sixty feet long in a hurry. And on the whole, you'd *want* to hurry.

She'd only ever giggled about the giant once, and that had been a very long time ago. There were really only four types of people in the world: men and women and wizards and witches. Wizards mostly lived in universities down in the big cities and weren't allowed to get married, although the reason why not totally escaped Tiffany. Anyway, you hardly ever saw them around here.

Witches were definitely women, but most of the older ones Tiffany knew hadn't gotten married either, largely because Nanny Ogg had already used up all the eligible husbands, but also probably because they didn't have time. Of

---

*Obviously, Tiffany thought, when jumping over a fire together, one ought to be concerned about wearing protective clothing and having people with a bucket of water on hand, just in case. Witches may be a lot of things, but first and foremost, they are practical.

course, every now and then, a witch might marry a grand husband, like Magrat Garlick of Lancre had done, although by all accounts she only did herbs these days. But the only young witch Tiffany knew who had even had time for courting was her best friend up in the mountains: Petulia, a witch who was now specializing in pig magic and was soon going to marry a nice young man who was shortly going to inherit his father's pig farm,* which meant he was practically an aristocrat.

But witches were not only very busy, they were also *apart*; Tiffany had learned that early on. You were among people, but not the *same* as them. There was always a kind of distance or separation. You didn't have to work at it—it happened anyway. Girls she had known when they were all so young they used to run about and play with only their undershirts on would make a tiny little curtsy to her when she passed them in the lane, and even elderly men would touch their forelock, or probably what they thought was their forelock, as she passed.

This wasn't just because of respect, but because of a kind of fear as well. Witches had secrets; they were there to help when babies were being born. When you got married, it was a good idea to have a witch standing by (even if you weren't sure if it was for good luck or to prevent bad luck), and when you died there would be a witch there too, to show you the way. Witches had secrets they never told . . . well, not to people who weren't witches. Among themselves, when they could get together on some hillside for a drink or two (or in the case of Mrs. Ogg, a drink or nine), they gossiped like geese.

But never about the real secrets, the ones you never told, about things done and heard and seen. So many secrets that you were afraid they might leak. Seeing a giant without his trousers was hardly worth commenting on compared to some of the things that a witch might see.

---

*Possibly Petulia's romantic ambitions had been helped by the mysterious way the young man's pigs were forever getting sick and requiring treatment for the scours, the blind heaves, brass neck, floating teeth, scribbling eyeball, grunge, the smarts, the twisting screws, swiveling, and gone knees. This was a terrible misfortune, since more than half of those ailments are normally never found in pigs, and one of them is a disease known only in freshwater fish. But the neighbors were impressed at the amount of work Petulia put in to relieve their stress. Her broomstick was coming and going at all hours of the day and night. Being a witch, after all, was about dedication.

No, Tiffany did not envy Petulia her romance, which surely must have taken place in big boots, unflattering rubber aprons, and the rain, not to mention an awful lot of *oink*.

She did, however, envy her for being so *sensible*. Petulia had it all worked out. She knew what she wanted her future to be, and had rolled up her sleeves and made it happen, up to her knees in *oink* if necessary.

Every family, even up in the mountains, kept at least one pig to act as a garbage can in the summer and as pork, bacon, ham, and sausages during the rest of the year. The pig was *important*; you might dose Granny with turpentine when she was poorly, but when the pig was ill, you sent immediately for a pig witch, and paid her too, and paid her well, generally in sausages.

On top of everything else, Petulia was a specialist pig borer, and indeed she was this year's champion in the noble art of boring. Tiffany thought you couldn't put it better; her friend could sit down with a pig and talk to it gently and calmly about extremely boring things until some strange pig mechanism took over, whereupon it would give a happy little yawn and fall over, no longer a living pig and ready to become a very important contribution to the family's diet for the following year. This might not appear the best of outcomes for the pig, but given the messy and above all noisy way pigs died *before* the invention of pig boring, it was definitely, in the great scheme of things, a much better deal all round.

Alone in the crowd, Tiffany sighed. It was hard, when you wore the black, pointy hat. Because, like it or not, the witch *was* the pointy hat, and the pointy hat was the witch. It made people *careful* about you. They would be respectful, oh, yes, and often a little bit nervous, as if they expected you to look inside their heads, which as a matter of fact you could probably do, using the good old witch's standbys of First Sight and Second Thoughts.* But these weren't really magic. Anyone could learn them if they had a lick of sense, but sometimes even a lick is hard to find. People are often so busy living that they never stopped to wonder *why*. Witches did, and that meant them being

---

*First Sight means that you can see what *really* is there, and Second Thoughts mean thinking about what you are thinking. And in Tiffany's case, there were sometimes Third Thoughts and Fourth Thoughts, although these were quite difficult to manage and sometimes led her to walk into doors.

needed: Oh, yes, needed—needed practically all the time, but not, in a very polite and definitely unspoken way, not *exactly* wanted.

This wasn't the mountains, where people were very used to witches; people on the Chalk could be friendly, but they weren't friends, not *actual* friends. The witch was different. The witch knew things that you did not. The witch was another kind of person. The witch was someone that perhaps you should not anger. The witch was not like other people.

Tiffany Aching was the witch, and she had made herself the witch because they needed one. Everybody needs a witch, but sometimes they just don't know it.

And it was working. The storybook pictures of the drooling hag were being wiped away, every time Tiffany helped a young mother with her first baby, or smoothed an old man's path to his grave. Nevertheless, old stories, old rumors, and old picture books still seemed to have their own hold on the memory of the world.

What made it more difficult was that there was no tradition of witches on the Chalk—none would ever have settled there when Granny Aching had been alive. Granny Aching, as everybody knew, was a wise woman, and wise enough not to be a witch. Nothing ever happened on the Chalk that Granny Aching disapproved of, at least not for more than about ten minutes.

So Tiffany was a witch alone.

And not only was there no longer any support from the mountain witches like Nanny Ogg, Granny Weatherwax, and Miss Level, but the people of the Chalk weren't very familiar with witches. Other witches would probably come and help if she asked, *of course*, but although they wouldn't say so, this might mean that you couldn't cope with responsibility, weren't up to the task, weren't sure, *weren't good enough*.

"Excuse me, miss?" There was a nervous giggle. Tiffany looked round, and there were two little girls in their best new frocks and straw hats. They were watching her eagerly, with perhaps just a hint of mischief in their eyes. She thought quickly and smiled at them.

"Oh, yes, Becky Pardon and Nancy Upright, yes? What can I do for the two of you?"

Becky Pardon shyly produced a small bouquet from behind her back and held it out. Tiffany recognized it, of course. She had made them herself for the older girls when she was younger, simply because it was what you did, it was part of the scouring: a little bunch of wildflowers picked from the down-land, tied in a bunch with—and this was the important bit, the magic bit—some of the grass pulled up as the fresh chalk was exposed.

"If you put this under your pillow tonight, you will dream of your beau," said Becky, her face quite serious now.

Tiffany took the slightly wilting bunch of flowers with care. "Let me see . . ." she said. "We have here sweet mumbles, ladies' pillows, seven-leaf clover—very lucky—a sprig of old man's trousers, jack-in-the-wall, oh—love-lies-bleeding, and . . ." She stared at the little white-and-red flowers.

The girls said, "Are you all right, miss?"

"Forget-me-lots!"* said Tiffany, more sharply than she had intended. But the girls hadn't noticed, so she continued to say, brightly, "Quite unusual to see it here. It must be a garden escapee. And, as I'm sure you both know, you have bound them all together with strips of candle rush, which once upon a time people used to make into rush lights. What a lovely surprise. Thank you both very much. I hope you have a lovely time at the fair. . . ."

Becky raised her hand. "Excuse me, miss?"

"Was there something else, Becky?"

Becky went pink, and had a hurried conversation with her friend. She turned back to Tiffany, looking slightly more pink but nevertheless deter-mined to see things through.

"You can't get into trouble for asking a question, can you, miss? I mean, just asking a question?"

It's going to be "How can I be a witch when I'm grown up?" Tiffany thought, because it generally was. The young girls saw her on her broomstick and thought that was what being a witch was. Out loud she said, "Not from me, at least. Do ask your question."

Becky Pardon looked down at her boots. "Do you have any passionate parts, miss?"

Another talent needful in a witch is the ability not to let your face show what you're thinking, and especially not allowing it, no matter what, to go

---

*The forget-me-lots is a pretty red-and-white flower usually given by young ladies to signal to their young men that they never want to see them again ever, or at least until they've learned to wash properly and gotten a job.

as stiff as a board. Tiffany managed to say, without a single wobble in her voice and no trace of an embarrassed smirk, "That is a very interesting question, Becky. Can I ask you why you want to know?"

The girl looked a lot happier now that the question was, as it were, out in the public domain.

"Well, miss, I asked my granny if I could be a witch when I was older, and she said I shouldn't want to, because witches have no passionate parts, miss."

Tiffany thought quickly in the face of the two solemn owlish stares. These are farm girls, she thought, so they had certainly seen a cat have kittens and a dog have puppies. They'd have seen the birth of lambs, and probably a cow have a calf, which is always a noisy affair that you can hardly miss. They know what they are asking me about.

At this point Nancy chimed in with "Only, if that is so, miss, we would quite like to have the flowers back, now that we've shown them to you, because perhaps it might be a bit of a waste, meaning no offense." She stepped back quickly.

Tiffany was surprised at her own laughter. It had been a long time since she had laughed. Heads turned to see what the joke was, and she managed to grab both the girls before they fled, and spun them round.

"Well done, the pair of you," she said. "I like to see some sensible thinking every now and again. Never hesitate to ask a question. And the answer to your question is that witches are the same as everybody else when it comes to passionate parts, but often they are so busy rushing around that they never have time to think about them."

The girls looked relieved that their work had not been entirely in vain, and Tiffany was ready for the next question, which came from Becky again. "So do you have a beau, miss?"

"Not right at the moment," Tiffany said briskly, clamping down on her expression lest it give anything away. She held up the little bouquet. "But who knows—if you've made this properly, then I'll get another one, and in that case you will be better witches than me, that is for certain." They both beamed at this dreadful piece of outright fluff, and it stopped the questions.

"And now," said Tiffany, "the cheese rolling will be starting at any minute. I'm sure you won't want to miss that."

"No, miss," they said in unison. Just before they left, full of relief and self-importance, Becky patted Tiffany on her hand. "Beaus can be very difficult, miss," she said with the assurance of, to Tiffany's certain knowledge, eight years in the world.

"Thank you," said Tiffany. "I shall definitely bear that in mind."

When it came to the entertainments offered at the fair, such as people making faces through a horse collar or fighting with pillows on the greasy pole or even the bobbing for frogs, well, Tiffany could take them or leave them alone, and in fact much preferred to leave them alone. But she always liked to see a good cheese roll—that is to say, a good cheese roll all the way down a slope of the hill, although not across the giant because no one would want to eat the cheese afterward.

They were hard cheeses, sometimes specially made for the cheese-rolling circuit, and the winning maker of the cheese that reached the bottom unscathed won a belt with a silver buckle and the admiration of all.

Tiffany was an expert cheesemaker, but she had never entered. Witches couldn't enter that sort of competition because if you won—and she knew she had made a cheese or two that *could* win—everyone would say that was unfair because you were a witch; well, that's what they would think, but very few would *say* it. And if you didn't win, people would say, "What kind of witch can't make a cheese that could be beat by simple cheeses made by simple folk like we?"

There was a gentle movement of the crowd to the start of the cheese rolling, although the frog-bobbing stall still had a big crowd, it being a very humorous and reliable source of entertainment, especially to those people who weren't actually bobbing. Regrettably, the man who put weasels down his trousers, and apparently had a personal best of nine weasels, hadn't been there this year, and people were wondering if he had lost his touch. But sooner or later everyone would drift over to the start line for the cheese rolling. It was a tradition.

The slope here was very steep indeed, and there was always a certain amount of boisterous rivalry between the cheese owners, which led to pushing and shoving and kicking and bruises; occasionally you got a broken arm or leg. All was going as normal as the waiting men lined up their cheeses, until Tiffany saw, and seemed to be the only one to see, a dangerous cheese roll up all by itself. It was black under the dust, and there was a piece of grubby blue-and-white cloth tied to it.

"Oh, no," she said. "Horace. And where you are, trouble can't be far behind." She spun around, carefully searching for signs of what should not be there. "Now you just listen to me," she said under her breath. "I know at least one of you must be somewhere near. This isn't for you; it's just about people. Understand?"

But it was too late. The Master of the Revels, in his big floppy hat with lace around the brim, blew his whistle and the cheese rolling, as he put it, *commenced*—which is a far grander word than "started." And a man with lace around his hat was never going to use a short word where a long word would do.

Tiffany hardly dared to look. The runners didn't so much run as roll and skid behind their cheeses. But she could hear the cries that went up when the black cheese not only shot into the lead but occasionally turned round and went back uphill again in order to bang into one of the ordinary innocent cheeses. She could just hear a faint grumbling noise coming from it as it almost shot to the top of the hill.

Cheese runners shouted at it, tried to grab at it, and flailed at it with sticks, but the piratical cheese scythed onward, reaching the bottom again just ahead of the terrible carnage of men and cheeses as they piled up. Then it rolled back up to the top and sat there demurely while still gently vibrating.

At the bottom of the slope, fights were breaking out among the cheese jockeys who were still capable of punching somebody, and since everyone was now watching that, Tiffany took the opportunity to snatch up Horace and shove him into her bag. After all, he was hers. Well, that was to say, she had made him, although something odd must've gotten into the mix since Horace was the only cheese that would eat mice and, if you didn't nail him down, other cheeses as well. No wonder he got on so well with the Nac Mac Feegles,* who had made him an honorary member of the clan. He was their kind of cheese.

---

*If you do not yet know who the Nac Mac Feegles are: 1) Be grateful for your uneventful life; and 2) Be prepared to beat a retreat if you hear anyone about as high as your ankle shout "Crivens!" They are, strictly speaking, one of the faerie folk, but it is probably not a good idea to tell them this if you are looking forward to a future in which you still have your teeth.

Surreptitiously, hoping that no one would notice, Tiffany held the bag up to her mouth and said, "Is this any way to behave? Aren't you ashamed?" The bag wobbled a little bit, but she knew that the word "shame" was not in Horace's vocabulary, and neither was anything else. She lowered the bag and moved a little way from the crowd and said, "I know you are here, Rob Anybody."

There he was, sitting on her shoulder. She could smell him. Despite the fact that they generally had little to do with bathing, except when it rained, the Nac Mac Feegles always smelled something like slightly drunk potatoes. "The kelda wanted me tae find out how ye were biding," said the Feegle chieftain. "You havena bin tae the mound to see her these past two weeks," he went on, "and I think she is afeared that a harm may come tae ye, ye are working sae hard an' all."

Tiffany groaned, but only to herself. She said, "That is very kind of her. There is always so much to do; surely the kelda knows this. It doesn't matter what I do, there is always more to be done. There is no end to the wanting. But there is nothing to worry about. I am doing fine. And please don't take Horace out again in public—you know he gets excited."

"Well, in point of fact, it says up on that banner over there that this is for the folk of these hills, and we is more than folk. We is *folklore*! Ye canna argue with the lore! Besides, I wanted tae come and pay my ain respects to the big yin without his breeks. He is a fine big wee laddie and nae mistake." Rob paused, and then said quietly, "So I can tell her that ye are quite well in yourself, aye?" There was a certain nervousness to him, as if he would have liked to say more but knew it wouldn't be welcome.

"Rob Anybody, I would be very grateful if you would do just that," said Tiffany, "because I have a lot of people to bandage, if I'm any judge."

Rob Anybody, suddenly looking like a man on a thankless errand, frantically said the words he had been told by his wife to say: "The kelda says there's plenty more fish in the sea, miss!"

And Tiffany stood perfectly still for a moment and then, without looking at Rob, said quietly, "Do thank the kelda for her angling information. I have to get on, if you don't mind, Rob. *Do* thank the kelda."

Most of the crowd was reaching the bottom of the slope by now, to gawk or rescue or possibly attempt some amateur first aid on the groaning cheese runners. For the onlookers, of course, it was just another show; you didn't often see a satisfying pileup of men and cheeses, and—who knew?—there might be some really interesting casualties.

Tiffany, glad of something to do, did not have to push her way through; the pointy black hat could create a path through a crowd faster than a holy man through a shallow sea. She waved the happy crowd away, with one or two forceful shoves for those of slow uptake. As a matter of fact, as it turned out, the butcher's bill wasn't too high this year, with one broken arm, one broken wrist, one broken leg, and an enormous number of bruises, cuts, and rashes being caused by people sliding most of the way down—grass isn't always your friend. There were several young men clearly in distress as a result, but they were absolutely definite that they were not going to discuss their injuries with a lady, thank you all the same. So she told them to put a cold compress on the afflicted area, wherever it was, when they got home, and watched them walk unsteadily away.

Well, she'd done all right, hadn't she? She had used her skills in front of the rubbernecking crowd and, according to what she overheard from the old men and women, had performed well enough. Perhaps she imagined that one or two people were embarrassed when an old man with a beard to his waist said with a grin, "A girl who can set bones would have no trouble finding a husband," but that passed, and with nothing else to do, people started the long climb back up the hill . . . and then the coach came past, and then, which was worse, it stopped.

It had the coat of arms of the Keepsake family on the side. A young man stepped out. Quite handsome in his way, but also so stiff in his way that you could have ironed sheets on him. This was Roland. He hadn't gone more than a step when a rather unpleasant voice from inside the coach told him that he should have waited for the footman to open the door for him and to hurry up, because they didn't have all day.

The young man hurried toward the crowd and there was a general smartening-up because, after all, here came the son of the Baron, who owned most of the Chalk and nearly all their houses, and although he was a decent old boy, as old boys go, a little politeness to his family was definitely a wise move. . . .

"What happened here? Is everybody all right?" he said.

Life on the Chalk was generally pleasant and the relationship between master and man was one of mutual respect; but nevertheless, the farmworkers had inherited the idea that it could be unwise to have too many words with powerful people, in case any of those words turned out to be a word out of place. After all, there was still a torture chamber in the castle, and even though it hadn't been used for hundreds of years . . . well, best to be on the safe side, best to stand back and let the witch do the talking. If she got into trouble, she could fly away.

"One of those accidents that was bound to happen, I'm afraid," said Tiffany, well aware that she was the only woman present who had not curtsied. "Some broken bones that will mend and a few red faces. All sorted out, thank you."

"So I see, so I see! Very well done, young lady!"

For a moment Tiffany thought she could taste her teeth. *Young lady*, from . . . him? It was almost, but not entirely, insulting. But no one else seemed to have noticed. It was, after all, the kind of language that nobs use when they are trying to be friendly and jolly. He's trying to talk to them like his father does, she thought, but his father did it by instinct and was good at it. You can't talk to people as though they are a public meeting. She said, "Thank you kindly, sir."

Well, not too bad so far, except that now the coach door opened again and one dainty white foot touched the flint. It was her: Angelica or Letitia or something else out of the garden; in fact Tiffany knew full well it was Letitia, but surely she could be excused just a tiny touch of nasty in the privacy of her own head? Letitia! What a name. Halfway between a salad and a sneeze. Besides, who was Letitia to keep Roland away from the scouring fair? He should have been there! His father would have been there if the old man possibly could! And look! Tiny white shoes! How long would they last on somebody who had to do a jot of work? She stopped herself there: *A bit* of nasty was enough.

Letitia looked at Tiffany and the crowd with something like fear and said, "Do let's get going, can we please? Mother is getting vexed."

And so the coach left and the hurdy-gurdy man thankfully left and the sun left, and in the warm shadows of the twilight some people stayed. But Tiffany flew home alone, up high where only bats and owls could see her face.

ABOUT THE AUTHOR

Knighted in 2009, Sir Terence "Terry" Pratchett is best known for his *Discworld* novel series. He has more than 65 million books in print. *I Shall Wear Midnight* was published by Gollancz, Harper.

INTRODUCTION

Here's this year's Rhysling Award winner in the short poem category.

TO THEIA

Ann K. Schwader

> *Theia, a hypothetical protoplanet, is central to the*
> *Great Impact Theory of the Moon's origin.*

That you were our meant earth, & not this other
flawed marble we crawl over, cling to, dream
in fits of leaving—surely this suspicion
once wove Atlantis through us, carved out Eden
between our ribs.

   That we are shattered creatures,
our sacred texts assure us, but not why
the iron that marks our blood is restless, seeking
some heart beyond our hearts.

   No second impact
remains to reunite our cores: Lagrange
holds only pebbled mercies, shooting stars
not worth the wishing on.

   Come summer midnights
when song dogs serenade your final shard,
we cannot help but raise our faces also
to that remotest of reflected blessings
& howl you, Theia, as the home we lost.

ABOUT THE AUTHOR

Ann K. Schwader's most recent collection of dark SF poems, *Wild Hunt of the Stars* (Sam's Dot Publishing, 2010), was a Bram Stoker Award finalist. A comprehensive collection of her weird verse, *Twisted In Dream* (edited by S. T. Joshi), is forthcoming from Hippocampus Press. Her poems have appeared in *Strange Horizons*, *Star*Line*, *Dreams & Nightmares*, *Weird Tales*, *Dark Wisdom*, *Tales of the Unanticipated*, *Weird Fiction Review*, and elsewhere in the small and pro press. She is an active member of SFWA, HWA, and SFPA. A Wyoming native, Schwader lives and writes in suburban Colorado. Her author's website is http:// home.earthlink .net/~schwader/

AUTHOR'S INTRODUCTION

I would love to say something mysterious about myself, but I'm afraid my life is rather mundane. I live in Bakersfield, California, home of the Fighting Drillers, with my husband (1), pet cats (3), and backyard full of strays (innumerable).

When I started writing "The Lady Who Plucked Red Flowers beneath the Queen's Window," I was wondering whether it would be possible to tell a coherent story from the perspective of a summoned creature. Since the creature would generally only be called in crises, it would be a story that flashed between moments of intense conflict, with much of the plot missing or happening behind the scenes.

At the time, I was also wondering how one might create an anthropologically believable matriarchy. Some sociobiologists claim that the kinds of male and female sex roles we see recurring in various cultures are based on inherent differences in male and female physiology—primarily the vulnerability that comes with being pregnant and nursing small children. That seems like a pretty valid thesis as these things go, so I tried to create a society that would eliminate that effect.

It was interesting writing the perspective of a character like Naeva, who would rather hurt people than admit her black-and-white views are wrong. I tried to find the places where I related with her, too: she's scared; she's manipulated; she's very powerful but often has no control. She's not a good person, but she is a human person, or at least I wanted her to be.

NEBULA AWARD, NOVELLA

THE LADY WHO PLUCKED RED FLOWERS BENEATH THE QUEEN'S WINDOW

Rachel Swirsky

My story should have ended on the day I died. Instead, it began there.

Sun pounded on my back as I rode through the Mountains where the Sun Rests. My horse's hooves beat in syncopation with those of the donkey that trotted in our shadow. The queen's midget Kyan turned his head toward me, sweat dripping down the red-and-blue protections painted across his malformed brow.

"Shouldn't . . . we . . . stop?" he panted.

Sunlight shone red across the craggy limestone cliffs. A bold eastern wind carried the scent of mountain blossoms. I pointed to a place where two large stones leaned across a narrow outcropping.

"There," I said, prodding my horse to go faster before Kyan could answer. He grunted and cursed at his donkey for falling behind.

I hated Kyan, and he hated me. But Queen Rayneh had ordered us to ride reconnaissance together, and we obeyed, out of love for her and for the Land of Flowered Hills.

We dismounted at the place I had indicated. There, between the mountain peaks, we could watch the enemy's forces in the valley below without being observed. The raiders spread out across the meadow below like ants on a rich meal. Their women's camp lay behind the main troops, a small dark blur. Even the smoke rising from their women's fires seemed timid. I scowled.

"Go out between the rocks," I directed Kyan. "Move as close to the edge as you can."

Kyan made a mocking gesture of deference. "As you wish, Great Lady," he sneered, swinging his twisted legs off the donkey. Shamans' bundles of stones and seeds, tied with twine, rattled at his ankles.

I refused to let his pretensions ignite my temper. "Watch the valley," I instructed. "I will take the vision of their camp from your mind and send it to the Queen's scrying pool. Be sure to keep still."

The midget edged toward the rocks, his eyes shifting back and forth as if he expected to encounter raiders up here in the mountains, in the Queen's dominion. I found myself amused and disgusted by how little provocation it took to reveal the midget's true, craven nature. At home in the Queen's castle, he strutted about, pompous and patronizing. He was like many birth-twisted men, arrogant in the limited magic to which his deformities gave him access. Rumors suggested that he imagined himself worthy enough to be in love with the Queen. I wondered what he thought of the men below. Did he day-dream about them conquering the Land? Did he think they'd make him pow-erful, that they'd put weapons in his twisted hands and let him strut among their ranks?

"Is your view clear?" I asked.

"It is."

I closed my eyes and saw, as he saw, the panorama of the valley below. I held his sight in my mind, and turned toward the eastern wind which carries the perfect expression of magic—flight—on its invisible eddies. I envisioned the battlefield unfurling before me like a scroll rolling out across a marble floor. With low, dissonant notes, I showed the image how to transform itself for my purposes. I taught it how to be length and width without depth, and how to be strokes of color and light reflected in water. When it knew these things, I sang the image into the water of the Queen's scrying pool.

Suddenly—too soon—the vision vanished from my inner eye. Something whistled through the air. I turned. Pain struck my chest like thunder.

I cried out. Kyan's bundles of seeds and stones rattled above me. My vision blurred red. Why was the midget near me? He should have been on the outcropping.

"You traitor!" I shouted. "How did the raiders find us?"

I writhed blindly on the ground, struggling to grab Kyan's legs. The midget caught my wrists. Weak with pain, I could not break free.

"Hold still," he said. "You're driving the arrow deeper."

"Let me go, you craven dwarf."

"I'm no traitor. This is woman's magic. Feel the arrow shaft."

Kyan guided my hand upward to touch the arrow buried in my chest. Through the pain, I felt the softness of one of the Queen's roc feathers. It was particularly rare and valuable, the length of my arm.

I let myself fall slack against the rock. "Woman's magic," I echoed, softly. "The Queen is betrayed. The Land is betrayed."

"Someone is betrayed, sure enough," said Kyan, his tone gloating.

"You must return to court and warn the Queen."

Kyan leaned closer to me. His breath blew on my neck, heavy with smoke and spices.

"No, Naeva. You can still help the Queen. She's given me the keystone to a spell—a piece of pure leucite, powerful enough to tug a spirit from its rest. If I blow its power into you, your spirit won't sink into sleep. It will only rest, waiting for her summons."

Blood welled in my mouth. "I won't let you bind me . . ."

His voice came even closer, his lips on my ear. "The Queen needs you, Naeva. Don't you love her?"

Love: the word caught me like a thread on a bramble. Oh, yes. I loved the queen. My will weakened, and I tumbled out of my body. Cold crystal drew me in like a great mouth, inhaling.

I was furious. I wanted to wrap my hands around the first neck I saw and squeeze. But my hands were tiny, half the size of the hands I remembered. My short, fragile fingers shook. Heavy musk seared my nostrils. I felt the heat of scented candles at my feet, heard the snap of flame devouring wick. I rushed forward and was abruptly halted. Red and black knots of string marked boundaries beyond which I could not pass.

"O, Great Lady Naeva," a voice intoned. "We seek your wisdom on behalf of Queen Rayneh and the Land of Flowered hills."

Murmurs rippled through the room. Through my blurred vision, I caught an impression of vaulted ceilings and frescoed walls. I heard people, but I could only make out woman-sized blurs—they could have been beggars, aristocrats, warriors, even males or broods.

I tried to roar. My voice fractured into a strangled sound like trapped wind. An old woman's sound.

"Great Lady Naeva, will you acknowledge me?"

I turned toward the high, mannered voice. A face came into focus, eyes flashing blue beneath a cowl. Dark stripes stretched from lower lip to chin: the tattoos of a death whisperer.

Terror cut into my rage for a single, clear instant. "I'm dead?"

"Let me handle this." Another voice, familiar this time. Calm, authoritative, quiet: the voice of someone who had never needed to shout in order to be heard. I swung my head back and forth trying to glimpse Queen Rayneh.

"Hear me, Lady Who Plucked Red Flowers beneath My Window. It is I, your Queen."

The formality of that voice! She spoke to me with titles instead of names? I blazed with fury.

Her voice dropped a register, tender and cajoling. "Listen to me, Naeva. I asked the death whisperers to chant your spirit up from the dead. You're inhabiting the body of an elder member of their order. Look down. See for yourself."

I looked down and saw embroidered rabbits leaping across the hem of a turquoise robe. Long, bony feet jutted out from beneath the silk. They were swaddled in the coarse wrappings that doctors prescribed for the elderly when it hurt them to stand.

They were not my feet. I had not lived long enough to have feet like that.

"I was shot by an enchanted arrow . . ." I recalled. "The midget said you might need me again . . ."

"And he was right, wasn't he? You've only been dead three years. Already, we need you."

The smugness of that voice. Rayneh's impervious assurance that no matter what happened, be it death or disgrace, her people's hearts would always sing with fealty.

"He enslaved me," I said bitterly. "He preyed upon my love for you."

"Ah, Lady Who Plucked Red Flowers beneath My Window, I always knew you loved me."

Oh yes, I had loved her. When she wanted heirs, it was I who placed my hand on her belly and used my magic to draw out her seedlings; I who nurtured the seedlings' spirits with the fertilizer of her chosen man; I who planted the seedlings in the womb of a fecund brood. Three times, the broods I catalyzed brought forth Rayneh's daughters. I'd not yet chosen to beget my own daughters, but there had always been an understanding between us that Rayneh would be the one to stand with my magic-worker as the seedling was drawn from me, mingled with man, and set into brood.

I was amazed to find that I loved her no longer. I remembered the emotion, but passion had died with my body.

"I want to see you," I said.

Alarmed, the death whisperer turned toward Rayneh's voice. Her nose jutted beak-like past the edge of her cowl. "It's possible for her to see you if you stand where I am," she said. "But if the spell goes wrong, I won't be able to—"

"It's all right, Lakitri. Let her see me."

Rustling, footsteps. Rayneh came into view. My blurred vision showed me frustratingly little except for the moon of her face. Her eyes sparkled black against her smooth, sienna skin. Amber and obsidian gems shone from her forehead, magically embedded in the triangular formation that symbolized the Land of Flowered Hills. I wanted to see her graceful belly, the muscular calves I'd loved to stroke—but below her chin, the world faded to grey.

"What do you want?" I asked. "Are the raiders nipping at your heels again?"

"We pushed the raiders back in the battle that you died to make happen. It was a rout. Thanks to you."

A smile lit on Rayneh's face. It was a smile I remembered. *You have served your Land and your Queen*, it seemed to say. *You may be proud.* I'd slept on Rayneh's leaf-patterned silk and eaten at her morning table too often to be deceived by such shallow manipulations.

Rayneh continued, "A usurper—a woman raised on our own grain and honey—has built an army of automatons to attack us. She's given each one a hummingbird's heart for speed, and a crane's feather for beauty, and a crow's brain for wit. They've marched from the Lake Where Women Wept all the way across the fields to the Valley of Tonha's Memory. They move faster than our most agile warriors. They seduce our farmers out of the fields. We must destroy them."

"A usurper?" I said.

"One who betrays us with our own spells."

The Queen directed me a lingering, narrow-lidded look, challenging me with her unspoken implications.

"The kind of woman who would shoot the Queen's sorceress with a roc feather?" I pressed.

Her glance darted sideways. "Perhaps."

Even with the tantalizing aroma of revenge wafting before me, I considered refusing Rayneh's plea. Why should I forgive her for chaining me to her service? She and her benighted death whisperers might have been able to chant my spirit into wakefulness, but let them try to stir my voice against my will.

But no—even without love drawing me into dark corners, I couldn't renounce Rayneh. I would help her as I always had from the time when we were girls riding together through my grandmother's fields. When she fell from her mount, it was always I who halted my mare, soothed her wounds, and eased her back into the saddle. Even as a child, I knew that she would never do the same for me.

"Give me something to kill," I said.

"What?"

"I want to kill. Give me something. Or should I kill your death whisperers?"

Rayneh turned toward the women. "Bring a sow!" she commanded.

Murmurs echoed through the high-ceilinged chamber, followed by rushing footsteps. Anxious hands entered my range of vision, dragging a fat, black-spotted shape. I looked toward the place where my ears told me the crowd of death whisperers stood, huddled and gossiping. I wasn't sure how vicious I could appear as a dowager with bound feet, but I snarled at them anyway. I was rewarded with the susurration of hems sliding backward over tile.

I approached the sow. My feet collided with the invisible boundaries of the summoning circle. "Move it closer," I ordered.

Hands pushed the sow forward. The creature grunted with surprise and fear. I knelt down and felt its bristly fur and smelled dry mud, but I couldn't see its torpid bulk.

I wrapped my bony hands around the creature's neck and twisted. My spirit's strength overcame the body's weakness. The animal's head snapped free in my hands. Blood engulfed the leaping rabbits on my hem.

I thrust the sow's head at Rayneh. It tumbled out of the summoning circle and thudded across the marble. Rayned doubled over, retching.

The crowd trembled and exclaimed. Over the din, I dictated the means to defeat the constructs. "Blend mustard seed and honey to slow their deceitful tongues. Add brine to ruin their beauty. Mix in crushed poppies to slow their fast-beating hearts. Release the concoction onto a strong wind and let it blow their destruction. Only a grain need touch them. Less than a grain—only a grain need touch a mosquito that lights on a flower they pass on the march. They will fall."

"Regard that! Remember it!" Rayneh shouted to the whisperers. Silk rustled. Rayneh regarded me levelly. "That's all we have to do?"

"Get Lakitri," I replied. "I wish to ask her a question."

A nervous voice spoke outside my field of vision. "I'm here, Great Lady."

"What will happen to this body after my spirit leaves?"

"Jada will die, Great Lady. Your spirit has chased hers away."

I felt the crookedness of Jada's hunched back and the pinch of the strips binding her feet. Such a back, such feet, I would never have. At least someone would die for disturbing my death.

Next I woke, rage simmered where before it had boiled. I stifled a snarl, and relaxed my clenched fists. My vision was clearer: I discerned the outlines of a tent filled with dark shapes that resembled pillows and furs. I discovered my boundaries close by, marked by wooden stakes painted with bands of cinnamon and white.

"Respected Aunt Naeva?"

My vision wavered. A shape: muscular biceps, hard thighs, robes of heir's green. It took me a moment to identify Queen Rayneh's eldest daughter, who I had inspired in her brood. At the time of my death, she'd been a flat-chested flitling, still learning how to ride.

"Tryce?" I asked. A bad thought: "Why are you here? Has the usurper taken the palace? Is the Queen dead?"

Tryce laughed. "You misunderstand, Respected Aunt. I am the usurper."

"You?" I scoffed. "What does a girl want with a woman's throne?"

"I want what is mine." Tryce drew herself up. She had her mother's mouth, stern and imperious. "If you don't believe me, look at the body you're wearing."

I looked down. My hands were the right size, but they were painted in Rayneh's blue and decked with rings of gold and silver. Strips of tanned human flesh adorned my breasts. I raised my fingertips to my collarbone and felt the raised edges of the brand I knew would be there. Scars formed the triangles that represented the Land of Flowered Hills.

"One of your mother's private guard," I murmured. "Which?"

"Okilanu."

I grinned. "I never liked the bitch."

"You know I'm telling the truth. A private guard is too valuable for anyone but a usurper to sacrifice. I'm holding this conference with honor, Respected Aunt. I'm meeting you alone, with only one automaton to guard me. My informants tell me that my mother surrounded herself with sorceresses so that she could coerce you. I hold you in more esteem."

"What do you want?"

"Help winning the throne that should be mine."

"Why should I betray my lover and my Land for a child with pretensions?"

"Because you have no reason to be loyal to my mother. Because I want what's best for this Land, and I know how to achieve it. Because those were my automatons you dismantled, and they were good, beautiful souls despite being creatures of spit and mud. Gudrin is the last of them."

Tryce held out her hand. The hand that accepted drew into my vision: slender with shapely fingers crafted of mud and tangled with sticks and pieces of nest. It was beautiful enough to send feathers of astonishment through my chest.

"Great Lady, you must listen to The Creator of Me and Mine," intoned the creature.

Its voice was a songbird trill. I grimaced in disgust. "You made male automatons?"

"Just one," said Tryce. "It's why he survived your spell."

"Yes," I said, pondering. "It never occurred to me that one would make male creatures."

"Will you listen, Respected Aunt?" asked Tryce.

"You must listen, Great Lady," echoed the automaton. His voice was as melodious as poetry to a depressed heart. The power of crane's feathers and crow's brains is great.

"Very well," I said.

Tryce raised her palms to show she was telling truth. I saw the shadow of her mother's face lurking in her wide-set eyes and broad, round forehead.

"Last autumn, when the wind blew red with fallen leaves, my mother expelled me from the castle. She threw my possessions into the river and had my servants beaten and turned out. She told me that I would have to learn to live like the birds migrating from place to place because she had decreed that no one was to give me a home. She said I was no longer her heir, and she would dress Darnisha or Peni in heir's green. Oh, Respected Aunt! How could either of them take a throne?"

I ignored Tryce's emotional outpouring. It was true that Tryce had always been more responsible than her sisters, but she had been born with an heir's heaviness upon her. I had lived long enough to see fluttering sparrows like Darnisha and Peni become eagles, over time.

"You omit something important," I said. "Why did your mother throw you out, Imprudent Child?"

"Because of this."

The automaton's hand held Tryce steady as she mounted a pile of pillows that raised her torso to my eye level. Her belly loomed large, ripe as a frog's inflated throat.

"You've gotten fat, Tryce."

"No," she said.

I realized: she had not.

"You're pregnant? Hosting a child like some brood? What's wrong with you, girl? I never knew you were a pervert. Worse than a pervert! Even the lowest worm-eater knows to chew mushrooms when she pushes with men."

"I am no pervert! I am a lover of woman. I am natural as breeze! But I say we must not halve our population by splitting our females into women and broods. The raiders nip at our heels. Yes, it's true, they are barbaric and weak—now. But they grow stronger. Their population increases so quickly that already they can match our numbers. When there are three times as many of them as us, or five times, or eight times, they'll flood us like a wave crashing on a naked beach. It's time for women to make children in ourselves as broods do. We need more daughters."

I scoffed. "The raiders keep their women like cows for the same reason we keep cows like cows, to encourage the production of calves. What do you think will happen if our men see great women swelling with young and feeding them from their bodies? They will see us as weak, and they will rebel, and the broods will support them for trinkets and candy."

"Broods will not threaten us," said Tryce. "They do as they are trained. We train them to obey."

Tryce stepped down from the pillows and dismissed the automaton into the shadows. I felt a murmur of sadness as the creature left my sight.

"It is not your place to make policy, Imprudent Child," I said. "You should have kept your belly flat."

"There is no time! Do the raiders wait? Will they chew rinds by the fire while I wait for my mother to die?"

"This is better? To split our land into factions and war against ourselves?"

"I have vowed to save the Land of Flowered Hills," said Tryce, "with my mother or despite her."

Tryce came yet closer to me so that I could see the triple scars where the gems that had once sealed her heirship had been carved out of her cheeks. They left angry, red triangles. Tryce's breath was hot; her eyes like oil, shining.

"Even without my automatons, I have enough resources to overwhelm the palace," Tryce continued, "except for one thing."

I waited.

"I need you to tell me how to unlock the protections you laid on the palace grounds and my mother's chambers."

"We return to the beginning. Why should I help you?"

Tryce closed her eyes and inhaled deeply. There was shyness in her posture now. She would not direct her gaze at mine.

She said, "I was young when you died, still young enough to think that our strength was unassailable. The battles after your death shattered my illusions. We barely won, and we lost many lives. I realized that we needed more power, and I thought that I could give us that power by becoming a sorceress to replace you." She paused. "During my studies, I researched your acts of magic, great and small. Inevitably, I came to the spell you cast before you died, when you sent the raiders' positions into the summoning pool."

It was then that I knew what she would say next. I wish I could say that my heart felt as immobile as a mountain, that I had always known to suspect the love of a Queen. But my heart drummed, and my mouth went dry, and I felt as if I were falling.

"Some of mother's advisers convinced her that you were plotting against her. They had little evidence to support their accusations, but once the idea rooted into mother's mind, she became obsessed. She violated the sanctity of woman's magic by teaching Kyan how to summon a roc feather enchanted to pierce your heart. She ordered him to wait until you had sent her the vision of the battleground, and then to kill you and punish your treachery by binding your soul so that you would always wander and wake."

I wanted to deny it, but what point would there be? Now that Tryce forced me to examine my death with a watcher's eye, I saw the coincidences that proved her truth. How else could I have been shot by an arrow not just shaped by woman's magic, but made from one of the Queen's roc feathers? Why else would a worm like Kyan have happened to have in his possession a piece of leucite more powerful than any I'd seen?

I clenched Okilanu's fists. "I never plotted against Rayneh."

"Of course not. She realized it herself, in time, and executed the women who had whispered against you. But she had your magic, and your restless spirit bound to her, and she believed that was all she needed."

For long moments, my grief battled my anger. When it was done, my resolve was hardened like a spear tempered by fire.

I lifted my palms in the gesture of truth telling. "To remove the protections on the palace grounds, you must lay yourself flat against the soil with your cheek against the dirt, so that it knows you. To it, you must say, 'The Lady Who Plucked Red Flowers beneath the Queen's Window loves the Queen from instant to eternity, from desire to regret.' And then you must kiss the soil as if it is the hem of your lover's robe. Wait until you feel the earth move beneath you and then the protections will be gone."

Tryce inclined her head. "I will do this."

I continued, "When you are done, you must flay off a strip of your skin and grind it into a fine powder. Bury it in an envelope of wind-silk beneath the Queen's window. Bury it quickly. If a single grain escapes, the protections on her chamber will hold."

"I will do this, too," said Tryce. She began to speak more, but I raised one of my ringed, blue fingers to silence her.

"There's another set of protections you don't know about. One cast on your mother. It can only be broken by the fresh life-blood of something you love. Throw the blood onto the Queen while saying, 'The Lady Who Plucked Red Flowers beneath Your Window has betrayed you.'"

"Life-blood? You mean, I need to kill—"

"Perhaps the automaton."

Tryce's expression clouded with distress. "Gudrin is the last one! Maybe the baby. I could conceive again—"

"If you can suggest the baby, you don't love it enough. It must be Gudrin."

Tryce closed her mouth. "Then it will be Gudrin," she agreed, but her eyes would not meet mine.

I folded my arms across Okilanu's flat bosom. "I've given you what you wanted. Now grant me a favor, Imprudent Child Who Would Be Queen. When you kill Rayneh, I want to be there."

Tryce lifted her head like the Queen she wanted to be. "I will summon you when it's time, Respected Aunt." She turned toward Gudrin in the shadows. "Disassemble the binding shapes," she ordered.

For the first time, I beheld Gudrin in his entirety. The creature was tree-tall and stick-slender, and yet he moved with astonishing grace. "Thank you on behalf of the Creator of Me and My Kind," he trilled in his beautiful voice, and I considered how unfortunate it was that the next time I saw him, he would be dead.

I smelled the iron-and-wet tang of blood. My view of the world skewed low, as if I'd been cut off at the knees. Women's bodies slumped across lush carpets. Red ran deep into the silk, bloodying woven leaves and flowers. I'd been in this chamber far too often to mistake it, even dead. It was Rayneh's.

It came to me then: my perspective was not like that of a woman forced to kneel. It was like a child's. Or a dwarf's.

I reached down and felt hairy knees and fringed ankle bracelets. "Ah, Kyan . . ."

"I thought you might like that." Tryce's voice. These were probably her legs before me, wrapped in loose green silk trousers that were tied above the calf with chains of copper beads. "A touch of irony for your pleasure. He bound your soul to restlessness. Now you'll chase his away."

277

I reached into his back-slung sheath and drew out the most functional of his ceremonial blades. It would feel good to flay his treacherous flesh.

"I wouldn't do that," said Tryce. "You'll be the one who feels the pain."

I sheathed the blade. "You took the castle?"

"Effortlessly." She paused. "I lie. Not effortlessly." She unknotted her right trouser leg and rolled up the silk. Blood stained the bandages on a carefully wrapped wound. "Your protections were strong."

"Yes. They were."

She re-tied her trouser leg and continued. "The Lady with Lichen Hair tried to block our way into the chamber." She kicked one of the corpses by my feet. "We killed her."

"Did you."

"Don't you care? She was your friend."

"Did she care when I died?"

Tryce shifted her weight, a kind of lower-body shrug. "I brought you another present." She dropped a severed head onto the floor. It rolled toward me, tongue lolling in its bloody face. It took me a moment to identify the high cheekbones and narrow eyes.

"The death whisperer? Why did you kill Lakitri?"

"You liked the blood of Jada and Okilanu, didn't you?"

"The only blood I care about now is your mother's. Where is she?"

"Bring my mother!" ordered Tryce.

One of Tryce's servants—her hands marked with the green dye of loyalty to the heir—dragged Rayneh into the chamber. The Queen's torn, bloody robe concealed the worst of her wounds, but couldn't hide the black and purple bruises blossoming on her arms and legs. Her eyes found mine, and despite her condition, a trace of her regal smile glossed her lips.

Her voice sounded thin. "That's you? Lady Who Plucked Red Flowers beneath My Window?"

"It's me."

She raised one bloody, shaking hand to the locket around her throat and pried it open. Dried petals scattered onto the carpets, the remnants of the red flowers I'd once gathered for her protection. While the spell lasted, they'd remained whole and fresh. Now they were dry and crumbling like what had passed for love between us.

"If you ever find rest, the world-lizard will crack your soul in its jaws for murdering your Queen," she said.

"I didn't kill you."

"You instigated my death."

"I was only repaying your favor."

The hint of her smile again. She smelled of wood smoke, rich and dark. I wanted to see her more clearly, but my poor vision blurred the red of her wounds into the sienna of her skin until the whole of her looked like raw, churned earth.

"I suppose our souls will freeze together." She paused. "That might be pleasant."

Somewhere in front of us, lost in the shadows, I heard Tryce and her women ransacking the Queen's chamber. Footsteps, sharp voices, cracking wood.

"I used to enjoy cold mornings," Rayneh said. "When we were girls. I liked lying in bed with you and opening the curtains to watch the snow fall."

"And sending servants out into the cold to fetch and carry."

"And then! When my brood let slip it was warmer to lie together naked under the sheets? Do you remember that?" She laughed aloud, and then paused. When she spoke again, her voice was quieter. "It's strange to remember lying together in the cold, and then to look up, and see you in that body. Oh, my beautiful Naeva, twisted into a worm. I deserve what you've done to me. How could I have sent a worm to kill my life's best love?"

She turned her face away, as if she could speak no more. Such a show of intimate, unroyal emotion. I could remember times when she'd been able to manipulate me by trusting me with a wince of pain or a supposedly accidental tear. As I grew more cynical, I realized that her royal pretense wasn't vanishing when she gave me a melancholy, regretful glance. Such things were calculated vulnerabilities, intended to bind me closer to her by suggesting intimacy and trust. She used them with many ladies at court, the ones who loved her.

This was far from the first time she'd tried to bind me to her by displaying weakness, but it was the first time she'd ever done so when I had no love to enthrall me.

Rayneh continued, her voice a whisper. "I regret it, Naeva. When Kyan came back, and I saw your body, cold and lifeless—I understood immediately that I'd been mistaken. I wept for days. I'm weeping still, inside my heart. But listen—" her voice hardened "—we can't let this be about you and me. Our Land is at stake. Do you know what Tryce is going to do? She'll destroy us all. You have to help me stop her—"

"Tryce!" I shouted. "I'm ready to see her bleed."

Footsteps thudded across silk carpets. Tryce drew a bone-handled knife and knelt over her mother like a farmer preparing to slaughter a pig. "Gudrin!" she called. "Throw open the doors. Let everyone see us."

Narrow, muddy legs strode past us. The twigs woven through the automaton's skin had lain fallow when I saw him in the winter. Now they blazed in a glory of emerald leaves and scarlet blossoms.

"You dunce!" I shouted at Tryce. "What have you done? You left him alive."

Tryce's gaze held fast on her mother's throat. "I sacrificed the baby."

Voices and footsteps gathered in the room as Tryce's soldiers escorted Rayneh's courtiers inside.

"You sacrificed the baby," I repeated. "What do you think ruling is? Do you think Queens always get what they want? You can't dictate to magic, Imprudent Child."

"Be silent." Tryce's voice thinned with anger. "I'm grateful for your help, Great Lady, but you must not speak this way to your Queen."

I shook my head. Let the foolish child do what she might. I braced myself for the inevitable backlash of the spell.

Tryce raised her knife in the air. "Let everyone gathered here behold that this is Queen Rayneh, the Queen Who Would Dictate to a Daughter. I am her heir, Tryce of the Bold Stride. Hear me. I do this for the Land of Flowered Hills, for our honor and our strength. Yet I also do it with regret. Mother, I hope you will be free in your death. May your spirit wing across sweet breezes with the great bird of the sun."

The knife slashed downward. Crimson poured across Rayneh's body, across the rugs, across Tryce's feet. For a moment, I thought I'd been wrong about Tryce's baby—perhaps she had loved it enough for the counter-spell to work—but as the blood poured over the dried petals Rayneh had scattered on the floor, a bright light flared through the room. Tryce flailed backward as if struck.

Rayneh's wound vanished. She stared up at me with startled, joyful eyes. "You didn't betray me!"

"Oh, I did," I said. "Your daughter is just inept."

I could see only one solution to the problem Tryce had created—the life's blood of something I loved was here, still saturating the carpets and pooling on the stone.

Magic is a little bit alive. Sometimes it prefers poetic truths to literal ones. I dipped my fingers into the Queen's spilled blood and pronounced, "The Lady Who Plucked Red Flowers beneath Your Window has betrayed you."

I cast the blood across the Queen. The dried petals disintegrated. The Queen cried out as my magical protections disappeared.

Tryce was at her mother's side again in an instant. Rayneh looked at me in the moment before Tryce's knife descended. I thought she might show me, just this once, a fraction of uncalculated vulnerability. But this time there was no vulnerability at all, no pain or betrayal or even weariness, only perfect regal equanimity.

Tryce struck for her mother's heart. She let her mother's body fall to the carpet.

"Behold my victory!" Tryce proclaimed. She turned toward her subjects. Her stance was strong: her feet planted firmly, ready for attack or defense. If her lower half was any indication, she'd be an excellent Queen.

I felt a rush of forgiveness and pleasure and regret and satisfaction all mixed together. I moved toward the boundaries of my imprisonment, my face near Rayneh's where she lay, inhaling her last ragged breaths.

"Be brave," I told her. "Soon we'll both be free."

Rayneh's lips moved slowly, her tongue thick around the words. "What makes you think . . . ?"

"You're going to die," I said, "and when I leave this body, Kyan will die, too. Without caster or intent, there won't be anything to sustain the spell."

Rayneh made a sound that I supposed was laughter. "Oh no, my dear Naeva . . . much more complicated than that . . ."

Panic constricted my throat. "Tryce! You have to find the piece of leucite—"

". . . even stronger than the rock. Nothing but death can lull your spirit to sleep . . . and you're already dead . . ."

She laughed again.

"Tryce!" I shouted. "Tryce!"

The girl turned. For a moment, my vision became as clear as it had been when I lived. I saw the Imprudent Child Queen standing with her automaton's arms around her waist, the both of them flushed with joy and triumph. Tryce turned to kiss the knot of wood that served as the automaton's mouth and my vision clouded again.

Rayneh died a moment afterward.

A moment after that, Tryce released me.

If my story could not end when I died, it should have ended there, in Rayneh's chamber, when I took my revenge.

It did not end there.

Tryce consulted me often during the early years of her reign. I familiarized myself with the blur of the paintings in her chamber, squinting to pick out placid scenes of songbirds settling on snowy branches, bathing in mountain springs, soaring through sun-struck skies.

"Don't you have counselors for this?" I snapped one day.

Tryce halted her pacing in front of me, blocking my view of a wren painted by The Artist without Pity.

"Do you understand what it's like for me? The court still calls me the Imprudent Child Who Would Be Queen. Because of you!"

Gudrin went to comfort her. She kept the creature close, pampered and petted, like a cat on a leash. She rested her head on his shoulder as he stroked her arms. It all looked too easy, too familiar. I wondered how often Tryce spun herself into these emotional whirlpools.

"It can be difficult for women to accept orders from their juniors," I said.

"I've borne two healthy girls," Tryce said petulantly. "When I talk to the other women about bearing, they still say they can't, that 'women's bodies aren't suited for childbirth.' Well, if women can't have children, then what does that make me?"

I forebore responding.

"They keep me busy with petty disputes over grazing rights and grain allotment. How can I plan for a war when they distract me with pedantry?

The raiders are still at our heels, and the daft old biddies won't accept what we must do to beat them back!"

The automaton thrummed with sympathy. Tryce shook him away and resumed pacing.

"At least I have you, Respected Aunt."

"For now. You must be running out of hosts." I raised my hand and inspected young, unfamiliar fingers. Dirt crusted the ragged nails. "Who is this? Anyone I know?"

"The death whisperers refuse to let me use their bodies. What time is this when dying old women won't blow out a few days early for the good of the Land?"

"Who is this?" I repeated.

"I had to summon you into the body of a common thief. You see how bad things are."

"What did you expect? That the wind would send a hundred songbirds to trill praises at your coronation? That sugared oranges would rain from the sky and flowers bloom on winter stalks?"

Tryce glared at me angrily. "Do not speak to me like that. I may be an Imprudent Child, but I am the Queen." She took a moment to regain her composure. "Enough chatter. Give me the spell I asked for."

Tryce called me in at official occasions, to bear witness from the body of a disfavored servant or a used-up brood. I attended each of the four ceremonies where Tryce, clad in regal blue, presented her infant daughters to the sun: four small, green-swathed bundles, each borne from the Queen's own body. It made me sick, but I held my silence.

She also summoned me to the court ceremony where she presented Gudrin with an official title she'd concocted to give him standing in the royal circle. Honored Zephyr or some such nonsense. They held the occasion in autumn when red and yellow leaves adorned Gudrin's shoulders like a cape. Tryce pretended to ignore the women's discontented mutterings, but they were growing louder.

The last time I saw Tryce, she summoned me in a panic. She stood in an unfamiliar room with bare stone walls and sharp wind creaking through slitted windows. Someone else's blood stained Tryce's robes. "My sisters betrayed me!" she said. "They told the women of the grasslands I was trying to make them into broods, and then led them in a revolt against the castle. A thousand women, marching! I had to slay them all. I suspected Darnisha all along. But Peni seemed content to waft. Last fall, she bore a child of her own body. It was a worm, true, but she might have gotten a daughter next. She said she wanted to try!"

"Is that their blood?"

She held out her reddened hands and stared at them ruefully as if they weren't really part of her. "Gudrin was helping them. I had to smash him into sticks. They must have cast a spell on him. I can't imagine . . ."

Her voice faltered. I gave her a moment to tame her undignified excess.

"You seem to have mastered the situation," I said. "A Queen must deal with such things from time to time. The important thing will be to show no weakness in front of your courtiers."

"You don't understand! It's much worse than that. While we women fought, the raiders attacked the Fields That Bask under Open Skies. They've taken half the Land. We're making a stand in the Castle Where Hope Flutters, but we can't keep them out forever. A few weeks, at most. I told them this would happen! We need more daughters to defend us! But they wouldn't listen to me!"

Rayneh would have known how to present her anger with queenly courage, but Tryce was rash and thoughtless. She wore her emotions like perfume. "Be calm," I admonished. "You must focus."

"The raiders sent a message describing what they'll do to me and my daughters when they take the castle. I captured the messenger and burned out his tongue and gave him to the broods, and when they were done with him, I took what was left of his body and catapulted it into the raiders' camp. I could do the same to every one of them, and it still wouldn't be enough to compensate for having to listen to their vile, cowardly threats."

I interrupted her tirade. "The Castle Where Hope Flutters is on high ground, but if you've already lost the eastern fields, it will be difficult to defend. Take your women to the Spires of Treachery where the herders feed their cattle. You won't be able to mount traditional defenses, but they won't be able to attack easily. You'll be reduced to meeting each other in small parties where woman's magic should give you the advantage."

"My commander suggested that," said Tryce. "There are too many of them. We might as well try to dam a river with silk."

"It's better than remaining here."

"Even if we fight to a stalemate in the Spires of Treachery, the raiders will have our fields to grow food in, and our broods to make children on. If they can't conquer us this year, they'll obliterate us in ten. I need something else."

"There is nothing else."

"Think of something!"

I thought.

I cast my mind back through my years of training. I remembered the locked room in my matriline's household where servants were never allowed to enter, which my cousins and I scrubbed every dawn and dusk to teach us to be constant and rigorous.

I remembered the cedar desk where my aunt Finis taught me to paint birds, first by using the most realistic detail that oils could achieve, and then by reducing my paintings to fewer and fewer brushstrokes until I could evoke the essence of bird without any brush at all.

I remembered the many-drawered red cabinets where we stored Leafspine and Winterbrew, powdered Errow and essence of Howl. I remembered my bossy cousin Alne skidding through the halls in a panic after she broke into a locked drawer and mixed together two herbs that we weren't supposed to touch. Her fearful grimace transformed into a beak that permanently silenced her sharp tongue.

I remembered the year I spent traveling to learn the magic of foreign lands. I was appalled by the rituals I encountered in places where women urinated on their thresholds to ward off spirits, and plucked their scalps bald when their eldest daughters reached majority. I walked with senders and weavers and whisperers and learned magic secrets that my people had misunderstood for centuries. I remembered the terror of the three nights I spent in the ancient ruins of The Desert which Should Not Have Been, begging the souls that haunted that place to surrender the secrets of their accursed city. One by one my companions died, and I spent the desert days digging graves for those the spirits found unworthy. On the third dawn, they blessed me with communion, and sent me away a wiser woman.

I remembered returning to the Land of Flowered Hills and making my own contribution to the lore contained in our matriline's locked rooms. I remembered all of this, and still I could think of nothing to tell Tryce.

Until a robin of memory hopped from an unexpected place—a piece of magic I learned traveling with herders, not spell-casters. It was an old magic, one that farmers cast when they needed to cull an inbred strain.

"You must concoct a plague," I began.

Tryce's eyes locked on me. I saw hope in her face, and I realized that she'd expected me to fail her, too.

"Find a sick baby and stop whatever treatment it is receiving. Feed it mosquito bellies and offal and dirty water to make it sicker. Give it sores and let them fill with pus. When its forehead has grown too hot for a woman to touch without flinching, kill the baby and dedicate its breath to the sun. The next morning, when the sun rises, a plague will spread with the sunlight."

"That will kill the raiders?"

"Many of them. If you create a truly virulent strain, it may kill most of them. And it will cut down their children like a scythe across wheat."

Tryce clapped her blood-stained hands. "Good."

"I should warn you. It will kill your babies as well."

"What?"

"A plague cooked in an infant will kill anyone's children. It is the way of things."

"Unacceptable! I come to you for help, and you send me to murder my daughters?"

"You killed one before, didn't you? To save your automaton?"

"You're as crazy as the crones at court! We need more babies, not fewer."

"You'll have to hope you can persuade your women to bear children so that you can rebuild your population faster than the raiders can rebuild theirs."

Tryce looked as though she wanted to level a thousand curses at me, but she stilled her tongue. Her eyes were dark and narrow. In a quiet, angry voice, she said, "Then it will be done."

They were the same words she'd used when she promised to kill Gudrin. That time I'd been able to save her despite her foolishness. This time, I might not be able to.

Next I was summoned, I could not see at all. I was ushered into the world by lowing, distant shouts, and the stench of animals packed too closely together.

A worried voice cut through the din. "Did it work? Are you there? Laverna, is that still you?"

Disoriented, I reached out to find a hint about my surroundings. My hands impacted a summoning barrier.

"Laverna, that's not you anymore, is it?"

The smell of manure stung my throat. I coughed. "My name is Naeva."

"Holy day, it worked. Please, Sleepless One, we need your help. There are men outside. I don't know how long we can hold them off."

"What happened? Is Queen Tryce dead?"

"Queen Tryce?"

"She didn't cast the plague, did she? Selfish brat. Where are the raiders now? Are you in the Spires of Treachery?"

"Sleepless One, slow down. I don't follow you."

"Where are you? How much land have the raiders taken?"

"There are no raiders here, just King Addric's army. His soldiers used to be happy as long as we paid our taxes and bowed our heads at processions. Now they want us to follow their ways, worship their god, let our men give us orders. Some of us rebelled by marching in front of the governor's theater, and now he's sent sorcerers after us. They burned our city with magical fire. We're making a last stand at the inn outside town. We set aside the stable for the summoning."

"Woman, you're mad. Men can't practice that kind of magic."

"These men can."

A nearby donkey brayed, and a fresh stench plopped into the air. Outside, I heard the noise of burning, and the shouts of men and children.

"It seems we've reached an impasse. You've never heard of the Land of Flowered Hills?"

"Never."

I had spent enough time pacing the ruins in the Desert which Should Not Have Been to understand the ways in which civilizations cracked and decayed. Women and time marched forward, relentless and uncaring as sand.

"I see."

"I'm sorry. I'm not doing this very well. It's my first summoning. My aunt Hetta used to do it but they slit her throat like you'd slaughter a pig and left her body to burn. Bardus says they're roasting the corpses and eating

287

them, but I don't think anyone could do that. Could they? Hetta showed me how to do this a dozen times, but I never got to practice. She would have done this better."

"That would explain why I can't see."

"No, that's the child, Laverna. She's blind. She does all the talking. Her twin Nammi can see, but she's dumb."

"Her twin?"

"Nammi's right here. Reach into the circle and touch your sister's hand, Nammi. That's a good girl."

A small hand clasped mine. It felt clammy with sweat. I squeezed back.

"It doesn't seem fair to take her sister away," I said.

"Why would anyone take Laverna away?"

"She'll die when I leave this body."

"No, she won't. Nammi's soul will call her back. Didn't your people use twins?"

"No. Our hosts died."

"Yours were a harsh people."

Another silence. She spoke the truth, though I'd never thought of it in such terms. We were a lawful people. We were an unflinching people.

"You want my help to defeat the shamans?" I asked.

"Aunt Hetta said that sometimes the Sleepless Ones can blink and douse all the magic within seven leagues. Or wave their hands and sweep a rank of men into a hurricane."

"Well, I can't."

She fell silent. I considered her situation.

"Do you have your people's livestock with you?" I asked.

"Everything that wouldn't fit into the stable is packed inside the inn. It's even less pleasant in there if you can imagine."

"Can you catch one of their soldiers?"

"We took some prisoners when we fled. We had to kill one but the others are tied up in the courtyard."

"Good. Kill them and mix their blood into the grain from your larder, and bake it into loaves of bread. Feed some of the bread to each of your animals. They will fill with a warrior's anger and hunt down your enemies."

The woman hesitated. I could hear her feet shifting on the hay-covered floor.

"If we do that, we won't have any grain or animals. How will we survive?"

"You would have had to desert your larder when the Worm-Pretending-to-Be-Queen sent reinforcements anyway. When you can safely flee, ask the blind child to lead you to the Place where the Sun Is Joyous. Whichever direction she chooses will be your safest choice."

"Thank you," said the woman. Her voice was taut and tired. It seemed clear that she'd hoped for an easier way, but she was wise enough to take what she received. "We'll have a wild path to tame."

"Yes."

The woman stepped forward. Her footsteps released the scent of dried hay. "You didn't know about your Land, did you?"

"I did not."

"I'm sorry for your loss. It must be—"

The dumb child whimpered. Outside, the shouts increased.

"I need to go," said the woman.

"Good luck," I said, and meant it.

I felt the child Laverna rush past me as I sank back into my restless sleep. Her spirit flashed as brightly as a coin left in the sun.

I never saw that woman or any of her people again. I like to think they did not die.

I did not like the way the world changed after the Land of Flowered Hills disappeared. For a long time, I was summoned only by men. Most were a sallow, unhealthy color with sharp narrow features and unnaturally light hair. Goateed sorcerers too proud of their paltry talents strove to dazzle me with pyrotechnics. They commanded me to reveal magical secrets that their peoples had forgotten. Sometimes I stayed silent. Sometimes I led them astray. Once, a hunched barbarian with a braided beard ordered me to give him the secret of flight. I told him to turn toward the prevailing wind and beg the Lover of the Sky for a favor. When the roc swooped down to eat him, I felt a wild kind of joy. At least the birds remembered how to punish worms who would steal women's magic.

I suffered for my minor victory. Without the barbarian to dismiss me, I was stuck on a tiny patch of grass, hemmed in by the rabbit heads he'd placed to mark the summoning circle. I shivered through the windy night until I finally thought to kick away one of the heads. It tumbled across the grass and my spirit sank into the ground.

Men treated me differently than women had. I had been accustomed to being summoned by Queens and commanders awaiting my advice on incipient battles. Men eschewed my consult; they sought to steal my powers. One summoned me into a box, hoping to trap me as if I were a minor demon that could be forced to grant his wishes. I chanted a rhyme to burn his fingers. When he pulled his hand away, the lid snapped shut and I was free.

Our magic had centered on birds and wind. These new sorcerers made pets of creatures of blood and snapping jaws, wolves and bears and jaguars. We had depicted the sun's grace along with its splendor, showing the red feathers of flaming light that arc into wings to sweep her across the sky. Their sun was a crude, jagged thing—a golden disk surrounded by spikes that twisted like the gaudy knives I'd seen in foreign cities where I traveled when I was young.

The men called me The Bitch Queen. They claimed I had hated my womb so much that I tried to curse all men to infertility, but the curse rebounded and struck me dead. Apparently, I had hanged myself. Or I'd tried to disembowel every male creature within a day's walk of my borders. Or I'd spelled my entire kingdom into a waking death in order to prevent myself from ever becoming pregnant. Apparently, I did all the same things out of revenge because I became pregnant. I eschewed men and impregnated women with sorcery. I married a thousand husbands and murdered them all. I murdered my husband, the King, and staked his head outside my castle, and then forced all the tearful women of my kingdom to do the same to their menfolk. I went crazy when my husband and son died and ordered all the men in my kingdom to be executed, declaring that no one would have the pleasure I'd been denied. I had been born a boy, but a rival of my father's castrated me, and so I hated all real men. I ordered that any woman caught breastfeeding should have her breasts cut off. I ordered my lover's genitals cut off and sewn on me. I ordered my vagina sewn shut so I could never give birth. I ordered everyone in my kingdom to call me a man.

They assumed my magic must originate with my genitals: they displayed surprise that I didn't strip naked to mix ingredients in my vagina or cast spells using menstrual blood. They also displayed surprise that I became angry when they asked me about such things.

The worst of them believed he could steal my magic by raping me. He summoned me into a worthless, skinny girl, the kind that we in the Land of Flowered Hills would have deemed too weak to be a woman and too frail to be a brood. In order to carry out his plans, he had to make the summoning circle large enough to accommodate the bed. When he forced himself on top of me, I twisted off his head.

The best of them summoned me soon after that. He was a young man with nervous, trembling fingers who innovated a way to summon my spirit into himself. Books and scrolls tumbled over the surfaces of his tiny, dim room, many of them stained with wax from unheeded candles. Talking to him was strange, the two of us communicating with the same mouth, looking out of the same eyes.

Before long, we realized that we didn't need words. Our knowledge seeped from one spirit to the other like dye poured into water. He watched me as a girl, riding with Rayneh, and felt the sun burning my back as I dug graves in the Desert which Should Not Have Been, and flinched as he witnessed the worm who attempted to rape me. I watched him and his five brothers, all orphaned and living on the street, as they struggled to find scraps. I saw how he had learned to read under the tutelage of a traveling scribe who carried his books with him from town to town. I felt his uncomfortable mixture of love, respect, and fear for the patron who had set him up as a scribe and petty magician in return for sex and servitude. *I didn't know it felt that way*, I said to him. *Neither did I*, he replied. We stared at each other cross-eyed through his big green eyes.

Pasha needed to find a way to stop the nearby volcano before it destroyed the tiny kingdom where he dwelled. Already, tremors rattled the buildings, foreshadowing the coming destruction.

Perhaps I should not have given Pasha the spell, but it was not deep woman's magic. Besides, things seemed different when I inhabited his mind, closer to him than I had been to anyone.

We went about enacting the spell together. As we collected ash from the fireplaces of one family from each of the kingdom's twelve towns, I asked him, *Why haven't you sent me back? Wouldn't it be easier to do this on your own?*

I'll die when your spirit goes, he answered, and I saw the knowledge of it which he had managed to keep from me.

I didn't want him to die. *Then I'll stay*, I said. *I won't interfere with your life. I'll retreat as much as I can.*

I can't keep up the spell much longer, he said. I felt his sadness and his resolve. Beneath, I glimpsed even deeper sadness at the plans he would no longer be able to fulfill. He'd wanted to teach his youngest brother to read and write so that the two of them could move out of this hamlet and set up shop in a city as scribes, perhaps even earn enough money to house and feed all their brothers.

I remembered Laverna and Nammi and tried to convince Pasha that we could convert the twins' magic to work for him and his brother. He said that we only had enough time to stop the volcano. *The kingdom is more important than I am*, he said.

We dug a hole near the volcano's base and poured in the ashes that we'd collected. We stirred them with a phoenix feather until they caught fire, in order to give the volcano the symbolic satisfaction of burning the kingdom's hearths. A dense cloud of smoke rushed up from the looming mountain and then the earth was still.

That's it, said Pasha, exhaustion and relief equally apparent in his mind. *We did it.*

We sat together until nightfall when Pasha's strength began to fail.

I have to let go now, he said.

No, I begged him, *Wait. Let us return to the city. We can find your brother. We'll find a way to save you.*

But the magic in his brain was unwinding. I was reminded of the ancient tapestries hanging in the Castle Where Hope Flutters, left too long to moths and weather. Pasha lost control of his feet, his fingers. His thoughts began to drift. They came slowly and far apart. His breath halted in his lungs. Before his life could end completely, my spirit sank away, leaving him to die alone.

After that, I did not have the courage to answer summons. When men called me, I kicked away the objects they'd used to bind me in place and disappeared again. Eventually, the summons stopped.

I had never before been aware of the time that I spent under the earth, but as the years between summons stretched, I began to feel vague sensations: swatches of grey and white along with muted, indefinable pain.

When a summons finally came, I almost felt relief. When I realized the summoner was a woman, I did feel surprise.

"I didn't expect that to work," said the woman. She was peach-skinned and round, a double chin gentling her jaw. She wore large spectacles with faceted green lenses like insect eyes. Spines like porcupine quills grew in a thin line from the bridge of her nose to the top of her skull before fanning into a mane. The aroma of smoke—whether the woman's personal scent or some spell remnant—hung acrid in the air.

I found myself simultaneously drawn to the vibrancy of the living world and disinclined to participate in it. I remained still, delighting in the smells and sights and sounds.

"No use pretending you're not there," said the woman. "The straw man doesn't usually blink on its own. Or breathe."

I looked down and saw a rudimentary body made of straw, joints knotted together with what appeared to be twine. I lifted my straw hand and stretched out each finger, amazed as the joints crinkled but did not break. "What is this?" My voice sounded dry and crackling, though I did not know whether that was a function of straw or disuse.

"I'm not surprised this is new to you. The straw men are a pretty new development. It saves a lot of stress and unpleasantness for the twins and the spirit rebounders and everyone else who gets the thankless job of putting up with Insomniacs taking over their bodies. Olin Nimble—that's the man who innovated the straw men—he and I completed our scholastic training the same year. Twenty years later? He's transfigured the whole field. And here's me, puttering around the library. But I suppose someone has to teach the students how to distinguish Pinder's Breath from Summer Twoflower."

The woman reached into my summoning circle and tugged my earlobe. Straw crackled.

"It's a gesture of greeting," she said. "Go on, tug mine."

I reached out hesitantly, expecting my gesture to be thwarted by the invisible summoning barrier. Instead, my fingers slid through unresisting air and grasped the woman's earlobe.

She grinned with an air of satisfaction that reminded me of the way my aunts had looked when showing me new spells. "I am Scholar Misa Meticulous." She lifted the crystal globe she carried and squinted at it. Magical etchings appeared, spelling words in an unfamiliar alphabet. "And you are the Great Lady Naeva who Picked Posies near the Queen's Chamber, of the Kingdom Where Women Rule?"

I frowned, or tried to, unsure whether it showed on my straw face. "The Land of Flowered Hills."

"Oh." She corrected the etching with a long, sharp implement. "Our earliest records have it the other way. This sort of thing is commoner than you'd think. Facts get mixed with rumor. Rumor becomes legend. Soon no one can remember what was history and what they made up to frighten the children. For instance, I'll bet your people didn't really have an underclass of women you kept in herds for bearing children."

"We called them broods."

"You called them—" Misa's eyes went round and horrified. As quickly as her shock had registered, it disappeared again. She snorted with forthright amusement. "We'll have to get one of the historians to talk to you. This is what they *live* for."

"Do they."

It was becoming increasingly clear that this woman viewed me as a relic. Indignation simmered; I was not an urn, half-buried in the desert. Yet, in a way, I was.

"I'm just a teacher who specializes in sniffing," Misa continued. "I find Insomniacs we haven't spoken to before. It can take years, tracking through records, piecing together bits of old spells. I've been following you for three years. You slept dark."

"Not dark enough."

She reached into the summoning circle to give me a sympathetic pat on the shoulder. "Eternity's a lonely place," she said. "Even the academy's lonely, and we only study eternity. Come on. Why don't we take a walk? I'll show you the library."

My straw eyes rustled as they blinked in surprise. "A walk?"

Misa laughed. "Try it out."

She laughed again as I took one precarious step forward and then another. The straw body's joints creaked with each stiff movement. I felt awkward and graceless, but I couldn't deny the pleasure of movement.

"Come on," Misa repeated, beckoning.

She led me down a corridor of gleaming white marble. Arcane symbols figured the walls. Spell-remnants scented the air with cinnamon and burnt herbs, mingling with the cool currents that swept down from the vaulted ceiling. Beneath our feet, the floor was worn from many footsteps and yet Misa and I walked alone. I wondered how it could be that a place built to accommodate hundreds was empty except for a low-ranking scholar and a dead woman summoned into an effigy.

My questions were soon answered when a group of students approached noisily from an intersecting passageway. They halted when they saw us, falling abruptly silent. Misa frowned. "Get on!" she said, waving them away. They looked relieved as they fled back the way they'd come.

The students' shaved heads and shapeless robes made it difficult to discern their forms, but it was clear I had seen something I hadn't been meant to.

"You train men here," I ascertained.

"Men, women, neuters," said Misa. "Anyone who comes. And qualifies, of course."

I felt the hiss of disappointment: another profane, degraded culture. I should have known better than to hope. "I see," I said, unable to conceal my resentment.

Misa did not seem to notice. "Many cultures have created separate systems of magic for the male and female. Your culture was extreme, but not unusual. Men work healing magic, and women sing weather magic, or vice versa. All very rigid, all very unscientific. Did they ever try to teach a man to wail for a midnight rain? Oh, maybe they did, but if he succeeded, then it was just that one man, and wasn't his spirit more womanly than masculine? They get noted as an exception to the rule, not a problem with the rule itself. Think Locas Follow with the crickets, or Petrin of Atscheko, or for an example on the female side, Queen Urté. And of course if the man you set up to sing love songs to hurricanes can't even stir up a breeze, well, there's your proof. Men can't sing the weather. Even if another man could. Rigor, that's the important thing. Until you have proof, anything can be wrong. We know now there's no difference between the magical capabilities of the sexes, but we'd have known it earlier if people had asked the right questions. Did you know there's a place in the northern wastes where they believe only people with both male and female genitals can work spells?"

"They're fools."

Misa shrugged. "Everyone's a fool, sooner or later. I make a game of it with my students. What do we believe that will be proven wrong in the future? I envy your ability to live forever so you can see."

"You should not," I said, surprised by my own bitterness. "People of the future are as likely to destroy your truths as to uncover your falsehoods."

She turned toward me, her face drawn with empathy. "You may be right."

We entered a vast, mahogany-paneled room, large enough to quarter a roc. Curving shelf towers formed an elaborate labyrinth. Misa led me through the narrow aisles with swift precision.

The shelves displayed prisms of various shapes and sizes. Crystal pyramids sat beside metal cylinders and spheres cut from obsidian. There were stranger things, too, shapes for which I possessed no words, woven out of steel threads or hardened lava.

Overhead, a transparent dome revealed a night sky strewn with stars. I recognized no patterns among the sparkling pinpricks; it was as if all the stars I'd known had been gathered in a giant's palm and then scattered carelessly into new designs.

Misa chattered as she walked. "This is the academy library. There are over three hundred thousand spells in this wing alone and we've almost filled the second. My students are taking bets on when they'll start construction on the third. They're also taking bets on whose statue will be by the door. Olin Nimble's the favorite, wouldn't you know."

We passed a number of carrel desks upon which lay maps of strange rivers and red-tinted deserts. Tubes containing more maps resided in cubby holes between the desks, their ends labeled in an unfamiliar alphabet.

"We make the first year students memorize world maps," said Misa. "A scholar has to understand how much there is to know."

I stopped by a carrel near the end of the row. The map's surface was ridged to show changes in elevation. I tried to imagine what the land it depicted would look like from above, on a roc's back. Could the Mountains where the Sun Rests be hidden among those jagged points?

Misa stopped behind me. "We're almost to the place I wanted to show you," she said. When we began walking again, she stayed quiet.

Presently, we approached a place where marble steps led down to a sunken area. We descended, and seemed to enter another room entirely, the arcs of the library shelves on the main level looming upward like a ring of ancient trees.

All around us, invisible from above, there stood statues of men and women. They held out spell spheres in their carved, upturned palms.

"This is the Circle of Insomniacs," said Misa. "Every Insomniac is depicted here. All the ones we've found, that is."

Amid hunched old women and bearded men with wild eyes, I caught sight of stranger things. Long, armored spikes jutted from a woman's spine. A man seemed to be wearing a helmet shaped like a sheep's head until I noticed that his ears twisted behind his head and became the ram's horns. A child opened his mouth to display a ring of needle-sharp teeth like a leech's.

"They aren't human," I said.

"They are," said Misa. "Or they were." She pointed me to the space between a toothless man and a soldier whose face fell in shadow behind a carved helmet. "Your statue will be there. The sculptor will want to speak with you. Or if you don't want to talk to him, you can talk to his assistant, and she'll make notes."

I looked aghast at the crowd of stone faces. "This—this is why you woke me? This sentimental memorial?"

Misa's eyes glittered with excitement. "The statue's only part of it. We want to know more about you and the Kingdom Where Women Rule. Sorry, the Land of Flowered Hills. We want to learn from you and teach you. We want you to stay!"

I could not help but laugh, harsh and mirthless. Would this woman ask a piece of ancient stone wall whether or not it wanted to be displayed in a museum? Not even the worms who tried to steal my spells had presumed so much.

"I'm sorry," said Misa. "I shouldn't have blurted it out like that. I'm good at sniffing. I'm terrible with people. Usually I find the Great Ones and then other people do the summoning and bring them to the library. The council asked me to do it myself this time because I lived in a women's colony before

I came to the academy. I'm what they call woman-centered. They thought we'd have something in common."

"Loving women is fundamental. It's natural as breeze. It's not some kind of shared diversion."

"Still. It's more than you'd have in common with Olin Nimble."

She paused, biting her lip. She was still transparently excited even though the conversation had begun to go badly.

"Will you stay a while at least?" she asked. "You've slept dark for millennia. What's a little time in the light?"

I scoffed and began to demand that she banish me back to the dark—but the scholar's excitement cast ripples in a pond that I'd believed had become permanently still.

What I'd learned from the unrecognizable maps and scattered constellations was that the wage of eternity was forgetfulness. I was lonely, achingly lonely. Besides, I had begun to like Misa's fumbling chatter. She had reawakened me to light and touch—and even, it seemed, to wonder.

If I was to stay, I told Misa, then she must understand that I'd had enough of worms and their attempts at magic. I did not want them crowding my time in the light.

The corners of Misa's mouth drew downward in disapproval, but she answered, "The academy puts us at the crossroads of myriad beliefs. Sometimes we must set aside our own." She reached out to touch me. "You're giving us a great gift by staying. We'll always respect that."

Misa and I worked closely during my first days at the academy. We argued over everything. Our roles switched rapidly and contentiously from master to apprentice and back again. She would begin by asking me questions, and then as I told her about what I'd learned in my matriline's locked rooms, she would interrupt to tell me I was wrong, her people had experimented with such things, and they never performed consistently. Within moments, we'd be shouting about what magic meant, and what it signified, and what it wanted—because one thing we agreed on was that magic was a little bit alive.

Misa suspended her teaching while she worked with me, so we had the days to ourselves in the vast salon where she taught. Her people's magic was more than superficially dissimilar from mine. They constructed their spells into physical geometries by mapping out elaborate equations that determined whether they would be cylinders or dodecahedrons, formed of garnet or lapis lazuli or cages of copper strands. Even their academy's construction reflected magical intentions, although Misa told me its effects were vague and diffuse.

"Magic is like architecture," she said. "You have to build the right container for magic to grow in. The right house for its heart."

"You fail to consider the poetry of magic," I contended. "It likes to be teased with images, cajoled with irony. It wants to match wits."

"Your spells are random!" Misa answered. "Even you don't understand how they work. You've admitted it yourself. The effects are variable, unpredictable. It lacks rigor!"

"And accomplishes grandeur," I said. "How many of your scholars can match me?"

I soon learned that Misa was not, as she claimed, an unimportant scholar. By agreement, we allowed her female pupils to enter the salon from time to time for consultations. The young women, who looked startlingly young in their loose white garments, approached Misa with an awe that verged on fear. Once, a very young girl who looked barely out of puberty, ended their session by giving a low bow and kissing Misa's hand. She turned vivid red and fled the salon.

Misa shook her head as the echoes of the girl's footsteps faded. "She just wishes she was taking from Olin Nimble."

"Why do you persist in this deception?" I asked. "You have as many spells in the library as he does. It is you, not he, who was asked to join the academy as a scholar."

She slid me a dubious look. "You've been talking to people?"

"I have been listening."

"I've been here a long time," said Misa. "They need people like me to do the little things so greater minds like Olin Nimble's can be kept clear."

But her words were clearly untrue. All of the academy's scholars, from the most renowned to the most inexperienced, sent to Misa for consultations. She greeted their pages with good humor and false humility, and then went to meet her fellow scholars elsewhere, leaving her salon to me so that I could study or contemplate as I wished.

In the Land of Flowered Hills, there had once been a famous scholar named The Woman Who Would Ask the Breeze for Whys and Wherefores. Misa was such a woman, relentlessly impractical, always half-occupied by her studies. We ate together, talked together, slept together in her chamber, and yet I never saw her focus fully on anything except when she was engrossed in transforming her abstract magical theories into complex, beautiful tangibles.

Sometimes, I paused to consider how different Misa was from my first love. Misa's scattered, self-effaced pursuit of knowledge was nothing like Rayneh's dignified exercise of power. Rayneh was like a statue, formed in a beautiful but permanent stasis, never learning or changing. Misa tumbled everywhere like a curious wind, seeking to understand and alter and collaborate, but never to master.

In our first days together, Misa and I shared an abundance of excruciating, contentious, awe-inspiring novelty. We were separated by cultures and centuries, and yet we were attracted to each other even more strongly because of the strangeness we brought into each other's lives.

The academy was controlled by a rotating council of scholars that was chosen annually by lots. They made their decisions by consensus and exercised control over issues great and small, including the selection of new mages who were invited to join the academy as scholars and thus enter the pool of people who might someday control it.

"I'm grateful every year when they don't draw my name," Misa said.

We were sitting in her salon during the late afternoon, relaxing on reclining couches and sipping a hot, sweet drink from celadon cups. One of Misa's students sat with us, a startle-eyed girl who kept her bald head powdered and smooth, whom Misa had confided she found promising. The drink smelled of oranges and cinnamon; I savored it, ever amazed by the abilities of my strange, straw body.

I looked to Misa. "Why?"

Misa shuddered. "Being on the council would be . . . terrible."

"Why?" I asked again, but she only repeated herself in a louder voice, growing increasingly frustrated with my questions.

Later, when Misa left to discuss a spell with one of the academy's male scholars, her student told me, "Misa doesn't want to be elevated over others. It's a very great taboo for her people."

"It is self-indulgent to avoid power," I said. "Someone must wield it. Better the strong than the weak."

Misa's student fidgeted uncomfortably. "Her people don't see it that way."

I sipped from my cup. "Then they are fools."

Misa's student said nothing in response, but she excused herself from the salon as soon as she finished her drink.

The council requested my presence when I had been at the academy for a year. They wished to formalize the terms of my stay. Sleepless Ones who remained were expected to hold their own classes and contribute to the institution's body of knowledge.

"I will teach," I told Misa, "but only women."

"Why!" demanded Misa. "What is your irrational attachment to this prejudice?"

"I will not desecrate women's magic by teaching it to men."

"How is it desecration?"

"Women's magic is meant for women. Putting it into men's hands is degrading."

"But why!"

Our argument intensified. I began to rage. Men are not worthy of woman's magic. They're small-skulled, and cringing, and animalistic. It would be wrong! *Why, why, why?* Misa demanded, quoting from philosophical dialogues, and describing experiments that supposedly proved there was no difference between men's and women's magic. We circled and struck at one another's arguments as if we were animals competing over territory. We tangled our horns and drew blood from insignificant wounds, but neither of us seemed able to strike a final blow.

"Enough!" I shouted. "You've always told me that the academy respects the sacred beliefs of other cultures. These are mine."

"They're absurd!"

"If you will not agree then I will not teach. Banish me back to the dark! It does not matter to me."

Of course, it did matter to me. I had grown too attached to chaos and clamor. And to Misa. But I refused to admit it.

In the end, Misa agreed to argue my intentions before the council. She looked at turns furious and miserable. "They won't agree," she said. "How can they? But I'll do what I can."

The next day, Misa rubbed dense, floral unguents into her scalp and decorated her fingers with arcane rings. Her quills trembled and fanned upward, displaying her anxiety.

The circular council room glowed with faint, magical light. Cold air mixed with the musky scents favored by high-ranking scholars, along with hints of smoke and herbs. Archways loomed at each of the cardinal directions. Misa led us through the eastern archway, which she explained was for negotiation, and into the center of the mosaic floor.

The council's scholars sat on raised couches arrayed around the circumference of the room. Each sat below a torch that guttered, red and gold, rendering the councilors' bodies vivid against the dim. I caught sight of a man in layered red and yellow robes, his head surmounted by a brass circlet that twinkled with lights that flared and then flitted out of existence, like winking stars. To his side sat a tall woman with mossy hair and bark-like skin, and beside her, a man with two heads and torsos mounted upon a single pair of legs. A woman raised her hand in greeting to Misa, and water cascaded from her arms like a waterfall, churning into a mist that evaporated before it touched the floor.

Misa had told me that older scholars were often changed by her people's magic, that it shaped their bodies in the way they shaped their spells. I had not understood her before.

A long, narrow man seemed to be the focal point of the other councilors' attention. Fine, sensory hairs covered his skin. They quivered in our direction like a small animal's sniffing. "What do you suggest?" he asked. "Shall we establish a woman-only library? Shall we inspect our students' genitalia to ensure there are no men-women or women-men or twin-sexed among them?"

"Never mind that," countered a voice behind us. I turned to see a pudgy woman garbed in heavy metal sheets. "It's irrelevant to object on the basis of pragmatism. This request is exclusionary."

"Worse," added the waterfall woman. "It's immoral."

The councilors around her nodded their heads in affirmation. Two identical-looking men in leather hoods fluttered their hands to show support.

Misa looked to each assenting scholar in turn. "You are correct. It is exclusionist and immoral. But I ask you to think about deeper issues. If we reject Naeva's conditions, then everything she knows will be lost. Isn't it better that some know than that everyone forgets?"

"Is it worth preserving knowledge if the price is bigotry?" asked the narrow man with the sensory hairs, but the other scholars' eyes fixed on Misa.

They continued to argue for sometime, but the conclusion had been foregone as soon as Misa spoke. There is nothing scholars love more than knowledge.

"Is it strange for you?" I asked Misa. "To spend so much time with someone trapped in the body of a doll?"

We were alone in the tiny, cluttered room where she slept. It was a roughly hewn underground cavity, its only entrance and exit by ladder. Misa admitted that the academy offered better accommodations, but claimed she preferred rooms like this one.

Misa exclaimed with mock surprise. "You're trapped in the body of a doll? I'd never noticed!"

She grinned in my direction. I rewarded her with laughter.

"I've gotten used to the straw men," she said more seriously. "When we talk, I'm thinking about spells and magic and the things you've seen. Not straw."

Nevertheless, straw remained inescapably cumbersome. Misa suggested games and spells and implements, but I refused objects that would estrange our intimacy. We lay together at night and traded words, her hands busy at giving her pleasure while I watched and whispered. Afterward, we lay close, but I could not give her the warmth of a body I did not possess.

One night, I woke long after our love-making to discover that she was no longer beside me. I found her in the salon, her equations spiraling across a row of crystal globes. A doll hung from the wall beside her, awkwardly suspended by its nape. Its skin was warm and soft and tinted the same sienna that mine had been so many eons ago. I raised its face and saw features matching the sketches that the sculptor's assistant had made during our sessions.

Misa looked up from her calclulations. She smiled with mild embarrassment.

"I should have known a simple adaptation wouldn't work," she said. "Otherwise, Olin Nimble would have discarded straw years ago. But I thought, if I worked it out . . ."

I moved behind her, and beheld the array of crystal globes, all showing spidery white equations. Below them lay a half-formed spell of polished wood and peridot chips.

Misa's quill mane quivered. "It's late," she said, taking my hand. "We should return to bed."

Misa often left her projects half-done and scattered. I like to think the doll would have been different. I like to think she would have finished it.

Instead, she was drawn into the whirl of events happening outside the academy. She began leaving me behind in her chambers while she spent all hours in her salon, almost sleepwalking through the brief periods when she returned to me, and then rising restless in the dark and returning to her work.

By choice, I remained unclear about the shape of the external cataclysm. I did not want to be drawn further into the academy's politics.

My lectures provided little distraction. The students were as preoccupied as Misa. "This is not a time for theory!" one woman complained when I tried to draw my students into a discussion of magic's predilections. She did not return the following morning. Eventually, no one else returned either.

Loneliness drove me where curiosity could not and I began following Misa to her salon. Since I refused to help with her spells, she acknowledged my presence with little more than a glance before returning to her labors. Absent her attention, I studied and paced.

Once, after leaving the salon for several hours, Misa returned with a bustle of scholars—both men and women—all brightly clad and shouting. They halted abruptly when they saw me.

"I forgot you were here," Misa said without much contrition.

I tensed, angry and alienated, but unwilling to show my rage before the worms. "I will return to your chamber," I said through tightened lips.

Before I even left the room, they began shouting again. Their voices weren't like scholars debating. They lashed at each other with their words. They were angry. They were afraid.

That night, I went to Misa and finally asked for explanations. It's a plague, she said. A plague that made its victims bleed from the skin and eyes and then swelled their tongues until they suffocated.

They couldn't cure it. They treated one symptom, only to find the others worsening. The patients died, and then the mages who treated them died, too.

I declared that the disease must be magic. Misa glared at me with unexpected anger and answered that, no! It was not magic! If it was magic, they would have cured it. This was something foul and deadly and *natural*.

She'd grown gaunt by then, the gentle cushions of fat at her chin and stomach disappearing as her ribs grew prominent. After she slept, her headrest was covered with quills that had fallen out during the night, their pointed tips lackluster and dulled.

I no longer had dialogues or magic or sex to occupy my time. I had only remote, distracted Misa. My world began to shape itself around her—my love for her, my concern for her, my dread that she wouldn't find a cure, and my fear of what I'd do if she didn't. She was weak, and she was leading me into weakness. My mind sketched patterns I didn't want to imagine. I heard the spirits in The Desert Which Should Not Have Been whispering about the deaths of civilizations, and about choices between honor and love.

Misa stopped sleeping. Instead, she sat on the bed in the dark, staring into the shadows and worrying her hands.

"There is no cure," she muttered.

I lay behind her, watching her silhouette.

"Of course there's a cure."

"Oh, *of course*," snapped Misa. "We're just too ignorant to find it!"

Such irrational anger. I never learned how to respond to a lover so easily swayed by her emotions.

"I did not say that you were ignorant."

"As long as you didn't *say* it."

Misa pulled to her feet and began pacing, footsteps thumping against the piled rugs.

I realized that in all my worrying, I'd never paused to consider where the plague had been, whether it had ravaged the communities where Misa had lived and loved. My people would have thought it a weakness to let such things affect them.

"Perhaps you are ignorant," I said. "Maybe you can't cure this plague by building little boxes. Have you thought of that?"

I expected Misa to look angry, but instead she turned back with an expression of awe. "Maybe that's it," she said slowly. "Maybe we need your kind of magic. Maybe we need poetry."

For the first time since the plague began, the lines of tension began to smooth from Misa's face. I loved her. I wanted to see her calm and curious, restored to the woman who marveled at new things and spent her nights beside me.

So I did what I knew I should not. I sat with her for the next hours and listened as she described the affliction. It had begun in a swamp far to the east, she said, in a humid tangle of roots and branches where a thousand sharp and biting things lurked beneath the water. It traveled west with summer's heat, sickening children and old people first, and then striking the young and healthy. The children and elderly sometimes recovered. The young and healthy never survived.

I thought back to diseases I'd known in my youth. A very different illness came to mind, a disease cast by a would-be usurper during my girlhood. It came to the Land of Flowered Hills with the winter wind and froze its victims into statues that would not shatter with blows or melt with heat. For years after Rayneh's mother killed the usurper and halted the disease, the Land of Flowered Hills was haunted by the glacial, ghostly remains of those once-loved. The Queen's sorceresses sought them out one by one and melted them with memories of passion. It was said that the survivors wept and cursed as their loved ones melted away, for they had grown to love the ever-present, icy memorials.

That illness was unlike what afflicted Misa's people in all ways but one—that disease, too, had spared the feeble and taken the strong.

I told Misa, "This is a plague that steals its victims' strength and uses it to kill them."

Misa's breaths came slowly and heavily. "Yes, that's it," she said. "That's what's happening."

"The victims must steal their strength back from the disease. They must cast their own cures."

"They must cast your kind of spells. Poetry spells."

"Yes," I said. "Poetry spells."

Misa's eyes closed as if she wanted to weep with relief. She looked so tired and frail. I wanted to lay her down on the bed and stroke her cheeks until she fell asleep.

Misa's shoulders shook but she didn't cry. Instead, she straightened her spectacles and plucked at her robes.

"With a bit of heat and . . . how would obsidian translate into poetry? . . ." she mused aloud. She started toward the ladder and then paused to look back. "Will you come help me, Naeva?"

She must have known what I would say.

"I'll come," I said quietly, "but this is woman's magic. It is not for men."

What followed was inevitable: the shudder that passed through Misa as her optimism turned ashen. "No. Naeva. You wouldn't let people die."

But I would. And she should have known that. If she knew me at all.

She brought it before the council. She said that was how things were to be decided. By discussion. By consensus.

We entered through the western arch, the arch of conflict. The scholars arrayed on their raised couches looked as haggard as Misa. Some seats were empty, others filled by men and women I'd not seen before.

"Why is this a problem?" asked one of the new scholars, an old woman whose face and breasts were stippled with tiny, fanged mouths. "Teach the spell to women. Have them cast it on the men."

"The victims must cast it themselves," Misa said.

The old woman scoffed. "Since when does a spell care who casts it?"

"It's old magic," Misa said. "Poetry magic."

"Then what is it like?" asked a voice from behind us.

We turned to see the narrow man with the fine, sensory hairs, who had demanded at my prior interrogation whether knowledge gained through bigotry was worth preserving. He lowered his gaze onto my face and his hairs extended toward me, rippling and seeking.

"Some of us have not had the opportunity to learn for ourselves," he added.

I hoped that Misa would intercede with an explanation, but she held her gaze away from mine. Her mouth was tight and narrow.

The man spoke again. "Unless you feel that it would violate your ethics to even *describe* the issue in my presence."

"No. It would not." I paused to prepare my words. "As I understand it, your people's magic imprisons spells in clever constructions. You alter the shape and texture of the spell as you alter the shape and texture of its casing."

Dissenting murmurs rose from the councilors.

"I realize that's an elementary description," I said. "However, it will suffice for contrast. My people attempted to court spells with poetry, using image and symbol and allusion as our tools. Your people give magic a place to dwell. Mine woo it to tryst awhile."

"What does that," interjected the many-mouthed old woman, "have to do with victims casting their own spells?"

Before I could answer, the narrow man spoke. "It must be poetry—the symmetry, if you will. Body and disease are battling for the body's strength. The body itself must win the battle."

"Is that so?" the old woman demanded of me.

I inclined my head in assent.

A woman dressed in robes of scarlet hair looked to Misa. "You're confident this will work?"

Misa's voice was strained and quiet. "I am."

The woman turned to regard me, scarlet tresses parting over her chest to reveal frog-like skin that glistened with damp. "You will not be moved? You won't relinquish the spell?"

I said, "No."

"Even if we promise to give it only to the women, and let the men die?"

I looked toward Misa. I knew what her people believed. The council might bend in matters of knowledge, but it would not bend in matters of life.

"I do not believe you would keep such promises."

The frog-skinned woman laughed. The inside of her mouth glittered like a cavern filled with crystals. "You're right, of course. We wouldn't." She looked to her fellow councilors. "I see no other option. I propose an Obligation."

"No," said Misa.

"I agree with Jian," said a fat scholar in red and yellow. "An Obligation."

"You can't violate her like that," said Misa. "The academy is founded on respect."

The frog-skinned woman raised her brows at Misa. "What is respect worth if we let thousands die?"

Misa took my hands. "Naeva, don't let this happen. Please, Naeva." She moved yet closer to me, her breath hot, her eyes desperate. "You know what men can be. You know they don't have to be ignorant worms or greedy brutes. You know they can be clever and noble! Remember Pasha. You gave him the spell he needed. Why won't you help us?"

Pasha—kin of my thoughts, closer than my own skin. It had seemed different then, inside his mind. But I was on my own feet now, looking out from my own eyes, and I knew what I knew.

When she'd been confronted by the inevitable destruction of our people, Tryce had made herself into a brood. She had chosen to degrade herself and her daughters in the name of survival. What would the Land of Flowered Hills have become if she'd succeeded? What would have happened to we hard and haughty people who commanded the sacred powers of wind and sun?

I would not desecrate our knowledge by putting it in the hands of animals. This was not just one man who would die from what he learned. This would be unlocking the door to my matriline's secret rooms and tearing open the many-drawered cupboards. It would be laying everything sacrosanct bare to corruption.

I broke away from Misa's touch. "I will tell you nothing!"

The council acted immediately and unanimously, accord reached without deliberation. The narrow man wrought a spell-shape using only his hands, which Misa had told me could be done, but rarely and only by great mages. When his fingers held the right configuration, he blew into their cage.

An Obligation.

It was like falling through blackness. I struggled for purchase, desperate to climb back into myself.

My mouth opened. It was not I who spoke.

"Bring them water from the swamp and damp their brows until they feel the humidity of the place where the disease was born. The spirit of the disease will seek its origins, as any born creature will. Let the victims seek with their souls' sight until they find the spirit of the disease standing before them. It will appear differently to each, vaporous and foul, or sly and sharp, but they will know it. Let the victims open the mouths of their souls and devour the disease until its spirit is inside their spirit as its body is inside their body. This time, they will be the conquerors. When they wake, they will be stronger than they had been before."

My words resonated through the chamber. Misa shuddered and began to retch. The frog-skinned woman detached a lock of her scarlet hair and gave it, along with a sphere etched with my declamation, to their fleetest page. My volition rushed back into me as if through a crashing dam. I swelled with my returning power.

Magic is a little bit alive. It loves irony and it loves passion. With all the fierceness of my dead Land, I began to tear apart my straw body with its own straw hands. The effigy's viscera fell, crushed and crackling, to the mosaic floor.

The narrow man, alone among the councilors, read my intentions. He sprang to his feet, forming a rapid protection spell between his fingers. It glimmered into being before I could complete my own magic, but I was ablaze with passion and poetry, and I knew that I would prevail.

The fire of my anger leapt from my eyes and tongue and caught upon the straw in which I'd been imprisoned. Fire. Magic. Fury. The academy became an inferno.

They summoned me into a carved rock that could see and hear and speak but could not move. They carried it through the Southern arch, the arch of retribution.

The narrow man addressed me. His fine, sensory hairs had burned away in the fire, leaving his form bald and pathetic.

"You are dangerous," he said. "The council has agreed you cannot remain."

The council room was in ruins. The reek of smoke hung like a dense fog over the rubble. Misa sat on one of the few remaining couches, her eyes averted, her body etched with thick ugly scars. She held her right hand in her lap, its fingers melted into a single claw.

I wanted to cradle Misa's ruined hand, to kiss and soothe it. It was an unworthy desire. I had no intention of indulging regret.

"You destroyed the academy, you bitch," snarled a woman to my left. I remembered that she had once gestured waterfalls, but now her arms were burned to stumps. "Libraries, students, spells . . ." her voice cracked.

"The council understands the grave injustice of an Obligation," the narrow man continued, as if she had not interjected. "We don't take the enslavement of a soul lightly, especially when it violates a promised trust. Though we believe we acted rightfully, we also acknowledge we have done you an injustice. For that we owe you our contrition.

"Nevertheless," he continued, "It is the council's agreement that you cannot be permitted to remain in the light. It is our duty to send you back into the dark and to bind you there so that you may never answer summons again."

I laughed. It was a grating sound. "You'll be granting my dearest wish."

He inclined his head. "It is always best when aims align."

He reached out to the women next to him and took their hands. The remaining council members joined them, bending their bodies until they, themselves, formed the shape of a spell. Misa turned to join them, the tough, shiny substance of her scar tissue catching the light. I knew from Misa's lessons that the texture of her skin would alter and shape the spell. I could recognize their brilliance in that, to understand magic so well that they could form it out of their own bodies.

As the last of the scholars moved into place, for a moment I understood the strange, distorted, perfect shape they made. I realized with a slash that I had finally begun to comprehend their magic. And then I sank into final, lasting dark.

I remembered.

I remembered Misa. I remembered Pasha. I remembered the time when men had summoned me into unknown lands.

Always and inevitably, my thoughts returned to the Land of Flowered Hills, the place I had been away from longest, but known best.

Misa and Rayneh. I betrayed one. One betrayed me. Two loves ending in tragedy. Perhaps all loves do.

I remembered the locked room in my matriline's household, all those tiny lacquered drawers filled with marvels. My aunt's hand fluttered above them like a pale butterfly as I wondered which drawer she would open. What wonder would she reveal from a world so vast I could never hope to understand it?

"To paint a bird, you must show the brush what it means to fly," my aunt told me, holding my fingers around the brush handle as I strove to echo the perfection of a feather. The brush trembled. Dip into the well, slant, and press. Bristles splay. Ink bleeds across the scroll and—there! One single graceful stroke aspiring toward flight.

What can a woman do when love and time and truth are all at odds with one another, clashing and screeching, wailing and weeping, begging you to enter worlds unlike any you've ever known and save this people, this people, this people from king's soldiers and guttering volcanoes and plagues? What can a woman do when beliefs that seemed as solid as stone have become dry leaves blowing in autumn wind? What can a woman cling to when she must betray her lovers' lives or her own?

A woman is not a bird. A woman needs ground.

All my aunts gathering in a circle around the winter fire to share news and gossip, their voices clat-clat-clatting at each other in comforting, indistinguishable sounds. The wind finds its way in through the cracks and we welcome our friend. It blows through me, carrying scents of pine and snow. I run across the creaking floor to my aunts' knees which are as tall as I am, my arms slipping around one dark soft leg and then another as I work my way around the circle like a wind, finding the promise of comfort in each new embrace.

Light returned and shaded me with grey.

I stood on a pedestal under a dark dome, the room around me eaten by shadow. My hands touched my robe which felt like silk. They encountered each other and felt flesh. I raised them before my face and saw my own hands, brown and short and nimble, the fingernails jagged where I'd caught them on the rocks while surveying with Kyan in the Mountains where the Sun Rests.

Around me, I saw more pedestals arranged in a circle, and atop them strange forms that I could barely distinguish from shade. As my eyes adjusted, I made out a soldier with his face shadowed beneath a horned helmet, and a woman armored with spines. Next to me stood a child who smelled of stale water and dead fish. His eyes slid in my direction and I saw they were strangely old and weary. He opened his mouth to yawn, and inside, I saw a ring of needle-sharp teeth.

Recognition rushed through me. These were the Insomniacs I'd seen in Misa's library, all of them living and embodied, except there were more of us, countless more, all perched and waiting.

Magic is a little bit alive. That was my first thought as the creature unfolded before us, its body a strange darkness like the unrelieved black between stars. It was adorned with windows and doors that gleamed with silver like starlight. They opened and closed like slow blinking, offering us portals into another darkness that hinted at something beyond.

The creature was nothing like the entities that I'd believed waited at the core of eternity. It was no frozen world lizard, waiting to crack traitors in his icy jaws, nor a burning sun welcoming joyous souls as feathers in her wings. And yet, somehow I knew then that this creature was the deepest essence of the universe—the strange, persistent thing that throbbed like a heart between stars.

Its voice was strange, choral, like many voices talking at once. At the same time, it did not sound like a voice at all. It said, "You are the ones who have reached the end of time. You are witnesses to the end of this universe."

As it spoke, it expanded outward. The fanged child staggered back as the darkness approached. He looked toward me with fear in his eyes, and then darkness swelled around me, too, and I was surrounded by shadow and pouring starlight.

The creature said, "From the death of this universe will come the birth of another. This has happened so many times before that it cannot be numbered, unfathomable universes blinking one into the next, outside of time. The only continuity lies in the essences that persist from one to the next."

Its voice faded. I stretched out my hands into the gentle dark. "You want us to be reborn?" I asked.

I wasn't sure if it could even hear me in its vastness. But it spoke.

"The new universe will be unlike anything in this one. It will be a strangeness. There will be no 'born,' no 'you.' One cannot speak of a new universe. It is anathema to language. One cannot even ponder it."

Above me, a window opened, and it was not a window, but part of this strange being. Soothing, silver brilliance poured from it like water. It rushed over me, tingling like fresh spring mornings and newly drawn breath.

I could feel the creature's expectancy around me. More windows opened and closed as other Sleepless Ones made their choices.

I thought of everything then—everything I had thought of during the millennia when I was bound, and everything I should have thought of then but did not have the courage to think. I saw my life from a dozen fractured perspectives. Rayneh condemning me for helping her daughter steal her throne, and dismissing my every subsequent act as a traitor's cowardice. Tryce sneering at my lack of will as she watched me spurn a hundred opportunities for seizing power during centuries of summons. Misa, her brows drawn down in inestimable disappointment, pleading with me to abandon everything I was and become like her instead.

They were all right. They were all wrong. My heart shattered into a million sins.

I thought of Pasha who I should never have saved. I thought of how he tried to shield me from the pain of his death, spending his last strength to soothe me before he died alone.

For millennia, I had sought oblivion and been denied. Now, as I approached the opportunity to dissipate at last . . . now I began to understand the desire for something unspeakably, unfathomably new.

I reached toward the window. The creature gathered me in its massive blackness and lifted me up, up, up. I became a woman painted in brushstrokes of starlight, fewer and fewer, until I was only a glimmer of silver that had once been a woman, now poised to take flight. I glittered like the stars over The Desert which Should Not Have Been, eternal witnesses to things long forgotten. The darkness beyond the window pulled me. I leapt toward it, and stretched, and changed.

ABOUT THE AUTHOR

Rachel Swirsky holds an MFA from the Iowa Writers Workshop. Her short fiction has been published in numerous magazines and anthologies, nominated for several awards, and won the Nebula. Her first collection, *Through the Drowsy Dark*, came out from Aqueduct Press in 2010.

2011 NEBULA AWARDS NOMINEES AND HONOREES

SHORT STORY

WINNER: "Ponies," Kij Johnson (Tor.com, January 17, 2010)

WINNER "How Interesting: A Tiny Man," Harlan Ellison (*Realms of Fantasy*, February 2010)

"Arvies," Adam-Troy Castro (*Lightspeed*, August 2010)

"I'm Alive, I Love You, I'll See You in Reno," Vylar Kaftan (*Lightspeed*, June 2010)

"The Green Book," Amal El-Mohtar (*Apex*, November 1, 2010)

"Ghosts of New York," Jennifer Pelland (*Dark Faith*)

"Conditional Love," Felicity Shoulders (*Asimov's*, January 2010)

NOVELETTE

WINNER: "That Leviathan, Whom Thou Hast Made," Eric James Stone (*Analog*, September 2010)

"Map of Seventeen," Christopher Barzak (*The Beastly Bride*)

"The Jaguar House, in Shadow," Aliette de Bodard (*Asimov's*, July 2010)

"Plus or Minus," James Patrick Kelly (*Asimov's*, December 2010)

"Pishaach," Shweta Narayan (*The Beastly Bride*)

"The Fortuitous Meeting of Gerard van Oost and Oludara," Christopher Kastensmidt (*Realms of Fantasy*, April 2010)

"Stone Wall Truth," Caroline M. Yoachim (*Asimov's*, February 2010)

NOVELLA

WINNER: "The Lady Who Plucked Red Flowers beneath the Queen's Window," Rachel Swirsky (*Subterranean Summer*, 2010)

The Alchemist, Paolo Bacigalupi (Audible; Subterranean)

"Iron Shoes," J. Kathleen Cheney (*Alembical 2*)

The Lifecycle of Software Objects, Ted Chiang (Subterranean)

"The Sultan of the Clouds," Geoffrey A. Landis (*Asimov's*, September 2010)

"Ghosts Doing the Orange Dance," Paul Park (*F&SF*, January/February 2010)

NOVEL

WINNER *Blackout/All Clear*, Connie Willis (Spectra)

The Native Star, M. K. Hobson (Spectra)

The Hundred Thousand Kingdoms, N. K. Jemisin (Orbit UK; Orbit US)

Shades of Milk and Honey, Mary Robinette Kowal (Tor)

Echo, Jack McDevitt (Ace)

Who Fears Death, Nnedi Okorafor (DAW)

BRADBURY AWARD
BEST DRAMATIC PRODUCTION

WINNER: *Inception*, Christopher Nolan (director), Christopher Nolan (screenplay) (Warner)

Despicable Me, Pierre Coffin and Chris Renaud (directors), Ken Daurio and Cinco Paul (screenplay), Sergio Pablos (story) (Illumination Entertainment)

Doctor Who: "Vincent and the Doctor," Richard Curtis (writer), Jonny Campbell (director)

How to Train Your Dragon, Dean DeBlois and Chris Sanders (directors), William Davies, Dean DeBlois, and Chris Sanders (screenplay) (DreamWorks Animation)

Scott Pilgrim vs. the World, Edgar Wright (director), Michael Bacall & Edgar Wright (screenplay) (Universal)

Toy Story 3, Lee Unkrich (director), Michael Arndt (screenplay), John Lasseter, Andrew Stanton, and Lee Unkrich (story) (Pixar/Disney)

ANDRE NORTON AWARD

WINNER: *I Shall Wear Midnight*, Terry Pratchett (Doubleday; Harper)

Ship Breaker, Paolo Bacigalupi (Little, Brown)

White Cat, Holly Black (McElderry)

Mockingjay, Suzanne Collins (Scholastic Press; Scholastic UK)

Hereville: How Mirka Got Her Sword, Barry Deutsch (Amulet)

The Boy from Ilysies, Pearl North (Tor Teen)

A Conspiracy of Kings, Megan Whalen Turner (Greenwillow)

Behemoth, Scott Westerfield (Simon Pulse; Simon & Schuster UK)

THE SOLSTICE AWARD (FOR IMPACT ON THE FIELD)

WINNER: Alice Sheldon/James Tiptree, Jr.

WINNER: Michael Whelan

SERVICE TO SFWA

WINNER: John E. Johnston III

PAST NEBULA WINNERS

1965

Novel: *Dune* by Frank Herbert

Novella: "He Who Shapes" by Roger Zelazny and "The Saliva Tree" by Brian Aldiss (tie)

Novelette: "The Doors of His Face, the Lamps of His Mouth" by Roger Zelazny

Short Story: "'Repent, Harlequin!' Said the Ticktockman" by Harlan Ellison

1966

Novel: *Babel-17* by Samuel R. Delany and *Flowers for Algernon* by Daniel Keyes (tie)

Novella: "The Last Castle" by Jack Vance

Novelette: "Call Him Lord" by Gordon R. Dickson Dead People Server

Short Story: "The Secret Place" by Richard McKenna

1967

Novel: *The Einstein Intersection* by Samuel R. Delany

Novella: "Behold the Man" by Michael Moorcock

Novelette: "Gonna Roll the Bones" by Fritz Leiber

Short Story: "Aye, and Gomorrah" by Samuel R. Delany

1968

Novel: *Rite of Passage* by Alexei Panshin
Novella: "Dragonrider" by Anne McCaffrey
Novelette: "Mother to the World" by Richard Wilson
Short Story: "The Planners" by Kate Wilhelm

1969

Novel: *The Left Hand of Darkness* by Ursula K. Le Guin
Novella: "A Boy and His Dog" by Harlan Ellison
Novelette: "Time Considered as a Helix of Semi-Precious Stones" by Samuel R. Delany
Short Story: "Passengers" by Robert Silverberg

1970

Novel: *Ringworld* by Larry Niven
Novella: "Ill Met in Lankhmar" by Fritz Leiber
Novelette: "Slow Sculpture" by Theodore Sturgeon
Short Story: No Award

1971

Novel: *A Time of Changes* by Robert Silverberg
Novella: "The Missing Man" by Katherine MacLean
Novelette: "The Queen of Air and Darkness" by Poul Anderson
Short Story: "Good News from the Vatican" by Robert Silverberg

1972

Novel: *The Gods Themselves* by Isaac Asimov
Novella: "A Meeting With Medusa" by Arthur C. Clarke
Novelette: "Goat Song" by Poul Anderson
Short Story: "When It Changed" by Joanna Russ

1973

Novel: *Rendezvous with Rama* by Arthur C. Clarke
Novella: "The Death of Doctor Island" by Gene Wolfe
Novelette: "Of Mist, and Grass, and Sand" by Vonda N. McIntyre
Short Story: "Love Is the Plan, the Plan Is Death" by James Tiptree, Jr.
Dramatic Presentation: *Soylent Green*

1974

Novel: *The Dispossessed* by Ursula K. Le Guin
Novella: "Born with the Dead" by Robert Silverberg
Novelette: "If the Stars Are Gods" by Gordon Eklund and Gregory Benford
Short Story: "The Day Before the Revolution" by Ursula K. Le Guin
Dramatic Presentation: *Sleeper* by Woody Allen
Grand Master: Robert Heinlein

1975

Novel: *The Forever War* by Joe Haldeman
Novella: "Home Is the Hangman" by Roger Zelazny
Novelette: "San Diego Lightfoot Sue" by Tom Reamy
Short Story: "Catch That Zeppelin" by Fritz Leiber
Dramatic Presentation: *Young Frankenstein* by Mel Brooks and Gene Wilder
Grand Master: Jack Williamson

1976

Novel: *Man Plus* by Frederik Pohl
Novella: "Houston, Houston, Do You Read?" by James Tiptree, Jr.
Novelette: "The Bicentennial Man" by Isaac Asimov
Short Story: "A Crowd of Shadows" by C. L. Grant
Grand Master: Clifford D. Simak

1977

Novel: *Gateway* by Frederik Pohl
Novella: "Stardance" by Spider and Jeanne Robinson
Novelette: "The Screwfly Solution" by Racoona Sheldon
Short Story: "Jeffty Is Five" by Harlan Ellison

1978

Novel: *Dreamsnake* by Vonda N. McIntyre
Novella: "The Persistence of Vision" by John Varley
Novelette: "A Glow of Candles, A Unicorn's Eye" by C. L. Grant
Short Story: "Stone" by Edward Bryant
Grand Master: L. Sprague de Camp

1979

Novel: *The Fountains of Paradise* by Arthur C. Clarke
Novella: "Enemy Mine" by Barry B. Longyear
Novelette: "Sandkings" by George R. R. Martin
Short Story: "GiANTS" by Edward Bryant

1980

Novel: *Timescape* by Gregory Benford
Novella: "Unicorn Tapestry" by Suzy McKee Charnas
Novelette: "The Ugly Chickens" by Howard Waldrop
Short Story: "Grotto of the Dancing Deer" by Clifford D. Simak
Grand Master: Fritz Leiber

1981

Novel: *The Claw of the Conciliator* by Gene Wolfe
Novella: "The Saturn Game" by Poul Anderson
Novelette: "The Quickening" by Michael Bishop
Short Story: "The Bone Flute" by Lisa Tuttle [declined by author]

1982

Novel: *No Enemy But Time* by Michael Bishop
Novella: "Another Orphan" by John Kessel
Novelette: "Fire Watch" by Connie Willis
Short Story: "A Letter from the Clearys" by Connie Willis

1983

Novel: *Startide Rising* by David Brin
Novella: "Hardfought" by Greg Bear
Novelette: "Blood Music" by Greg Bear
Short Story: "The Peacemaker" by Gardner Dozois
Grand Master: Andre Norton

1984

Novel: *Neuromancer* by William Gibson
Novella: "Press Enter []" by John Varley
Novelette: "Blood Child" by Octavia Butler
Short Story: "Morning Child" by Gardner Dozois

1985

Novel: *Ender's Game* by Orson Scott Card
Novella: "Sailing to Byzantium" by Robert Silverberg
Novelette: "Portraits of His Children" by George R. R. Martin
Short Story: "Out of All Them Bright Stars" by Nancy Kress
Grand Master: Arthur C. Clarke

1986

Novel: *Speaker for the Dead* by Orson Scott Card
Novella: "R&R" by Lucius Shepard
Novelette: "The Girl Who Fell into the Sky" by Kate Wilhelm
Short Story: "Tangents" by Greg Bear
Grand Master: Isaac Asimov

1987

Novel: *The Falling Woman* by Pat Murphy
Novella: "The Blind Geometer" by Kim Stanley Robinson
Novelette: "Rachel in Love" by Pat Murphy
Short Story: "Forever Yours, Anna" by Kate Wilhelm
Grand Master: Alfred Bester

1988

Novel: *Falling Free* by Lois McMaster Bujold
Novella: "The Last of the Winnebagos" by Connie Willis
Novelette: "Schrödinger's Kitten" by George Alec Effinger
Short Story: "Bible Stories for Adults, No. 17: The Deluge" by James Morrow
Grand Master: Ray Bradbury

1989

Novel: *The Healer's War* by Elizabeth Ann Scarborough
Novella: "The Mountains of Mourning" by Lois McMaster Bujold
Novelette: "At the Rialto" by Connie Willis
Short Story: "Ripples in the Dirac Sea" by Geoffrey A. Landis

1990

Novel: *Tehanu: The Last Book of Earthsea* by Ursula K. Le Guin
Novella: "The Hemingway Hoax" by Joe Haldeman
Novelette: "Tower of Babylon" by Ted Chiang
Short Story: "Bears Discover Fire" by Terry Bisson
Grand Master: Lester del Rey

1991

Novel: *Stations of the Tide* by Michael Swanwick
Novella: "Beggars in Spain" by Nancy Kress
Novelette: "Guide Dog" by Mike Conner
Short Story: "Ma Qui" by Alan Brennert

1992

Novel: *Doomsday Book* by Connie Willis
Novella: "City of Truth" by James Morrow
Novelette: "Danny Goes to Mars" by Pamela Sargent
Short Story: "Even the Queen" by Connie Willis
Grand Master: Fred Pohl

1993

Novel: *Red Mars* by Kim Stanley Robinson
Novella: "The Night We Buried Road Dog" by Jack Cady
Novelette: "Georgia on My Mind" by Charles Sheffield
Short Story: "Graves" by Joe Haldeman

1994

The 1994 Nebulas were awarded at a ceremony in New York City in late April 1995.

Novel: *Moving Mars* by Greg Bear
Novella: "Seven Views of Olduvai Gorge" by Mike Resnick
Novelette: "The Martian Child" by David Gerrold
Short Story: "A Defense of the Social Contracts" by Martha Soukup
Grand Master: Damon Knight
Author Emeritus: Emil Petaja

1995

Novel: *The Terminal Experiment* by Robert J. Sawyer
Novella: "Last Summer at Mars Hill" by Elizabeth Hand
Novelette: "Solitude" by Ursula K. Le Guin
Short Story: "Death and the Librarian" by Esther M. Friesner
Grand Master: A. E. van Vogt
Author Emeritus: Wilson "Bob" Tucker

1996

Novel: *Slow River* by Nicola Griffith
Novella: "Da Vinci Rising" by Jack Dann
Novelette: "Lifeboat on a Burning Sea" by Bruce Holland Rogers
Short Story: "A Birthday" by Esther M. Friesner
Grand Master: Jack Vance
Author Emeritus: Judith Merril

1997

Novel: *The Moon and the Sun* by Vonda N. McIntyre
Novella: "Abandon in Place" by Jerry Oltion
Novelette: "Flowers of Aulit Prison" by Nancy Kress
Short Story: "Sister Emily's Lightship" by Jane Yolen
Grand Master: Poul Anderson
Author Emeritus: Nelson Slade Bond

1998

Novel: *Forever Peace* by Joe Haldeman
Novella: "Reading the Bones" by Sheila Finch
Novelette: "Lost Girls" by Jane Yolen
Short Story: "Thirteen Ways to Water" by Bruce Holland Rogers
Grand Master: Hal Clement (Harry Stubbs)
Author Emeritus: William Tenn (Philip Klass)

1999

Novel: *Parable of the Talents* by Octavia E. Butler
Novella: "Story of Your Life" by Ted Chiang
Novelette: "Mars Is No Place for Children" by Mary A. Turzillo
Short Story: "The Cost of Doing Business" by Leslie What
Script: *The Sixth Sense* by M. Night Shyamalan
Grand Master: Brian W. Aldiss
Author Emeritus: Daniel Keyes

2000

Novel: *Darwin's Radio* by Greg Bear
Novella: "Goddesses" by Linda Nagata
Novelette: "Daddy's World" by Walter Jon Williams
Short Story: "macs" by Terry Bisson
Script: *Galaxy Quest* by Robert Gordon and David Howard
Bradbury Award: Yuri Rasovsky and Harlan Ellison
Grand Master: Philip José Farmer
Author Emeritus: Robert Sheckley

2001

Novel: *The Quantum Rose* by Catherine Asaro
Novella: "The Ultimate Earth" by Jack Williamson
Novelette: "Louise's Ghost" by Kelly Link
Short Story: "The Cure for Everything" by Severna Park
Script: *Crouching Tiger, Hidden Dragon* by James Schamus, Kuo Jung Tsai, and Hui-Ling Wang
President's Award: Betty Ballantine

2002

Novel: *American Gods* by Neil Gaiman
Novella: "Bronte's Egg" by Richard Chwedyk
Novelette: "Hell Is the Absence of God" by Ted Chiang
Short Story: "Creature" by Carol Emshwiller
Script: *Lord of the Rings: The Fellowship of the Ring* by Frances Walsh, Phillipa Boyens, and Peter Jackson
Grand Master: Ursula K. Le Guin
Author Emeritus: Katherine MacLean

2003

Novel: *Speed of Dark* by Elizabeth Moon
Novella: "Coraline" by Neil Gaiman
Novelette: "The Empire of Ice Cream" by Jeffrey Ford
Short Story: "What I Didn't See" by Karen Joy Fowler
Script: *Lord of the Rings: The Two Towers* by Frances Walsh, Phillipa Boyens, Stephen Sinclair, and Peter Jackson
Grand Master: Robert Silverberg
Author Emeritus: Charles L. Harness

2004

Novel: *Paladin of Souls* by Lois McMaster Bujold
Novella: "The Green Leopard Plague" by Walter Jon Williams
Novelette: "Basement Magic" by Ellen Klages
Short Story: "Coming to Terms" by Eileen Gunn
Script: *Lord of the Rings: Return of the King* by Frances Walsh, Phillipa Boyens, and Peter Jackson
Grand Master: Anne McCaffrey

2005

Novel: *Camouflage* by Joe Haldeman
Novella: "Magic for Beginners" by Kelly Link
Novelette: "The Faery Handbag" by Kelly Link
Short Story: "I Live with You" by Carol Emshwiller
Script: *Serenity* by Joss Whedon
Grand Master: Harlan Ellison
Author Emeritus: William F. Nolan

2006

Novel: *Seeker* by Jack McDevitt
Novella: "Burn" by James Patrick Kelly
Novelette: "Two Hearts" by Peter S. Beagle
Short Story: "Echo" by Elizabeth Hand
Script: *Howl's Moving Castle* by Hayao Miyazaki, Cindy Davis Hewitt, and Donald H. Hewitt
Andre Norton Award: *Magic or Madness* by Justine Larbalestier
Grand Master: James Gunn
Author Emeritus: D. G. Compton

2007

Novel: *The Yiddish Policemen's Union* by Michael Chabon
Novella: "Fountain of Age" by Nancy Kress
Novelette: "The Merchant and the Alchemist's Gate" by Ted Chiang
Short Story: "Always" by Karen Joy Fowler
Script: *Pan's Labyrinth* by Guillermo del Toro
Andre Norton Award for Young Adult Science Fiction and Fantasy: *Harry Potter and the Deathly Hallows* by J. K. Rowling
Grand Master: Michael Moorcock
Author Emeritus: Ardath Mayhar
SFWA Service Awards: Melisa Michaels and Graham P. Collins

2008

Novel: *Powers* by Ursula K. Le Guin
Novella: "The Spacetime Pool" by Catherine Asaro
Novelette: "Pride and Prometheus" by John Kessel
Short Story: "Trophy Wives" by Nina Kiriki Hoffman
Script: *WALL-E* by Andrew Stanton and Jim Reardon. Original story by Andrew Stanton and Pete Docter
Andre Norton Award for Young Adult Science Fiction and Fantasy: *Flora's Dare: How a Girl of Spirit Gambles All to Expand Her Vocabulary, Confront a Bouncing Boy Terror, and Try to Save Califa from a Shaky Doom (Despite Being Confined to Her Room)* by Ysabeau S. Wilce
Grand Master: Harry Harrison
Author Emeritus: M. J. Engh
Solstice: Kate Wilhelm, Martin H. Greenberg, and the late Algis Budrys
SFWA Service Award: Victoria Strauss

2009

Novel: *The Windup Girl* by Paolo Bacigalupi
Novella: "The Women of Nell Gwynne's" by Kage Baker
Novelette: "Sinner, Baker, Fabulist, Priest; Red Mask, Black Mask, Gentleman, Beast" by Eugie Foster
Short Story: "Spar" by Kij Johnson
Ray Bradbury Award: *District 9* by Neill Blomkamp and Terri Tatchell
Andre Norton Award: *The Girl Who Circumnavigated Fairyland in a Ship of Her Own Making* by Catherynne M. Valente
Grand Master: Joe Haldeman
Author Emeritus: Neal Barrett, Jr.
Solstice Award: Tom Doherty, Terri Windling, and the late Donald A. Wollheim
SFWA Service Awards: Vonda N. McIntyre and Keith Stokes

ABOUT THE COVER

The cover of *The 2011 Nebula Awards Showcase* is by this year's second Solstice Award winner, the renowned artist and illustrator Michael Whelan.

Since 1980, Mr. Whelan, a fifteen-time winner of the Hugo Award, has been one of the world's premier fantasy and science fiction artists. In the past three decades his art has graced the covers of books written by Grand Masters and Nebula winners, including Isaac Asimov, Robert A. Heinlein, and Sir Arthur C. Clarke. His vision has not only provided a glimpse into the worlds science fiction and fantasy writers imagine, but has also served to draw readers, old and new, into the genre and has inspired artists whose work is featured on countless covers of SFWA members' books today. In June 2009, he was inducted into the Science Fiction Hall of Fame, the first living artist so honored.

ABOUT THE EDITORS

James Patrick Kelly has written novels, short stories, essays, reviews, poetry, plays, and planetarium shows. His books include *The Wreck of the Godspeed*, *Think Like a Dinosaur*, *Wildlife*, and *Look into the Sun*. His short novel *Burn* won the Science Fiction Writers of America's Nebula Award in 2007. He has won the World Science Fiction Society's Hugo Award twice, for the novelettes "Think Like a Dinosaur" and "Ten to the Sixteenth to One." He writes a column on the Internet for *Asimov's Science Fiction Magazine* and is on the faculty of the Stonecoast Creative Writing MFA Program at the University of Southern Maine. His most recent publishing venture is the e-zine *James Patrick Kelly's Strangeways*.

John Kessel teaches creative writing and American literature at North Carolina State University in Raleigh. A two-time winner of the Nebula Award, he has also received the Theodore Sturgeon Award, the Locus Award, the Shirley Jackson Award, and the James Tiptree, Jr. Award. His books include the novels *Good News from Outer Space* and *Corrupting Dr. Nice*, and the collections *Meeting in Infinity* and *The Pure Product*. With James Patrick Kelly he edited the anthologies *Feeling Very Strange: The Slipstream Anthology*, *Rewired: The Post-Cyberpunk Anthology*, *The Secret History of Science Fiction*, and *Kafkaesque*. His recent collection *The Baum Plan for Financial Independence and Other Stories* contains the winner of the 2008 Nebula Award for best novelette, "Pride and Prometheus."